This is an excellent mystery and whodunit with well-developed characters, an interesting backstory and great potential. The action is fast paced but nicely interspersed with moments of stillness and humanity....Well written, enjoyable reading. I literally can't wait for the next one to see where Ms. Maiorisi takes us with both the crime-fighting team and the prospective romance.

-Lesbian Reading Room

This book was a long time in the pipeline for Catherine Maiorisi, and it shows. The pacing is perfect, and there has clearly been a lot of work done over a long period on making sure that everything is just right. As a result, this is a really easy read that will hold your interest until the final page.

-The Lesbian Review

The Blood Runs Cold

While I did not read the first book in Catherine Maiorisi's Chiara Corelli series, this did not prevent me from thoroughly enjoying *The Blood Runs Cold*. Maiorisi populates her story with some much-needed diversity, but never strays into exhortative territory: these characters feel like individuals rather than stereotypes intended to fill a role (or purpose). The mystery is suitably complex, sure to keep readers guessing until late in the game.

-The Bolo Books Review

In most cases, I will say readers can start with the current book and not miss anything. With Chiara ostracized by other members of the department, readers should start with *A Matter of Blood* to get the full effect and the background of Chiara and PJ working together. Both books are fast-paced thrillers, where every minute could be their last, with no one to trust and nowhere to hide... Love page-turner thrillers? Pick these books up—then try to keep up with Chiara. It'll be a breathtaking ride.

-Kings River Life Magazine

An excellent police procedural with twists, turns and surprises. Looking forward to other mysteries featuring Chiara Corelli.

-Map Your Mystery

The Disappearance of Lindy James

This is not your typical Catherine Maiorisi book. It is a deeply involved fictional look at mental illness and how it affects the life, family and friends of Quincy, Lindy and their two young daughters. The story is told through two narrators, Quincy and Lindy. We are inside Lindy's head as she devolves and it is a scary place. As well we are privy to the emotional ride Quincy faces as her family slips away. This is by no means a light read. The writing is solid with exceptional moments when describing the inner workings of Lindy's mind as she loses touch with reality. The storyline is intensely interesting as Quincy and Lindy's lives diverge...I could not put this book down. And although this may be a challenging read for some due to triggers, this is an engaging story.

-Della B., NetGalley

4.25 stars. I'm a fan of the Corelli mystery series, however this is such a completely different theme, so I was curious to see how it would work for me. It was a tough read, but surprisingly good! Like in the mystery series, Maiorisi is not afraid to show the ugliness of the world, but in the end this book is about unwavering love... This is not an easy read and contains many triggers concerning religion in combination with homosexuality, so this might not be for everybody. It is a book I will remember though, it's very well written and I thought the insights in postpartum psychosis were very interesting and well done (to my limited knowledge on the subject) and their love for each other is something you can really feel even during the darkest parts of their relationship, which is quite exceptional. Recommend!

-Meike V., NetGalley

Love Among the Ruins

Catherine Maiorisi

About the Author

Catherine Maiorisi lives in New York City with her wife, Sherry.

Catherine is passionate about writing. And when she's not writing, she's reading or cooking. Italian is her favorite but she's always on the lookout for good recipes in any cuisine.

Love Among the Ruins is her fifth romance. Other romances are: *Matters of the Heart, No One But You, Ready for Love* and *Taking a Chance on Love*.

Catherine is also the author of the NYPD Detective Chiara Corelli Mystery series—*A Matter of Blood* (2019 Lambda Literary Award Finalist), *The Blood Runs Cold* (2020 Goldie and Lambda Literary Award Finalist), *A Message in Blood* and *Legacy in the Blood*.

The Disappearance of Lindy James, Catherine's first general fiction book, won the 2022 Goldie for Best General Fiction.

Catherine also writes mystery and romance short stories.

She is an active member of Sisters in Crime and Mystery Writers of America.

Love Among the Ruins

Catherine Maiorisi

2023

Bella Books, Inc.
P.O. Box 10543
Tallahassee, FL 32302

Printed in the United States of America on acid-free paper.

First Edition - 2023

Editor: Medora MacDougall
Cover Designer: Heather Honeywell

ISBN: 978-1-64247-464-0

Acknowledgments

I missed traveling to Italy during the pandemic so I wrote *Love Among the Ruins* and revisited all the places I love with Callie and Dana.

Thank you to my wife, first reader, and travel mate for her ongoing support of me and my writing.

And thank you to my editor, Medora MacDougall, for her patience and willingness to go through this long manuscript many times. As always, you made it better, and you made me a better writer.

And, finally, thank you Jessica, Linda, and everyone at Bella Books for everything you do.

Dedication

For Sherry, who shares my love of Italy

CHAPTER ONE

At the crack of dawn, as she had every single day for the last eighteen years, Callie DeAndre opened her eyes to the glorious chorus of birds singing outside her window. Some days her heart soared hearing the birds' songs. Other days the chorus was painful. Did the birds feel the way she did? Did they also wait, expect, hope, for Abby to walk in the house, bringing life and love and happiness with her? Or was she the only one? She yawned, stretched, and then it hit her. Today was the one-year anniversary of Abby's death. She covered her face with her arm, but it didn't stop the tears leaking from her eyes. Or the birds from singing.

The toilet in the guest bathroom flushed. Callie groaned. Creature of habit that Angela was, she always woke with the dawn too. Right on schedule. *Tap, tap.* Her door opened. "Good morning, Callie. Coffee will be ready in a few minutes." Angela walked away humming. On days like today when Callie wanted to curl up and forget it all, Angela's chirpy morning attitude was annoying. Nevertheless, she appreciated having her in her life and in her house. If it hadn't been for Angela, and Erin and Bonnie, two college friends, urging her to get out of bed, shower, dress, eat, and relate to them, she might have slipped into the blackness that beckoned.

She dried her tears on the sheet. Knowing Angela would harass her until she was up and dressed, she got out of bed to start the first day of her second year without Abby. Another lonely, painful day longing for something she could never have. Oblivious, the cheerful chorus of birdsong continued in the background.

She walked into the kitchen and sat at the table. Angela handed her a cup of coffee.

"Thanks." At least Angela got that Callie needed time to wake up so she was blessedly silent as she prepared their breakfast.

Callie had no appetite to speak of, but she'd learned to eat a little at meals to keep her friends from worrying. She took a couple of bites of the fried egg and nibbled on the slice of toast Angela placed in front of her, then pushed her plate away. "Thanks for breakfast." She carried her dish to the sink.

Angela eyed the partially eaten breakfast Callie scraped into the garbage but didn't comment.

"Put yours in the sink too, Angela. I'll clean up so you can get to work."

"Thanks." As she turned from the sink, her cell rang. "Angela Fortuna," she said, in her business voice.

Assuming it was someone from Angela's financial services firm calling, Callie put their breakfast dishes and silverware in the dishwasher and reached for the frying pan.

"Callie, it's for you."

She froze. "You know I don't want to talk to anyone." She made no attempt to hide her anger.

"It's Sarah." Angela held the phone out. "She said you've been ignoring her emails and she *must* talk to you."

Callie shook her head.

"Stop being so damned selfish."

Callie was shocked. Angela never got mad at her.

"She's your friend and you've pushed her away along with everyone else. But she's kept Danville House Books off your back for more than a year, and now your actions are jeopardizing her livelihood. And yours."

What could be so bad that her agent was in trouble? She backed away, but Angela followed. "You owe her, Callie. It won't kill you to talk to her."

She scowled at Angela, then took the phone. She bit her lip. "Hello."

"It's muted."

At least Sarah hadn't heard her churlish refusal.

She put the phone on speaker. "Hi, Sarah."

"Callie. I'm so sorry to pressure you." Sarah sounded tentative. "I've missed you." Callie felt guilty for causing the sadness she heard in her voice.

"I'm sorry—"

"Don't apologize, Callie. It's a statement of fact, not an attempt to guilt-trip you." Strong and direct. That was the Sarah she knew and why she loved her as a friend and as her agent.

Despite the fact that it had been a year since they last spoke, she felt the same warmth and connection with Sarah that she'd had from their very first phone call seventeen years ago.

"How is Ben? I never thanked him for what he did at the cemetery."

She'd been dazed at the funeral home and even more out of it in the church, and by the time they got to the cemetery she was totally disoriented. Propped up by Angela at the gravesite, she stared at the coffin perched on a fake green carpet over the hole she knew they would lower Abby into. Then her gaze fell on the pile of dirt nearby, and she imagined the *thump, thump, thump* of dirt being shoveled on top of Abby. Suddenly she couldn't breathe. She woke in Angela's arms on the ground, surrounded by her friends. At a nod from Angela, Sarah's husband, Ben, picked her up and carried her to the limousine.

"He doesn't need to be thanked. But he misses you." Sarah hesitated. "And Abby, his favorite birding partner."

She couldn't talk about Abby. "How are the kids?" The three, a college junior, a high school senior, and a sixth grader, had been close to her and Abby.

"They miss you. Natalie asks about you every time she calls. Laurie came out to us a couple of months ago, and she wants to talk to you about being a lesbian. And Devon doesn't quite understand why he can't call Abby with questions about dinosaurs."

Tears threatened. She felt a pang of regret. A year in their young lives gone.

Unsure what to say, she remained silent. They listened to each other breathe on the phone for a few seconds before Sarah spoke.

"A couple of weeks before Abby died, she asked me to make sure Danville House Books didn't pressure you to produce. She wanted to be sure you would have time to mourn and heal. And I've managed to do that. Finishing the romance you put aside when Abby started to decline appeased them for a while, but a couple of months ago they started pushing me for a delivery date on the romance in Italy book. It's already on the schedule for next year and they have big plans for it, including a huge publicity campaign starting months before it's released. We're contractually obligated, Callie. And they might let the date slip a bit, but they won't let you off the hook."

"Could I write something else?" Her gaze skipped from Angela to the frying pan on the stove to the carton of eggs and the loaf of bread on the counter. "How about, um, the story of a recluse who hires a chef and finds love in her own house? We could call it *Love on the Menu*."

Sarah laughed. "Not a bad idea. But they want what you proposed, a romance set in Italy. If you don't deliver, both our reputations will take a hit."

"You know I can't write about a place I haven't been. And you know I've barely left the house since Abby's funeral. What you don't know is that even going out to the backyard will, more often than not, trigger an anxiety attack. So how the hell am I supposed to fly to Italy, where I don't speak the language, then negotiate multiple unfamiliar cities while dealing with strangers and crowds? Abby and I were meant to do this trip together. I can't do it alone."

Sarah sighed. "I've kept in touch with Angela so I do know. I hope *you* know I wouldn't be asking you to do this if I thought I could delay them any longer. I'll take the hit with you if you absolutely can't do it. But will you at least give it some thought?"

She already knew she couldn't do it. Why lie? She looked up. Angela was sitting across from her, nodding. "All right. I'll think about it."

That seemed to satisfy Sarah, so they made a plan to speak again in a few days and hung up.

She handed the phone to Angela. "I don't want to talk about it now." She quickly scrubbed the frying pan, put the eggs, bread, and butter away, and then went to her office. She was pissed. Angela knew Abby was supposed to go to Italy with her so they could discover the romance of Italy together and she could write the book. Surely Angela didn't believe she could suddenly stroll out the door by herself, sit in a congested airport, fly in a crowded airplane to a country where she knew no one and didn't speak the language, stay at hotels, go to restaurants, and visit romantic places surrounded by crowds of strangers? She'd been working twice a week with her therapist, Maggie, for months and had made some progress. She was able to go out to her backyard with Maggie now, sometimes without having an attack, able to take drives with Maggie, and, though she'd had an attack each time, able to sit with Maggie in a small café and have coffee, twice. But she still couldn't leave the house on her own.

She closed her office door and cried. For Abby, for the wonderful life they'd planned, for the trip to Italy they would never take, and because she was afraid. Afraid she was forgetting Abby's voice, her strong, beautiful face, her smile, and her confident manner. Perhaps Maggie was right when she said that, subconsciously, Callie equated leaving the house with leaving Abby behind, starting her life without her.

She spent the day looking at pictures and videos of birthdays, vacations, and special events like Abby's PhD party, the launch party for Callie's first published book, and their wedding. As the light faded, she heard Angela in the kitchen, probably preparing the lasagna she had requested. It was Abby's favorite. She must have dozed off because when she opened her eyes in the semidark room she was in Abby's arms. Realizing it was a dream, that Abby was gone, and she was alone, she curled in a ball and sobbed.

The door opened and Angela was framed in the light from the hall. She turned on the lamp next to Callie, wrapped her in her arms, and held her as she cried. When the tears stopped and Callie pulled away, Angela handed her a tissue, then used one to wipe her own eyes. She took Callie's hands in hers.

"I know you're hurting, honey. Losing Abby was and is a tremendous loss. But she's dead and you're alive. I'm not saying you shouldn't or can't continue to mourn. That takes as long as it takes. But it's time for you to start living again."

"I know." Callie wasn't surprised to receive the gentle encouragement. Angela, Erin, and Bonnie had been more than patient with her. "A year *is* a long time and I appreciate all you've done for me, Angela, but I think you should get back to your life. I'll be all right by myself."

"Oh, honey, it's not me who needs to get back to her life. It's you. It's time. You can't wander around this house like a ghost for the rest of your life. I think Abby would be appalled if she could see you now. Have you looked in the mirror lately?"

Yes. In fact, she had accidently caught a glimpse of herself in the mirror this morning. She'd panicked at having a stranger in the bathroom with her, then quickly looked away when she realized it was her reflection. Her once shiny and luxurious blond hair was lackluster and limp. The racoon-like dark circles around her dull blue eyes, the too-large pajamas hanging off her always-slender frame, her protruding clavicle bones and dry dull skin brought to mind pictures she'd seen of starved and abused women. *Lifeless* was the word that fit.

"I don't know how to live without her, Angela."

Angela tightened her hold on Callie's hands. "You're one of the strongest, most determined women I've ever met, Callie. I have no doubt you can reclaim your life and go back to being the magnificent person you've become in the years we've been friends. But you have to want to live, despite the pain. You have to be willing to walk out the door despite the anxiety attacks. And you have to be willing to go on, despite being alone. You know Abby would never want you to give up on life because of her. And yet, that's what you've done."

The tears came again. She'd cried enough to refill the Great Salt Lake. No wonder she looked like a desiccated apple.

Angela had said her piece. Now she would give Callie the space to think about it. She was right, of course. Not only had Callie lost Abby, she'd also lost the desire to create and the desire to live. She was merely existing.

Angela stood. "I'm going to finish prepping dinner. Come talk to me."

"I need a few minutes to pull myself together." Avoiding the mirror, she washed her tear-stained face and dabbed cold water on her swollen eyes. It was true. Abby had encouraged her many times in the last weeks before she lost the ability to speak, to take the trip to Italy they'd planned. Could she go alone?

She tried to imagine walking out the door to the taxi. And remembered instead the first time she tried to leave the house after the funeral to go to Maggie's office for her therapy appointment. She'd stepped out onto the porch and suddenly she couldn't breathe. Gasping for air, dizzy, she started sweating. Her heart galloped, her hands and arms tingled, she lost control of her bladder and started to black out. She was having a heart attack. She was going to die right there in front of her house. Strong arms caught her as she was going down. Angela. She vaguely heard her on the phone with Maggie, then Angela was rubbing her arms, telling her to look at her, to look at the blue sky, the green grass, the leaves on the tree, telling her that she was safe. When she finally could breathe, she realized she was in Angela's arms on the floor of the porch. She was safe, but embarrassed. She blinked. It was a memory.

"Callie."

"I'm coming, Angela." Callie wiped her tears and went into the bathroom to wash her face again.

In the kitchen, Callie eyed the open door to the backyard.

"Go ahead, go outside."

Callie didn't like to be told what to do. "Why?"

"Because it's time, Callie. You can't just give into the fear. You have to keep pushing against it. At least try again."

"No." Callie knew she sounded harsh. Angela was her best friend, she reminded herself. Not her enemy. And this year had taken a toll on her too. Could she do what Angela suggested, walk out the door knowing she might have an anxiety attack? Could she face the fear head-on? It was safer to stay inside but she'd gone into her yard with Maggie several times recently and she didn't always have an attack. Angela would be there if she went outside now. Maybe she could do it. "Okay, I'll try."

Callie moved to the doorway and stared into the darkness. She jumped when Angela snapped on the outside lights.

"I'm right here, Callie. You'll be safe."

Callie swallowed. This was her backyard. Nothing to fear. She could do it. She stepped onto the patio. The cool air felt good. Heart racing, she took another step into the night. Her gaze fell on the firepit Abby loved. Suddenly she was sweating, shaking, and gasping for air. Angela dragged her into the house, held her and talked her down from the anxiety attack.

"I'm sorry for pushing you, Callie."

"You push because you want the best for me." She stepped out of Angela's embrace. "You know, I really thought I was going to die during that first attack last year. But the recent ones in the backyard have felt less intense. So maybe there's hope."

Angela smiled. "I've believed in you since that day in fourth grade when you got between me and that nasty boy who was bullying me. I have no doubt that you'll get past this." She kissed Callie's forehead. "I need to get back to prepping dinner."

Happy that Angela was leaving her to her own thoughts, Callie slumped in her chair while Angela made a salad and prepared garlic bread for dinner. Angela looked up at the sound of the front door opening and closing. "Hopefully that was Bonnie and Erin coming in, not thieves. I'm going to put the lasagna in the oven, then let's go visit with them while we wait for dinner to be ready."

Callie took a deep breath and followed Angela to the living room. Without Angela, her oldest friend, and Bonnie and Erin, her closest friends from college, she wouldn't have made it through this last year. The newcomers greeted her with hugs, and though she was sure they could see her exhaustion, neither commented on it. Spotting the bottle of Abby's favorite sauvignon blanc and the four glasses on the coffee table in front of the sofa, Callie filled with rage.

"This isn't a celebration. Don't you get it. She's gone. Dead. Never to return." She knew she was being irrational and ungrateful. They'd all lost a close friend, yet they'd been there for her while she mourned for the last year. Embarrassed by her outburst, she gazed at her hands in her lap.

Angela's calm voice broke the tense silence. "I'm sorry, Callie, but I do want to celebrate Abby, to share how important she was to me and to remember the many ways she helped me." She picked up a glass of the wine.

Bonnie and Erin raised their glasses. Callie hesitated, then did the same.

Angela continued, "She may not be here physically, but she is here, in my heart, in all of our hearts, and in the hearts of the many people who loved her and will never forget her."

Erin lifted her glass. "To Abby, who not only showed me how to love and live by example but also helped me and Bonnie acknowledge that our love for each other was more than friendship. There's not a day when I don't ask myself, what would Abby do?"

Bonnie wiped her eyes and lifted her glass. "Abby helped me become who I am and who I wanted to be. I'll always love her, but she was adamant that I, that we all, needed to move on with our lives. She was so loving and giving that even as she faced death, she thought about us. We were truly blessed to have her in our lives."

The three turned to Callie. She wasn't sure she could speak, but then the words flowed.

"She's not in my heart because she took it with her along with my soul. I'm an empty shell without her, useless. If it wasn't for the incessant singing of those damned birds and you three I think I might have killed myself. I was so lucky to have her in my life. I loved her so much. How can I go on without her?"

After another round of hugs and tears, Angela placed a page from the travel section of the *New York Times* in front of her. "We think this is how, Callie."

Callie read the description of the "Romantic Italy" group tour, thirty-one days that seemed tailor-made for her. Not only did it include all the places she and Abby planned to visit, it also included others they hadn't considered, and the amount of time in each place was pretty close to the times in the itinerary she'd outlined in the book proposal.

It was expensive, but the large advance she received when she signed the contract would more than cover the cost. It would be a small group, only twelve. She shuddered. Although the tour promised lots of time on her own, she'd still be trapped in a bus with eleven people, eleven strangers who would want to know all about her, why she was on a romantic tour alone, and what she thought about the places they were seeing. It was impossible. Other than her conversation with Sarah today and a weekly conversation with her mom, she hadn't spoken to anyone but Angela, Erin, Bonnie, and her therapist, Maggie, for a year.

As she started to put the paper down, the highlighted passages caught her eye. The travel agency would take care of everything. She wouldn't have to think about getting from place to place or worry about luggage or where to eat or where to stay. Could she do it? The memory of the fear, the embarrassment, and the exhaustion she felt the only time she'd tried to walk out the front door, hit her again. No way could she chance that with eleven strangers. Or even one.

She scowled at Angela. "I presume this morning wasn't the first time Sarah talked to you about the Italy book."

"No, it wasn't. We've talked about it often over the last few months as Danville House has increased the pressure, but I put her, and them, off. I think you're ready now."

Callie tossed the ad on the table. "Not only can I not write a romance without Abby, I also don't do groups. You know that." She glared at them. "And even if I was willing to try a tour, who am I kidding? Travel alone to Italy for a month? I can't even walk out the door without being incapacitated by an anxiety attack."

A bell rang in the kitchen. Angela stood. "I'll get the lasagna but I need a volunteer to carry the salad and wine to the dining room table." She met Callie's eyes. "Let's enjoy dinner and discuss the trip after we eat."

The lasagna. It was delicious, but she had no appetite. So she did what she always did, ate a few bites and pushed the rest around on her dish, hoping no one would notice. She was blessed to have three caring friends with her. Blessed that they had all loved Abby and she had loved them. She relaxed and let their gentle conversation, laughter, and affection warm her and ease her loneliness. Abby was there in all of them. She'd lied earlier. Abby was in her heart, would always be in her heart. She would never forget her. That was the good news and the bad because remembering her was painful.

They moved back into the living room for dessert. Angela sipped her coffee and watched Callie over the rim of her cup. "Abby wanted to take this trip with you, but she made it clear that if she couldn't she wanted you to do it without her. She hoped that if you went to new places and met new people you might find someone and be happy again. Who knows what could happen if you do this tour?"

In the months leading up to her death, Abby had tried to help Callie deal with it. "You're too young to be a widow," she'd said, stroking her face. "I hope you'll never forget me, but I don't want you to mourn more than six months. I love you so much, Callie, and I want you to find someone who makes you happy. Promise?"

"How am I supposed to do this alone, Angela? She made me promise to find someone else, but she didn't tell me how to stop loving and missing her. And you saw less than an hour ago what happens the minute I step outside."

"And you told me less than an hour ago that the attacks were less intense now. You can't hide forever." Angela stood. "I'll be right back. I have something for you." She returned a few minutes later with an envelope. "Abby left this for you."

Callie stared at the envelope, then looked at the other two women. It was clear they knew about the letter.

Her hands were shaking as she took the envelope. Abby had written on it in her bold script "For Callie if she's still mourning me after a year." She smiled through her tears. "Abby always was a sucker for the romantic gesture." She carefully tore the envelope, wanting to preserve all of this last gift.

My Dearest Callie,

I hope getting a letter from the dead doesn't freak you out too much but if Angela has given you this letter, it's a year later and you're still not living your life and that calls for drastic measures.

You are the love of my life, my soul mate, and I know you feel the same. We both thought and hoped we would have many more joyful years than the twenty we were granted. I probably should say nineteen and a half since the last six months haven't held much joy. But they have held much love and having you there with me every step of the way has made it easier to bear the physical pain of the cancer and the emotional pain of losing you, of knowing I was leaving you to find your way without me. It's good that I'm the one dying because I don't think I could exist without you. We both know that you are so much stronger than I am, so much more capable of going on alone. I know it doesn't feel that way but it's the truth and if you let yourself, you'll see I'm right – aren't I always, my love?

I'm sorry to leave you, but I'll be eternally grateful that we found each other, that I loved you, and that you loved me with all your heart. I meant what I said. I don't want you to ever forget me, but I don't want you to live your life with only the memories, no matter how happy and loving those memories are.

Please, dearest Callie, do it for me. Go out into the world and live. Take that trip to Italy. Be happy, find someone to love, celebrate life. It's what I want for you. It's what I would want for myself if I'd lost you.

But think of me as you travel through life. When you feel the warmth of the sun or the gentle kiss of rain, when you smell new mown grass or the fragrance of flowers, when you see the sparkle of new fallen snow or experience a beautiful sunrise or sunset, when you hear the rustle of leaves or the wildness of the wind. And, wherever you are, think of me when you see birds, hear the gentle flapping of their wings and their excited songs because you know, my love, if it's possible I will come back as a bird and watch over you.

Shakespeare was wrong. Parting is not such sweet sorrow. It sucks. But part we must. I must die and you must live. So get your sweet ass out there.

All my love forever, Abby

She broke down again. And her friends embraced and held her until her sobs subsided. Erin, a social worker, pushed the hair off Callie's face and spoke frankly as always.

"She's gone, Callie. Spending the rest of your life in this house won't change that. Take this trip to Italy. It's perfect for you in so many ways."

"If I leave here, she'll truly be gone. Besides, what about the panic attacks?"

Bonnie, a nurse and yoga instructor, supported Erin. "You've been meditating, right? I know you didn't like the way the anxiety medication made you feel, but maybe you could start taking it again. Between the two you should be able to manage on the tour."

"No medication. Even when I'm not anxious, it makes me feel miserable so I'm not sure I'd be able to absorb the atmosphere I need to write the book."

"But it might help you get back on the path to life and to writing," Angela said. "Abby would want you to try. I believe that was the point of her letter."

Writing was her life. She'd never not delivered, so she'd have to write the book. But if she hadn't experienced the romantic atmosphere herself, the book wouldn't have the authenticity, the real feeling for the setting that her readers had come to expect. She needed to go to Italy, wanted to go. If the half hour drive from Montclair to Newark Airport seemed overwhelming, though, how in the world could she fly to Italy and then spend a month confined with eleven strangers? Would she have to talk about Abby? About herself? Could she protect the privacy she'd fought so hard for?

Callie's eyes fell on the letter lying on the table and the last sentence jumped out at her. "So get your sweet ass out there." She could see the mischievous glint in Abby's eyes and the smirk that surely would have been there when she wrote that sentence, knowing she would recall the many times in their life together she'd followed a pep talk with those very words.

Abby was her muse and her sounding board. Her love for her, the sexual passion they shared, had inspired her romantic imagination. Could she write a romance about two unlikely people who fall in love on a tour of the romantic sights in Italy without Abby? She doubted it. But Abby would insist she at least try.

She took a deep breath. "You know they book these ads way in advance. The tour starts May first, just sixteen days from today, and it's probably sold out by now." Callie held her hand up to forestall any more efforts to convince her. "But I'll try to book it tomorrow."

Hoping she was right, that the tour was sold out, she called the next morning. As luck would have it, they'd had a cancellation less than an hour earlier. With Abby's last words, "Get your sweet ass out there," echoing in her head, she took a deep breath and booked the trip.

Then, after a good cry, she sent a group text to Angela, Erin, Bonnie, Sarah, her mom, and her therapist, Maggie. *Yikes. I'm going to Italy in two weeks!!!*

Comforted by their loving responses, she meditated to push back the hovering anxiety attack.

CHAPTER TWO

With a little more than two weeks to prepare, her three friends and Maggie sprang into action. Maggie came every day. They not only got beyond the front steps, but soon were taking long, sometimes shaky walks on busy streets and making forays into department stores to purchase things she needed and into supermarkets to shop for groceries. Instead of cooking for her or picking up takeout, Angela, Bonnie, or Erin took her out every night for dinner and more walks. The panic attacks came frequently, but her support team got her through them.

Exhausted by the attacks, Callie was stressed, but, to her surprise, also excited about the trip. She slept a lot, but in between naps and forays to the outside world she focused on packing her backpack, selecting the items she would need to write and take notes in addition to her MacBook Air, her password book, and her favorite Mont Blanc fountain pen with black ink cartridges. Her iPhone would do triple duty as a phone, camera, and recorder so she checked to make sure her plan covered international calls, and purchased an Italian current converter and a portable power bank to charge the phone on the fly. She downloaded the Italian-English

Dictionary and Translator App and an Italian phrasebook app from the Apple Store. She included a sketchbook, a trip notebook, a journal she'd dedicate to ideas and tidbits for the romance book, a couple of extra notebooks in case she needed them, a box of her favorite colored pencils, a dozen black and a dozen red pilot #5 fine point pens, a box of sharpened #2 pencils and several erasers.

Finally, she eyed the well-worn guidebook she and Abby had used to map out the trip, with the sticky notes poking out of it and their handwritten notes on the pages. The backpack was stuffed and she could look up what she needed on the Internet, so she put the guidebook aside. She would throw in her Kindle and its charger, her passport, wallet, sunglasses, lipstick, keys, and phone charger at the last minute.

Packing her clothing entailed its own challenges. The tour limited each guest to two suitcases no larger than the standard airline carry-on. The day before her departure Angela watched her sort through the clothing and underwear she usually wore, all of it white, gray, or black since Abby's death.

"We should have bought you some more colorful clothing, Cal. And you might want to pack some fancier underwear."

"I don't need fancier underwear." She stared at the tops and pants she'd put on the bed to pack. "This is what I wear. I don't want bright colors."

"I didn't say bright. I said colorful. Wearing colorful clothing doesn't mean you've forgotten Abby. It means you're alive and in the world. We still have time to run to the store."

Callie shook her head. "No. I'm good."

"Okay. But you haven't packed any sundresses or dresses for evenings out. Didn't the suggested list of items to pack include something dressy for a night at the opera and a fancy dinner?"

"It said the group would be going to the opera and a dressy dinner. That doesn't mean I'll go. But I'll bring something dressy as an option."

Angela got off the bed and walked into Callie's closet. She pulled out several black dresses, several sun dresses in muted colors, and the sexy sapphire-blue dress Callie had bought for a dinner in her honor.

Callie selected the black dress she'd purchased online recently for the planned unveiling of a memorial to Abby at her university at the end of June and the black dress she'd worn to the funeral and folded them into the suitcase along with a pair of low-heeled black sandals. She waved a hand at the remaining dresses. "I'll try those on before I go to bed or when I get up tomorrow."

Later that night, she tried on the sundresses. They were big, though because of the design they didn't look too bad. Still, the idea of wearing a color offended her. And just so she could say she had, she put on the sapphire-blue dress.

If she needed proof of the radical change the year of mourning had wrought, the dress made it clear. When she'd tried it on, Abby had swooned, "Oh, my God, Callie, it fits like a glove. You look so damned sexy they'll be sniffing after you as you walk to the podium." She'd never felt as sexy and desirable as she did in that dress. The color heightened the blue of her eyes and made her skin look like alabaster. It clung to her, emphasized every curve, and showed just enough cleavage to tantalize. She'd bought the dress and they'd gone home and made love all afternoon. The tags were still on it because two days before the event Abby started to decline and she hadn't attended. The award had arrived after the funeral.

She stared at herself in the mirror. Now she looked like a crack or meth addict wearing a stolen dress two sizes too large. She appeared bloodless, beaten, washed out. In fact, she looked worse than Abby had after months of illness. Turning away from the mirror, she stripped off the dress and hung it and the sundresses in the back of her closet.

The early part of the next day seemed unending and then suddenly it was time to get ready. While Callie was in the shower, Angela packed the last few items on the bed and closed the suitcases. Callie dressed, zipped her backpack, hung the small purse with her passport and wallet over her shoulder and headed for the door. Spotting the guidebook on her night table, she hesitated, then added it to her backpack. Reading Abby's handwritten notes would make it feel like she was with her.

Erin and Bonnie came by to wish her luck. Maggie arrived, and a few minutes later the chauffeured car provided by Emirates Airlines pulled up. Angela pulled the luggage to the curb. The chauffeur loaded her bags in the trunk, then helped the three of them into the car.

It turned out there were no direct first class flights to Milan from Newark Airport so she was flying out of JFK on an Emirates flight departing at 10:20 p.m. And because they were driving in rush hour, the car service suggested picking her up a five thirty rather than six in order to arrive three hours prior to departure, as required for an international flight.

Callie stared out the window, seeing the world for the first time in a year. It looked the same. The chauffeur negotiated the heavy traffic through New Jersey to the George Washington Bridge. As they crossed the bridge, she gazed at New York City glowing in the still-bright sunlight, remembering the many visits to Abby's doctors and the daily visits to New York Presbyterian Hospital for radiation treatments.

Angela took her hand. "You're pretty quiet. How are you holding up?"

"I'm seeing the city for the first time in more than a year. I'd forgotten how beautiful it is." She squeezed Angela's hand. "And I'm remembering all the medical appointments with Abby and how she always insisted we do something to make the visit fun or at least enjoyable. Until she got too weak."

Angela squeezed back. "The view of the city I see every day on my way to work awes me every time. And it brings back memories of the days I was able to join the two of you for the fun things."

Traffic was heavy but except for a brief stop as they merged onto the Van Wyck Expressway to the airport, it moved and they arrived in plenty of time. The chauffeur unloaded her luggage and helped them out of the car. Check-in was fast and easy. Somehow Maggie had wrangled permission for the two of them to escort her through the TSA Precheck security line and wait with her until she boarded.

Instead of the gate, they were escorted to the Emirates lounge, which was low-key and elegant. Angela and Maggie accepted the offered drinks while Callie asked for water. Angela sat on one side of her and Maggie on the other, each holding her hand. Around her people were speaking quietly in various languages. Every now and then a burst of Italian drifted over from a nearby group and Callie panicked, realizing there was no way she'd be able to negotiate traveling in a country where she didn't speak the language. Maggie and Angela made light conversation, trying to keep her calm, but she worked herself up and had an anxiety attack. Luckily with the two of them there it passed quickly, but, as usual, it left her feeling exhausted and she fought to stay awake.

Maggie had asked the woman at the desk to let her know when they were getting close to boarding and when she did, Callie took a Valium. She clung to Angela and Maggie until a flight attendant trained to work with anxiety attacks arrived to escort her onto the plane. She introduced herself as Zara. One last hug and Callie and Zara exited the lounge and boarded the plane along with the few other early boarding passengers.

Zara led Callie up to the second level in the plane and helped her settle into her very comfortable window seat. She glanced around. Angela had said they would remain in the lounge until her plane took off. She could still leave.

"The seat converts to a bed and if you like I'll come back with pillows, sheets, a blanket, and pajamas right after takeoff."

Pajamas? Really? "Thank you, but I think I'd feel exposed, so I'll sleep sitting up."

"You won't be exposed if you close the privacy doors." Zara pressed a button on the arm of the seat.

Callie watched in awe as the decorative panel on the wall beside her, slid over and enclosed her seat, converting it to a small private room. She pressed the button and the door opened. "I'm impressed."

Zara grinned. "We also have a shower if you feel the need. And as you can see, each seat has its own minibar and widescreen TV. Use that tablet"—she pointed—"to order drinks or dinner any time you're hungry. Would you like something to drink now, before I need to attend to other passengers?"

"If the minibar has water, I'll be fine." Between the unusual activity of the day, the attack, and the tranquilizer, Callie was having trouble keeping her eyes open.

"You look tired. Would you like me to make up the bed now? Or should I wait until you call for service."

Right now, she couldn't think of anything more terrible than getting up from this sumptuous leather armchair. "Let's wait until later. Thank you." She pressed the button to close the doors, and lay back in her seat.

Angela had booked the flight. It was expensive, but it was the only direct first class flight she could find and she knew there was no way Callie could fly in economy. She was so right. While Abby, with her WASP sensibilities, insisted on flying in coach, maintaining that flying first class was an unseemly flaunting of wealth, she also would only stay in luxury hotels. Callie didn't understand the distinction, but traveling in economy hadn't felt like a hardship. It might from now on, though.

It was wonderful to not have to watch people stream onto the plane and even better to have her own private room so she wouldn't have to talk to strangers. She even had Zara at her beck and call, though she hoped she wouldn't need her.

She was semidozing when the doors closed and the safety instructions were delivered. By the time the plane took off, the Valium had fully kicked in and she slept for several hours. When she woke up, she used the tablet to order a cup of soup.

Zara delivered her dinner. "Would you like me to come back and make up your bed?"

"Thank you, Zara. I'll be fine with just a pillow and a blanket."

She ate the soup and a few bites of the roll served with it. Zara returned with the pillow and blanket and removed the dinner tray. Callie closed the privacy doors again and slept until the window brightened. She ate half a slice of toast, took another Valium, and meditated until the wheels of the plane touched down in Milan.

Once the plane emptied, Zara led her out to the wheelchair Maggie had arranged to take her through Customs. They picked up her luggage, she answered a few questions and was waved through. The woman she'd hired through the travel agency to escort her to the hotel was waiting, holding a sign with DeAndre written on it. The woman introduced herself, spoke to the wheelchair guy in Italian, and led them outside to a waiting car. Callie tipped the guy and he helped her into the car while the driver loaded her luggage in the trunk. The woman slid into the car and explained that depending on traffic the drive would be about forty-five minutes. Happily, the woman didn't feel it was necessary to chat so Callie sat back on the comfortable leather seat and dozed until the woman called her name to wake her.

As arranged, the woman checked her into the hotel, escorted her to her room, and asked if she'd like help unpacking. Callie refused but thanked her. Finally alone, she sat in the chair near the window, exhausted but triumphant. It had required a lot of support and some medication, but she'd done it. She was in Italy. Her younger self, the self before Abby died, would have been horrified at the amount of money and the number of people it had taken to get her here.

And now she was on her own. Would she be able to function without that level of support? She'd find out soon enough. Unless she had a sudden urge to sightsee, which she doubted, she planned to spend the rest of today and all day tomorrow in the room of her luxury hotel, reading, adjusting to the time difference and steeling herself for the next challenge. Eleven strangers.

She pulled out her phone and sent a group text to Angela, Bonnie, Erin, her mom, and Maggie. *Relaxing in my room. IN ITALY!*

She smiled reading the congratulatory texts that came in as each person woke up.

Angela. *YES. I knew you could do it!!! I'm here if you need me.*

Bonnie. *Yay. Have fun. We're here if you need us.*

Erin. *Super. Now focus on enjoying it. Call anytime.*

Maggie. *Congrats. Meditate. Medicate if needed. Above all enjoy.*

Mom. *Great news baby. Be careful. Have fun.*

She gazed out the window. Italy was out there, waiting for her to explore it. Would she be brave enough in two days to leave this room, meet eleven strangers, and travel with them in a bus for a month? That was the plan. But it wasn't too late to go home.

She retrieved her backpack and pulled out her journal and the Italy guidebook. She turned to Milan. They'd spent hours discussing this trip while Callie wrote the proposal. A month later Abby was diagnosed. She stared at Abby's strong script.

The Duomo is a must. I climbed to the roof during my trip between college and graduate school. I hope you're not too old to do it. Callie smiled. Abby was older than her.

Let's check this out, she had written next to the Galleria Vittorio Emanuele. *I didn't see the Last Supper, so make reservations. Nothing romantic in Milan that I remember but a good starting point.*

CHAPTER THREE

Callie had always been a travel snob. She and Abby had been to Greece, Spain, England, and the Scandinavian countries but never on a tour. She sneered at group tours, looked down on people who were afraid to travel on their own, and ridiculed the groups of tourists who never stepped out of their American bubble to experience the countries they visited. Now, unable to be out on her own, she was one of them.

Meditating this morning had calmed her some. But her heart was racing as she prepared to leave the safety of her room. She closed her eyes and breathed in and out slowly. She hadn't had an anxiety attack since the one in JFK Airport, but she'd been escorted and medicated and she hadn't left her room since she arrived two days ago. Now she was alone, and it was time to meet the group she would be traveling with for the next thirty-one days. She took a deep breath and let it out slowly. Could she do this? She'd know soon enough. She grabbed her backpack.

Luck was with her. It was just her and another woman in the elevator and the woman paid her no attention. The elevator called out the number of each floor but didn't stop to pick up any more passengers. The door slid open. She took a deep breath and stepped out into the lobby. Angela's ringtone blared.

Callie pulled her phone out. "Hi, Angela. It's the middle of the night in New Jersey. Why are you awake?"

"I set my alarm so I could wish you good luck today. How are you doing?"

Angela to the rescue as usual. "I just arrived in the lobby and as you'd expect, I'm nervous." She scanned the area, spotted the sign for the group, and headed in that direction.

"You can do this, Callie. Did you take a Valium this morning?"

"No. I didn't want to be groggy. Listen, I'm approaching the group. Thanks for being here for me as usual. Wish me luck. Love you, talk later."

Callie ended the call, but instead of joining the group she hung back, not quite hiding behind a plant but almost, observing the other scaredy-cats she'd be traveling with. She counted three men and seven women, all of whom appeared to range in age from their fifties to seventies, and the eleventh, a man, in his thirties, maybe early forties, who had tracked her progress from the elevator. At first she thought he was checking her out, but as she got closer he seemed to be looking at her with pity. Maybe he thought she was a drug addict. Creepy. But he didn't look creepy. He was tall and slender with strong-looking shoulders, piercing eyes, and dark hair. Although she would have preferred a woman, she was glad at least one person on the tour was close to her age.

Oh, boy, Abby would bop her on the head for her judging and her ageism. Like it or not, she was part of this group and would be for the next thirty-one days. If she lasted.

A slender guy with a gray ponytail, wearing a too-tight T-shirt and skinny jeans stared or, more precisely, leered at her. His eyes raked her from head to toe, held at her breasts, then met her gaze with an oily smile. She flushed.

Ponytail man looked at her like a starving man seeing a steak. Overcome by a wave of fear, she started trembling. The room spun. Her heart pounded. She gasped for air. *Breathe*, she reminded herself, but her body couldn't seem to follow the instruction. Breathless, she closed her eyes. She was going to die in Italy.

"You can breathe." The soothing voice was very close. "Open your eyes." Callie forced herself to obey and gazed into gray-blue eyes filled with warmth and compassion and caring. "This will be over in a few minutes. Nod if it's all right for me to touch you."

She nodded.

The tall woman gently gripped Callie's forearms. "Is it okay if I continue to talk to you?"

Callie nodded again.

"Do you want to sit?"

No way could she move. She shook her head.

The woman took a deep breath. "You can breathe. You're safe with me. I won't leave until you tell me to go. This will be over in a few minutes. You're safe."

The woman's hands anchored her and her soft but compelling voice soothed Callie as she reassured her again, "You're safe. I'm here with you."

Her heart slowed, breathing became easier. She unclenched her jaw, relaxed. And looked away, embarrassed that this stranger had seen her paralyzed by anxiety, yet thankful she was there. She should have taken the Valium.

"I'm all right now, thank you."

"Are you with the tour?"

"Yes."

"I'm standing in front of you so I doubt anyone in our group noticed. If anybody asks, say we recognized each other from college. Now, I'm going to remove my hands and step back."

With a little distance Callie was able to see the woman's caring face, not just her kind eyes. The eleventh member of the group was a woman, not a man. And she seemed unfazed by Callie's inability to function in public. But that was now. What about the next thirty days?

Traveling with a group where the only thing she had to think about was getting herself up and out every day seemed like a good idea, but five minutes out of her room she'd had an attack. What was she thinking? She backed away.

"I can't do this."

"Don't leave." The woman's voice stopped her. "Give it a chance. I'll help you if it happens again. What have you got to lose? You've already paid for the trip so you can leave at any time if it becomes too difficult."

She must be the other single on the trip. But Callie was puzzled why whether she stayed mattered to this total stranger. "Why do you care?"

The woman glanced over her shoulder, then lowered her voice before answering, "To be frank, I'm not sure I'm staying either."

"Really?"

She looked at the group again. "But I'd like to do the trip if I can. We're both alone and, I'd guess, about the same age. Maybe we can help each other. I'll stay if you do."

Callie followed her gaze to the group. "I can't. This was a mistake. Everybody is pointing and laughing at me. I can't do it." She backed away, toward the elevators.

"It's not you. It's the bird."

"Bird?"

The woman pointed toward the ceiling.

Callie looked up. A small brown and white bird, probably a sparrow, was swooping, dipping, and soaring up and around her head. She'd been so wrapped up in her angst she hadn't noticed. But everyone else was smiling. A group of hotel employees approached, waving their arms, shooing the bird toward the open door. It looked as if they were succeeding until the bird turned sharply and dove back toward Callie and the others on the tour. It circled Callie, singing a cheery song, swooped over the tall woman standing near her, sang for a few seconds, then returned to fly around Callie, warbling happily.

Callie laughed. *Is that you, Abby? Are you telling me to stay?* It felt like a sign. Then, almost as if the bird knew she'd made a decision, it darted through the open door to freedom. She took a deep breath and slowly exhaled.

"A friend of yours?" The tall woman smiled.

Callie faced her, grinning. "Maybe." When she'd agreed to the tour, she'd given herself permission to walk away if it got to be too much. If this woman was offering to help, she'd give the tour a day or two and then decide whether to stay.

"All right. I'll try it a couple of days. I can't thank you—"

"I'm happy to help. I'm Dana. And you are?"

"Callie. Sorry about the freak-out. I don't know what came over me." She'd hoped to avoid talking about her condition to anyone on the trip.

"Really?" Dana raised her eyebrows. "It looked like an anxiety attack to me."

Dana had helped her and didn't seem at all turned off, so Callie went with her gut reaction. "Busted." They laughed. Dana had a lovely laugh.

"How are you feeling? Fatigue? Nausea?"

Callie hesitated to share, but why hide when Dana had seen the attack and seemed to know what followed? "Fatigued and thirsty."

Dana reached into the bag at her feet and pulled out a bottle of water. She twisted off the cap and handed it to Callie. "Drink." She pulled a chair over. "Sit."

"Are you always this bossy?" Callie did as she was told, enjoying the distraction.

"Only when necessary." Dana watched her drink.

They both looked up as an attractive blond thirty-something woman wearing a crisp blue shirt with Romantic Italy embroidered above her left breast and a big smile on her face moved into the middle of the group.

"Hi, welcome to the Romantic Italy tour. I'm Camilla. Feel free to call me Millie."

Callie detected a slight Italian accent.

Millie looked at each of them. "As stated in the contract you signed, to protect your privacy we only use first names on the tour. Of course, you may reveal your full name whenever you choose. When I call your name, please hand me your trip voucher."

Callie retrieved the voucher from her backpack.

Millie looked at the clipboard in her hand. "Callie." Her gaze traveled over everyone standing nearby.

Callie froze. She hadn't expected to be the first one called.

Hearing no response, Millie went on. "Carl."

"Here." A tall older man stepped forward.

Millie smiled and accepted his voucher. "Dana."

Dana hesitated, glanced at Callie, and, seeming to have made a decision, she stepped forward with her voucher. "Here." Callie felt bad. Dana said she'd give it a chance if Callie did, so she was probably wondering why Callie hadn't responded.

When the eleven others were accounted for, Millie read Callie's name again. It was now or never. Callie took a deep breath. "Here."

Twelve heads swiveled in her direction. Red-faced, she handed over her trip voucher and sat again.

"I was afraid you were abandoning me already." Dana spoke softly. She looked relieved.

Dana seemed sweet. Callie couldn't help but smile back.

"Okay, folks, we're all here, so let's get started." The woman's voice was strong and clear. "Welcome to Milan and the first day of the Romantic Italy tour. As I said, I'm Millie. I'll be your guide for the next month as we travel through Italy on our comfortable luxury bus.

"First order of business is to make sure your cell phones are always charged and on because I'll text reminders, a half hour and fifteen minutes, before we depart any place we visit. You can plug in on the bus if necessary." She gave them a minute to check their phones. "And though we allow ample free time on the tour, the second is, whenever you are not with the group you must text me periodically to let me know where you are so I know you're safe.

"As you probably remember, our first day is packed with the wonderful sights of Milan. From here, we'll go directly to a guided tour of the Duomo di Milano, the first of several lovely gothic cathedrals you'll see while in Italy. After the tour, I suggest those who enjoy being on their own climb or take the elevator to the top of the cathedral and enjoy the spectacular views of Milan, then, walk across the street to the Galleria Vittorio Emanuele, an indoor shopping mall, for shopping and lunch."

She stopped to check they were all listening. "Those of you who don't want to go to the top of the cathedral and prefer a guided walk and a group lunch stay with me when we leave the Duomo. The bus will be in front of the cathedral at two thirty to drive us to the church of Santa Maria delle Grazie for our 3:15 viewing of Leonardo Da Vinci's *Last Supper*." She took a breath.

"After that, there's an optional walk on the Via Dante before returning to the hotel to rest and change. We'll meet in the lobby at five thirty to walk to the restaurant for dinner and from there walk to La Scala opera house for a performance of *Carmen*.

"It's a lot for one day, I know, but we like to kick off the trip with a bang. Let me know if you decide to skip any of the activities. The Daily Info Packet"—she held up a sheaf of papers—"which you should have received electronically earlier and in hard copy when you checked into the hotel, contains today's schedule, a map of Milan, information about the places we'll visit today and some recommendations for places to eat lunch.

"My cell number is also in the packet. If you haven't already put it in your phone, please do it as soon as you're seated in the bus. Call me any time, day or night, if you have a problem during the trip. At the end of each day, I'll leave a packet with information about the next day's activities and any vouchers or passes at the hotel desk. I'll also email a copy of the itinerary.

"And, speaking of the bus, Enzo, our driver for the month has arrived."

The young man wearing a blue Romantic Italy T-shirt waved and bowed.

"Please follow him to the bus in front of the hotel."

The members of the group gathered their things and straggled after Enzo. Confined to a bus with thirteen strangers? Callie felt her blood drain. What made her think she could do this? She stood and faced Dana. "I'm sorry. I can't do this. I'm going back to my room to book a flight home."

Dana studied her. "What's changed?"

Millie came over. "Is everything all right?"

Dana stepped back, allowing Callie to handle it.

"I was thinking I might not do the tour and Dana was helping me decide." She started to shake.

Dana moved closer. "Give us a few minutes, Millie."

Concern on her face, Millie addressed Callie. "It's really a great tour. I hope you'll stay. But you can still join us tomorrow if you don't want to do today. The bus is right outside, so please decide quickly." She left them alone.

"My offer still stands, Callie. I won't leave you alone, so I'll be there if you have an attack. And if you decide to leave, I promise to help you book a flight and a room at the closest airport and arrange for transportation to the airport. Come on, give it a couple of days."

Callie didn't understand why Dana was so invested in her staying, but she seemed to be. Why not accept her offer? She had nothing to lose and a great deal to gain. If she stayed she could do the research necessary to write her book. And wasn't the bird in the lobby a sign from Abby that she should do the tour? "All right."

Dana nodded. "If you're sure, we should head out to the bus."

Millie was standing in front of the bus when they arrived. Callie smiled. "Thank you for waiting. I hope I haven't delayed us too long."

"Not at all. I'm glad you're staying."

Dana asked Millie a question. Callie climbed into the bus. It really was luxurious. There were six groups of two nicely cushioned recliners with seatbelts spaced to provide plenty of legroom and privacy for each twosome. Only two seats were free, one next to Ponytail Man and the other next to the sour-faced woman who had started complaining as she left the lobby of the hotel.

Callie hesitated. Ponytail Man waved with a sleazy grin and pointed to the seat next to him. She didn't want to sit with him, but she didn't want to be rude. He stood. "Take the window seat. I'm James. And you are?"

He was being so friendly she had no choice. "Callie." Damn, she would be trapped. She moved past him and shifted as she sat trying to get as far from him as she could, hoping she could just ignore him. He dropped into the seat next to her. She could hear him breathing and felt him shift closer. The sweet scent of his cologne flooded her senses. She glanced out the window. She couldn't bear being next to him. Not only did he seem predatory but based on the little conversation she'd overheard, he was a pedantic boor. Should she leave? Taking a deep breath, she was about to ask him to get up when she heard that soothing voice.

"Would you be a dear, James, isn't it? Callie and I haven't seen each other in ages. We would be forever in your debt if you would move so we could sit together. Right, Cal?"

"Oh. I'd rather..." He looked at Dana, who was looming over him, then at Callie cowering against the window, then offered a smile which he probably thought was seductive. "Of, course, lovely ladies." He rose, looked around, then sat next to the sour puss.

Dana slid into the seat and spoke softly. "I hope it's all right with you. I couldn't bear sitting next to the complainer. And I thought you might feel the same about you-know-who."

"More than all right. That's twice you've saved me in less than half an hour." She breathed deeply. "Is it Saint Dana?"

"You're not the first to call me that, but you are the first to mean it positively." Dana leaned in close. "I shouldn't make snap judgments, but in the short time we were in the lobby, she was bitching about every little thing, and he was hanging all over me until he spotted you. I turned to see why he was drooling, and that's when I saw you. I think he's hot for the beautiful, blond, blue-eyed cheerleader type and obviously thinks he's so sexy you'd be happy to have him."

"I'm far from a beautiful blond cheerleader." *It might have been true before Abby died but not now.* "Actually, I look more like a drug addict these days." Why had she said that? "But I'm not. An addict." She flushed. "And for the record, flattery from a saint is a turnoff."

The color drained from Dana's face. "I'm so sorry, Callie. I'm just as offensive as him. You don't have to explain anything. I'll shut up now. Let's see if we can relax and enjoy this very expensive tour."

Dana had been so generous Callie wanted to ease her discomfort. "I'm all right. I'm just sensitive about how I look. But you're right. Let's forget everything and focus on the tour. Are you still willing to be my protector if I stay for the rest of the trip?"

"Of course. And don't worry about him. I've read the way these things work is that people tend to take the same seats over and over again, and I'm positive the next thirty days will be a lot more enjoyable sitting next to you than either of those two."

"Anxiety and all?"

Dana smiled and patted her hand. "Anxiety and all."

"How did you know I was having an anxiety attack?"

"Been there, done that."

Callie was curious, but she wasn't willing to talk about Abby and she knew if she asked what had triggered Dana's anxiety, she would be opening herself to Dana's questions. Besides, the important thing was that Dana knew what to do and seemed willing to help her deal with her anxiety. And, to her surprise, she felt safe with Dana sitting next to her.

She gazed out the window, not quite believing she was in Milan and enjoying the company of a virtual stranger. A flock of birds swirling in the sky brought the bird from the hotel to mind. It might have been a coincidence, but Abby had said if she could, she'd come back as a bird and watch over her. And there was no denying the bird had flown into the hotel and paid particular attention to her. Could it have been Abby? Angela, Erin, Bonnie, and Maggie would have a good laugh over this development.

The bus stopped in front of what could only be the Duomo. It was magnificent. She turned from the window. People were getting off the bus yet Dana hadn't moved to leave. Why?

"I thought it would be best if we were behind everyone in case you get anxious. Is that all right?" Was it a coincidence that Dana answered her unspoken question? Or was she tuned in to her?

"Good thinking. Thank you." Callie pulled her phone out of her backpack. She always took photos of the places she might include in a book so she could reference them along with her notes while writing.

Dana moved into the aisle. "Should I go before or after you?"

Callie took a deep breath. "I'd feel better if I could see you."

"Sure." Dana led her out to the plaza in front of the cathedral. Like everyone else the rest of the tour group was looking up, trying to take in the gorgeous building. Callie snapped a few pictures before Millie led them inside the Duomo and introduced their guide.

The young man was great, putting what they were seeing in context with descriptions, stories and tidbits that brought it all alive. Fascinated, Callie managed to forget herself and be in the moment until she got caught in the middle of the group. Dana noticed her shaking, pulled her close to shield her, and quietly talked her down before she had a full-on attack. After that they stayed at the outer edge of the group, close enough to hear but far enough back so she didn't have to deal with all those bodies touching her.

When they'd completed the full circuit of the cathedral, Millie reminded them they could go with her to the Galleria and lunch, go to the roof of the cathedral, or take some free time on their own. Callie dropped into a nearby pew. The cathedral was beautiful. She and Abby had planned this trip. Now, though, she was alone and obligated to write a romance—when fear was the strongest emotion she was feeling. Members of the group followed Millie out. She didn't want to go with the group and getting in an elevator to go to the top of the Duomo seemed beyond her. She wanted to wander and discover. But what if she had an attack when she was alone?

Dana sat beside her. "Want to go to the roof with me?"

"I can't. Being in an elevator pressed up against people makes me anxious."

"Want to try? Maybe it would help if you faced me and looked only at me?"

Callie studied Dana. The roof of the cathedral was one of her and Abby's don't-miss places. One of several possible romantic places she'd identified for her lovers to meet. Could she chance it? "You're willing to go on the elevator with me?"

"I'll do the elevator if that's what you want. But walking up would be better for you. Aerobic exercise changes your brain chemistry and decreases muscle tension. Both are good for people who suffer anxiety, but I get that the idea of so many steps might be too scary for you."

Callie eyed Dana. "That sounded like a challenge."

Dana smiled and lifted her shoulders. "Your choice. Trust that I won't let anything bad happen to you. I am your protector, after all."

I hope you're not too old to do it, Abby had written in the guidebook, issuing a sort of challenge. Abby really knew how to push Callie's competitive buttons.

"I can't believe I'm even entertaining the idea of walking." Callie chewed her lip. She heard Angela's voice. *You're one of the strongest people I know.*

Maggie had pushed her to exercise for her physical and mental health, and, though in the beginning she often didn't have the energy to stand, forget walking on the treadmill, she'd managed some exercise in the last six months.

"I'm really out of shape, Dana. Starting with two hundred and fifty steps might be pushing it." Dana waited patiently while she made her decision. "What if I can't make it?"

"If you're willing to try, I'll make sure you get to the roof."

For some reason she trusted Dana would take care of her. She nodded.

Luck was with them. The steps weren't super crowded. Dana set a reasonable pace and managed to distract her by describing what she'd read about the Duomo. They stopped often to hydrate, giving Callie a chance to catch her breath and let others squeeze past them. By the time the end was in sight, however, her legs felt like tree stumps and getting to the top seemed impossible.

"I can't do it."

Dana looked from Callie to the landing above. "Is it alright if I put my arms around you to help you up?"

"Yes," Callie breathed out.

"I can help if you'd like," offered the man behind them. He had been patient, almost protective on the way up. "It would be easier with two of us."

Dana leaned and spoke softly. "I can do it alone if you don't want him to touch you."

She didn't want to make this any more difficult than necessary for Dana. "That's very kind of you. I'm sure my friend would appreciate the help."

Dana and the man carried her up the last thirty steps. When they emerged onto the roof, the man warned, "I'm going to let go now."

Her legs were wobbly, but she could stand on her own. "I'm good. Thank you so much."

"No problem." He smiled and walked away before she had a chance to feel more awkward. She made a mental note to include a similar act of kindness in her book.

She was hot and sweaty and exhausted but triumphant. She'd needed help, but Dana had challenged her to move past her fear and she had. They drank some water, then sat side by side, grinning at each other. A text came in from Angela. *Have you on my mind. I hope it's going well.*

"Sorry to be rude, Dana. I hope you don't mind if I text my friend back and brag a little."

"Be my guest. You've earned bragging rights."

Callie typed, *So far so good. Just walked up 200+ steps to the roof of Milan's Duomo. Talk later.*

After about ten minutes Callie recovered, and they walked around the roof enjoying the spectacular views and the sculptures. They took selfies alone and together on each of their phones, and Dana used Callie's phone to snap several pictures of her with gorgeous views in the background. When they found an open spot near where other tourists were resting, Dana removed her jacket and stretched out in the sun with her eyes closed.

Callie took the opportunity to send her friends a group text with a picture of her with the view behind her. She snapped a couple of pictures of Dana, then pulled her trip journal and her Mont Blanc pen from her backpack and made notes about her day so far. Thinking about the bird in the lobby brought tears to her eyes. But she smiled as she described it circling everyone in the group but seeming to single out her and Dana. It really did seem to be Abby. She described the anxiety attack in the lobby and Dana coming to her rescue, the attack during the tour of the Duomo, her impressions of the Duomo, her pride in accepting Dana's challenge to walk up, and the kindness of the stranger who had helped Dana get her to the top. Would Abby have made it all the way?

She recorded her first impressions of the other members of their little group as well. The offensive ponytail guy and the complaining woman, who seemed to be singles. The middle-aged heterosexual couple who were so into each other they must be new. The couple that looked to be in their seventies who seemed close, though while the woman seemed relaxed and related, the man seemed distant. The two women who held hands and touched often, obviously a lesbian couple. The other two women who looked so alike they must be sisters. One seemed miserable and withdrawn while the other oscillated between focusing on the art and architecture of the cathedral and comforting her.

And then there was Dana. Strong but gentle, kind and caring. She would make a fantastic character. Her pen in midair, Callie froze. Dana as one of the lovers? Why not? She slid the trip journal into her backpack, pulled out her book journal and wrote down her impressions of the woman. *Dana is kind and easy to be with. She had challenged her but left room for her to set limits. Her back and arms are muscled and her legs long. She looks like a swimmer. She's probably also a runner because she had had no problem walking up the steps and, if she was honest about those last steps, carrying her. With her gleaming dark hair, her large luminous gray-blue eyes, the gentle curve of her eyebrows, the fullness of her lips and the sculpted planes of her face she was beautiful but not in a girlie way. She was willowy, seemed comfortable in her body and carried herself with confidence and grace. In her jeans, white button-down shirt, and blue blazer with gold buttons, she looked businesslike, yet casual. And sexy.*

Sexy? That thought surprised her. It was just an observation and didn't mean anything. Yet she felt guilty for noticing.

Dana opened her eyes and caught Callie staring. She pretended to be thinking and made a note in her book. "You writing about me?"

"What?" How had Dana figured it out? "Don't flatter yourself, Saint Dana. I've been keeping a diary since I was nine years old." She shot her a small smile, hoping it conveyed that she was teasing. "I always make notes about what I'm seeing and feeling when I travel."

She entered another note. *The lovers could meet on the steps when he helps her up the last flight to the roof. Or even on the roof when they are both resting from the walk and he drops his wallet or phone or something and she picks it up. Who are they and why are they there?* She underlined the last sentence.

"Ready to go down?" Dana stood and slipped into her jacket.

Callie let out a breath. Dana wasn't offended. "Yes, ma'am. And, ready for lunch."

Dana looked around. "It looks like most people have cleared out. Let's check the elevator situation."

Happily, there were only two other people waiting. "I'll be all right with just the four of us as long as I can hold on to you and not see the others."

As they descended, Dana stood with her back to the elevator wall. Callie faced her and grasped her arms, but she avoided looking into her eyes. How lucky was she to find someone with whom she felt safe and who was able to help and willing to put up with her? Maybe Abby *had* arranged this. It was that or divine intervention that brought her and Dana together.

Before they entered the Galleria, Dana read from Millie's briefing. "The Galleria Vittorio Emanuele II dates from the 1870s and is Italy's oldest active shopping mall."

"A mall? Really?" Callie put her hands on her hips. "I could have stayed in New Jersey if I wanted to spend time in a shopping mall."

Dana put her hand up. "But this one not only has a glass and steel ceiling but it's embellished with mosaics and stone carvings of draped female figures around windows and balconies, something I'm sure your local mall doesn't have." She extended her arm. "Shall we?"

They took a minute in the entryway to study the ceiling before walking in. It was beautiful and unusual. But the heat, the noise, and the press of people was intense, and when they were suddenly surrounded by a large tour group pushing past to stay close to their leader, Callie started hyperventilating. Sweat broke out on her forehead.

"Let's get out of here. Is it okay if I put my arm around you so we can stay close?" Dana spoke softly in her ear, reassuring her as she eased them through the crowd. Callie was shaking by the time they were outside in the sunshine. Dana steered her to a quiet spot and turned her so they were face-to-face.

"I'm going to touch you again, Callie. You can breathe. I'm here. You're safe with me." She repeated the comforting phrases over and over.

Callie inhaled and exhaled the way Maggie had taught her until she felt in control. She stepped back, wiped the sweat from her face, and leaned against the building, exhausted. "Thank you." She touched Dana's arm. "I can't tell you how much I appreciate—"

"I'm happy to help, Callie. It almost feels like fate put us together on this tour. I'm enjoying your company and if I can help you with your anxiety, all the better. Why don't we sit on that bench"—she tipped her head—"until you feel ready to walk?"

Callie drank some water and after sitting for about ten minutes she felt better. "I'm ready. Let's find someplace to have lunch."

Dana extended a hand and pulled Callie up. "The restaurants in the Galleria and right near the Duomo seem noisy and geared to tourists, which usually means not so great food and higher prices. I'll bet we'll find better, quieter options a couple of blocks in any direction."

"That's a wonderful idea. The thing I loved about traveling when I was younger was finding the out-of-the-way spots most tourists avoid. But thanks for encouraging me to go inside the Galleria. It's overwhelming but beautiful and I'm happy I saw it."

Callie could feel her energy flagging again as they wandered. "I haven't walked this much in…a long time, Dana. I'm going to need to sit soon." She smiled weakly. "Unless you want to carry me back to the bus."

"I'll need to refuel before I can carry you, so let's keep our eyes open. You might find it easier to continue if you hold on to me."

She extended her arm. They walked another block and turned a corner. Dana pointed to a pretty little restaurant across the street. She glanced at Millie's list. "Trattoria Tomassino isn't on Millie's list of lunch places, but I'm game if you are."

They sat in the shade of several trees and looked at the menu. Dana ordered the three-course price-fixed lunch—risotto Milanese, osso buco, and fresh fruit. Callie selected the cold antipasto.

Dana sipped her sparkling water. "It sounds like you've done a bit of travel in the past. Is this your first tour?"

Callie laughed. "Is my snobbery showing? Yes. My first. I've always looked down on people who need guides to travel because I like to explore and discover rather than be told what to look at. But the anxiety attacks made a tour the only option. Romantic Italy seemed perfect because of the smallness of the group, the flexibility in terms of restaurants and menus, and the amount of free time to explore on my own. But even on this tour I couldn't have gotten this far without you." She looked away to hide the tears threatening to fall. Happily, the waiter delivered Dana's risotto and her antipasto. Callie stared at the huge platter he placed in front of her—olives, balls of fresh mozzarella cheese, salami, prosciutto, stuffed sweet cherry peppers, marinated mushrooms, eggplant, and a couple of things she didn't recognize.

Dana touched Callie's hand and spoke softly so the diners at nearby tables couldn't hear. "It's only been a few hours, but I've enjoyed being with you. We seem to have similar tastes and interests. I'm looking forward to spending time getting to know you. And please know, helping you is not a burden. Hopefully you'll become more comfortable around crowds and the attacks will diminish. That's what happened with me."

"I hope you're right." Callie hadn't realized the antipasto platter would be so large. She placed a selection on a small plate and pushed the large platter over to Dana. "Please help me with this, it's too much for me."

Dana eyed the small plate in front of Callie. "Thanks. But it goes two ways. Here, try the risotto." She held out her fork.

Callie gazed at Dana. She looked innocent but somehow Callie knew Dana understood her. Well, one forkful wouldn't kill her. "That's good. Thank you. There's something wonderful about eating outdoors. Everything seems to taste better, and, for some reason, I don't feel guilty about eavesdropping on conversations. Especially when I don't understand a word they're saying."

They ate in silence, both paying attention to the activity in the restaurant and people walking past. When the waiter delivered her osso buco, Dana eyed Callie's plate. "I don't mean to be intrusive, but you've barely touched the little food you put on that little plate. I've eaten more of your lunch than you have."

"I don't have much of an appetite." Callie cut a small piece off the stuffed pepper with her fork. She gazed at Dana. "Though that might change if you keep exercising me the way you have today." She chewed the stuffed pepper.

Dana snapped her fingers. "Two hundred and fifty steps were just to warm us up. Wait until tomorrow." They laughed.

"You'll need fuel to keep up with me." Dana held out a forkful of her veal. "Taste this. It's delicious."

Callie hesitated, then opened her mouth. She chewed. "Yum, it's wonderful."

As they chatted about what they'd seen and liked in the Duomo and looked at the pictures they'd taken on the roof, Dana fed her a little more of her osso buco.

The service was leisurely. The waiter cleared their dishes but seemed distressed by the amount of food remaining on Callie's plate. She mimed that it wasn't the food, but she didn't speak Italian and his English was minimal, so she wasn't sure he got it. She thought about the app she'd downloaded, but she hadn't used it yet and didn't want to embarrass herself.

Dana took her phone out of her backpack, entered something, then spoke to him in shaky Italian. He looked puzzled so she pointed to her phone. He glanced at Callie sympathetically and said something.

"What did you say to him? And what did he say to you."

"I told him you didn't feel well." Dana laughed. "Of course, as you saw, he had no idea what I said until he read the phrase on the phone. I think he said you need to eat more."

"You're making that up."

"No, really. If you don't do better, I'll have to eat all your food and mine so we don't insult the waiters."

It occurred to Callie that Dana had sneakily fed her from her plate. "Hey, missy, don't think I didn't notice you tricked me into sharing your veal shank."

"You really do need to eat if we're going to be walking around, but I guess it was presumptuous of me to make that decision for you. Are you mad?"

"No." Callie smiled. "I just don't know why you care. About me, I mean."

Dana shrugged. "My best friend, Ellen, says I'm a caretaker, so maybe that's it. Or maybe it's because I feel connected to you and I'm enjoying being with you."

"I'm also feeling connected and enjoying being with you." Interesting. The only things they knew about each other were their first names, that they both suffered anxiety attacks, and that neither of them could speak Italian. "It's terrible being here and not speaking the language. I downloaded an online phrase book but that really isn't enough." *I should have spent the last year learning Italian.*

"I intended to study Italian before the tour started and I actually bought three Italian Language programs—Pimsleur, Duolingo, and Babbel. But then life got in the way and I was preoccupied with…other things." Dana paused to acknowledge the waiter as he placed the fresh fruit they'd ordered on the table. "*Grazie.*"

She smiled at Callie. "At least I know how to say thank you." Her face brightened. "Would you be interested in studying together? I mean using the software, then speaking to each other and, as much as we can, to Italians?"

"Not knowing the language was one of my issues with taking the tour. Do you think we can learn enough in such a short time?"

Dana lifted her hands. "Who knows? We'll probably get a lot of blank stares like I got when I tried to tell the waiter you were sick but what better place to try?"

"I'd like to do it. If I stay with the tour."

"Oh," Dana said. "I forgot you're not sure about continuing." She focused on the fruit, avoiding Callie's gaze.

Callie hated disappointing Dana. "You've made it possible for me to have an almost normal day, but I'm not sure I can do a month." A month was a long time to ask a stranger, no matter how generous, to be her caretaker. "Let's see how the rest of the day goes."

"Sure. We can discuss it when you're ready." Dana reached for a piece of melon.

Callie picked at the fruit while Dana slowly ate the rest, but the silence between them felt awkward. She hadn't known her long, but hurting Dana was the last thing she wanted. She wasn't sure how to reconnect, though.

Dana looked at her phone then waved the waiter over. "*Posso avere il conto, per favore?*" She slowly read from her phone, then showed it to him.

"*Un minuto.*" He picked up the empty fruit plate. And smiled. "*Hai mangiato tutta la frutta, molto bene.*" He walked away.

"You're very brave, Dana. Am I right that he was complimenting us on eating all the fruit?"

"I think so." Dana grinned. "I really want to do this."

Callie realized she really wanted to do it too. Dana was fun and made her want to do things outside her comfort zone. She was tending toward staying but she'd give herself tonight to decide.

"*Il conto.*" The waiter dropped the check on the table and walked away.

Callie insisted they split the check and suggested leaving several extra euros for the waiter's patience. The meal was not only delicious, but inexpensive. Callie was elated. She loved stumbling over unknown places. This kind of experience was what she feared she'd miss as part of a tour group.

"Would you mind if I take a few minutes to make notes about the restaurant?"

They'd both skipped wine with lunch to avoid getting sleepy. Dana raised her glass of sparkling water. "Be my guest." It seemed that the interaction with the waiter had eased the tension between them.

Callie recorded the facts about and her impressions of the restaurant. The leisurely lunch had restored her flagging energy, and after she completed her notes they strolled, checking out the buildings and fountains and statues they encountered and looking in store windows. They found a thousand things to talk about. Dana was interested in many things, as was Callie, but it seemed, history wasn't one of them.

Callie's phone pinged. A text from Bonnie. *Thinking of you. How's it going?*

She looked up from her phone. "I don't want to be rude, Dana, but my friends back home are worried about me so I'm going to text back to reassure them."

"It's nice you have friends who care." Dana looked away, then turned back. "Feel free."

Callie didn't know Dana well, but she was sure she'd looked sad before she turned away. What was that about?

Callie texted Bonnie. *Better than I imagined. More tonight.*

Dana's prediction proved correct. When they got on the bus, everyone sat in the same seats they'd taken that morning and they had no problem sitting together. As the day wore on, it seemed Callie and Dana were totally in sync. Neither enjoyed the restricted viewing of the *Last Supper* and both chose not to walk on the Via Dante, Callie because she was tired and Dana because she'd spent some time there over the weekend.

Hearing her name repeated softly Callie opened her eyes, surprised to see Dana smiling at her. She'd fallen asleep in the bus on the way back to the hotel. She straightened up. "I'm mortified."

Dana laughed. "You aren't the only one." She tilted her head and Callie turned to see several others still sleeping. "Don't worry. It's probably jet lag. Or the unusual activity."

Back in her room, Callie set her alarm and lay on the bed, but sleep now eluded her. She reviewed the day and realized that although she'd had three anxiety attacks, she'd had a good time. Dana was an intelligent, witty, caring woman and she'd enjoyed her company.

But was she ready to spend the evening with the other ten people in a setting that would require conversation? Not really. Yet, if she was going to continue with the group, avoiding tonight would only put off the inevitable. Meeting them when they were all new to each other might be easier.

She dozed, and when her alarm sounded, she showered and changed into the black dress she'd bought recently for the dedication of the memorial to Abby at her university. Angela was right about packing the dresses. She made a mental note to thank her.

Callie sat next to Dana at the round table for twelve and ordered dinner from the regular menu. Millie and Enzo were seated nearby at a table for two. The food was delicious. Dana must have noticed she was mostly pushing the food around on her plate rather than eating it, and whispered in her ear, "If you don't eat a little more you won't be strong enough for tomorrow's challenges." For some reason, the playful way she said it didn't put Callie off. She took another bite, elbowed Dana, then took another.

"Good job." Dana said it softly so only she heard.

It had been almost two years since she'd had this kind of back-and-forth with Abby, or anyone, and she was enjoying it. And though she didn't contribute much, she was comfortable and interested in the lively conversation about what they'd seen today. She'd started to put names to the faces, too.

Loretta and Carl, the couple celebrating their fiftieth anniversary, seemed oddly matched. While he was held back and didn't speak at all, she was relaxed, related, and happy to discuss art, music and the opera.

On the other hand, Miriam, a warm, upbeat woman who laughed easily, and the easygoing Lou, who were on their honeymoon, seemed perfectly matched. Both were fluent in history and politics. Fran, an architect, shared her knowledge of the architecture of Milan, while her wife, Susan, an historian, offered tidbits of the history of Milan. Serena spoke enthusiastically about the art in the cathedral and her disappointment about only having fifteen minutes to view *The Last Supper*. Ellie, her unhappy sister, stared into space.

Vanessa, also known as Miss Grumpy, was British. She interjected occasionally but seemed content to listen. Ponytail Man, James, was his creepy self and mostly focused on her and Dana.

And Dana, who Callie had started to realize was brilliant, seemed interested and involved and able to contribute in some way to every conversation, no matter the topic. Callie had such a good time she forgot to worry about having an attack.

Italians were not known for their willingness to form orderly lines so she shouldn't have been surprised that the crowd pressed around them as they entered the opera house. She was, though, and she started to hyperventilate. Happily, Dana caught on immediately, pulled her aside, grounded her, and waited with her until the crowd thinned and they could enter.

As they took their seats, Callie filled with sadness. Abby had introduced her to opera and tonight, for the first time in twenty years, she was in an opera house without her. She thumbed through her program, hiding her tears.

The performance at La Scala was exceptional, but, exhausted by the panic attacks and such an active day, Callie dozed off as soon as the lights dimmed for the second act. She was embarrassed to find her head on Dana's shoulder when the applause and the cheering woke her. "Oh, damn, now I'm using you as a bed. I hope I didn't drool on you."

Dana stood and stretched. "No worries. You're a neat sleeper." The rest of their group filed out and she texted Millie to say they would be a few minutes late. "I didn't know whether I'd like opera, but I enjoyed the performance."

"I'm glad you enjoyed it. I have a subscription to the Metropolitan Opera in New York City and I assure you, I usually manage to stay awake."

"I'm sure you do. But jet lag, a couple of anxiety attacks, and a very busy day would exhaust most of us. I'm amazed you were awake for the first act." Less than one day together and Callie knew Dana would be supportive.

When the crowd thinned, they left their seats and met the group out front for the walk back to the hotel.

Peopled out and tired from all the activity, Callie passed on a nightcap but agreed to meet Dana for breakfast at eight a.m. Dana walked her to her room before heading to the bar to have a drink with the others. Callie got ready for bed. Although she felt drained, it was still early in New York City, so she texted Angela, Bonnie, and Erin. *Ready to drop. Let's have a short Zoom session.*

They listened without interruption while she described her day. Angela was the first to comment. "I'm so glad you had a good day. I love the bird fluttering around the lobby. It almost makes me believe in reincarnation."

Erin spoke next. "Dana sounds absolutely wonderful. I'm so happy she's there and willing and able to handle your anxiety."

Bonnie looked thoughtful. "That bird is a little creepy. Do you really think it could be Abby? In any case, I'm glad you stayed and I'm glad you made a new friend."

"Dana makes me feel safe. I enjoy her company and I think we could be friends, but it's too early to be sure. Be truthful now. Did any of you or Maggie arrange for Dana to travel with me?"

Angela glanced at the other two. "Absolutely not. But you know, it's exactly the kind of thing Abby would have done."

She was so right. "Oh, God, yes." Callie couldn't stop laughing. "But unless we assume she was the bird checking on things or that she's still arranging my life from heaven or wherever she is, it seems the universe sent someone who knows how to deal with panic attacks and is kind enough to volunteer."

"You have such a beautiful laugh, Callie. I can't tell you how wonderful it is to hear it again." Angela grabbed a tissue and wiped her eyes. "You know, however it happened, Dana seems to be exactly what you need to make this trip work for you."

Callie yawned. "I can't keep my eyes open so I'm going to say good night."

She crawled into bed feeling hopeful. She'd been tense and wary most of the day, but she'd totally relaxed enough times—on the roof of the Duomo, during lunch and the stroll after, during dinner, and, though she'd fallen asleep, at the opera—to call it a success. She closed her eyes. She could see Dana's smiling face, hear her voice, her laugh. With Dana at her side today, Callie had faced down her fears, ventured out into the world, and had fun. Angela was right. One day down, thirty to go. She *could* do this. She *wanted* to do this. On the bus tomorrow she would tell Dana.

So far so good, Abs, but I wish you were here with me. Overwhelmed by a wave of sadness, feeling the loss, feeling alone, Callie cried herself to sleep.

CHAPTER FOUR

Callie was depositing her second suitcase near the door of her room when Dana knocked, a few minutes to eight. "You weren't at breakfast yesterday so I thought you might have trouble finding the breakfast room."

Dana was so thoughtful. "Thanks. You've probably saved me from getting lost and having another attack. Give me a second to get my things." She grabbed her hat, sunglasses, and backpack, then did a quick scan of the room before closing the door behind her.

They stood shoulder to shoulder gazing at the elevator. Dana seemed muted this morning. On the chance that her uncertainty about the tour was the reason for Dana's distress, Callie opted to assure her now. "I'd love to study Italian with you, Dana."

Dana whipped around to face her. "Does that mean you're staying with the tour?"

"I am if you're still willing to be my protector."

"A saint never backs out of a commitment." Dana's shoulders dropped and she seemed to brighten and lighten. "Learning Italian with you will be fun."

The elevator door slid open and they entered. Callie side-eyed Dana, who had miraculously transformed to the relaxed woman of yesterday. No doubt they'd both enjoyed their time together yesterday, but would Dana really have left the tour if she did? She'd explore that some other time. Right now seeing her smile was enough.

Dana led Callie to the breakfast room behind the elevators in the lobby. They sat at the long table with all the others from the tour. Not exactly the table for two Callie had pictured on her way down in the elevator but maybe a good idea since Maggie said the more connected she felt to the others the less likely she'd have an anxiety attack around them. Besides, to her surprise she'd enjoyed the conversation during the group dinner last night.

Callie greeted everyone and, after ordering a cappuccino from the waiter, went to the buffet and selected an orange, a slice of cheese, and a cornetto, the Italian version of a croissant. When she rejoined the group, she learned she wasn't the only one who had dozed off during the opera. "The opera has just been added to the schedule," Millie said. "I'm going to let the head office know that such a long day on the first day of the tour isn't a good idea."

Callie and Dana settled into their seats on the bus as the others trickled in. James, who hadn't been at breakfast, seemed breathless as he climbed on board and stopped in front of them.

"Hey, Dana! I thought I recognized you from that picture in the *Wall Street Journal* last year." James smirked. "You know, the one with your arm around that sexy actress. The one in the article that described you as a software genius and entrepreneur."

Dana tensed and stared into the distance as James plowed ahead. "You using Dana threw me off, but then I remembered your real name, Danielle Wittman, and when I Googled you last night I found rumors that something big is brewing at your company. I'm a stockbroker. Got any insider tips?"

Callie jerked back as Dana popped up from her seat.

"You scummy son of a bitch!" She pushed James and pinned his shoulders to the wall of the bus. "I'm on vacation, damn it, and I expected my privacy to be respected. Insider trading is illegal, and I don't do illegal. And I don't deal with crooks. I should report you and have you blacklisted."

She lifted a fisted hand as if to hit him, but Carl, the man from the couple celebrating their fiftieth anniversary, was standing beside her and grabbed her arm. "Don't. He's not worth it."

Callie moved behind Dana and put her arms around her waist, trying to pull her back to her seat. She looked around. Everyone seemed concerned for Dana.

"Come sit down, Dana." Dana looked over her shoulder at Callie, inhaled, and stepped back.

"And one other thing, asshole, stop staring at Callie like a hungry dog with a steak in front of him."

"Get in your seat, man." Carl pushed James toward the back of the bus and he and the others behind him, followed.

Once they were all in their seats, Millie came to speak to Dana. "What he did was outrageous. Privacy is the reason we only use first names." She looked at Callie. "I'm sorry, too, that I didn't realize he was harassing you."

Callie lifted a shoulder. "Mostly he just stares at me, but he makes me uncomfortable. I hoped he'd get bored eventually."

Millie walked back to James. "Your behavior is unacceptable. I'm going to ask the home office for permission to remove you from the tour."

He paled and started to say something. She held her hand up. "Just sit and be quiet or I'll make the decision on my own and leave you here." He nodded.

Millie walked to the front of the bus and turned on the mic. "Please settle down. I'd apologize for James's inappropriate behavior, but that's up to him. She paused. "The Daily Info Packet contains everything you need to know about the next three days on the Italian Riviera. The drive to Portofino will take about two and a half hours. Once we're there you'll be on your own until three p.m. when we leave to catch the ferry to the Cinque Terre. You'll be free to stroll around the town, walk up the hill for spectacular views of the lighthouse, Castello Brown and Portofino's tiny church, then have lunch in one of the many restaurants on the water." She turned to Enzo. "Okay, let's go."

The bus moved forward and Millie steadied herself before continuing. "From Portofino we'll drive on the coast to Bonassola, then take a boat to Monterosso al Mare, the largest of the five coastal villages that make up the Cinque Terre. We'll spend three nights there. Any questions?" Seeing none, she turned off her mic and sat down.

James's idiocy seemed to have thrown a pall over the group, and except for Millie pointing out the occasional sight along the way, the drive to Portofino was quiet. Dana was staring at her Kindle, but unless she was using mind control to turn the pages, she wasn't reading. Callie had been so focused on herself, her fears, her reason for being here that she hadn't given much thought to who Dana was other than her guardian angel. That she was a lesbian didn't surprise her. It really didn't matter. Though yesterday had had its ups and downs, she'd had fun and laughed more than she had in the three months Abby suffered before she died, and the year since. She'd enjoyed the no pressure time she'd spent with Dana and had started to relate to the others in the group at dinner last night and breakfast this morning. Other than creepy James, who hopefully wouldn't be around too long, the group seemed okay. She could see herself spending time with some of the others. But Dana and the other group members aside, she wasn't on the tour to make friends. She was here to do research for her book, to explore what her characters would see, to imagine what they would feel, and to absorb the romantic atmosphere. So, time to get to work.

She reviewed Millie's itinerary on her phone and wondered why Portofino was included. Granted, the former fishing village was the current playground of the rich and famous, but it didn't seem particularly romantic. Or authentic. The buildings were standard concrete blocks painted with trompe l'oeil designs to make them look historic. And the few attractions she had highlighted—the lighthouse, the Castello Brown and the tiny church—seemed boring.

Callie put her phone aside and tried to nap, but she couldn't get James's comments out of her mind. Dana was still spaced out, so she pulled out her writing journal and Monte Blanc pen and jotted down her thoughts.

Danielle Wittman. A pretty name shortened to Dana, which is more suitable for the relaxed woman I'm starting to know, but it does convey sophistication and power. A computer software entrepreneur seems fitting since she is smart and has an air of confidence about her. But aren't software people all introverts? She doesn't seem the type to date sexy actresses. But why not? She's sexy herself. Characters need to have contradictions like Dana seems to have.

Millie announced they would arrive in ten minutes and Callie put her journal away, then lightened her backpack by placing her MacBook, her Kindle, extra notebooks, the guidebook, extra pens and pencils, and miscellaneous other things she didn't need when walking around, into the small lockbox next to her chair. She turned to Dana. "Ready?"

Dana blinked. "Sure." She quickly stowed her Kindle and her laptop in her own lockbox. "Do you want to hang out together again?"

Callie was surprised. Dana was so kind and sensitive and, despite her anger at James, caring. She was aware that Callie wouldn't get far without her yet she didn't assume. She let her decide.

Callie didn't hesitate. "I'd love to. But"—she formed a cross with a finger from each hand and held it in front of her as if warding off a vampire—"just so you know, I am not climbing to the top of that lighthouse, no way." She hoped Dana would respond to humor.

Dana laughed. "Hey, it's for your own good, but I promise I won't challenge you today."

As they walked away from the bus, Callie noticed James in deep discussion with Millie.

Their few hours in Portofino were relaxed. It helped that it was May 2nd. The heavy tourist season wouldn't start until Memorial Day, so while there were lots of people it was nowhere nearly as crowded as the Galleria had been yesterday. Dana steered them a little off the beaten path and they ambled along, in the sunshine, enjoying the views of the sea and the fresh seaside air.

Dana was quiet and withdrawn again. Callie sensed she was uneasy about her interaction with James, but she didn't want to be intrusive. She jumped when Dana spoke suddenly.

"I'm not a violent person. It's just that I've been feeling vulnerable, and James pushed all the wrong buttons. I overreacted and now I'm feeling doubly exposed." Her voice was full of pain.

Callie's instinct was to take Dana in her arms to comfort her, but they were virtually strangers, and she wasn't sure Dana would welcome it. "I'm sorry he did that to you."

"Do you think I overreacted?"

"Absolutely not. Not only did he invade your privacy by digging up information about you, he made sure everyone heard it and then asked you to do something illegal. I probably would have reacted the same way. And from what I saw, the rest of the group is behind you. James is the one exposed, not you."

Dana nodded but didn't comment. They continued walking in silence until she spoke again. "Thank you, Callie." She stopped. "Want to walk to the water and look for a place to eat?"

Callie was relieved that the pain was gone from Dana's voice. "Did you read Millie's notes?"

Dana shook her head.

"She warned that the seafood here is frozen and almost all the restaurants have the same expensive price-fixed menus. She recommends the food and prices of Lo Stella, a family-owned restaurant facing the harbor."

They had no trouble finding the restaurant and a table with a beautiful view of the water. While they were studying the menu, four women from the tour group asked to join them. Dana looked to Callie to make the decision. She panicked a second, then realized ignoring them would seem hostile. "Yes, please do, we have plenty of room."

Just as they sat, Loretta and Carl appeared. "May we join you?" She'd noticed Loretta's pretty Southern accent last night.

In for a penny, in for a pound. What difference would two more make? Especially since Carl had kept Dana from hitting James, something she would surely have regretted doing. "Yes, we'd love to have you."

Pesto was a local specialty and they all ordered the Lasagna Pesto, Millie's recommendation. Callie tuned in but didn't participate while some of the others expressed outrage at James's behavior. Dana thanked them, then asked everyone where they were from. Ellie, the woman who looked beaten and depressed, and her sister Serena were from Chicago. Fran and Susan, the lesbian couple, were from Pittsburgh, and Loretta and Carl were from Lake View, South Carolina. That Dana was from New York was a nice surprise.

While the conversation about their various cities flowed around her, Callie picked at her lasagna, listened to the squawking of the seagulls and watched the smaller birds, Italian sparrows as she'd confirmed on Google, flit around on the ground pecking at food left behind by careless tourists. None of the birds seemed particularly interested in her, and her tablemates respected her silence so she sat back and observed.

Carl seemed attentive but comfortable behind the invisible wall between him and the world. Ellie also appeared to be in her own world but in pain. Callie hadn't said a single word to the woman but she felt her distress. And their appetites appeared to be similar. Ellie was also nibbling and mostly pushing the food around on her plate. She must have noticed Callie watching because she dropped her gaze to Callie's plate, then looked up and met Callie's eyes with an ever-so-small smirk. An acknowledgement?

Callie studied Dana, the way she focused on whoever was speaking, listening attentively, asking questions, and responding when she had something to say, not just to hear herself talk, how she drew everyone in so no one dominated, and, how knowledgeable she was about so many things. She was tempted, but she knew it would be rude to take out her notebook and jot down some of these observations as ideas for her character. Oh, well. Dana was being Dana, so this wouldn't be the last time she displayed these characteristics.

Callie steeled herself for questions about why she was on the tour alone, but no one asked her or Dana, and neither offered. As the meal continued, Callie relaxed and joined in the wide-ranging conversation.

A few minutes before three, the eight of them boarded the bus for the hour-long drive down the coast to the beach town of Bonassola. As soon as Dana seemed involved with something on her computer, Callie began to write in her journal.

Dana relates to everyone, pulls them in, contributes to every conversation. Contrary to my stereotype, she really is an extrovert. Nice dichotomy for the character. Both Carl and Ellie are pulled back from the group for different reasons. He seems an observer and she seems to be suffering. Interesting for one or both characters.

The drive was timed so they would only have to wait fifteen or twenty minutes to board the ferry to Monterosso al Mare, the largest of the five centuries-old fishing villages collectively known as the Cinque Terre. Enzo dropped them off and left to drive the bus and their luggage overland to the hotel. While they waited for the ferry to arrive, Callie scanned the itinerary on her phone.

The Cinque Terre appeared more in line with her expectations. Three nights in the Hotel Porto Roco, built on a cliff overlooking the sea. Now that sounded romantic. The terraced restaurant specialized in the fresh seafood of the area, the pool, and the beach just two minutes away were pluses. The center of town was five minutes away and provided easy access to the ferry or trains to the other four towns. Or they could hike the Blue Trail, which connected the five towns. Six hours to complete? *Nope.* Not her thing. But wait. There was a hike that would be perfect for the book—the Via dell'Amore, a flat mile-long trail on the side of the cliff along the water, famous for its kissing statue and tunnel covered with declarations of love.

Callie put her phone away. She'd overlooked the Cinque Terre in her research for the book and planned to go directly to Venice from Milan. That would have been a mistake. She reached for her journal but looked up at the sound of throat clearing.

James was standing in front of them. "Dana, Callie, I realize I have no right to ask, but can we speak privately?" He spoke softly.

Callie assumed Dana would refuse, but she nodded. "You seemed to feel fine talking in front of the group this morning. So just say what you have to say." She didn't speak softly. The members of their group circled them. Carl positioned himself next to Dana.

James flushed, but he didn't look away. "I apologize. I was way, way out of line. I let my need to be cool get the better of me. I don't do illegal trades either. I'm so sorry I invaded your privacy."

He turned to Callie. "And I apologize for making you uncomfortable." He watched the ferry docking. "Millie said it's up to the two of you whether I can stay on the tour." His eyes filled. "I'm not a bad guy. I know there's no excuse for my behavior, but my wife dumped me four months ago for a younger guy, and I came on the tour hoping to meet someone younger, like you two. I meant to be hip or, as they say these days, dope, but I guess I've been an ass. I would understand if either of you says no, but I hope you'll give me another chance. I promise you won't regret it."

Dana studied him as if trying to see into his heart. "I'll talk it over with Callie. We'll let you know tonight or tomorrow morning."

"Okay, folks, let's get on the ferry." Millie herded them along.

The Daily Info Packet failed to mention the breathtaking approach to the five towns. It helped that it was a gorgeous sunny day, the sky was deep blue, and the water sparkled as if blue-green emeralds were riding the waves. Callie's spirits soared seeing the colorful stacked houses tumbling down the mountainside to the water's edge and the neat terraces bursting with lush green crops. The fine mist blowing back as the boat powered forward, the taste of salt, and the thrill of the wind whipping her hair filled her with happiness, with the joy of being alive.

"Oh, Abby, it's so beautiful, we're going to love it." Callie turned and hugged…

Oh God, not Abby. Dana gasped. *Damn.* She'd hugged Dana, called her Abby, and acted like they were a "we" and not two individuals who barely knew each other.

"Oh my God, I'm so sorry."

Red-faced, she pulled away and stared straight ahead, not seeing through her tears. For just a minute, in her excitement, she'd forgotten it wasn't Abby standing next to her. Now she was filled with sorrow. Abby was gone, and they would never again share something so beautiful. She shook, and gasped for air.

Dana responded immediately, speaking softly from next to her. "You're safe, Callie. I'm right here. Nod if I can touch you." She nodded. Dana turned and put her arms around her. "Do you want to sit?" Gasping, she shook her head.

"Look up and out. Focus on the beauty, the colors, the freshness of the air, the sun on the water. You're not alone, I'm here. You're safe." Dana repeated the words over and over while encouraging Callie to not hunch her body forward and keep her air passages open.

Yes. The green gardens, the blue sky, the white froth on the blue water and the calm blue-gray of Dana's eyes, the mist on her face, the safety of Dana's arms. She sucked in air, then did it again and again. Her heart slowed. Her body relaxed.

Dana pulled a tissue from her bag and wiped the tears off Callie's face. "Feeling better?"

"Yes. Thanks to you. Again." Callie shifted away from Dana. "Sorry about physically attacking you. I was blown away by the beauty of the place." She gestured to the harbor as they neared. "And I wanted to share it, but it was inappropriate to touch you. I didn't stop to think, I just acted."

"Hey, you surprised me, that's all. No reason to have an anxiety attack. Besides, I'd never turn down a hug from a beautiful woman."

Callie smiled. "Come on, Dana, we've talked about this and we both know I look like shit. And the hug was inappropriate." It seemed like Dana hadn't heard her call her Abby and thought it was the hug that had freaked her out. Good. She wasn't going to have to explain about Abby. But Dana was a lesbian. Was she flirting or just being nice?

Dana put a finger on Callie's chin, lifted her face, and looked into her eyes. "I see your inner beauty. And hugging is what old college friends do."

Her ever-changing gray-blue eyes looked green in this light and were so tender Callie was tempted to hug her again, but this time her, not Abby. The comment about seeing her inner beauty warmed her. "Thank you."

"Let's sit." Dana pointed at some empty seats. "You should rest."

The silence between them was easy, giving Callie the space to think. The attention of everyone in their group was focused on the view, not her. But had anyone else witnessed her attack?

As the boat docked in Monterosso, Dana remained seated. "No rush. Millie will wait for us."

Sure enough, Millie and the group were standing together. "Okay, we're all here. Follow me. The path up to the hotel is kind of steep, so take your time. You can't get lost."

Dana hung back. "Why don't we stop for a cool drink first?" Callie gazed at her. She looked innocent, but Callie guessed she sensed how exhausted she was from the attack and was being protective again, suggesting time for her to rest a bit.

"I'd like that."

Dana let Millie know they'd follow later, then they sat at the nearest outdoor café. When their cold nonalcoholic drinks arrived, Callie asked, "What do you think we should do about James?"

"He seemed sincere. What he did was stupid and insensitive, but anyone can make a mistake. I'm inclined to give him a second chance. I'd like to get a feel for what some of the others think and confirm with Millie that if we give him a second chance we can boot him later if he gets out of line or I find out he's exposed me in some way. What about you?"

Dana really was kind. Callie wasn't sure she could be so forgiving if he'd exposed her the way he'd exposed Dana. "I also feel he was sincere in his apology, but I'm not sure he can control his impulse to be cool. So he might do something else to offend one of us again. But I'll go along with a second chance if Millie agrees we have the option to ask him to leave later."

"Okay, I'll chat with a couple of the others to get their opinions. Let's forget him and relax for a while."

They sipped their drinks and people-watched, commenting now and then. Callie opened her mouth to thank Dana for her support and for understanding her need to recuperate after an attack, but Dana spoke first. "I wasn't sure you would stay but cockeyed optimist that I am I laid out an Italian study plan last night. Want to take a minute to talk about it?"

"Hey, your"—she simulated quote marks with her fingers— "'cockeyed optimism' is a plus as far as I'm concerned." Callie hated that Dana seemed to put herself down. "I'm eager to get started. Tell me."

Dana scooted around so she was next to Callie, pulled her MacBook out of her backpack, and put it on the table. "The Italians articulate every letter in a word, so we'll start with the Italian pronunciation of the letters of the alphabet. I suggest we each study vocabulary—nouns and verbs—and the tenses separately, then quiz each other." She opened the computer and scrolled through several pages. "These are the basics—nouns, pronouns, adjectives, and the present tense of verbs—plus some exercises creating sentences. We can practice speaking with each other on the bus and at lunch, if it's just us, and before or after dinner if we feel like. Doing it together will be fun."

Dana's enthusiasm energized Callie and she couldn't wait to get started. "Sounds good. I'll give you my email address so I can download everything onto my phone and computer later. Let's start tonight."

Dana stowed her computer into her pack. "I'm ready if you are."

The gradual but steep hill up to the Hotel Porto Roco was well worth the effort. The hotel was truly spectacular, not just the views but the building itself, the terrace dining room, the gardens, and the pool. Millie waved them over from the bar in the lobby and invited them to join her and a couple of the others from the tour. When they declined, she handed them their keycards. Their rooms were on the second floor next to each other. They made plans to meet for a drink and dinner at the hotel's terrace restaurant, then separated.

As the door to the junior suite clicked shut behind her, Callie gaped. The tour was expensive, but the company hadn't stinted on accommodations. Light and airy, the room was decorated in white with blue highlights and had a king bed, a sofa, a desk, a large bright bathroom and, best of all, a balcony overlooking the sea, with a table, four chairs, two lounges, and lots of flowering plants. She could happily spend the next few days curled up on one of the lounges with a book.

Her suitcases were on the luggage racks ready for her to unpack. She was starting to appreciate the benefits of traveling with a tour—no need to check-in, no need to worry about luggage, and getting from place to place was a breeze. Of course, this was a small luxury tour designed to cater to the wealthy, but it was exactly what she needed. She unpacked slowly and laughed when she got to the bottom of the second suitcase and found the sapphire-blue dress, the matching shoes, four sundresses, and the five sets of coordinated sexy bras and panties she'd refused to pack. Angela was such an optimist. She hung the dresses and moved the underwear into the drawer with her cotton bras and briefs.

Speaking of optimists. Her mind wandered. She knew why she was on this tour alone, but what about Dana? She was attractive, intelligent, caring, kind and fun to be with. Was the sexy actress that James mentioned when he outed Dana her girlfriend? If so, why was she on a romantic tour alone, seeming happy to be hanging out with and taking care of her. She would love to know, but she reminded herself that asking Dana to talk about her reasons for being on the tour would lead to questions about why she was here, and she wasn't ready to discuss Abby and the impact her death had on her. She also wasn't ready to disclose her identity to her or anyone or that she was writing a book about a couple who find love on a tour. Maybe they would reveal more about themselves when they knew each other better.

She kicked off her sandals, grabbed a bottle of water from the fridge and her journal and pen, then stretched out on the chaise lounge to enjoy the late afternoon sun and the beautiful water view from the terrace. The light breeze was refreshing and the sound of the waves breaking on the rocks below relaxing. Only two days on the tour and she was starting to feel less tense. The only glitch so far was that ass, James. She picked up her pen.

Main character: Sensitivity, resilience, and optimism, three characteristics she shares with Dana. Also, easygoing like Dana, but as shown by Dana's physical response to James she can be provoked to anger. Complex and forgiving, like Dana.

But what about her partner? What would he need to be like to balance her, provide conflict?

Callie capped her pen and closed her eyes, trying to imagine a hero for her heroine.

CHAPTER FIVE

During breakfast on the hotel terrace, Callie discussed options for the day with Dana. "The pool and the beach are tempting but I'd like to do this walk. It sounds wonderful." She read aloud from the info packet. "'Stroll down Via dell'Amore between Riomaggiore and Manarola and seal your eternal love at Lover's Lock or enjoy a kiss or two on the Love Seat. View the famous forty-foot cliff jumps into the Mediterranean.'"

She flushed realizing what she just implied. "I didn't mean we should kiss."

"I knew what you meant." Dana laughed. "But jumping off the forty-foot cliff sounds intriguing. As I've said, exercise is good for you."

Callie stared at Dana. "You're kidding right? I'll watch, but there's absolutely no chance I'm jumping off a cliff."

"Okay, no jumping. What about hiking either the hard or the moderate trail and coming back along the lover's lane?"

With Dana's assistance she'd managed to do the steps in the Duomo in Milan, but she'd never enjoyed hiking and didn't have hiking shoes with her. She thought about lying, but what would that accomplish other than calluses and sore muscles?

"To tell you the truth, I enjoy walking, but I'm not a hardcore hiker. And I only have sneakers with me."

Dana took a sip of her cappuccino. "Then let's do the easy hikes. I'm sure we can get the flavor of the place and see most of it that way." She continued eating her cornetto.

"Are you sure? I mean you don't have to stay with me. Even college friends separate sometimes when traveling together." Callie wanted to let Dana off the hook, but the idea of going separate ways made her anxious.

Dana met her eyes over her coffee cup. "It's always more fun seeing and experiencing things with someone else and I enjoy being with you, so unless you're looking for time alone, I'd like to trail along with you."

That Dana was choosing to be with her and not go off on her own made Callie lightheaded. Her reaction confused her. Was it relief that Dana would be there to help her in case of an anxiety attack? Or the idea that she wanted to be with her? She couldn't think about that now. "I would prefer to be with you too, but I think protocol requires that Saint Dana walk next to me instead of trailing behind. All right?"

Dana extended her hand. "Next to you it is."

Callie shook her hand, then gestured to the view in front of them. "It's gorgeous up here. Eating on the terrace last night was lovely and dinner was delicious. But let's not get in a rut. Are you up for spending the day roaming, eating lunch and dinner at restaurants in one of the towns, then coming back here for a nightcap?"

Dana grinned.

Callie's face flamed. "I've done it again, haven't I?" Her hand flew to her cheek. "Sorry. I'm assuming." She looked away.

Dana put her hand over Callie's and with her other hand turned her face so they were looking at each other. "It's fine, Callie. I really enjoy your company and I like that you enjoy mine. So can we agree that from now on we'll just assume we'll be doing everything together unless one of us says different?"

"You're sure? After all, you didn't sign on to this tour to take care of me. Or did you?"

"No, I didn't. Honestly? I thought I'd sulk silently on the outside of the group for a few days, then leave in boredom. So, finding someone I can have a real conversation with, someone knowledgeable about so many things, someone I enjoy being with, is an amazing gift. The fact that I'm able to help you with the anxiety attacks is a bonus."

Callie blushed. "Thank you. I feel the same. I just don't want to impose."

"Believe me, you'll know when I'm feeling imposed on."

"Oh, now you're scaring me."

Dana patted Callie's hand. "I'll be gentle." She picked up her fork and resumed eating the fruit and the cheese on her plate. "So, since this is a tour of romantic Italy, I propose after breakfast we go find the Via dell'Amore with its kissing statue and the tunnel covered with declarations of love. No kisses or cliff jumps required."

Before they left the hotel they spoke to Millie. The others on the tour that Dana spoke to agreed James should have a second chance with the proviso they could dump him if he proved to be a problem later.

Millie seemed relieved. "I've never had to ask someone to leave a tour, and I do think he realizes he was being a prick. Oh, excuse the language."

"Don't apologize." Dana laughed. "Prick describes him perfectly. Will you let him know he can stay but will be booted if he doesn't behave?"

Millie typed a note into her iPad. "Sure. And you have a great day. And don't forget to text me so I know where you are."

They bought Cinque Terre Cards, which covered the entrance to all the walking trails and unlimited train travel. On the train to Riomaggiore they ran into Marian and Lou, the couple on the tour who they'd chatted with at dinner last night. It turned out they planned to take the same walk, so they joined forces. The couple, both professors at Rutgers University in New Jersey, looked to be in their late fifties or early sixties. She taught American history and he taught political science. They were on the tour celebrating their recent marriage.

"Thanks to Asshole James we all know what Dana does for a living," Lou said. "What about you, Callie?"

She'd thought about how to handle this question, so she didn't hesitate. "I'm in publishing." Though she had prepared to provide details, like "I deal with agents and editors," no one asked, and she relaxed.

The four of them were evenly matched in terms of wit and intelligence and they laughed a lot during the short train ride. Callie hadn't been so relaxed, so herself, since Abby was diagnosed. Often though, in the midst of laughing she would think about Abby and how much she would have enjoyed these people and be overcome with sadness.

The trail from the Via dell'Amore to Manarola was paved and had handrails and benches along the way. It hugged the side of the cliff and had spectacular views of vineyards on one side and the sea on the other. Even in the bright sunlight, even with other people walking nearby, the path was truly romantic. Abby would have loved the walk and, romantic soul and sexual being that she was, would have taken every opportunity for a passionate kiss or two.

Callie fought back the tears that appeared whenever Abby came into her consciousness and she felt the pain of loss again. But each time they stopped to take pictures, or one of her three companions said something funny or interesting, or the chirping of the birds flitting around the terraced gardens reminded her of Abby's letter telling her to live, she would be dragged back from her sadness. She appreciated that the others who clearly sensed her fading in and out didn't make a big deal of it, just let her feel what she was feeling.

By the end of the walk she was exhausted—a good exhaustion, not the post-anxiety attack kind. Dana claimed to need a nap and the other two agreed. Callie saw through Dana's pretense but went along with it because she really did need to rest.

Back at the hotel, they went to their separate rooms. Callie showered and lay down to nap, but sleep eluded her. She picked up her journal and pen from the night table and wrote down her thoughts.

Well, Abby, you were right as usual. This trip was exactly what I needed. You would have loved today. I wish we could have shared it. I feel guilty because I had fun. I do wonder if somehow you arranged for Dana to be here to take care of me. Whether you did it or not, we're very compatible. She's been great about helping me deal with the anxiety I've experienced since you left me. Her presence is a big part of why I've enjoyed the trip so far. Hopefully, our connection will continue.

Giving up on sleep, she went out to the terrace and spent forty-five minutes making notes in her journal about what they'd seen, trying to capture the warm companionship and the beauty and the romance of the place. She was thrilled that she was already seeing glimmers of the story she would write. Her lovers would definitely walk the Via dell'Amore and stop for a kiss or two. But she was having trouble imagining a suitable man for her heroine.

Would he be older and like James have been dumped by his wife for a younger man? Or a widower? An age-gap romance might be fun, Dana needed someone strong but gentle, someone intelligent and playful, someone...

Wait! Not Dana, the character. She put her journal down.

When her phone alarm went off, she dressed for dinner and went to meet Dana. They'd changed their plans and were having dinner at the hotel with Marian and Lou.

She knocked on Dana's door and they went to the restaurant together. Marian and Lou were already at the table. Lou stood, but the waiters were fast and slid their chairs in.

"I hope you don't mind. I invited Loretta and Carl to join us for dinner." Dana waved in the direction of the entrance. "There they are, in fact."

When Loretta and Carl arrived, the four early arrivals briefed them on what they were talking about—the state of political discourse in the United States. Callie had always been interested in politics, but once Abby got sick she couldn't deal with the additional anxiety the disintegration of normal discourse generated and she'd not watched or listen to any news since. Loretta and Carl were more conservative than the other four, but the fact that the group was able to discuss things without arguing or spewing hate kept Callie listening and asking questions to clarify. There was no pressure to participate and she felt like she was getting a catch-up course.

As their appetizers were served, Dana focused on Carl. "You mentioned sustainable farming. What is it?"

Carl lit up.

"Oh, oh, don't get him started." Loretta laughed. "Keep it short, honey, or we'll be here all night."

Carl patted her hand and gave them the CliffsNotes version. And though Callie could see Dana was dying to get into it, she managed to curb her curiosity. "This is fascinating, Carl, I want to hear more but I can wait." They all laughed.

By the time their main courses arrived, they'd moved on to literature and history related to places they would visit and things they would see. And to that conversation she was able to contribute a great deal. So was Carl, who was well-read in history, mainly American but early Roman history as well.

The next morning Callie and Dana took the train to each of the five towns and wandered around, absorbing the beauty and easing into vacation relaxation mode. After lunch at a restaurant in Monterosso al Mare, the town they were staying in, they spent the afternoon at the hotel's pool, dozing, reading, and, in Callie's case, making notes about what they'd seen, the people on the tour, and her feelings.

She looked up and found Dana watching her through half-closed eyes. What was she seeing? What was she thinking? It didn't escape Callie that many of the notes she made were about Dana, who was definitely the model for the main character in her book. What would Dana write about her?

CHAPTER SIX

Since they would only spend the afternoon and the night in Bellagio on Lake Como, they had an earlier than usual breakfast, then boarded the ferry back to Bonassola, where they would meet the bus and their luggage. Callie appreciated a last look at the five towns from the water and took pictures of each. She took selfies with Dana and surprised herself by taking selfies with Marian and Lou, who were fast becoming friends.

The bus was waiting when they docked and everyone settled into their usual seats for the three-and-a-half-hour drive to Lake Como, where they would meet the ferry for what Millie described as a scenic two-hour trip to Bellagio.

As the ferry slowly made its way along the lake, Callie lounged in a chair on the deck, enjoying the warmth of the sun and the gentle breeze, the gorgeous green hills and mountains surrounding the lake, and an unusual feeling of peace. Dana seemed to sense her contentment and gave her, or maybe, took some space. Leaning casually on the railing, she chatted with various members of the tour.

Callie's mind wandered and when she focused on Dana again she was in what looked like a very intense conversation with Ellie, the depressed sister from Chicago. Callie was trying to recall what she knew about the woman when Serena sat in the lounge next to her. Her gaze was on her sister.

Callie could feel her agitation. "Everything all right?" She surprised herself by reaching out.

Serena leaned in and spoke softly. "Today is Ellie's eighteenth wedding anniversary. She booked this trip as a celebration for the two of them, but three days before they were supposed to depart, the bastard told her he'd taken a job, rented a house in Seattle, and was filing for a divorce. She was in total shock. Since she'd already paid for the tour and had arranged for our parents to care for their eleven-year-old twin daughters, I convinced her to take the trip to get some distance and give herself time to deal with her feelings. As it happened, I'm off for the entire summer trying to use some of my vacation time, and I jumped at the opportunity when she asked me to come with her for support. It hit her hard today."

Callie shifted her gaze to Ellie. She had a hand on Dana's arm and seem to be talking nonstop. Dana listened attentively and nodded occasionally. Ellie sure picked the right one to talk to. "That's awful. How are her daughters dealing with it?"

"They don't know yet." Serena shook her head. "He'd packed his car with everything he was taking before he told Ellie, and he left without saying goodbye to the girls. They were already with our mom and dad so she decided to let them enjoy the month and tell them when she gets back."

They watched Ellie straighten, wipe her eyes, touch Dana's shoulder, and then walk inside. Serena jumped up. "Please don't tell anyone what I shared."

"Don't worry. Go to her." Callie closed her eyes. Abby had left her but not willingly, and she still felt gutted. It must be even more painful having someone you love and thought you had a life with change their mind and abandon you and your children. What does that do to your self-image, your self-confidence? She was having a hard time dealing with her loss, but she was intact. Well, almost intact. How do you ever heal from being tossed aside like a dirty tissue? She recognized Dana's cologne as she sat in the lounge next to her.

"*Bellagio in dieci minuti,*" the PA system announced. *Ten minutes.* Callie opened her eyes. Land was in sight. She yawned and smiled at Dana. Millie had briefed them on the bus. Lunch was on their own. They could either follow her to the Hotel Belvedere, where they were booked for the night, or wander the charming alleys and shops.

As they waited to disembark, Dana did a quick check-in with the group. Everyone was going directly to the hotel. She turned to Callie. "Still up for wandering and having lunch before we go to the hotel?"

"Yes." Picking up her backpack and popping her sunglasses on the top of her head, Callie took a moment to take in the beauty of the lake and the mountains. Bellagio was called "the pearl of the lake" for a reason.

From the ferry they strolled uphill, wandering up and down narrow cobblestone streets and alleys, in and out of shops. In the bright sunlight Bellagio's colorful buildings, greenery, and flowers were welcoming and beautiful. At the top of the narrow winding street they were following, Callie gasped. "Oh."

"What?" Dana followed Callie's gaze over the rooftops to the lake and the mountains beyond. "Wow. What a gorgeous view."

They began to photograph the scene and then, with the view behind them, took selfies together and then photographed each other. They wandered until they were hungry, then they sat outside under an umbrella at a wine bar, sipped a delicious local wine, and shared a fabulous charcuterie board. As was their habit when alone, Dana offered Callie bits of cheese and the various cured meats. She insisted she just wanted Callie to taste everything, but Callie was pretty sure she was trying to fatten her up. She liked Dana's teasing and playful attempts to encourage her to eat more. It made her feel taken care of. And, as was becoming their habit, they drilled each other on Italian verbs and the present tense.

The next morning as they boarded the bus for a few days in Venice the complainer grumbled about having to make another stop.

"Really, Vanessa?" Dana sounded incredulous. "How could a romantic tour not visit Verona where Shakespeare set his great romantic story, *Romeo and Juliet*? Besides, Verona is a UNESCO World Heritage Site and should be worth seeing."

"Yes, yes, of course you're right," Vanessa responded with a smile, the first one they'd seen, albeit one that looked a little pained.

Callie studied the information in the packet and Millie's plan for the time in Verona. So many things to do and see. She stared out the window. She hadn't had a single anxiety attack yesterday, so she was feeling optimistic about being on her own. She turned to Dana, who was also reviewing the information as they neared their destination.

"I'm not interested in the museum or the Juliet balcony or any of these recommended tourist sites. I prefer to wander around, absorb the atmosphere, and stop to look at anything that interests me, but you should feel free to go with the group. I'll be fine on my own so do what feels right to you."

Dana frowned. "You don't like museums or monuments?"

"I love museums. But you don't find romance in museums or public buildings. Or at least I don't." Callie didn't want to reveal too much, but she wanted Dana to understand. "Absorbing that atmosphere is what this trip is about for me. The streets, the smells, the sounds, the people, and imagining the past of the places we visit are what make it romantic for me."

Damn. Dancing around the subject to avoid revealing she was writing a romance that takes place on a romantic tour, was awkward.

"I see what you mean." Dana didn't sound like she got it at all.

"Okay, folks, if you're going to the Casa di Giulietta, the museum, and the Duomo di Verona follow me. If not, remember we meet back here at three." Milly exited the bus and the others streamed after her.

Dana studied Callie. "If you're really all right being alone, I'll go with the group. I could happily skip everything Juliet, but I'm interested in the museum and the Romanesque carvings in the cathedral." She picked up her backpack. "Where are you headed?"

"I thought I'd go to, the main square, Piazza delle Erbe." She pointed on her map. "Would you let Millie know?"

"Sure. You have my cell. Call me if you need me. Okay?"

"Yes, thank you."

Callie gathered her things and left the bus. She watched Dana run to catch up with the group walking to Juliet's house or at least what the tourist board claimed was the balcony from which she spoke to Romeo. Apparently, it was a thing for people to rub the right breast of a bronze statue said to be Juliet and stare at the balcony, sighing. To each their own.

Alone on the street in Italy for the first time, she suddenly felt afraid. Enzo was still there in the bus. Maybe she should sit with him and wait for everyone to return.

She closed her eyes and breathed deeply. According to Millie's map the Piazza was close, a direct route from here. Surely she could walk a few blocks on her own. And, if not, Dana would come to her rescue. She pulled out her phone and set up a text to Dana, *Please come Piazza delle Erbe.* If she had an attack she could just hit send.

Aware that Enzo was watching, she waved goodbye and walked the three blocks to the piazza. It was still early and relatively few people were about. She was breathing heavily when she arrived at the square, but she didn't feel an attack coming on. She took a minute to select a café, then sat at a table under a tree and ordered a cappuccino and a pastry. She'd done it. She was on her own in Italy and she hadn't had an anxiety attack. She closed her eyes and imagined Dana's warm, sexy voice encouraging her to relax. When her breathing had slowed to normal she opened her eyes and pulled her journal, her sketch pad, and pens and pencils out of her backpack.

Interesting that it was Dana's voice that had soothed her and not that of her therapist or any of her friends, who had been doing it much longer. In just four days, Dana had become her guardian angel. She sipped her coffee, nibbled her pastry, and recorded her feelings about being out on her own before exchanging her journal for her sketchbook. She wasn't a very good artist, but the process, using her eyes as well as her hand to capture the details, helped her see in a different way, and she often referred to her drawings while writing the book.

The sketch of the square finished, she turned back to her journal to write her observations of a young couple sitting nearby. Totally immersed in each other, they were speaking Italian, and though she couldn't understand what they were saying, their body language communicated their feelings loud and clear. That's what she needed to capture. One of the ubiquitous Italian sparrows hopped onto her table, chirped, and pecked at the crumbs on the plate she'd pushed aside, then stared at her. She stared back.

"If that's you, Abs, I'm doing it. I—"

A sudden movement and the rasp of a chair being moved startled Callie. Her heart pounding, she pushed her chair away from the table.

"Whoa, it's me. Relax."

"Geez, Dana, you scared me. Why are you here?"

"Sorry. I should have warned you." Dana dropped into the chair.

Callie blew out a breath. Her heart slowed. She moved her chair closer to the table. "It's all right. I was deep in thought. I wasn't expecting to relate to you. Or anyone."

"Really?" Dana squeezed her hand. "I thought you were discussing your abs with that bird." She tilted her chin to the bird now eyeing her from the back of the chair across the table.

Damn, how to explain talking to a bird without bringing Abby into it. Humor would do it. "I assure you I don't discuss my exercise routine or my body parts with just any bird."

Dana laughed. "I'm sure you're particular about the birds you share with."

"I didn't expect to see you. What happened?"

"I realized the museum and the Duomo would be interesting, but I can look at the pictures of the treasures in a book or do a virtual tour of the museum any time. What I've enjoyed most so far is strolling with you and experiencing places in a relaxed manner. I'd rather tag along with you?"

"Are you sure?" Callie worried she was taking advantage of Dana's good nature. "If wandering is what you'd really enjoy and not your way of taking care of me, I would welcome your company."

"Namaste." Dana clasped her hands in the prayer position. "I'm here because I want to wander with you."

They looked at Millie's map. The Piazza delle Erbe, the heart of Verona's historic medieval old town, was surrounded on three sides by the Adige River. The packet described it as "a stunning third century BC Romanesque town center that reflects the warm sun on its red, pink and white marble walkways." It really was impressive. As was the Torre di Lamberti, a 275-foot tower dating back to 1172, across the square.

"Millie recommends taking the elevator to the top of the tower for spectacular views of the surrounding area. But if they have stairs we could walk to the top, get you some cardio," Dana said, with a mischievous glint in her eye.

Callie elbowed Dana. "I think I'll forego that little adventure. But if you're dying to walk up, I'll wait here for you."

They picked a direction and meandered around the rectangular piazza, stopping to admire the beautiful medieval buildings, the remnants of the city's Roman forum, and the nicely preserved frescoes on the facades of the surrounding houses. After a quick look at the ancient fountain topped by a statue, they strolled through an arch with, of all things, a whale rib hanging down from it. The Arco della Costa led them to the Piazza dei Signori, a smaller square with a statue of Dante in its center. From there they wandered along the cobblestone streets and explored winding side streets, marveling at the warm yellow and orange buildings and the many Romanesque statues overlooking the streets from the tops of buildings. They ducked into churches for a quick look, stopped to view statues and sculptures, gazed at beautiful bridges and arches and castles, and discussed the information Dana read from the guidebook on her iPad.

When they were hungry, they found a trattoria and, as usual, selected items they both found appealing to share. With Dana's gentle encouragement Callie was eating more but still not nearly as much as before Abby was diagnosed.

While waiting for their food, Callie looked around. "Looking at the design of the buildings and the open spaces, the frescoes and statues on the buildings, and the fountains and statues in open spaces, I'm struck by how much art and beauty were a part of everyday living when Verona was built. It's gorgeous. No wonder it's a World Heritage site."

Dana shifted her gaze from Callie to the area around them. "It does seem as if art and beauty were integrated into everyday life, not something experienced separately, in a museum. And here we are hundreds of years later enjoying it the way the Italians did."

They ate slowly, discussing what they'd seen. When they received Millie's thirty-minute text alert they paid the bill and headed back to the bus. Warm and tired, they were happy to accept the bottles of ice-cold water Enzo was handing out, and sank into their seats in the air-conditioned bus to wait for the other members of the group.

As they started the hour-and-a-half drive to Venice, Millie gave them a brief introduction. "Venice, like Verona, is a World Heritage Site. It's built on one hundred and eighteen small islands and seems to float on the water surrounding them. Its history, environment, and architecture are unique and for centuries, its enchanting mysterious and dreamy atmosphere has cast a spell on tourists and artists, inspiring painters, sculptors, architects, and designers to create the beauty and splendor that we see today. We'll be there for four days and nights. I recommend you join the group for the Doge's Palace Secrets tour and the trip to the islands of Murano, where you'll learn about glassblowing, and Burano, where you'll see lace fabric being made. Today's packet includes a map of Venice, a four-day public waterbus travel card for the vaporetto, and vouchers for a two-hour boat tour of the Grand Canal and a gondola ride for two. I'll speak again when we're closer." She clicked off the mic.

Moving as if choreographed, Dana and Callie retrieved their phones and reviewed the information in the daily packet. Callie read aloud. "'The Doge's Palace will provide some history of Venice, including its brutal legal system, and give you access to the hidden torture chambers, Casanova's jail cell, and areas of the Palace restricted to the general public. You'll also learn about the Bridge of Sighs and even cross it.'"

Callie elbowed Dana. "Bridge of Sighs sounds romantic. Torture chambers, not so much."

Dana poked her back. "It's all relative, my dear. Those into S&M probably think the torture chambers sound more romantic."

"I have a piece of Murano glass at home so I'm interested in the Murano tour"—she wrinkled her nose—"but lace, not so much."

"I've noticed you're not the lace type." Dana smirked. "But who knows what lacy red things lurk beneath your monochromatic clothing."

Callie blushed. "And I'll never tell." An image of the sexy, lacy underwear Angela had packed for her popped into her mind. Was Dana flirting or commenting on her boring gray and black clothing? Or just teasing? To avoid any further discussion of her underwear, Callie pulled out her journal.

Millie came back on the mic. "In about fifteen minutes we'll arrive at Piazzale Roma, where we'll leave the bus and board water taxis to our hotel on the banks of the Grand Canal. Once we arrive, the rest of the day is on your own but I'm available for a walking tour this afternoon, and I've arranged for a group dinner tonight at a restaurant near the hotel for those interested. Please let me know in advance when you plan to accompany me and when you intend to join the group meals. As always, I'm staying at the hotel with you and I'm always available by phone if you need me. Let me know about your plans."

CHAPTER SEVEN

When the bus dropped them off at the vaporetto stop in the Piazzale Roma, Enzo supervised the loading of their luggage onto one of the three water taxis arranged for them, and Callie and the members of the tour boarded the other two waiting taxis. Venice in the bright sunlight was breathtaking. As they made their way through the many boats on the Grand Canal, Callie turned to Dana and Marian. "I've seen so many photographs of this but seeing it in real life is...is magic. I almost feel like we're in a painting."

Fifteen minutes later the water taxi delivered them to the front door of the luxury four-star boutique hotel, Sina Palazzo Sant'Angelo. They disembarked onto a red-carpeted ramp and walked through the double glass doors into the posh marble-floored lobby. Millie went to the front desk and returned with their room keys.

"Anyone interested in a walk to St Mark's Square meet me down here in a half hour. After, we'll come back to the hotel so you can rest before we go out for dinner. As usual, the walk and dinner are optional, but if you're on your own, remember it's extremely easy to get lost in Venice. Be careful, but if you do get lost ask for directions to the Grand Canal and take the vaporetto to the hotel."

Dana elbowed Callie. "Let's start out with the group to get our bearings, then branch off on our own when it feels right."

"Sounds like a plan."

A half hour later, Millie did a quick count. "Vanessa isn't coming so we're all here. It's only a fifteen-minute walk, but it involves going up and down quite a few steps. If you don't think you can do the steps we can hop on the vaporetto, but I need to know now." She made eye contact with Carl and Loretta, the couple in their seventies.

"We're both fine with steps," Carl said.

Carl and Loretta were holding hands. Celebrating their fiftieth anniversary and still in love. Callie swallowed. She and Abby used to laugh and imagine themselves in their nineties propping each other up, holding hands and still making out whenever they had the chance. Now she was alone.

"You all right?" Dana whispered.

The woman was really tuned in to her. She started to lie but decided to not deny what Dana obviously sensed. "Just sad."

Dana squeezed her hand but didn't ask for an explanation. Once again Callie marveled at her luck. Dana was perfect.

"Okay, no problems with steps?" Millie waited a few seconds. "Up to now we haven't encountered many tourists, but Venice is always crowded, so try to stay close together. Follow me." She led them out the door.

Callie spoke softly so only Dana could hear. "I'm nervous about the crowds."

"Stay close to me. Hang on to my arm if it makes you feel secure. And remember, I'll be right there if you need me."

It occurred to Callie as they strolled through narrow alleyways and streets, up and down steps, with their group mates surrounding them, that she felt comfortable with these people. Everyone was friendly and no one pressed for more personal information than she was willing to share. Even James no longer felt like a threat. Dana had gone out of her way to relate to him in public and the group had followed her lead. He had relaxed, and he, Serena, and the grump, Vanessa, seemed to hit it off.

Millie must have taken this route many times because she didn't hesitate at all on the twists and turns. She set a nice pace, not so fast that Callie wasn't able to take in the surrounding buildings and waterways and not so slow that it felt tiresome. They emerged onto

St. Mark's suddenly, and Callie pulled up short at the roar of the crowd milling about the piazza in front of the famous Caffè Florian and what must be the Doge's Palace. Millie had warned them but, lulled by the few tourists they'd encountered in the Cinque Terre and Bellagio, Callie hadn't imagined this...this nightmare. Dana gently touched her back. "Let's stay with them."

They moved forward, but lost sight of their group in the crush of shouting, laughing, pushing people and pigeons who seemed unafraid of the humans walking amongst them. Callie started to sweat. Then without warning the hundreds of pigeons in the piazza rose into the air, flapping their wings and circling just above their heads. The people in the crowd screamed, waved their arms to avoid the brush of wings, and pressed forward trying to get away. Callie panicked. Shaking, unable to move, her vision narrowed and she began to sink into darkness. She was vaguely aware of strong arms holding her and a comforting voice drawing her back. "You're safe, I have you, you're safe, look at the blue sky, look at me, this will be over in a few minutes. Hold on to me. I've got you."

As Dana's calm voice repeated the reassuring words, the darkness slowly became light, the shaking stopped, her breathing evened out, and, in the midst of the clamor, Callie relaxed. Dana held her tight until she whispered, "I'm okay. You can let go."

Dana loosened her grip but continued to hold her. "I hope it's okay I grabbed you without your consent, but I thought you were too far gone."

Callie wiped her eyes. "Thank you. I was hoping the attacks were in the past. And, for the record, you always have my permission to touch me when you think it's necessary."

Dana stepped back. "You've made a great deal of progress. Not one attack yesterday. Be patient with yourself." She looked around. "This place is insane. I doubt we'll be able to find the group. She dug in her backpack for her phone. "I'm texting Millie to let her know we haven't been kidnapped, and then I suggest we get out of here." She sent the text and pocketed her phone. "Are you up for riding the vaporetto until we find a stop we like, then wandering until we need to go back to the hotel?"

"Yes."

Dana checked her map. "The vaporetto stops on the other side of the Giardini Reali, over there behind the Caffè Florian." With

Dana's protective arm over Callie's shoulders, they skirted the crowd and moved toward the café.

The vaporetto was crowded but not horribly so. Still holding her close, Dana steered them to what seemed to be the less desirable side of the boat. Facing the water with the people behind them, Callie stood with the wall of the boat on one side and Dana on the other. Out of sight, out of mind? Well, it worked.

Exhausted, Callie leaned into Dana, her elbows on the railing and her eyes on the buildings on the opposite shore. She owed Dana. She wouldn't have lasted a day on this trip without her. Why was someone so kind, considerate, intelligent and interesting single? Dana would definitely be the model for the hero in the romance. But what was her motivation for being on this trip alone? Wait. Dana was just the inspiration, not the real character, so her reason for being here alone was irrelevant.

Dana pointed to a building and Callie turned to listen to her describe what she'd read about it. "We're coming to the stop for our hotel. Do you want to go back or shall we continue?"

"Let's continue. I'm enjoying the sun and the water and the sheer beauty of the city. What a marvel. It seems unchanged from centuries ago. One could easily imagine living here in the fifteenth century. Or earlier or later, for that matter." Her dad's family, the DeAndres, originated here in Venice centuries ago, but, fearing sharing her last name might give her away, she didn't mention it.

"I guess that's why so many books are set here." Dana laughed. "I had great plans to read books set in the various places we're visiting before the trip, then life got in the way. Have you read any books that take place in Venice?"

"I've read many over the years, but none specifically for this trip. The ones that immediately come to mind are Donna Leon's mysteries, all of which take place here, Thomas Mann's *Death in Venice*, but I don't remember much of it, and *The Talented Mr. Ripley* by Patricia Highsmith."

"So you're a fan of mysteries?"

"I am. But I read widely. Romance, sci-fi, literary fiction, history, biography, politics, and just about anything that appeals." Callie considered telling Dana that she was a writer, that she wrote romance, romantic suspense, mystery, and general fiction depending on her mood. That she was here to write a romance which she'd proposed almost two years ago when she was capable of feeling. But then she'd have to explain why she was no longer capable of feeling.

"We have that in common. I'll read any fiction that catches my eye, regardless of genre, but I'm more discriminating with nonfiction. I like to dig in and learn as much as I can about subjects that interest me, so I read a lot of politics, anthropology, and psychology."

"Look." Callie pointed. "We're back at the Piazzale Roma where we arrived earlier. It's the last stop. Let's walk on the same side of the canal as our hotel."

"Sure."

On the dock they studied their maps for a few minutes before heading out. The city belonged to pedestrians. It had an intimate, immediate feel as they wandered in and through claustrophobic alleyways, some that opened suddenly to wide squares with a few trees and a few outside tables belonging to tiny restaurants, others that led to wider streets lined with stores and restaurants. It seemed as if there were ancient buildings, churches housing the works of famous artists, and museums on every corner. In between those were the stores that provided the basics for living, little grocery stores, a liquor store, a pharmacy, a hairdresser, vintage and modern clothing stores, a shoe repair shop, a bank, and of course stores selling trinkets and souvenirs.

They stopped to purchase bottled water and sit a few times but after more than an hour, Dana suggested they head back to the hotel to rest before dinner. Though it took a while to find it, their hotel was not that far.

They went up to their rooms, junior suites next to each other again. She wondered for the hundredth time whether Dana and this whole arrangement were set up by Angela and Maggie. At the room's entrance Callie paused to admire the classic silk red-striped wallpaper, red carpeting, contrasting white bedding, the desk, and a small sitting area with a red couch and two side chairs with a small end table between them. Her luggage awaited on luggage racks.

She peered into the bathroom. It had white-and-green marble walls, and the white fixtures included a jacuzzi bathtub. The room's windows overlooked the garden rather than the canal, but it would probably be a lot quieter and that was good.

She sat on the bed. Abby would have enjoyed this trip, a month of luxury and beauty and romance, the pleasure of someplace different. Callie smiled. If Abby was alive and they were traveling together, she would have insisted on this level of luxury. The acute ache for Abby that returned the minute she was alone hit her. The tears followed. She dozed, and when she woke her thoughts drifted back to leaning into Dana on the vaporetto earlier, but she brushed away the thought that holding on to Dana was part of the reason she was enjoying the trip.

She reached for her journal.

Strong arms grasped her and held her up. She opened her eyes and looked into the eyes of her rescuer, the eyes of a beautiful woman. Warmth flooded her system. She felt lightheaded. It must be due to the attack because she'd never responded to a woman this way.

Wait. Her female character was reacting to a woman? This was a gamechanger and she needed to think it through. And what better place to relax and cogitate than a jacuzzi. She moved her pen and journal to the small table next to the tub for easy access in case she was inspired, turned on the water, and stripped.

She eased into the tub and let her mind wander until it was time to get ready for dinner. She felt refreshed when she joined Dana to meet the others. But when she ended up sitting with Dana on her left and Vanessa, better known as Miss Grumpy on her right, she steeled herself for an unpleasant evening.

Callie was drawn to the Venetian specialties. After all when in Rome...or Venice. Not a fan of liver of any kind, though, she nixed the *Fegato alla Veneziana* and settled on a first course of *sarde in saor*, fried sardine fillets marinated in a sweet-sour sauce of vinegar, onions, raisins, and pine nuts with a second course of *risotto al nero di sepia*, rice in squid ink, and fresh fruit for dessert.

Vanessa commented that the recipe for sarde in saor was developed in the Middle Ages by Venetian fishermen as a way of preserving fish. To Callie's surprise, Vanessa was a professor of medieval history at Oxford and an interesting dinner companion with extensive knowledge of Venice's history and its food. The group was enthralled. Callie asked questions, contributed what she could, and for the first time, really engaged with the group. Not only had she had a wonderful time, she also felt more like herself than she had in almost two years.

James helped Venessa stand. She groaned, then looked at Dana and Callie. "Sorry, I have arthritis, and I get stiff if I sit too long."

Dana looked the way Callie felt, embarrassed that they'd called her Ms. Grump when she had a physical problem, not a sour personality, as they'd imagined.

CHAPTER EIGHT

Callie and Dana met at five a.m. and walked to the Rialto Bridge so Callie could see it without having to deal with the crush of tourists usually at the popular site. They'd read that early mornings and late nights were the loveliest and most romantic times to wander through the streets of Venice, especially for couples. But even though they weren't a couple, walking through the nearly empty streets in the swirling, predawn fog and quiet was enchanting. She'd have her lovers hold hands and stop to kiss from time to time in the privacy afforded by the heavy mist. She glanced at Dana, trying to gauge her reaction. Was she feeling the romance of Venice, thinking about kissing?

Suddenly the sky brightened, the mist drifted away, and the bridge arched in front of them like a huge whale breaching the surf. Callie pointed to the staircase facing Piazza San Marco and they walked onto the bridge. The sunrise was breathtaking. She resisted the urge to reach out and take Dana's hand.

Dana glanced at her phone. "It's beautiful, but we'd better get back to the hotel if we want to eat before we leave for Burano. Come on, let's get some exercise." She grabbed Callie's hand and they jogged to the hotel.

At breakfast Millie overheard them practicing Italian. "Ah, you're learning my language."

Callie laughed. "That's the goal."

"From time to time I've helped guests with conversation. If you're interested, I'd be happy to spend twenty minutes to a half hour when we have time, just talking."

Dana's eyes were dancing. "Yes, yes. We'd love it. Right, Callie?"

Callie wanted to hug Dana. She loved her enthusiasm. "That would be terrific, Millie."

After breakfast, Dana and Callie, Marian and Lou, Ellie and Serena, and Susan and Fran took a water taxi to Burano where they would meet Gennaro, the local guide for the kayak tour of the Venetian Lagoon they'd all opted to take.

Gennaro met them at the dock and escorted them to the boatyard where he helped them store their bags and settle into the brightly colored solo kayaks. Since Susan, Fran, and Serena had never kayaked, he spent a few minutes instructing them while the others looked on. Callie found it a helpful refresher. Finally, they pushed off, navigated through a narrow boat-clogged canal lined on both sides by pastel-colored houses, and paddled out to the lagoon.

Because of the early hour there wasn't much boat traffic. The trip was magical. For two hours, with Gennaro leading and narrating what they were seeing, their kayaks skimmed noiselessly through the beautiful landscape, the silence broken only by the guide's voice and their comments. Stopping to rest occasionally and to take pictures of egrets and herons gliding into and out of the water, they explored islands that could only be reached by the flat-bottom kayaks because of the shallow water.

Callie enjoyed the peacefulness, the almost silence, a welcome respite from the hectic activity and noise of tourist-jammed Venice. She gazed at her tour mates spread out around her, each in their own world, and watched Dana for a few seconds, her paddle lifted, her eyes closed, drifting to her thoughts. She looked peaceful. Was she in the moment or remembering something?

Dana drifted, a dreamy expression on her face. Was she feeling the sweet tension between them? Did she also yearn to kiss, to touch?

Whoa! Dana was the model for one of her characters, but if fragments of the story were going to start popping into her mind, she needed to come up with another name for the character sooner rather than later. She retrieved her journal and fountain pen from the waterproof bag Gennaro had supplied for things that couldn't be left behind and wrote down the fragment. She secured the bag again, then closed her eyes and sat back, listening to the quiet and the occasional bird song. Abby loved kayaking. She would have loved it here, would have been fascinated by the natural life. In fact, she probably would have become an expert on the lagoon and the canals and the birds of Venice before they arrived.

Callie's eyes popped open. For the first time since Abby was diagnosed, thinking about her didn't devastate her. Instead, she felt happy.

By the time they returned to Burano, Callie was tired from the unusual exertion, but she felt centered in a way she hadn't felt since Abby's diagnosis. They returned to the boat club, where they had the opportunity to take showers, use the toilet and/or change clothes. It turned out that even the most inexperienced kayakers had enjoyed the exercise and had managed to stay dry, so other than toilets, they all passed on the facilities and immediately set out for lunch at a restaurant Gennaro recommended.

Dana fell into step beside Callie as they followed the directions to the restaurant. "Feeling good? You look happy."

"I'm tired, but I do feel good. Like when you made me walk up all those steps in Milan." She gently elbowed Dana. "Let's remember to do as much physical stuff as we can on the rest of the trip."

"I told you cardio is good for anxiety and I'm open to whatever outdoor opportunities we have. I feel good too. What do you think about skipping lunch here, hopping on the vaporetto, and finding a place to have lunch in a new neighborhood?"

"Sounds good to me. Let's invite the others."

The rest of the group was happy with the plan to have lunch in Burano, so the two of them headed to the vaporetto. They got off at a stop on the side of the canal they hadn't explored yet and began to wander.

"I'd love to try some *cicchetti*."

Callie had no idea what Dana was talking about. She'd done no reading about the trip other than the itinerary and she had been too stressed or too busy writing notes at night to read the guidebook she'd brought with her. "What are 'cich-etti'?"

"You make them sound like a rare disease," Dana said. "Actually, they're little bites of things. They can be meat, fish, or vegetables. You buy them by the piece. I read that Venetians stroll from one bar to another, eating a cicchetti and chasing each bite with a tiny glass of wine, translated as a shadow of wine. I'm not suggesting we do that. But I say we find a place and take a look at what they have to offer. Interested?"

"No doubt we have many multicourse meals in our future so something light sounds good."

After wandering a bit more they stumbled across the Madagio Caffe and Wine Bar. Next to a church and a narrow alley, it had a canal view. Attracted by the local vibe and the warm lighting, they peered in through the open door at the patterned marble floor, wood beam ceiling, and modern glass and chrome showcases. They entered. Seeing the large variety of delicious-looking cicchetti in the display case, they decided this was the place. Each cicchetti was 1.5 Euros and five were seven Euros, so they each ordered five, pointing at the ones that appealed to them. Dana asked for an IPA beer and Callie an Aperol spritz, a drink containing prosecco amongst other things. They went outside, claimed one of the high-top tables, and sat and waited for their food and drinks. What a feast. And so lovely, sitting outside in the sunshine, eating delicious food, chatting, and people watching.

Callie watched Dana, her face sparking with the pleasure she took in this simple food, for that's what it was, simple Venetian food, and speaking enthusiastically about these ancient surroundings filled with art and history.

"To me," Dana said, "Venice's beauty, its history, its architecture is overwhelming. It feels timeless, enduring. It's almost as if we're time travelers. Like we've woken up in the thirteenth, fourteenth, or fifteenth century, and if I narrow my eyes I can see the people of those times going about their lives, walking where we walk, eating what we're eating in small osterias, hearing the voices and sounds on the canal, and smelling the same smells."

"For someone who didn't mention history as one of her interests, you really seem to be into history, at least Venice's history."

Dana sipped her beer. "I guess I am. There's something about this place. It's…it's that I can feel and see and imagine the history, which is different than reading somebody's description of the past. The history is alive here. How do you feel about it?"

"I'm stunned by the beauty. I also feel like we've stepped back in time. It's impossible not to feel the history, to imagine people of other times living here, but I don't know enough about it. I'm thinking of buying a history of Venice. But I was expecting to feel the romance of the places we visit and so far, for the most part, I haven't." She looked up at Dana. "Have you?"

Dana moved her empty beer glass in circles on the table, giving it some thought. "Being out in the fog early this morning felt romantic but for the most part, I haven't felt it either. Was it just me or did you feel it this morning?"

"I felt it when we were in the dense fog." Had Dana also felt the desire to kiss this morning?

"Maybe we're thinking about it the wrong way, Callie. Maybe it has less to do with the place or its history and more to do with who you share it with. Do you think we don't feel the romance generally because we're not coupled? Interesting that we both felt it when we were the only people out this morning."

"Hmm. I'm not sure." She was going to have to mull over the question. When she'd proposed the book, Callie was thinking she would be with Abby and the places would feel romantic. Now she believed that though the places they were visiting were beautiful and filled with history, in and of themselves, they weren't romantic. Did they only feel romantic to connected couples, people in love? No doubt it would have felt different with Abby.

"Let's pay and head back. I think this morning's exercise has caught up with me. I'm really tired." She waved the waiter over. "*Il conto, per favore.*"

CHAPTER NINE

Remembering the crowd and the pigeons in the Piazza San Marco, Callie was having second thoughts about the private Secret Itineraries Tour of the Doges Palace when the group gathered for breakfast at seven thirty. She was feeling more connected to the people in the group, but she wasn't ready to chance an anxiety attack with their eyes on her. She leaned closer to Dana. "If I skip the tour and stay at the hotel, will you come back for me so we can have lunch and meet up for the street art tour later?"

Dana eyed her as she finished chewing. "If it's what you really want." She sipped her cappuccino. "Are you afraid the crowds and the pigeons will set you off?"

Callie was tempted to say she just wanted some time alone at the hotel, but she figured Dana knew the truth. "Just thinking about it makes me anxious."

"Millie did say she chose the first tour to avoid the crowd in the piazza *and* the palace. That doesn't mean the pigeons won't be there, but I'll bet there will be fewer of them too. You've been looking forward to seeing the inside of the palace, especially the secret places. Come. I'll do my best to shield you." She ate some of the berries she'd selected from the buffet. "You know, everyone has gotten to know and like you, and I'm sure they'd be able to deal with you having an anxiety attack. Ellie had a meltdown on the ferry to Bellagio and everyone was concerned, not condemning her. Think about it. I'm good either way." Dana turned to answer a question from Susan.

Callie sipped her double espresso and thought about it. The anxiety attacks were coming less frequently and with Dana's help they were briefer. She *had* been looking forward to seeing the rooms and chambers of the palace and learning some of the political history. She felt safe with Dana. And if she had an attack, Dana would be there for her.

Dana's laugh got Callie's attention. She pulled out her pen and journal and jotted some notes about her teasing interaction with Ellie and Carl, the two most withdrawn members of the group. Dana really was everything the heroine in her romance should be. *Except.*

Damn, she couldn't imagine Dana with a man, and all her romances had a hero and a heroine. Her mind wandered while she doodled, drawing hearts and flowers. Her agent and her publisher knew she was a lesbian and were happy with her writing heterosexual characters, which was great, because heterosexual romances were the big sellers.

The contract she'd signed for this book, like all the others, didn't specify a heterosexual couple. It was assumed based on what she'd always written. Did she dare write a lesbian couple? Would her publisher go for it? Would her readers? Did she really care? Her books sold very well and lingered on the bestseller lists, so her royalty income was more than enough for her to live comfortably. Plus, she was Abby's beneficiary on several insurance policies and her trust fund, so even if she never earned another penny she would be more than fine.

She made a note to call her agent to discuss it. Then she crossed it out. No. Better to follow her muse and present it as a fait accompli than waste her breath fighting a battle she didn't intend to lose. There would be no discussion. She would write *her* book, and they could take it or leave it. She would self-publish it if necessary.

"You're smiling." Dana had turned back to her. "Does that mean you're coming on the tour?"

The temptation to share her thoughts with Dana was great, but Callie didn't want to make her self-conscious about being studied. "That's what it means."

At the completion of the Doge's Palace tour Millie led the group away from the now-crowded Piazza San Marco to a small café in a quiet alley so they could relax and eat lunch before the art tour. Callie ordered a glass of fresh orange juice and Dana tried Italian lemon soda.

"Thank you for encouraging me to come, Dana. I loved it."

"Which parts?" Dana asked.

Suddenly all eyes were on Callie. She looked at the twelve attentive faces and realized she felt comfortable enough to answer. "I was surprised at how beautiful the public rooms still are after all these years. And a little taken aback by the prisons. The vast difference in the quality of the prison cells in the same building, the small wet cells on the ground floor and the cells directly under the roof used for prisoners accused of political crimes or those awaiting sentence or serving short prison terms. Also, I was impressed by the efficiency of linking the Chamber of Torment directly with the prisons and holding the interrogations there in the presence of the judges. The weapons also surprised me. The idea that the crossbows and lances and the precious metal arms, shields, and gauntlets displayed in the weapons room were not replicas but actually used by men hundreds of years ago."

She sipped her orange juice. "Of course, I found the secret chambers and staircases fascinating, but what really held my interest was the history. The idea that the Venetians set up the Chamber of the Inquisitors in 1539 to protect State secrets, that the inquisitors could obtain information using any means, including informers and torture, but that any information they discovered had to be kept secret. Wow. That's a little scary. Overall, I was, and am, impressed with how well they were organized and how well the government functioned."

As soon as Callie stopped, conversations broke out around the table, everyone anxious to talk about their favorite parts. She listened with half an ear, wondering whether she had it in her to write a historical novel based in Venice in the sixteenth century. She already visualized several scenes in her head like a movie. Now she just needed characters and a story. Maybe two women, a noble and a pirate, secretly in love. Were there women pirates here? She'd never attempted to write a historical and wasn't sure she had the skills to do extensive research and turn it into an engrossing novel. But her imagination was engaged in a way that it hadn't been since Abby was diagnosed, and it felt good to have the creative juices running again. First things first, though. She still had to write the Italy romance.

After lunch, everyone opted for the private three-hour walking tour of the art of Venice that Millie had arranged. The guide, Sara, an art historian, led them through the narrow streets and alleys, pointing out and explaining the interesting art and architecture of the city. The group had varied interests and Sara patiently answered all Serena's questions about the art, Fran's questions about the architecture, Dana's questions about the historical context of what they were seeing, and many questions about the history. It was fascinating looking at the city through the lens of the art integrated throughout.

Later the group went out for dinner together, and Callie and Dana sat across from Carl and Loretta. Dana's enthusiasm pulled the older couple into a discussion of what they'd seen that day. Their interesting and different perspectives made for a lively discussion and soon everyone at the table was sharing their thoughts and ideas. They'd lucked out with the people in the group. Even James was interesting once he stopped acting like an ass and just let himself be.

The next day was Millie's second scheduled tour. They were going to Murano to learn about glassblowing. After a boat trip of twenty minutes or so, she led them to a glassmaking factory. Callie had researched the Murano glassblowing tours last night and was prepared to be disappointed, but she wanted to buy some glass pieces as gifts for Angela, Erin, Bonnie, Maggie, and her agent, Sarah, so she went along.

She was pleasantly surprised. Rather than the generic demonstration, Romantic Italy had arranged an extended private demonstration by a fifth-generation master glassblower. Each step of the process was thoroughly explained, and members were asked to assist at points. The master started by making a simple hollow vase, followed by a solid elephant. He then went on to create several birds, a sculpture of two women embracing, and an intricate vase.

When all their questions had been answered, they were given the opportunity to create a small keepsake from various colored glass beads. Callie and Dana chose the beads for their bracelets and, with the help of one of the assistants, tied off the ends. They slipped the bracelets on, extended their arms, and congratulated each other on their creative genius. The bracelets were a simple but lovely keepsake to remember the day.

From the workshop they were steered into the gift shop, where many blown-glass items were on sale. They weren't cheap but they were gorgeous. Though it was crowded it was quiet, so Callie relaxed into browsing and picking out gifts. She gasped.

Dana grabbed her arm. "What is it?"

"I'm all right. It's just…" She pointed at the sculpture in front of her, five colorful glass birds perched on a glass branch. "I have that exact sculpture. The birds are different colors, but otherwise it's exactly the same, the size, the branch, the gold leaf."

Abby had reluctantly responded to Callie's nagging about taking some clothing and books to the Thrift Shop, but when she came home with the sculpture, she was euphoric. She had displayed it in her office at the university, but after her death it was returned to Callie with her other belongings, and it now sat in the place of honor in her home office.

Dana read the tag aloud. "Sculpture of five birds embellished with real gold leaf, worked freehand in solid glass. Ground and polished by hand. Made and signed by the master. Two thousand dollars."

"Mine cost twenty-five dollars in a thrift shop."

"Whoa. Talk about bargains." Dana stared at the birds perched on a glass branch. "It's lovely."

"Yes, it is." Callie closed her eyes as she was enveloped in Abby's perfume. Her heart skipped a beat as Abby's arms encircled her body. No. it couldn't be. She opened her eyes. Not Abby. A stranger's arms, a stranger's perfume.

She started shaking. She heard Dana in the distance. "Move, lady." Felt the stranger pull away.

"Callie, look at me. You're safe. I'm going to touch you now."

She opened her eyes and focused on Dana's gentle voice, repeating those words over and over, guiding her through the attack, until finally she could breathe easily.

"Thank you." Embarrassed, she glanced at the people gathered around the two of them. It took a minute to register, but she realized that the members of their group were shielding her from the crowd of strangers still milling around them. She looked for judgment or disgust and found relief and caring. She inhaled.

"And thank you all for your support. I'm okay now. I just need some air and then I'll be back to finish shopping."

Dana followed her outside. "Do you know what set you off? Was it the sculpture?"

Callie didn't want to talk about the reasons here, but she owed it to Dana to tell her about Abby, maybe tonight during their gondola ride. "That woman reaching around me with both arms was wearing perfume that I'm familiar with. I think the combination of being touched by a stranger and the memories brought up by the fragrance did it." She took Dana's hand. "I know I've been reticent, but I'll explain soon."

Dana looked into Callie's eyes. "I only need to know what you want to share. Neither of us has been particularly forthcoming about our past."

Millie stepped outside. "I'd like to wrap up here, so it would be good if you're able to go back and pay for the things you've selected and fill out the shipping and Customs forms."

It was their last night in Venice. Callie had enjoyed almost every minute so far. Despite today's attack, her level of anxiety was dropping day by day, and she was looking forward to the rest of the trip.

Ellie sat next to her at dinner. "I've had a couple of anxiety attacks since my husband dropped his bomb on me and I know they can take a lot out of you. How are you feeling?"

Callie was still not totally comfortable talking about her anxiety, but now that everyone had witnessed her attack it was out on the table. "I took a nap when we got back to the hotel so I'm fine. Thanks for stepping in to help care for me."

Ellie sipped her prosecco. "I didn't do anything but get between you and the strangers in the gallery. It was Dana who ripped that woman off you and helped you through the attack. She's quite protective of you. I think she would have torn the woman to pieces if she'd hung around."

"Really?" She'd been so deep into her attack she hadn't registered what was happening around her. Dana *was* protective, aware of what might trigger her, there when she needed her, but she wasn't smothering or controlling.

"Yes. You're lucky to have Dana as a friend." Ellie turned her attention to the waiter as he placed her first course in front of her.

Lucky indeed. Whether it was the universe or Maggie and Angela or Abby that brought them together, Callie knew she was lucky to have Dana with her on this trip. And in her life.

Ellie turned back to Callie. "Just so you know, I'm happy to help if Dana's not around. I'd like to think we're becoming friends."

Callie flushed with pleasure. "Thank you, Ellie, I feel the same. And I know you're dealing with your husband's leaving so the offer goes both ways."

Ellie nodded. "Yeah, I guess everyone knows since my meltdown on the ferry to Bellagio. But I'm happy to report I'm at the rage stage of grief. You know, I can almost accept that he just walked away from me without any warning or discussion, but how he could do that to his eleven-year-old daughters is beyond me. The man I thought I married would never have treated me or them that way. I wonder if I ever really knew him."

She sipped her wine. "I'm so glad Serena convinced me to take this trip rather than cancel it. It's been hard, but it's a lot better than being home alone. I'm using the time to work through the desire to kill him and to figure out what to tell the girls. Best of all, I'm making new friends and having a great time."

Callie grasped Ellie's arm. "I'm glad you're here too, especially if it means you'll avoid murdering him. Your girls will need you even more now." They laughed.

Callie was fully present for the entire dinner again, joining in the discussions and the laughter. It turned out she and Dana were the only ones who'd left the gondola ride for their last evening in Venice. Everyone else had opted for a daytime ride. Happily, it was a beautiful night, warm and clear.

They'd paid extra for a private late evening ride, hoping to experience the famous Venice fog, but as they strolled to the prearranged spot to meet their gondolier the evening was warm and the sky clear. The slender man wearing the standard uniform of a red-striped shirt, navy pants, white sneakers but no straw hat, helped Callie in first. Before she could decide where to sit, Dana said from the dock, "Let's sit next to each other facing front so we can see the same things at the same time."

The nonsinging gondolier they'd chosen propelled them through the water, quietly pointing out the sights, taking them down narrow canals, giving them the history of what they were seeing. Toward the end of their hour, wisps of fog drifted up from the water, adding a mysterious feeling to the evening.

She glanced at Dana. Did she feel it? Probably not. She was focused on the gondolier, intent as usual on learning as much as she could. Maybe it was the darkness and the fog seeming to enclose the two of them or maybe it was the many movies she'd seen and the many books about romance in Venice she'd read, but it felt romantic to Callie. She imagined a couple holding hands, heads together, kissing in some of the darker, narrow lanes.

It felt like a dream, sliding through the dimly lit canal, quiet except for the sound of her own breathing and the rhythmic dipping of the oar in and out of the water as the gondolier propelled them forward. She leaned in, wanting Dana's soft lips on hers, wanting…

She glanced at Dana again. This time Dana smiled. Was Dana feeling romantic? Of course not. They were friends, not lovers. She forced herself to concentrate on the beauty of their surroundings, on the quiet of the small side lanes, of the soft sounds of the oar dipping in and out of the water, and her connection and feeling of ease with Dana.

CHAPTER TEN

The bus was buzzing with conversations, good-natured ribbing, and bonhomie that hadn't been there until this morning. Callie couldn't decide whether it was the magic of Venice or the result of having been together for ten days. She felt connected to the group, but Dana seemed distant, there but not there, which was unusual. She'd noticed the change at breakfast, but she knew Dana sometimes worked at night so she chalked it up to her being tired. No one else seemed to notice.

Her absence created a void for Callie, though, leaving her feeling lonely, something she hadn't felt since that first day in Milan. Not wanting to intrude, she debated ignoring it. But Dana seemed to be suffering, and she wouldn't let her suffer in silence.

"Are you all right?" Callie spoke softly so only Dana would hear.

Staring straight ahead, hands resting on her thighs, she said, "I'm fine." Her tone warned Callie away.

Callie covered Dana's hand. "I can see you're upset. After all you've done for me, please let me help."

Dana tried to extract her hand.

"Uh-uh. You don't get to ignore me."

Dana tensed. Callie knew she was pushing it. She and Dana were not best friends, they were little more than acquaintances, so there was no obligation to share. Had she'd gone too far? If Dana objected, she'd let it go. But she didn't want to. She cared about Dana and really did want to ease whatever was troubling the usually chipper, empathetic woman.

Giving Dana space to respond, she turned to stare out the window. There wasn't much to see as they zipped along the highway at high speed, snaking in and out to pass. Italians were crazy drivers. She was glad Enzo was behind the wheel, not her.

Dana cleared her throat. "It's a business problem."

Callie turned. Not a lot of information, but at least she was willing to share. "Would it help to talk it out?"

"I'm not sure." She lifted a shoulder. "Maybe. But not now. After lunch in Bologna if that's okay?" She sounded apologetic.

"Of course. Whenever you feel comfortable."

Dana smiled, seeming more relaxed. Callie smiled back, but her mind was on Dana's lips. She'd never noticed the sweetness of her smile or the plumpness of her lips. She closed her eyes, blocking the sight. *Where the hell did that thought come from?*

About an hour later instead of going into Bologna they left the highway and drove on a local road for about fifteen minutes, then stopped in front of an unpretentious stone building. Millie stood. "This is a two-starred Michelin restaurant. The menu includes traditional Bolognese specialties and variations on the specialties, so read it carefully. The food is excellent and so are the local wines they'll serve with the meal. We have a table outside on the terrace. The restrooms are inside."

As dessert was being served Dana's phone rang. She moved to the edge of the terrace to take the call. While she was far enough away from their tables that her conversation was private, Callie stared, fascinated by her body language. She paced, raked her hand through her hair, waved her arm, and even seemed to stomp at one point. Clearly things were not going well.

Millie stood. "Please be on the bus in ten minutes so we can leave on time."

Dana had her back to the group and Callie didn't want Millie or anyone to intrude and hear something she might not want to share. "I'll tell Dana."

Dana was listening, rather than talking, and when Callie touched her shoulder and held up ten fingers, she gave her a thumbs-up.

Dana was the last one on the bus. "Sorry, Millie, I hope I didn't hold us up." She buckled herself into her seat and leaned toward Callie. "We'll talk when we get to the hotel."

Once they were on their way, Millie took a minute to brief them.

"Today and the next two days, we'll be in a small hotel on a working vineyard about fifteen minutes outside of Florence. It's beautiful and quiet. As you know, Florence is filled with history and beautiful art and architecture—"

"Excuse me, Millie, but three days doesn't seem nearly long enough to take in the architecture, forget the art."

"You're right, Fran. Anyone interested in architecture or the arts could spend weeks here, but it's always really crowded, even at this time of the year, and we've found most of our guests prefer a short visit." Millie held her hands out as if to apologize. "I'm sorry." She looked at each of them. When no one else commented, she continued.

"We'll have the entire hotel to ourselves. You can go to the pool or walk the grounds this afternoon. There's a wine-tasting there at six p.m. and dinner later at the Michelin star restaurant on site. Or, if you'd rather, Enzo will drive you into Florence after we check in and pick you up when you're ready to return."

A crowded, hot city. Yuck! All Callie wanted was to talk to Dana, then relax, write in her journal, and read. "Want to talk, then go to the pool?" she whispered to Dana.

"Sounds good."

"Tomorrow morning we'll tour the Uffizi and the day after we'll visit Michelangelo's *David*. I recommend you do both tours with the group since getting into the popular sites is difficult.

"Other than that, you're on your own. The packet contains a Florence City Hop-on-Hop-Off Tour pass. The buses stop at eighteen of the top attractions. I've also included a map of Florence, plus a route and information for a walking tour for those who prefer more relaxed sightseeing. And if you're interested in buying gold jewelry, I've recommended two shops on the Ponte Vecchio that we've found to be honest."

"Are you saying we shouldn't buy at the other shops?" Loretta asked.

Millie hesitated before answering. "Of course you can shop wherever you like, Loretta. But Florence is a very touristy city and many are ready to take advantage of people who don't speak Italian. These two shops have English-speaking clerks and, as I said, we've found them to be honest.

"Dinner tomorrow is on your own and I've included some restaurant recommendations in the packet as well. Make a note of where we park the bus in the morning and meet us there at ten p.m. to go back to the hotel. You can take a taxi if you want to return earlier. If you'd rather skip Florence, I've included recommendation for some day tours you can do on your own. Any questions?"

She waited a minute. "Okay, as usual I'll check you in, so see me later for your room keys."

An hour or so later they left the highway and traveled on hilly local roads lined with vineyards, olive groves, and cypress trees. The rambling castle-like hotel perched on the top of a hill overlooking row after row of neatly tended grape vines appeared after a turn. The tan stone of the buildings, the blue water in the large pool, and the green of the well-maintained grounds seemed to sparkle in the brilliant sunlight. An honor guard of cypress trees lined the long winding driveway up the hill. Vines and olive trees marched down rolling hills as far as the eyes could see.

"Feel free to walk the grounds or have a drink on the terrace," Millie announced as they stepped off the van.

Dana looked around before turning to Callie. "How about a walk in the garden, then a drink on the terrace?"

"Sounds good to me." Callie followed Dana.

Once they were out of earshot of the group, Dana spoke quickly as if she couldn't wait to get it all out. "Thanks to James you know about my actress girlfriend and that I'm a software entrepreneur, but you don't know anything about my business or why I'm on this trip alone. I'm going to reveal some of that now, but it doesn't mean you're obligated to share anything about your life. I trust that you'll keep what I say confidential."

She took a breath. "I'm the chief executive officer of Integrated Bank Financial Software, a firm I founded ten years ago. I worked as a programmer in a bank all during college and I saw a lot of ways to use computers to improve their processing, but they weren't interested in my ideas. I developed parts of the system as class projects and then continued writing code on my own time. A year after I graduated, I sold the first application to a small bank and I brought in two college friends, Linda and Artie, to help with training and management and marketing to grow the company while I continued to develop the system. After a year or so of success, I gave each of them a thirty percent interest in the business in exchange for one dollar and kept forty percent for myself. In the last nine years with me managing the software and interfacing with customers, Linda managing personnel, training and accounting, and Artie managing marketing and sales, IBFS has become a major player in the banking industry. We've all made lots of money."

She stopped and seemed to go inward. "A couple of months ago I became aware that Linda and Artie were planning to oust me and take control of the company."

Callie gasped. "How awful."

Dana nodded. "It was a shock and yet it wasn't. I'd sensed the resentment building as the business grew and I became the face of the company. But the betrayal hurt. Thanks to Ellen, my best friend and attorney, there's a clause in the contracts they signed that confirms my total ownership of the code and without the code the company is a shell. They either hadn't noticed or didn't care at the time. They hired a powerhouse law firm to fight me, but I'm protected, and it's just a matter of time before I get them out. I came on this trip to get away while things played out."

She looked into the distance, then took a deep breath. "But I've been closely monitoring all the corporate computer systems, and last night I discovered they're stealing from the company, diverting about twenty percent of all income to offshore accounts. Our auditors are either in on it or totally inept. Ellen wants me to hire an audit team that represents me to go in and review everything. She's asking her partners for recommendations, but it's really on me to come up with an auditing firm. I don't want one of the big five or whatever the number is these days and I'm stumped. There's more to the story, but that's the problem in a nutshell."

"No wonder you're upset."

Angela could help Dana, but if she introduced them it was likely she'd no longer be able to keep her life secret. Callie chewed her lip. She probably should stay out of it. But Dana was exposing herself by sharing the betrayal of her partners. And really, how could she not help the woman who'd made this trip possible for her?

She broke the silence. "My best friend might be able to help. Her name is Angela Fortuna. She's a CPA and the managing partner of Fortuna, Melloni, and Carter. They have offices in New York City, Chicago, Miami, and San Francisco. If her firm can't handle the audit, she probably could recommend one. I'd trust her with my life." *In fact, I have for the last year.* "If you're interested, I'll call her and see what she thinks."

"Can you call right now?"

Callie checked her phone. Four thirty in the afternoon here would be ten thirty in the morning there. "All right." She punched a number and waited. "Good morning, Angela. No, no, everything is fine. I've mentioned Dana to you several times—yes, that Dana. She's looking for a CPA firm for her business and I thought you might be able to help." She listened for a few seconds. "I don't know, but rather than get in the middle, I'm going to hang up and have her call you right back. Speak to you tonight."

Callie ended the call, dictated Angela's number to Dana, then pointed to a nearby bench. "I'll sit over there while you talk."

Forty-five minutes later Dana dropped onto the bench. "Thank you. She's sure they can handle the problem, so she's going to send me and Ellen a proposal with information about her firm and some client references. I'll review it later, and if Ellen and I agree, Ellen will sign on my behalf tomorrow and we'll put the audit in motion."

She pulled Callie off the bench. "Come on. I'm going to buy you a drink."

The terrace overlooked the rolling hills of the valley below. As soon as they sat, Millie brought them their room keycards, reminded them of the wine tasting at six p.m., and hurried back to her own table. They both ordered prosecco and nibbled the olives the waiter left on the table.

"Angela sounds nice and very professional. She grasped the problem right away and immediately proposed an approach that I think will help lower their guard. Do you and Angela spend much time together?"

How much to reveal? It would all come out in the end, so she might as well rip the bandage off and be done with it. "We're very close. We've been best friends since third grade. And she moved in with me a little over a year ago just before…when my wife was dying."

"Abby?"

Callie's eyes widened. "Did Angela tell you?"

Dana shook her head. "No. She thanked me for taking care of you, but otherwise we didn't discuss you. You called me Abby that day on the boat in the Cinque Terre. You were so excited I guess you forgot she wasn't there. You said Abby and turned and hugged me."

She had forgotten that. "Right. I thought you hadn't heard me so, after my anxiety attack, I forgot the whole thing. How come you never asked about her?"

"We weren't sharing much about our lives at that time, and I figured when you wanted me to know about her you would tell me. But I am interested."

Callie rubbed her chin. They were already friends and getting closer by the day. Now Dana and Angela would be working together and Dana would probably hear the story in dribs and drabs, so why not. She took a deep breath. She spoke about their love, their commitment, Abby's illness, and how her death had devastated her. She told her about the letter and the last-minute decision to take the tour.

Dana hadn't said a word while Callie told her story. "You'd hardly left your home for an entire year until two weeks before you left for Milan?"

"Other than going out to my backyard and lots of desensitizing excursions in those last two weeks, that's correct."

"You're very brave, Callie, to do the tour on your own under those circumstances."

Callie dabbed at the tears on her face. "I wouldn't have lasted an hour if it hadn't been for you. Angela and I have joked during our nightly telephone calls that Abby arranged for you to be here to take care of me."

Dana took her hand. "I don't know if it was Abby, but I believe the universe had a hand in our meeting. I'm on the tour alone because the betrayal of my business partners resulted in another betrayal. And it's the reason the twelfth seat on the tour was available the moment you decided to come."

She took a breath and let it out slowly. "I planned this trip as a surprise thirty-third birthday present for Sandra, the 'sexy actress'

James mentioned, someone I was involved with for nearly three years. I intended to propose at the end. But, as it turned out, Sandy assumed losing control of the company meant I was, or would be, broke and powerless and she dumped me. That she immediately took up with Linda, who, it seemed, had lusted after whatever I had, completed the betrayal and shattered me."

Callie reached for Dana's hand. "What a horrible person."

Dana entwined their fingers. "I was clueless. But I got off easy. It would have been much worse if I'd married her. When I learned about the coup, I started having anxiety attacks. After Sandy defected, they got worse, so I took my friend Ellen's advice and went into therapy."

Callie watched Dana take a breath, then another and then relax and assumed she'd learned to do that in therapy.

"Jean, my therapist, asked lots of questions." She smiled. "I quickly learned that the raised eyebrows meant she wasn't buying my story. She forced me to think about myself and the people I chose to have in my life. And why I thought it necessary to give more than half my business away. When she asked what I missed about Sandy the only things I could come up with—other than her shopping for my clothing and packing for me—were having someone beautiful on my arm and, when Sandy was in the mood, good sex. Jean's eyebrows almost launched into space when I admitted I often felt lonely when I was with Sandy. Pathetic right?"

Callie didn't know how to respond so she punted. "So why did you decide to come on the tour alone?"

"Jean helped me identify my self-worth and trust issues, asked me to think about my willingness to settle for such a shallow relationship, and encouraged me to come on the tour alone to think about who I am and who I want to be. When Ellen said the same thing, I decided it would be good to get away from all the drama, and two weeks before the start of the tour I cancelled Sandra's ticket."

Callie squeezed Dana's hand. "Thank you for trusting me with that. I'm sorry to hear about the business, but hearing about Sandra makes me angry. You deserve better. The timing is amazing, though. You cancel, then I call an hour later and get Sandra's seat."

Dana smiled. "You know what? I'm having a much better time with you than I would have had with Sandra. I realized after a couple of days that Sandra would have hated everyone and everything about the tour. And she would have made me feel stupid for arranging it. I doubt we'd have lasted more than two days before she made me so uncomfortable that I'd have agreed to leave."

Callie was stunned. "I need some time to absorb everything you've shared, but I'm overjoyed how events unfolded. Abby or the universe sent you when I needed help. But more than that, I love traveling with you and I'm thrilled we've become friends."

Marian appeared at their table. "Hey, you two, we're going down to the wine tasting. Are you coming?"

Callie looked at Dana. "I don't know about you, but I could use the distraction and the wine."

Dana stood. "Me too."

The wine tasting was fun. They were given small glasses of different wines to taste, then discard, but Callie found herself drinking the ones she liked a lot and dumping the others. In between she drank water. There was much kidding and laughing and from time to time she and Dana, who'd ended up at the other end of the table, locked eyes. Sharing their stories had brought them closer. It was nice to feel so connected.

Afterward, there was just enough time to find their rooms and change for dinner. Callie's room was beautiful and had huge windows and a spectacular view of the rolling hills. The sun was setting as Callie and Dana walked over to the restaurant. Bathed in the sunset's warm reds and pinks and blues, they stopped to watch nature's dramatic end to a dramatic day. Neither spoke, but Dana's hand on the small of Callie's back indicated that Callie wasn't the only one feeling closer, more connected.

The dinner was the usual delicious feast, a variety of appetizers including locally cured meats, a smorgasbord of local specialties like tripe, steak alla Fiorentina, pappardelle pasta in boar meat sauce, tagliatelle pasta with porcini mushrooms and truffles, plus fresh vegetables, and fresh fruit and gelato for dessert. Callie's appetite had improved, but she still ate moderately, tasting a little bit of everything. The group was mellow from the wine tasting so the conversation was quiet and relaxing.

Back in her room after dinner, Callie took a shower and washed her hair, made some notes about her thoughts for the romance, then settled in with a mystery to wait for Angela's nightly call. She didn't get much reading done because her mind kept going back to her earlier conversation with Dana.

Interesting that they'd both suffered immense losses. She'd been devastated by Abby's death. And Dana had been traumatized by the betrayal of her two best friends followed by the woman she thought she loved abandoning her. She was just starting to fall asleep when her phone jolted her awake. She glanced at the clock on the night table. It was much later than usual.

"Hey, Angela. Working late?"

Angela laughed. "I've been in a Zoom meeting with Dana and Ellen, her attorney, for hours ironing out the details of our contract."

Callie sat up. "You're doing it? You're going to audit her company?"

"Yes. I owe you big for the referral, Cal. This is a huge deal for my firm. It could open doors for work at major banks. And that means the big time and big bucks."

"Hey, I'll never be able to pay you back for what you've done for me, so don't worry about it. What did you think of Dana?"

"I already knew she was a good person, but after meeting her I think she's brilliant, has a good business head, and seems in command of all aspects of the company. You failed to mention that she's sexy and great-looking."

Callie blushed. "I lucked out having her on this trip. I'm glad you've met her. You were talking business, so I doubt you heard the whole story. Let me tell you how it came about."

They spent a half hour discussing Dana and her situation, then hung up. Callie turned off the light and got into bed. It was the first night Angela hadn't had to encourage her to stay on the trip.

CHAPTER ELEVEN

They'd all groaned when Millie called for an early breakfast because their tour of the Uffizi Gallery was scheduled for the first time slot of the day. But judging by the crowd milling around outside the gallery in the Piazza delle Signori and the crush of people waiting to buy tickets before the booth even opened, the early start was a smart move.

With Dana at her side and surrounded by her friends, Callie entered the museum without stress. She'd considered skipping the gallery to avoid the crowds, but since the attack in the glass factory in Murano her tour mates had been quietly protective of her, so it didn't feel so scary. Besides, she didn't want to miss the opportunity to see Botticelli's *The Birth of Venus*, in the flesh. She wasn't disappointed. The group spent almost ten minutes gazing at the luminous depiction of the naked goddess of beauty and love emerging from the sea on a clamshell, modestly covering her privates with her golden hair.

As Callie studied the late fifteenth-century canvas, a wave of sadness washed over her. Abby had called her "my Botticelli Venus" in their courting days.

"Are you all right?" Dana whispered.

Grateful to be seen, Callie reached for Dana's hand. "Yes, thanks. It was just a moment of sadness from a memory that popped up." She squeezed and then dropped Dana's hand. Happy to be with Dana, happy she never pushed for details.

They moved on from the Botticelli to equally gorgeous masterpieces by Leonardo, Michelangelo, Caravaggio, Artemisia Gentileschi, and Giotto. She enjoyed learning, but after an hour of listening to the tour guide she was bleary-eyed. Her brain was saturated with so much beauty, and the escalating cacophony of tour guides shouting to be heard over the chatter of the increasing number of tourists made her feel as if her head was going to explode. She tugged on Dana's arm. "I need to get out of here."

"I'm more than ready. I'll let Millie know." As the guide moved to the next painting, Dana spoke to Millie. "Callie and I are leaving. We'll see you at the bus later." Millie nodded and continued onto the next room with the group.

Dana held Callie close and eased them through the overcrowded gallery to the exit. The Piazza della Signoria was even more crowded than earlier, people jammed together with no obvious objective, holding cameras up to photograph the many sculptures and historic buildings. The noise was ear shattering. They took a few seconds to breathe and scan the L-shaped piazza for an exit.

"There." Callie pointed. "There's an opening next to that café."

Dana took Callie's hand and interlaced their fingers. "Okay, try to focus on my hand rather than the crowd and the noise."

Callie glanced at their hands and concentrated on the warmth and strength of their connection as Dana led her around and through the groups of tourists. She blinked at the sudden quiet, surprised to see they'd left the square and were moving along the Via Vaccchereccia.

"I can't believe I got through the crowds and noise in and outside the Uffizi without an attack. Thank you."

Dana held up their clasped hands. "I thought anchoring you might help you feel safe." Callie missed the connection as soon as Dana let go of her hand.

The farther they got from the square the fewer people they encountered, and when they found a tiny café in a quiet street Callie sank into a chair at a shaded table and closed her eyes, savoring the quiet. Dana ordered a large bottle of sparkling water and two espressos.

Hearing the gurgle of water being poured, Callie opened her eyes. Dana handed her a glass. "How are you doing?"

"Other than being thirsty as hell and tired from standing too long, I'm good." Callie emptied her glass and poured another.

"Congratulations." Dana lifted her glass. "Being in the middle of screaming crowds of strangers and not having an anxiety attack is worth celebrating."

Callie straightened. "I hope it means the anxiety is gone for good. Is that what happened with your attacks?"

"Kind of. After Ellen helped me understand I have the legal upper hand in the attempted coup and my therapist helped me recognize that I was embarrassed by Sandra's betrayal but better off without her, I felt in control. And once I started taking action, the attacks just dribbled away, like yours seemed to be doing."

The waiter placed an espresso and a tiny cookie in front of each of them, then left. While Callie stirred sugar into her coffee and considered what Dana said, two birds landed on the table. One flew away, but the other stared at Callie.

"These Italian sparrows are so brazen." She pushed her cookie toward the bird. Its little head swiveled from her to the cookie, then looked at Dana, then at Callie and back to the cookie. It chirped, picked up the treat, and flew onto the overhead branch.

Abby? She hadn't told Dana about Abby saying she would come back as a bird and she didn't want to get into it now.

Dana laughed. "They sure are aggressive."

Callie sipped her coffee. "Do you think the disappearing anxiety means I'm accepting Abby's death?"

Dana considered the question. "I doubt you'll ever accept her death, Callie. But maybe coming on this trip was your way of taking control of your life again. Maybe the anxiety is going because you're allowing yourself to have a life without Abby."

The bird landed on their table, dropped a piece of the cookie in front of Callie, and sang a happy song. She was mesmerized.

"Hey, there, we were wondering where you two had gone." Susan and Fran looked as tired and frazzled as they had been when they'd arrived here. The bird flew away.

Callie would think about the bird and what Dana said, but it could wait until later when she was alone. They hadn't spent a lot of time alone with this couple, but they were lesbians and they seemed nice so she wanted to be friendly. She hoped Dana felt the same. "Join us."

"Thanks. We've been looking for a place to rest and plan a walking tour." The waiter appeared and they ordered.

"We're going to do a walking tour as well, but more of an ambling, see where we end up rather than following any of the recommended routes." Dana glanced at Callie. "We're close to the Ponte Vecchio so we'll start there, look in the gold shops Millie told us about, then walk across the bridge to the other side of the Arno where it's probably less crowded and see some of those sights like the Piazzale Michelangelo, which is supposed to have a stunning view of the city and the cathedral. You're welcome to join us."

"Ordinarily we would, but Fran is an architect and I'm a historian, and we both have specific buildings and places we want to see while we're here, so no ambling for us. Maybe we can hang out in Rome." Susan spoke for the two of them and Fran tipped her head to indicate her agreement.

After some time in the jewelry shops, Dana bought a beautiful gold pendant with a ruby stone for Ellen and Callie bought a beautiful ring with fire opal in an intricate gold setting for Angela, gold earrings with emeralds for Erin, a gold bracelet for Bonnie, and a gold pendant with a sapphire stone for Maggie. They tucked their purchases into their backpacks, walked over the bridge, then along the Arno River until the Piazza Poggi, where they started uphill. They stopped along the way at the Giardino delle Rose, a terraced rose garden billed as one of the loveliest and most romantic gardens in Florence. Pretty? Yes. Fragrant? Yes. Romantic? Not to Callie.

They left the garden and continued to the Piazzale Michelangelo. They checked out the copies of Michelangelo's *David* and the four allegories of the Medici Chapel of San Lorenzo, then sat on the steps and gazed at the spectacular panoramic view of the whole city of Florence—the hills of Fiesole and Settignano in the background, the Ponte Vecchio over the winding Arno, the orange rooftops, the Brunelleschi dome, the Palazzo Vecchio, and the Basilica di Santa Croce. It was breathtaking. And timeless.

Dana pulled her backpack to her and removed her sketch pad and colored pencils. "I hope you don't mind if I try to sketch this. It helps me see things I might miss otherwise."

"Please do. I do the same thing. You know, people sitting here centuries ago had pretty much the same view. And think about it. We walked on the same streets and looked at the same buildings as Michelangelo and so many other famous artists. We're just a minute in the life of this city."

Dana shifted to look at Callie. "The view is gorgeous. But you're right, thinking about the history makes me feel insignificant. And trying to sketch when talking about Michelangelo makes me feel ridiculous."

Callie laughed. "Unless you imagine you're going to sell one of your sketches for millions, I say go for it."

Dana sketched and Callie retreated into her thoughts, the silence companionable and comfortable. Callie felt the way she felt with Abby when bird-watching or hanging out at the firepit in their backyard, just being together and close without needing to speak or touch. "Sitting like this reminds me of times with Abby. Did you ever just sit quietly with Sandra and yet feel together and close?"

Dana took so long to answer that Callie thought she hadn't heard. Or was ignoring the question.

"I only felt connected with Sandra during sex. Other than that we were rarely alone. And if we were, she'd sleep or be focused on her phone, talking, doing email, or whatever."

"Were you aware of the, um, disconnect?"

"Yes, on some level. I think that's why I planned this tour, to give us time to focus on each other." Dana shook her head. "Talk about being out of touch with reality." She stared at the view, but Callie sensed she was seeing something else. "I never acknowledged to myself how lonely I felt when I was with her." She brushed her eyes.

Callie put her hand on Dana's thigh but didn't comment. Dana covered her hand. They sat like that for a long while in silence. Callie felt content. She hoped Dana didn't feel lonely with her. She took a long drink from her bottle of water. "I'm ready to walk back to the city, whenever you are."

"Good idea." Dana packed her sketch pad and pencils, stood, and extended her hand to pull Callie up. "You know, getting back to the people who lived here centuries ago I wonder how they managed to build these beautiful buildings without the tools we have today. It's amazing."

After they made their way back over the Arno, they scanned the map and Millie's listing of things to see. "We've already got great pictures of Florence from high up. So can we skip climbing the four hundred and sixty-three steps to the Duomo's dome to see the glorious city vista?"

Dana laughed. "Do I always have to remind you that aerobic exercise is good for you?"

Callie tapped her forehead, pretending to think. "Duh, I thought walking was aerobic too. And we've been doing it for hours."

"You're right. Let's walk." And they did, stopping occasionally to look closer at a building or a sculpture. They would have gone into the Museo dell'Opera to see the original Ghiberti's bronze doors displayed there, but the line was long so they settled for seeing the replacement casts hanging on the Baptistery.

When they came across the Mercato Centrale, Dana read Millie's description to Callie. "'Don't miss the heart of the food scene in Florence, the trendy Industrial Age, steel-and-glass Central Market. Start on the ground floor and take in the fabulous displays of the vendors selling meat, fish, produce, and other staples. And then go upstairs to the bustling food court for a meal.' Might as well, huh?"

They wandered through the market, stopping to check out small specialty shops selling local olive oils, meats, cheeses, and more, but the food court was noisy and though tripe was a Florentine specialty, a cow stomach sandwich didn't appeal, so they left.

They found a small, quiet trattoria they liked the look of, took an outdoor table, and ordered a pizza and a hot and cold antipasto platter to share. Callie decided on a carafe of the local chianti and Dana a beer.

"You know—" They spoke at the same time.

Callie waved a hand, inviting Dana to speak first.

"I'm tired. There are way too many tourists here so it's hard to even get close enough to look at things from the outside, forget getting in anywhere. I'm sure if we wander long enough we'll find places that are not so crowded, but I'd really like to lie at the pool and read. If you want to stay, I'll hook you up with some of the others in the group before I get a taxi to the hotel."

"You took the words right out of my mouth, Dana. Florence is beautiful, but it's hard to feel the charm because of the crowds. If I ever come back, it will be in winter, when I hope there will be far fewer tourists. I'd love to go back to the hotel. I'll text Millie to let her know."

As Callie made her way to the pool later, she could see Dana already engaged with someone lying in a lounge chair. Actually, it was Marian and Lou.

Marian waved. "Hey, we were just asking Dana how you did with the crowds in Florence."

After her very public anxiety attack in the gallery on Murano, the group had become protective of her and this morning in the Uffizi, had surrounded her as the crowd grew and the noise level escalated. Maybe she hadn't had another attack because the group had protected her, or maybe it was because she was accepting Abby's death. Or maybe both.

"I was fine. You all made me feel safe in the Uffizi and Dana grounded and protected me walking through the crowds outside. I'd like to think Murano was my last attack, but I guess time will tell. Thanks for asking. What brought you back here so early?"

Lou sat up and signaled the waiter. "As beautiful and historic as Florence is, it's crowded and noisy and doesn't fit with the relaxed, romantic vacation we signed up for. What about you?"

The waiter came over and they all ordered drinks.

"That's exactly why we came back to hang out at the pool." Callie went on to ask the question she'd been wrestling with. "What makes a place romantic for you?"

The couple looked at each other, then Marian answered.

"I can tell you what *isn't* romantic for me. Being jostled, fighting my way through crowds, and not being able to hear myself think. As for what is, I find candlelight or moonlight, soft music, and flowers romantic, but only if I'm with someone I care about."

The waiter handed them their drinks. "I think Callie was asking more about the cities on the tour." Dana sipped her beer. "What makes them romantic? Is it being with someone you're attracted to or the beauty of the place?"

"I'm not sure." Marian turned the question back. "You two are close and you've been experiencing the places we're visiting just like us, so what are you finding romantic?"

Callie flushed. "We just met on the tour."

Marian raised her eyebrows. "Really? You seem so close. I thought you were together, I mean, a couple. I did wonder at the separate rooms, though."

Dana cleared her throat. "We're just friends."

Marian turned to her husband. "What do you think makes a place romantic, Lou?"

"I'm not sure either. Ask me at the end of the tour. In the meantime, I'm going back to my book." He slipped down onto the lounge chair and picked up his novel.

The women followed suit. Callie stared at her book, but she couldn't stop thinking about Marian's assumption that they were a couple. Dana was in the lounge next to her, ostensibly reading. Though there didn't seem to be a lot of page turning activity for her either.

She and Dana were compatible travel mates. They liked the same things and enjoyed relaxed wandering, breathing in a city, rather than intense sightseeing. Abby, on the other hand, always took a more academic approach, trying to learn everything, visit every museum and church and statue, study every building. In some ways, at least when traveling, Callie was more compatible with Dana than with Abby. She felt a stab of pain. *No.* Her eyes filled. Her breathing sped up. How could she think that? No one could replace Abby. The bile rose into her throat.

Dana must have sensed her agitation. Without looking at her, she put her hand on Callie's thigh. "Okay?"

Callie struggled out of the lounge chair. "I'm too hot. I'm going to my room."

Dana sat up. "Can I help?"

Callie shook her head and stumbled to the hotel. She hoped and feared Dana would follow her.

It took her a few seconds for her shaking hands to open the door to her room. She rushed into the bathroom and threw up in the toilet. She remained on her knees on the cool tiles until her tears stopped and the nausea passed, then after washing her face and brushing her teeth, she texted Angela. *R u free to talk?*

A couple of minutes later Callie's phone rang. "Hey, Callie, I'm strategizing with my team about your girlfriend Dana's project so I can't talk long. What's up?"

"That's what's wrong. She's not my girlfriend. I'm not replacing Abby."

"Whoa. That was just a figure of speech. I know you're not ready for another relationship. What brought this on, Cal?"

"Some of the people on the tour think we're a couple, and it made me realize that we're good together, compatible in ways that Abby and I were not." She took a breath. "And it freaked me out to think that."

"So you're feeling disloyal? Guilty?"

"Yes. Abby and I were great together. I'll never have that with anyone else." She walked to the sliding glass door and stared out. She laughed. "And now I'm looking out my door for a bird to reassure me that Abby isn't mad at me. Am I nuts?"

Angela laughed. "Listen to me, hon. You and Abby were deeply in love. You were compatible in all the things that mattered to both of you. Your relationship was wonderful. But there were ways you didn't fit together. That doesn't negate what you had."

Angela hesitated, then continued, "I'm just getting to know Dana, but I like her a lot. And from what you've said she seems to care about you and has helped make this trip possible. She's a good fit as a friend and maybe more, eventually. But liking someone and feeling close to them is just that. It's not a zero-sum game, Cal. Fitting together, enjoying being with Dana, doesn't take away from your connection to Abby. Read her letter again, Callie. She wanted you to keep her in your heart but find someone to love. Maybe Dana is that someone. Maybe not. But I think it's fantastic that while still dealing with the loss of Abby, you've allowed Dana to get close. Also, let me remind you that so far on this trip the birds have been supportive of her and you spending time together."

Callie laughed. "It's true. They have." The birds hopping and pecking outside her room now were showing no interest in her, however. Was Abby mad?

"And now you have me wondering whether being ignored by the birds outside really means Abby is mad at me." She laughed again. "Thanks, for taking the time to talk me down, Ang. I'll let you go back to work."

The birds continued to ignore her, so she dug the much-read copy of Abby's letter out of her bag and sat on the bed. Abby's voice was in her head, speaking the words she'd written.

I don't want you to ever forget me, but I don't want you to live your life with only the memories, no matter how happy and loving those memories are.

Callie wiped the tears blurring her vision.

Please, dearest Callie, do it for me, go out into the world and live. Be happy, find someone to love. Celebrate life. It's what I want for you. It's what I would want for myself if I'd lost you.

She fell back and stared at the ceiling, recalling those painful, teary conversations with Abby as she was dying. They'd only had a little more than twenty years instead of the forever they'd promised each other, but they were happy years, a wonderful life. There were many happy memories. And because of how deeply Abby had loved her, she'd not only given her permission to live and love again but had encouraged her to do it.

She'd overreacted to Marian's comment. She and Dana were close and to an outside eye it probably looked like more than friendship. But Dana was her friend. Period. She picked up her phone and texted Dana.

What time shall we meet for dinner?

CHAPTER TWELVE

Callie and Dana decided to sleep in rather than go to Florence with the bus. They'd take a taxi later if they felt like it. Over a leisurely breakfast they discussed the day.

"I was thinking we could rent a couple of motorcycles, take a ride into the countryside, have lunch and do a little sightseeing."

Callie shook her head. "I've never ridden a motorcycle. I assume you have?"

"I've ridden since I was in college. I own one. Two, actually. I got a second one for Sandy, but the princess refused to go with me after our first excursion because the helmet flattened her hair. If you'd chance riding behind me, I think it would be fun."

Callie felt woozy, as if all her blood had drained from her brain.

"Oh, geez, you just turned snow white. Forget the motorcycle." Dana looked flustered. "We can hire a guide with a car to take us on a private tour."

The idea of being on the back of a motorcycle frightened her, but that didn't mean she couldn't do it. She'd enjoyed pushing her boundaries so far. Dana was an experienced biker. And Callie liked the idea of zipping around the countryside just the two of them. Why not try?

"It makes me anxious, but you haven't steered me—oops, no pun intended—wrong so far and I trust you to keep me safe." She blew out a breath. "Let's do it."

"I'm really okay doing something else."

"If you can put up with a nervous nelly behind you, I'm willing to try."

"You'll relax after a few miles and, if not, we'll come back and hire a car. Let me see what I can arrange at the desk." Visibly excited, Dana jumped up.

Callie sipped her coffee. Was she making a mistake?

A half hour later Dana returned. "All set. I ordered a Ducati Multistrada 1200 S Touring D-air, the exact model I have at home. I also got us both helmets and special jackets and vests that offer airbag protection in case of a serious accident. They'll deliver everything in about an hour."

The rental agency provided several sizes of the helmets and the special clothing, and when they were both well-fitted, Dana straddled the bike and the rental agent helped Callie climb on.

"I'm going to ride around the parking lot for a few minutes so you can get accustomed to the feel of the bike. Put your arms around my waist and hold me tight. Try not to tense on curves. Just let your body follow my body."

After about fifteen minutes riding in figure eights to give Callie a sense of how the turns would feel, Dana stopped and shifted to look at her.

"You did great. Ready to hit the road?"

She felt surprisingly comfortable on the bike. "Yes."

Dana grinned, revved the bike, and headed to the long drive that would take them out to the road. The route on the map the motorcycle rental agency provided took them on scenic and less trafficked local roads that twisted and turned and went up and down hill. Callie relaxed into the curves and the hills and delighted in the sight and fragrance of the vineyards, wheat and corn fields, groves of olive trees, and fields of sunflowers and lavender they passed. But what she enjoyed most was being close to Dana, arms wrapped around her waist, inhaling her heady fragrance—a mixture of her cologne, the smell of leather and something fruity, maybe her shampoo or soap. She jerked at the electric shock she felt when she leaned into a curve and one of her hands slid under Dana's jacket and T-shirt. Judging by Dana's reaction, she felt it too.

She considered removing her hand, but the tautness of Dana's belly, the softness of her skin, and the pleasure of touching her were too tempting, so she pretended she didn't notice she was holding on to bare skin. The next time Dana slowed and shifted to confirm Callie was enjoying the ride and point out something of interest, her hand slid out.

Back to grasping Dana through her clothing, Callie felt a pang of loss, followed by a flush of shame. Just because she hadn't had that kind of physical contact with anyone in the year since Abby died didn't mean she had the right to surreptitiously touch Dana like some creepy guy getting his rocks off. *Abby was right, though. Memories are good but living is better.* Perhaps it was a good sign that she was loving being close to and touching a woman's body.

They stopped frequently to stretch, so it took almost two hours to arrive at the walled hill town of Castellina in Chianti. Following the GPS instructions, they cruised through its narrow, winding streets, passed markets filled with colorful fresh fruits and vegetables, cafés, and fragrant bakeries until they arrived at Le Tre Porte, the restaurant recommended by the motorcycle rental guy. Seated on a pine-shaded patio overlooking terraced vineyards, they ordered a platter of mixed appetizers, pappardelle pasta in a wild boar sauce, several vegetables, and an assortment of flavors of gelato for dessert. They had sparkling water but no wine or beer since they were on the motorcycle.

Dana watched Callie help herself to a little bit of everything from the antipasto platter, then did the same. "It seems like you're eating more."

"Am I not leaving enough for you?"

Dana laughed. "Not a problem since I've been ordering more."

Callie considered the issue as she chewed.

"I hadn't noticed, but I am hungry more often and I've gained some weight, so yes, I am eating more. It's probably the delicious Italian food combined with you spoon-feeding me so much. Or it could be that the way we've settled into sharing fits the way I like to eat, a little bit of this and a little bit of that."

"I like it too." Dana tasted the stuffed cherry pepper, then extended her fork with a bite on it. "Here try this."

Callie steadied Dana's hand, put the fork in her mouth, and slowly chewed the pepper. "Spicy but good."

"How are you feeling about being on the bike?"

Callie put her fork down. "I'm loving it. I feel like I'm *in* the countryside rather than looking out at it. I like the wind in my face, the different smells as we move through different areas, and even the vibration of the bike. I don't like the noise, but the helmet and the steady speed help with that. And because I'm hugging you it feels like we're sharing the sights."

They chatted easily as usual, enjoying each other, the delicious food, and the pleasant atmosphere. After eating they wandered around the town for a while before getting back on the bike to ride to the medieval hill town of San Gimignano.

Only residents were allowed to drive in San Gimignano, so they left the motorcycle in the first public parking lot they encountered and walked into the historic center. They strolled around the town's triangular main square, Piazza della Cisterna, observing several of the many surviving square towers built by rival families as both status symbols and fortified homes. They walked along the thirteenth-century walls surrounding the center, then, curious, they visited the Museum of Torture.

Dana was agog at the impressive collection of actual historic torture devices, some familiar like the guillotine, the rack, the chastity belt, and some lesser known, like the iron maiden, the inquisitorial chair, and the heretic's fork.

Callie stared at the iron maiden, a coffin-like box topped by the decorative carved head of a woman. It had two doors fitted with spikes on the inside that pierced the victim when the doors were shut. The card describing the device said it had a thick lining so the screams of the victim couldn't be heard.

Dana took her hand. "Just imagining it is horrible, isn't it?"

Callie shivered. "It's hard to believe people would do this to each other."

Dana put her arm over Callie's shoulder and moved them to the next exhibit, the Inquisitor's Chair. She read the description. "The chair has thirteen hundred spikes. The naked victim was seated and the straps were slowly tightened, so that the spikes penetrated the flesh."

Callie's stomach clenched and the bile rose. "I need to get out of here before I throw up. I'll be outside in the piazza."

"I'm coming with you. I don't need to see the last couple of exhibits to get the message that torture is horrible." Dana took her hand and they quickly exited.

Out in the bright sunshine and feeling the warmth of the sun, Callie breathed deeply, trying to settle her stomach. She consciously pushed the images of torture out of her mind and focused on Dana's firm grip on her hand and the familiar feeling of comfort and safety she provided. The memory of touching the soft skin on her belly filled her and brought with it a jolt of warmth, a shortage of air, and a yearning to do it again. Did Dana feel the need to touch her?

Dana's voice interrupted Callie's thoughts. "I'm ready to leave San Gimignano if you are."

"Let's go." They took a second or two to get their bearings and headed in the direction of the lot where they'd parked the motorcycle.

Dana put her arm around Callie's waist and pulled her closer, as if to protect her. "You know, we pretend we're more civilized than people in medieval times, but we're equally barbaric. Think about things like the electric chair, the horrors of uncontrolled gun ownership, the use of rape as a weapon of war, and the kinds of torture conducted behind closed doors in foreign countries and, for all we know, in the US, that we don't hear about."

In Callie's life and in her fantasy world she didn't think about torture. And in her self-imposed exile from the world for almost the last sixteen months she'd avoided watching or reading the news, so she'd been blissfully ignorant about such horrors. The discussions of world events at meals recently had brought her into the present. But there was something to be said for being oblivious.

The ride back was slow and easy with frequent stops to enjoy the scenery, take pictures and talk about history, about good and bad humans, about life. Being with Dana was always interesting.

Back at the hotel, they dismounted and removed their helmets.

"Would you like me to take your picture?" The doorman smiled and held out his hand. Dana glanced at Callie. "We should memorialize this moment." She gave him her phone.

Callie hesitated, then handed him her phone as well. "Let's stand next to the bike."

Dana threw a hand over Callie's shoulder, and they posed for the first picture. They took a few more in different poses, then several of each of them alone. Dana gave the guy a generous tip, and they left the rented clothing, helmets, and the motorcycle with him for pickup later.

Callie followed her impulse and kissed Dana's cheek. "Thank you. Today was wonderful. I loved riding with you. It's a fabulous way to see things. And I can't thank you enough for once again helping me push my limits."

Dana touched her fingers to her cheek. "I enjoyed it too. I was afraid you'd be too nervous to enjoy it, but you seemed to settle right away. We'll have to do it again. If not on this trip, then when we get back to New York."

Callie smiled. That was the first time either of them mentioned seeing each other after the tour.

"Hey, let's go to the terrace and I'll buy you a drink. And then I want to text the pictures to Angela, Bonnie, and Erin."

"Okay, but I suggest you take a long hot bath later, because you're going to be sore in places you don't expect. It's been a while for me, so I'll do the same."

Callie blinked as her brain jumped to images of Dana naked in the bathtub. *Whoa. Where did that come from?* She shook her head and followed Dana to the terrace. She definitely needed a drink. Or two.

CHAPTER THIRTEEN

By one p.m. the next day they were in their rooms at the Hotel Exellente Roma near the Spanish Steps. As usual, the accommodations were top-notch, lovely junior suites with terraces overlooking the park of the Villa Borghese. Except for tonight's group dinner and the two scheduled tours—St. Peter's and the Sistine Chapel first and then the Colosseum and Forum—they were on their own for the three days in Rome.

Callie arranged to meet Dana in the lobby for a leisurely stroll and lunch, then went down to pick up some tissues in the hotel store. Waiting for Dana, she leaned against a pillar near the elevators, took out her notebook, and jotted down a thought about Dana's love interest in the romance she was planning. *Oops!* She really should give the character a name and stop thinking of her as Dana. While Dana would be the starting point, the character that appeared on the page would be someone Callie created to fit the needs of the story. As would Dana's love interest, though so far she hadn't been able to visualize that person.

A burst of sound caught her attention. People were streaming out of two elevators that had arrived simultaneously, and her gaze found Dana snaking around clusters of people toward her. Their eyes locked. Dana pushed her short hair out of her eyes, a familiar gesture, and grinned. Warmth spread through Callie's body. What the hell was that? A hot flash?

She looked away from Dana, focused on her journal and wrote:

Wearing a crisp white shirt, navy jeans that hung perfectly on her slim hips and a navy blazer she looked like and moved with the confidence of an executive. She was tall for a woman, at ease in her body, no hunched shoulders attempting to hide her height or the full, rounded breasts whose shape was visible under her jacket. Draped from one shoulder was the backpack she always carried, filled with her compact, top-of-the-line camera, sketch pad, colored pencils, guidebook, and e-reader. Her smile was irresistible.

As Dana neared, Callie slipped the journal into her backpack, then looked up and smiled.

Outside, in front of the hotel, Dana extended her map. "Okay, let's pick a direction. Behind us is the Villa Borghese and its gardens. In front of us is the Tiber River. We can cross over it and head in the direction of the Vatican or go south to the old working-class neighborhood of Trastevere, which, according to the guidebook, is"—she opened her iPad and read—"romantic, charming and beautiful, one of the most authentic Roman neighborhoods, a place to experience the real Rome and eat traditional Roman food."

Callie elbowed Dana. "You had to ask? Trastevere, of course."

"Good choice. It says there are lots of restaurants, so we can have lunch while soaking up the wonderful old Italian atmosphere." Dana glanced at her map. "I'm thinking of using the GPS to plot a route to the neighborhood so we don't wander forever. Once we're there we can stroll aimlessly as usual."

"It's a great idea. Rome is so big we could easily get turned around. And I'm getting hungry."

The route was relatively straight and level so a half hour later they turned onto the Ponte Sisto, a stone footbridge over the Tiber, and entered Trastevere. Dana pocketed her phone. "The guidebook said the farther away from the river, the quieter it is."

"I'm all for quiet. And lunch."

Dana jumped away from Callie. "Hey, you're not going to chew on my arm, are you?"

Callie laughed. "I can't promise, but you'll be safe if you find us a pretty restaurant with great food, in a quiet place. Soon."

"I can do that. Let's go."

They stuck to the side streets, strolling through alleys, arches, and narrow cobblestone lanes lined with colorful buildings, some crumbling, whose balconies dripped with ivy, bougainvillea, and geraniums. The shutters on some bars were covered in graffiti, but the plants and religious shrines lining the streets and the many artisan shops, most still closed for *riposo* or siesta, gave Trastevere an artsy feel.

When they came across a small trattoria with an interesting menu in one of the narrow lanes, Callie lifted her chin toward the laundry flapping in the breeze over the tables. "Ah, here's the Italian atmosphere you mentioned."

"Yep, it's authentic Italian. And the purple wisteria mixed in with the undies is a lovely touch." Dana placed her hand on Callie's back and steered her to a chair at one of the tables spread out along the outside wall of the building.

Callie observed her as she ordered in Italian—a large bottle of carbonated water to share, a beer for herself, and a local wine for Callie. Was Dana touching her more recently? Or was she just more aware of it? She scanned the menu written on the chalkboard placed on a chair near the entrance to the restaurant, pleased that most of the offerings were Roman specialties. "I'm interested in either the *pasta alla carbonara* or the *tonnarelli cacio e pepe*. And, if I remember correctly that *carciofi* means artichoke, the *carciofi alla Romana*. What about you?"

"I've read a lot about the pasta with bacon and eggs so let's have the carbonara and the artichoke sounds good too. I'm going to add a small cold antipasto."

After they ordered, Dana picked up her beer. "What are your impressions so far?"

Morgan lifted her beer to her soft, kissable mouth, then lowered the glass and ran her tongue over her glistening lips. Jane was mesmerized. Her heart raced. All she could think about was that mouth, kissing Morgan, the taste of beer on her tongue—

"Callie?" Her head jerked up. Dana was grinning.

"What?" Callie had been so focused on Dana's lips, thinking about describing them in her journal, that she hadn't heard the question. She'd thought naming the characters would provide some distance but apparently not.

"I asked what you think of Trastevere?"

Damn. Had Dana caught her staring at her lips? "Oh, it's beautiful and charming. And, dare I say, romantic?"

"This a first. What makes it feel romantic?"

Callie had no idea. The words had just popped out. But it was true, it did feel romantic.

"I'm not sure. We've seen a lot of beautiful places, but something about the winding alleys and all the flowers makes me feel like I'm in the Rome of olden days." She shrugged. "Maybe that's it." Was looking at Dana as the love interest in her romance making her feel romantic? "Or maybe it's the laundry flapping over our heads."

They laughed. And dug into the antipasto the waiter placed on the table.

After a leisurely lunch, they continued to explore the neighborhood until they stumbled on the Piazzi di Santa Maria.

Dana checked the map and Millie's notes. "Ah, this piazza is considered the beating heart of Trastevere." They sat on the steps of the fountain in the square, surrounded by medieval buildings and other tourists sitting and passing nearby. Callie liked places like this, places to people-watch and think about the past. But her thoughts kept going back to the scene between Morgan and Jane she'd imagined earlier and she was itching to write it down. "Would you think I'm an awful person if I write in my journal now?"

"You mean you don't want to relate to me every second of every day? I can't imagine why, but, no, I'd still think you were the best thing since someone invented beer." Dana gently pressed her shoulder to Callie's shoulder. "Go on. I'm good."

Callie closed her eyes, imagining the scene, watching Dana lift her glass and drink, then swipe her tongue over the foam on her lips, the feeling of her heart racing, of wanting to kiss Dana.

Her eyes popped open. Is that what happened? What came first? Had her thoughts about the book come first and her thoughts about Dana after? Was she confusing herself by using Dana as the model for Morgan?

She glanced at Dana. She was totally focused on her sketch pad, one leg extended, the other bent to support the pad. The pencil in her long, slender fingers moved quickly over the page, creating a picture of two women holding hands, looking into each other's eyes, heads tilted as if ready to kiss. Unlike her, Dana was a talented artist.

Callie followed Dana's gaze to the subjects of her drawing. She'd caught them perfectly—except the real women were deep in conversation, not leaning in for a kiss. The women were Dana's inspiration, but the drawing was what Dana saw, not a photograph.

Just like her character. Dana was the perfect inspiration for Morgan, but Callie was creating Morgan. Perhaps the problem was that she'd been totally focused on Morgan and therefore Dana and was confusing her brain as a result. Perhaps she needed to work on Jane, who she was, what she was like, what did Morgan like about her and vice versa. Both characters needed to be fully alive for her if they were going to be alive for her readers, and she'd hardly given Jane a thought besides naming her.

Callie put her journal into her bag. She looked up, surprised to find Dana watching her. Dana smiled. "Did you get it all down?"

"I did." She appreciated that Dana never pried and asked what she was writing, never presumed to be entitled to Callie's private thoughts. But that was Dana, wasn't it? Thoughtful, caring, and considerate. A lovely person and a good friend. That's it, a good friend.

"Your drawing is quite good. Are you a trained artist?"

Dana gripped her sketch pad. "I've loved to draw since someone in daycare put a crayon in my hand. I was about four, I think. Other than one painting class in college, though, I've never had any training." She put her pad and pencils in her backpack and stood.

"Shall we mosey on?"

As they walked, something Dana said set Callie off laughing and she put a pretend microphone in front of Dana and asked in a what she considered a TV reporter's voice, "So, Dana, tell us how you're enjoying your travels in Italy so far."

Dana got right into the game. She put on a serious face. "To be frank, Callie, I've never taken a sightseeing vacation trip before. I—"

Callie pretended to push the mic closer. "Really? The world wants to know what kinds of vacations you went on, Dana."

"Well, if you really want to know, my vacations were centered around the outdoors, playing tennis, swimming, hiking, skiing, and things like that. Nothing close to walking around romantic historic cities and towns."

"So, healthy, wholesome activities?"

Dana laughed. "Healthy and wholesome by day, but alcohol-filled dinner parties with dancing and much sexual activity by night."

"Oh." Callie lowered the hand with the pretend mic. "Sorry. I didn't mean to pry."

Dana took Callie's hand and gazed into her eyes. "Hey, you weren't prying. I brought it up. It all seems so empty now. Until I started spending time with you, talking and laughing and learning and...just being, I didn't understand the wonder of connecting with someone. I've been happier, felt more whole since we met than any time I can remember."

Callie closed her eyes.

Heat flushed through Jane, her heart pounded in her ears and her legs shook at the intensity of Morgan's gaze, the affirmation of her words. She too was happy, happier than she had a right to be.

She'd had the thoughts of her characters running rampant through her head from time to time while writing. But this was the first time she'd ever felt what they were feeling. And she hadn't even started writing in earnest. She needed space to think. She opened her eyes. "All right, this interview is being interrupted because of breaking news. Callie needs a nap before dinner." She grinned. "Let's head back to the hotel."

Dana's eyebrows shot up. "First I need to know what your usual vacation was like."

Callie was aware that Dana had made herself vulnerable by sharing her feelings about being together and she'd abruptly changed the subject, but she wasn't ready to discuss her own feelings or share them. She could talk about vacations, though.

"Generally, like you, Abby and I took vacations centered around outdoor activities. We both liked hiking and skiing and we also enjoyed tennis and swimming in pools and the ocean and walking on the beach. Abby was an avid bird-watcher, of course, and always made time for it whether we were in the mountains, at a lake or at the ocean, and though it wasn't my thing, I enjoyed sharing it with her. No wild parties or meaningless sex, however."

They stopped in the middle of the Ponte Sisto to take in the view. "I guess you would have thought us boring. But we were happy."

"It doesn't sound boring to me. It sounds real. My life was hollow. And I can't deny that before I understood how superficial it was and how alone and unworthy I felt, I probably *would* have considered your life boring. But my life was meaningless. Therapy opened my eyes and after connecting with you on so many levels I know better now. I'll never settle for anything less. Maybe someday I'll get lucky and find the kind of love and life you had with Abby."

Her heart ached for Dana. That she, who had so much to give, had been willing to settle for so little. She was such a beautiful person it was sad she'd never experienced real love. Callie responded to the impulse to comfort Dana by taking her hand. Dana gazed at Callie for a second before interlacing their fingers. Hand in hand they walked over the footbridge and made their way back to the hotel.

The food served at the group dinner included traditional Roman dishes as well as other tasty options. And the conversation, as had become the norm, was interesting, challenging, and filled with witty and lively banter. Laughing and still engaged in conversation, the group left the restaurant and meandered through the winding streets of Rome in the direction of the hotel. And then, as happened frequently in these old Italian cities and towns, they turned a corner and came to an abrupt halt, awed by the sight of the magnificent baroque fountain directly in front of them.

"Ah, the Fontana di Trevi. What a wonderful surprise," Vanessa said, as the group moved closer.

Callie leaned into Dana. "I've seen pictures, but in my mind it was freestanding, in the middle of the piazza like most fountains we've seen, not so huge, not part of a building. It's beautiful and with the lighting it feels…romantic."

"Look at those sculptures." Dana turned to Callie. "Do you think it's romantic because that's how it's always depicted in the movies?"

"Marian and I are married," Lou said, "but we'd like to return to Rome." They each tossed a coin into the fountain. Others around them were doing the same.

Vanessa turned to Callie and Dana. "We know you've already found love, so throw three coins in so you can return and marry."

Callie froze. "What? We're just friends."

"Ha. Out with the truth," James said. "We all saw you holding hands on your walk this afternoon."

Abby. Callie flooded with guilt. The warmth and connection she'd felt holding Dana's hand on their way back from Trastevere was so much more than she'd ever felt for someone who was just a friend. But it was Abby she wanted, not Dana. She turned and fled from the group. She hurried, hoping Dana wouldn't follow.

"Callie." Millie appeared at her side. She must have run to catch up, but she didn't seem out of breath. "I was afraid you'd get lost. I hope you don't mind if I walk with you and guide you to the hotel."

Callie bit her lip. "Good idea. I'd probably end up in the catacombs or something." Damn, that came out sarcastic. Millie was just doing her job. "Thank you."

As they walked in silence, Callie realized she needed a break from the group to process her feelings. "Millie, I hope it's all right if I pass on the tours tomorrow. I'd like to spend the day alone at the hotel."

"It's almost always all right to do what you want on this tour, Callie. Why don't I arrange a spa day for you at the hotel? The package includes a massage, a facial, a manicure, and time at the pool and in the gym. It might help you relax."

"I'm not sure I'm up to it, Millie."

As they entered the hotel, Millie put her hand on Callie's arm. "I'll arrange it, and if you're not in the mood, you can cancel it in the morning. I really think it would help."

She had nothing to lose by having it as an option. "Okay, set it up for any time after ten, and I'll decide in the morning."

"Great. I'll do it now and text you the information about time and place and the number to call to cancel or ask questions. Get some sleep. I'm sure you'll feel better tomorrow."

Callie knew sleep would elude her, but Millie had managed to be there and support her without asking why she was upset so she didn't feel the need to share her feelings. "Thanks, Millie. I appreciate you escorting me back and arranging the spa appointment. Good night."

Once she was alone in her room, Callie sank into the chair by the window and let the tears she'd been holding back flow. She started at the knock on the door. She should have expected it. If she opened the door, Dana would see her red eyes and swollen face, but she knew Callie was upset so did it matter?

"Hey, Callie, it's Dana. Can I do anything for you? Are you mad at me?" Dana sounded upset. Knowing her, she'd worry all night if Callie didn't assure her she was all right.

Callie opened the door. "Dana." She had started toward her own room but turned hearing her name.

Callie peered at her through the partially opened door, puffy eyes and swollen nose be damned. "Why would I be mad at you? You didn't do anything wrong." Callie dabbed at her eyes with a tissue. "I'm all right. I just need some time to process…things. I'm sorry I ran away."

"You don't have to apologize. I just wanted to be sure you were okay." Dana looked like she wanted to dash in to hold and comfort her. Part of Callie wanted that too, but she remained behind the door.

"I'm all right, really."

"Okay then, I'll see you at breakfast. And if you don't feel up to Millie's tour of the Vatican Museum, the Sistine Chapel, and St. Peter's, we can do something else."

"I won't be at breakfast. I need time by myself. Millie has arranged a spa day for me here at the hotel. But you should go with the group. Knock when you get back. Maybe we can have dinner together tomorrow. Of course, you're free to make other plans if you'd rather."

Dana paled. "You're not thinking of leaving, are you?" Her words came out in a rush, in a voice an octave higher than usual.

"No." Callie's heart went out to Dana. She would feel the same panic if she thought Dana was leaving the tour. "I just need time alone to think and work through some issues. Abby issues."

"Oh." Dana's shoulders dropped. "Enjoy your spa day. A little pampering can go a long way when you're stressed. I'll check about dinner when we get back."

"Thanks." Callie closed the door and picked up her phone. She texted Maggie. *Need 2 talk R U available?*

She washed her face, changed into pajamas, and went back to the chair by the window. A few minutes later her phone signaled a FaceTime call from Maggie.

"Hey, Callie, good timing. I'm in a two-hour break so we can talk now if you're ready."

"I'm ready." Callie couldn't suppress the sob that rushed out. "Sorry."

"Tell me what's going on."

Callie explained what had happened.

Maggie jotted a note. "So how did you come to be holding hands with Dana while walking around Rome?"

"Dana revealed some intimate feelings about her life and I was concerned and touched she trusted me enough to confide in me. I took her hand to comfort her. She laced our fingers together and we held hands all the way back to the hotel." Callie hesitated, seeing the whole scene clearly for the first time. "Wow, I hadn't realized I was the one to initiate the physical contact."

"And how do you feel about that? About initiating?"

Callie ran her fingers through her hair. "I'm not sure. I was uneasy when I thought it was Dana who took my hand. But maybe that's where my guilt is coming from. That I reached out to touch, to hold hands with another woman, feels like betraying Abby."

"Reaching out to comfort a friend is not betraying Abby. I'm sure she'd expect nothing less of you. Dana has helped you through your anxiety attacks and from what you've said, you enjoy her company. It sounds like you've made a good friend. Are you attracted to Dana?"

"What? No." She flushed, remembering the lure of Dana's lips earlier today. "Well. To be honest. I'm not sure."

Maggie was silent, giving her the space to get in touch with her feelings.

"Maybe. We rented a motorcycle the other day and I was behind Dana holding on with my arms around her waist. Her jacket rode up and I ended up with my hand on her bare belly. And I liked touching her. I didn't want to let go."

When Maggie didn't comment, Callie continued, "Dana is the model for one of the main characters in the romance I'm planning, so I've been observing her and every now and then thoughts of her from the perspective of the other main character pop into my mind and I write them down."

She reached for her journal and flipped to the page she'd written in Trastevere. "Here's the last one." Callie read the passage.

"'Heat flushed through Jane, her heart pounded in her ears, and her legs shook at the intensity of Morgan's gaze, the affirmation of her words. She too was happy, happier than she had a right to be.'"

"This is a lesbian romance?"

"It appears to be. I haven't told my agent or publisher, so please don't tell anyone."

"Come on, Callie. You know everything we discuss is confidential. Who is Jane modeled on?"

Callie put the journal down. "I have no idea who Jane is. I just plugged in a name because that character is responding to Morgan and a name makes it easier."

Maggie nodded. "When these passages come to you, are you Callie responding to Dana and writing it down as if your characters are experiencing the feelings?"

"Maybe." Callie blew out a breath. "Probably." She laughed. "Yes. Sometimes. She's attractive and nice. I'm human."

"I never doubted that." Maggie smiled. "Am I right that you experienced the heat, the pounding heart, the shaking legs, and the happiness that Jane was feeling?"

"Yes. It scares me. I love Abby." She grabbed a tissue from the box on the night table and dabbed at her eyes, trying to stem the flow of tears. "I'm not ready to be attracted to Dana. Or anyone."

Maggie gave her a moment to get control. "Remember, Abby encouraged you to live, to find love. But aside from that, as you said, you're human. You've spent an entire year cut off from everyone except me and your three best friends, totally focused on mourning Abby. Now you're out in the world and you're spending time with a woman you like a lot. Whom you find attractive. It doesn't mean you're abandoning Abby. Feelings are feelings. We can't control what we feel, but we can control how we respond to the feelings. I encourage you to recognize what you're feeling, enjoy the attraction, and use it as you wish."

Callie thought about that. "You're suggesting letting myself enjoy being with Dana and use my feelings to inspire Morgan in my book?"

"Yes. Take the pressure off. Repressing your feelings might trigger your anxiety."

"That's a good incentive. The anxiety attacks have tapered off and I'd rather not go there again."

"Let's finish up about tonight. How did you feel walking back to the hotel holding hands with Dana?"

"I felt fine. It seemed so natural that I didn't give it a thought. It wasn't until later, after a fun dinner, when Vanessa and the others thought we were a couple that I freaked and ran away. Millie arranged a spa day for me tomorrow so I won't have to face them again until dinner. But I'm not looking forward to seeing them again. What do I say?"

Maggie held up a hand. "Let's unpack that. From what you've told me, you and Dana are together constantly so your fellow travelers assumed you were a couple. It was a natural mistake. But you could have just laughed or explained that you're just friends. Why did you react so strongly?"

Callie flushed. "I felt exposed, like I had been caught doing something bad."

"Have you fantasized about being a couple with Dana?"

Had she? Callie considered the question. Most of the snippets she'd recorded for the book were about being attracted, not about being a couple.

"Not consciously. But I feel so connected to her. We've done everything on the tour together and we've shared so much of our personal history and feelings that it's easy to forget that we're not a couple. And I guess the feeling of closeness that led to us holding hands was still with me when Vanessa made that remark."

"Do you think you've done something bad?"

The tears flowed again. "I miss her so much." A sob escaped despite Callie's best efforts. "I'm frightened that I'm losing her."

"You're afraid you'll lose Abby if you let yourself feel something for Dana?" Seeing Callie's nod, Maggie went on. "That fear is a natural part of grieving, Callie. But Abby is in your heart. She's a part of you in many ways and you'll never lose her. Your heart doesn't have limited space for love. You'll always love Abby, but it doesn't mean you can't love someone else as well. She knew that. And that's why she wrote the letter giving you permission—no, urging you—to love again. You need to focus on that."

"I'll try. Any advice on how to deal with the group? I'm embarrassed about running away."

Maggie didn't hesitate. "I'd confront the issue head-on, explain why you ran. But think about it and only do it if it feels right."

They set up their next appointment and said good night. Feeling better, Callie went out to sit on the terrace. She had a lot to think about, but her brain seemed focused on the fact that Dana was in bed in the room next to hers.

CHAPTER FOURTEEN

Callie stretched. Last night when Millie suggested a spa treatment, she was still racked with guilt about Dana and not sure she wanted to do it. But she was glad she had let Millie arrange it. She'd slept well after last night's telephone therapy session, and she felt calm and centered when she woke. The massage, the hair and skin beauty treatments, and the solitary day spent swimming and lounging at the pool had added to her feeling of well-being.

An unexpected benefit was catching a glimpse of herself in the mirror in the dressing room. She was surprised at how much better she looked after only two weeks on the tour. The racoon eyes and hollowed-out look were gone, her face had color, her hair had life, and, with the weight she'd gained, she no longer looked like an addict. Now she felt positive, confident, and relaxed. She was actually looking forward to dinner.

Her stomach fluttered a bit when Dana knocked. She needed to make sure they were good before they went to dinner. After a few deep breaths she opened the door.

"Hi, come in."

Callie could see that Dana was apprehensive, not sure what to expect. But tuned in to her as always, Dana immediately registered Callie's upbeat mood. "Hey. Feeling better?"

"I am. Let's sit on the balcony and talk for a few minutes."

As Maggie had suggested, she planned to deal with the incident head-on, and so when they settled at the table, she spoke.

"I want to apologize for running away last night."

"That's—"

Callie raised her hand. "Please let me finish, Dana. I need to do this. My immediate response to the comments about us being a couple was to feel guilty, as if I was cheating on Abby, and scared that if we *were* a couple, I would lose her." Callie took a deep breath. "Those feelings rushed in, even though I know neither of us thinks we're a couple. I feel many things for you. You've made this trip possible for me and I'm grateful for your care and attention. I love being with you and you've become someone I think of as a very close friend. I took your hand yesterday because you shared some very intimate, powerful feelings with me, and I wanted to offer you comfort just as you've offered it to me."

She blew out a breath. "That's what I wanted to say. You can talk now."

Dana leaned forward and took Callie's hand. "Thank you for telling me. I thought you might be feeling guilty about Abby. It's a natural reaction. Holding hands was an expression of the closeness we were feeling. I felt comforted and comfortable. I care for you and feel close too. We laugh and have fun and talk about everything. I shouldn't be surprised that our friendship developed so quickly, but given that emotionally I'm in a space that makes it hard for me to trust anyone, I am surprised." She smiled. "Are we on for dinner?"

"In my therapy session last night Maggie suggested that I not slink around avoiding the group, so if you're amenable I'd like to join them for dinner and put this to bed."

Dana's eyes widened. "What are you going to tell them?"

"I'm going to talk about Abby and about our friendship."

"And you're up to exposing yourself, answering questions?"

"I'm nervous, but Maggie suggested that coming out of the 'widow closet' would free me so I'm giving it a shot." Callie met

Dana's eyes. "I've already let Millie know we're joining them for dinner."

They were the last to arrive at the restaurant, and the tension at the table was palpable. Hoping to reassure everyone she was in a better place, she smiled. "Hi."

Millie responded in her usual cheerful manner. Ellie waved and said hello, but most of the others mumbled what sounded like a greeting and raised the large menus in front of them.

"Just do it," Dana whispered.

Right. Rip the bandage off and feel the pain. She could do that. She tapped her water glass with her knife. "Can I have your attention for a minute?" She waited until all the menus were lowered. "Thanks. I'm sorry about running off last night. My response to the comments about me and Dana being a couple was overboard. It was a natural assumption, but though Dana and I have become close friends, we are not a couple."

She bit her lip, then forged on. "You all know I suffer anxiety attacks." She forced herself to look each of them in the eyes. "But you don't know they were brought on by my wife's death a little over a year ago. And you had no way of knowing your teasing would make me feel guilty, guilty for something I wasn't even doing. My therapist reassured me it's a normal part of grieving. I'm really enjoying traveling with the eleven"—her gaze moved to Millie—"no, the twelve of you, and I hope we can put the incident behind us and go back to the way we were."

No one said anything, then Ellie who was sitting next to her, leaned over and hugged her. "I'm so sorry about your wife. Thank you for sharing."

One by one the others came to her, took her hand or hugged her and expressed the same sentiments as Ellie. Vanessa and James waited for the others to take their seats before going to Callie. She took their hands. "Are we good?"

"If you're good, we're good." Vanessa hugged her.

James shuffled forward, hesitated, then took her hand. "Sorry."

Callie sensed his discomfort had as much to do with his behavior when they first met as with his mistaken assumption about her relationship with Dana. She smiled.

"It's okay, James." Still holding his hand, she waited for him to look at her. "In a way you all have helped me take a step toward accepting Abby's death. I've only told Dana about her and talking about her tonight feels liberating. So maybe I should thank you."

She squeezed his hand before letting go of it. He smiled, looking boyish. "Thanks for saying that, Callie." He took his seat next to Vanessa. Callie didn't miss the look of relief they shared.

As the waiter wove around the table serving each of them prosecco, the conversation picked up. Dana leaned in. "You were wonderful."

"Thanks. I wasn't sure I could talk about Abby without breaking down." Callie sipped her prosecco. "I'm surprised no one asked about her."

"My guess is you'll get questions once they've had time to think about it."

Bringing Abby into the open made her feel closer to Dana and to the other members of the group. "I didn't have a chance to toss any coins into the Trevi Fountain and I'd like to go back there with you after dinner, if you're willing."

They moved through the crowd around the fountain until they had a clear pathway. Callie chewed her lip and sent a silent prayer up to Abby. *If you're here, sweetheart, please know I'll always love you. No one will ever replace you. I'll just expand my heart to hold the two of you.*

Callie felt Dana's eyes on her as she tossed in a coin indicating she was hoping to return to Rome. After admitting to Maggie last night that she didn't want to live her life alone, she'd thought about Abby, about their love, and several times during the day, she'd read the letter she'd left. Abby had not only given her permission to find someone else, she'd encouraged her to fall in love again and be happy. Then Callie had acknowledged to Abby, and herself, that her feelings for Dana went beyond friendship.

She heard Dana's soft gasp as she tossed a second coin which meant she wanted to fall in love, though not necessarily with an Italian as the legend predicted. She glanced at Dana as she tossed the third coin, wishing to marry the person she met. Dana elbowed her. "Welcome to the three coins in the fountain club. I joined last night."

Callie blew out a breath. "It's scary, but it feels right. I'm glad you're a member too." Taking Maggie's advice, she was letting herself feel what she felt. She slipped her arm through Dana's.

"I'm ready to go to bed." Realizing what she'd said, she blushed. As attracted as she was to Dana, she wasn't ready for sex with her. Or anyone for that matter. "I mean I'm ready to go back to the hotel."

Dana pressed Callie's arm closer. "I knew what you meant."

The evening was clear and warm, the lighting dim, and except for the murmur of the few people they passed, the only sound was the echo of their footsteps. Callie felt as if they were encased in their own private bubble. Did Dana feel the connection? It was more than just the warmth she felt where their bodies touched. It felt...romantic.

She side-eyed Dana. She looked far away. Was she feeling romantic too? Lost in their own thoughts neither spoke until they were standing in the hallway outside their rooms.

Dana cleared her throat. "About tomorrow. I'm interested in the tour of the Colosseum and the Forum. What about you?"

"Definitely. I had enough me time today and it sounds intriguing. Meet for breakfast as usual?"

CHAPTER FIFTEEN

Dana was pensive over breakfast, not as hyped about the Colosseum Underground tour as Callie expected. No one else seemed to notice, but she and Dana were tuned in to each other in a way that the other's weren't. She hoped Dana's mood was related to business issues rather than Callie flaunting her new attitude toward life by tossing three coins in the Trevi Fountain last night.

Callie pulled Dana aside as they walked to the Colosseum. "Okay, what's wrong?"

Dana blinked. "Why do you think something is wrong?"

"Because I know you. Is it me?"

"Ego much?" Dana laughed. "It's business." She looked around. They were trailing the group, so they had privacy. "One of Angela's guys uncovered more fraud. Apparently, my partners are holding back the system-generated invoices for some clients, printing inflated invoices on a standalone computer and sending those out. Angela believes they're either pulling the checks for those accounts when they come in or they have them mailed to a separate lockbox. But however they capture them, they have an accomplice in Accounts Receivable who is applying the correct amount to the original invoice and allocating the difference to a special bank account, probably one of the offshore accounts I discovered."

"So not only are they stealing from the company, they're also stealing from your clients?"

"Exactly."

Callie was puzzled. "You said you all make a lot of money. Why would they take such risks?"

"Good question. I hired a private investigator recommended by Angela to look into Linda and Artie's finances and dig into the offshore accounts. And I've asked Angela and Ellen to find someone to investigate Linda's private life. She and Sandy are together now, and I want to know what happened to her wife, M.J., and their three kids and what's going on that she needs money?"

Callie put a hand on Dana's arm. "I am so sorry you have to deal with this."

Dana placed her hand over Callie's. "It's embarrassing. I feel like an ass for trusting them."

"People and circumstances change, Dana. I'm sure they were trustworthy when you brought them in."

Dana was silent and Callie knew her so well now, knew she was processing the comment. "You're right. We had a lot of good productive years. This behavior is recent. Thanks, Cal." Dana smiled. "Look, we're here."

Callie eyed the long ticket line at the entrance to the Colosseum and though anxiety attacks seem to be in her past, she was thankful they would bypass it and be a group unto themselves. Millie introduced their guide, Marco, a slender man probably in his thirties. He waved them closer.

"Hi. Before we go in, let me assure you I teach European and Italian history at the college level and I've also received special training to lead this tour. I hope to bring the history alive for you." His English was excellent. "So, we will tour the Colosseum Underground, the Arena Floor, the Roman Forum, and the Palatine Hill. I will share fascinating facts about what we see and what we know about it, describe how the various parts of the Colosseum were used, talk about the mechanics of gladiator battles, and try to communicate a sense of what it felt like to be a gladiator before a match to the death. Please follow me and stay with the group."

Dana grinned. "This sounds wonderful."

Marco led them through the Gate of Death onto the arena floor, also known as the stage. "From here we see the amphitheater from the gladiators' point of view. Facing us in those marble seats close to the arena floor are the Roman senators. Imagine having to fight for your life while up to seventy thousand spectators are screaming for blood. Your blood."

He gave them a few seconds to think about it. Callie glanced at Dana who looked as if she was hearing the roar of the spectators. He signaled them to follow him. "Come this way, please."

"Construction of the Colosseum was completed in 80 AD, but the underground—also known as the *hypogeum*—where we are about to go, was not part of the original construction." They followed him down and then through the system of tunnels. "Nearly two thousand years ago, gladiators would have walked from their gym and training areas through a tunnel into this backstage area where we're standing and would have been preparing to fight for their lives. Depending on the type of fight, two gladiators, a gladiator against a beast or two animals fighting, tearing each other apart, these elevators"—he pointed to several vertical shafts— "transported the fighters and the beasts onto the arena floor, where the roar of thousands of spectators, each screaming for their favorites, would greet them."

Dana was back to her animated, engaged self, asking questions and appearing fascinated by the tale Marco was weaving. Callie felt a wave of affection for her. She, who had initially professed no interest in the history of the places they visited, seemed to be turning into a history nerd. Dana moved closer to Marco as he ushered them along the wooden walkways, which he explained were there to protect the original herringbone paving beneath.

"They didn't have electricity so how did the elevators work?" Dana asked.

"They were powered by slaves."

Dana looked puzzled. "The gladiators were slaves?"

"No, they were prisoners of war. Many signed ten-year contracts that promised them freedom if they survived. I guess you could say they had no choice or nothing to lose. Even though the emperors like to show mercy and spared the lives of most losers, many gladiators died from infected wounds after the games, and those who survived only lived to fight another day. In the end few made it to freedom. Any questions?"

Of course, Dana and Carl and several of the others had a ton of questions.

Marco patiently answered every one of them, then led them to the public toilets near the entry. "Take a ten-minute break before we go to the Roman Forum and Palatine Hill for the last hour of the tour."

The group scattered but Dana continued to engage with Marco and then handed him her phone.

Callie felt uneasy. Damn, her body felt hot, her heart raced, and she felt lightheaded. An anxiety attack? No. This felt different. It was... She didn't know what it was. Was Dana bisexual? She'd never been territorial with a friend, so why was Dana's interest in Marco making her uncomfortable? Maggie's voice echoed in her mind. *Own your feelings, Callie.*

Dana turned and smiled at her. She focused on the breathing exercises she used to avert an anxiety attack. And then Dana was at her side. "Are you having an attack?"

"No. I just felt lightheaded. Maybe too much time underground?"

Dana eyed her, as if not believing her. And why should she since it was a lie? She took Callie's hand. "Remember. I'm here."

Ha! Now she understood why Victorian ladies had fainting spells. Good way to keep the attention on them. "I know. You seem to be enjoying the tour so far."

Dana grinned. "Am I ever. I never knew history could be so fascinating. Marco is going to email me the names of some books on Roman history that he thinks I'd enjoy. You know, I was so focused on computers when I was in college that I didn't give history a thought. I always got good grades on tests and papers, but before this trip history was just dead stuff to me. It started in Verona, but then in Venice, Florence, and now Rome, imagining the people who built and lived in these ancient buildings, thinking about their lives, has brought history alive for me. I owe that to you."

At the appointed time the group came back together and headed for the Forum. It was hot and dusty and by the end of the hour, Callie was exhausted. She wanted lunch, a drink, and a nap in that order and happily trailed Millie as she led them to the restaurant for lunch. The amount of information Marco had stuffed into the three hours left her with mush brain, but Dana, who had stuck close to Marco and seemed engrossed in whatever they were talking about, was alert and energized.

The shaded courtyard of the restaurant was a welcome relief from walking around the ruins in the sun for more than an hour. Ready to be off her feet, Callie sank into a chair between Vanessa and Ellie, across the table from Dana. She downed the glass of sparkling water placed in front of her, then refilled her glass. Feeling a little more human, she focused on the conversations around her.

Dana, still hyped from the tour, was deep in discussion with Vanessa, picking her brain about medieval history. Her enthusiasm, her energy, the light in her eyes, and her apparent hunger to learn all there was to know mesmerized Callie. Along with everyone at their end of the table, Callie listened as Dana questioned Vanessa about the history of Rome. Dana listened so intently that when the waiter asked for her order she seemed confused about where she was and what he was asking.

Callie waved to get the waiter's attention. *"Ordineremo insieme."* She wasn't sure how to say I'll order for her, but she figured saying they'd order together would get the message across. Dana flashed a smile and focused on Vanessa once more.

The waiter hesitated, then came around to Callie. *"Condivideremo tutto,"* she said, letting him know they would be sharing everything, then ordered a hot antipasto platter, fried artichokes, pasta alla carbonara, *picchiapò*, a beer for Dana and a small carafe of white wine for her.

"Brava, Callie." Millie gave her a thumbs-up. Everyone clapped.

Callie blushed. Their conversation sessions with Millie were helping her feel comfortable with speaking. And ordering in a restaurant was relatively easy.

The applause stopped and she looked up. Ellie was staring at her. "What? It's just baby Italian."

Ellie flushed. "Nothing. I…" She shook her head.

Callie was puzzled. "Clearly it's something. What are you thinking?"

Ellie shifted to face her and spoke softly. "I don't want you to freak out again, but I was wondering how you know Dana so well after two weeks that you can order for her."

"It's simple. We like the same things. We often share what we've ordered so I know if I like it so will she."

"Are you like that with all your friends?"

Callie thought about Angela, Erin, and Bonnie, her three closest friends. "No. Only with Abby."

Before Ellie could comment, the waiter appeared with their appetizers and James asked her, "What is picchiapò?"

"That sounds like a Jeopardy answer." Callie laughed. "It's a beef stew. It's really good. You can taste it when it comes."

Dana smiled and mouthed "thanks" as Callie put about two-thirds of the antipasto in front of her, but she continued to focus on Vanessa. Callie watched her take a forkful of eggplant and slowly chew as she listened. She felt lighter, happier than she'd felt in a long time. Taking care of Dana felt good. She was as in tune with her as she had been with Abby.

Morgan cocked her head in that sexy way that made you feel you were the only person in the world, listening, questioning, absorbing. Jane couldn't take her eyes off her, her feelings for Morgan were undeniable.

Itching to write down her thoughts, Callie reached for her backpack, but the sound of flapping wings caught her attention and she looked up. A bird was circling her head. Vanessa tensed. The bird flew over to Dana and circled her head, then flew back to Callie. It took another turn or two, then Callie watched it disappear into the nearby tree.

Abby, is that you? Do you approve?

Ellie poked her. "What is it with you and birds, Callie?"

"Yes, remember the one in the hotel in Milan?" James said. "That was weird. But this was weirder."

What would they think if she said it might be her dead wife watching over her?

"I don't know, Italian birds just seem to like me. And Dana." She looked up at the chirping birds. *You must be having a good laugh at my expense wherever you are, Abby.* She dug into her lunch, hoping someone would change the subject. At the ping of a message arriving, phones became the focus.

"It's me," Dana said. "Marco just texted the titles of a couple of Roman history books in English." She leaned in and glanced down the table. "Millie, do you know of a bookstore between here and the hotel?"

"There's one near the Spanish Steps that carries English books. We can stop on the way back. It's about a mile and a half. Is everyone up to walking or should I have Enzo pick us up after lunch?" The consensus seemed to be for walking.

The beef stew arrived. Callie passed a plate with half of it to Dana, who was still deep in discussion with Vanessa, gave James a taste of hers, then passed her half around so anyone interested could taste it.

Ellie snorted. "I just love that you two are so close. I could not order for my bastard of a husband of eighteen years without getting into a fight."

Callie picked up on Ellie's anger. "So it wasn't that you didn't know what he would like but that he didn't want you to order for him?"

"That's right. He never recovered from the blow to his ego when I made the cut as a surgeon and he didn't. And he was very sensitive about being the"—she made quotes with her fingers—"man in our relationship."

Callie took the dish with the remaining stew from Ellie but didn't eat any. The appetizers and some of the pasta were more than enough for her. "What about after the girls were born?"

"It got worse. He refused to change diapers, wouldn't carry them or their diaper bag, or do anything around the house." She put a hand on Callie's arm. "I should have kicked him out long before he left, but truthfully, rather than rock the boat I turned a blind eye to his inadequacies for the sake of the twins. And in the end, he sank the boat without a thought for the girls or me. So much for appeasement."

"What happens now?" Callie felt for Ellie, but being a first-class surgeon wasn't for the weak, and now that she seemed to be over the shock of his dumping her, she sounded strong and confident.

"Our attorneys are dealing with it. But he's willing to give up all rights to the girls, our house, my income, and my retirement assets if I don't request alimony, child support, or a share of his retirement assets or other investments. My attorney thinks he probably sold his practice and has hidden investments that he's trying to protect, but I don't want or need his money. And since he hasn't been a real dad up to now and I can't force him to be one, I'm inclined to agree just to be rid of him."

Callie felt bad for Ellie. She and Abby had been lucky to find each other, and she was lucky to have twenty years of mostly happy memories. Abby was right about that.

The sound of chairs scraping pulled her from her reverie about Abby. She was surprised to see she'd eaten the few bites of her half of the stew left in the bowl. Listening to Ellie's story and then daydreaming had diverted her attention. The group was leaving. Dana appeared at her side, still excited about what they'd seen and learned today and hyped about getting books on the subject. They walked to the bookstore with Loretta and Carl. She chatted with Loretta while Dana and Carl chewed over Roman history. Carl was much more outgoing and personable then he'd seemed originally. He seemed to really enjoy Dana.

It was nice to stretch and exercise after a big lunch and before she knew it they'd arrived at the bookstore.

"Look, it's Callie!" someone screamed.

She turned to the voice. Fran and Susan were pointing to the poster of her face covering the entire window of the store. *Damn it.* She'd totally forgotten her latest book was being released in Europe today. This wasn't how she wanted her new friends to learn she was an author. A fairly famous author. Twelve sets of eyes settled on her. What did they expect her to say?

Dana broke the silence. "You're Calliope DeAndre?"

Fighting her impulse to run, Callie raised her eyes to the gigantic picture of her face in the window. No use denying it. "Yes, that's me, all right."

Marian looked flustered. "I'm a huge fan and I had no idea you were, are, Calliope DeAndre."

"I know."

There was a burst of chatter, and then everyone except Dana dashed into the bookstore.

"I've told you so much about my life, Callie. You could have told me who you are. All those notes. Are you writing about the group? About me?"

"No. Not exactly. That's not how I work. I create my characters. Sometimes I borrow a characteristic or mannerism from someone I know, but my characters are my creation, not real people."

Except... Wasn't that what she was doing with Dana? She would explore that in depth when she had some time alone. And make sure she didn't fall into that trap. Now she needed to reassure Dana.

"I'm sorry for keeping it from you. You know at first I was reluctant to talk about myself and then it didn't seem relevant. It's nice sometimes just being Callie and not Calliope, the *New York Times* best-selling author. As you can see, people look at me differently when they know. Even if I'd thought about it, which I didn't, I might not have told you because I want you to know me, Callie."

Dana rubbed her eyes. "I think I understand. But I'm a big fan and it was a shock to find out this way." She took Callie's hand. "Sorry if I came across pissy."

"Hey, I get it." Dana was so generous, so sensitive, and so forgiving that she was apologizing for her anger even though Callie deserved it. She fought back the tears threatening. "Didn't you want to get some history books?"

"Oh, yeah. You coming in?"

"I'll wait outside. Otherwise the bookstore may ask me to sign every book they have and I'll be here for hours and end up talking to fans, which I'd rather not do right now."

Dana released Callie's hand and headed for the store.

"Dana, please quietly let the others know they're invited to my room five-ish this afternoon. I'll order some prosecco and snacks, answer questions, and sign books for anyone who wants me to."

CHAPTER SIXTEEN

Ciao, Roma. They were en route to the Amalfi Coast. Dana was deep into one of her new history books and Callie was pretending to sleep. She was flattered that almost everyone was reading her book, but seeing her face staring at her from the back covers was unsettling.

The worst was hearing the whispered questions and comments about the story. Readers were entitled to their reactions and opinions about the events and characters she'd portrayed, but every word in every book came from her heart and being exposed to their feelings made her feel vulnerable. Her publisher would continue to bitch, but this experience confirmed her decision to not have her picture on her books or used for publicity in the United States.

At least yesterday afternoon had gone well. She'd ordered prosecco and a couple of charcuterie boards and in the privacy of her room signed everyone's books plus a couple bought for friends in the States.

Dana was the last one to present her copy to be signed. Callie froze for a second. She wanted to say something personal but not too personal. She picked up her pen, looked at Dana, and wrote in black ink:

To my new friend, Dana, I will be forever grateful to Abby, the universe, or whoever, for bringing us together. Thank you for taking care of me. Thank you for making Romantic Italy possible for me. It's a privilege to have you in my life. Love, Callie (Calliope DeAndre).

She handed the book to Dana, who closed it without reading the inscription. Perhaps she was as nervous about what it said as Callie was writing it.

She'd posed for pictures with those who asked, answered questions, and explained that they hadn't recognized her because she protected her privacy by prohibiting her picture from appearing on her books, being used for publicity, or at her readings in the US. It had never mattered in Europe so she'd allowed it.

And, she explained, though the next book would be a romance set in Italy, the people on the tour would not be appearing as characters. Good natured boos, teasing comments, and much laughter followed that announcement. She was surprised how much she enjoyed the attention. And pleased that by the time they met for dinner in the hotel restaurant, things were back to normal and she was just Callie again.

Before going to sleep she'd read through all her notes for the new book. Actually, there was little of Dana in there. It was mostly her, or Jane's, feelings about Dana. Did it mean something that she was looking at Dana as a possible love interest through the eyes of a character? With her heterosexual characters she always had distance. Their emotions were theirs, separate from hers. But here, in black and white, she could see she was emotionally involved with her characters. At least the one who was seeing Dana as a love interest.

What did it mean? She knew she cared for Dana. Knew she found her attractive physically and enjoyed being with her. Knew they had formed a strong bond in a very short period of time. She'd been positive she'd never consider another relationship. But. She was.

Dana poked her. "You're not really sleeping, are you?"

"Just hiding," Callie whispered. "Being surrounded by people reading my book is kind of embarrassing. I keep waiting for someone to say it's a piece of shit."

"I doubt that will happen. Just so you know, I started it last night and I love it so far, but I thought reading it while sitting next to you might be awkward for both of us, so"—she held up her book—"I'm forced to read Roman history."

"A likely story. But your thoughtfulness is one of the things I love about you." Her words echoed in her head. *That doesn't imply I'm in love with her, does it?*

Dana didn't seem to notice. "I didn't want to ask in the group last night, but why is it you write books about straight people and not lesbians or others on the LGBTQI spectrum?"

This question had come up a lot in her extended LGBTQI circle of friends and from fans, and she'd found the truth was the simplest answer. "When I started out, I wrote what I knew, romantic suspense with lesbian main characters, and submitted it to agents. Of the hundred fifty plus agents I queried most didn't even send rejections and only one responded positively. Sarah Diller emailed to get my phone number, then called. 'I love the story,' she said, 'but publishers won't buy it. If you rewrite it as a heterosexual romantic suspense, I can almost guarantee you a six-figure advance. It's a big ask but think about it. If you decide to make the change, I'll take you on as a client and work with you to strengthen the manuscript.'

"I was tired. I'd been working at jobs I didn't want to do that paid peanuts but allowed me time to write. Abby convinced me I wasn't betraying anything or anyone by writing straight characters. And I figured once I was established, I could write whatever I wanted, so I decided to give it a try. The rest is history."

"It probably wasn't too bad, right? Changing the name and pronouns of one of the characters couldn't take too long."

"Actually, it was a huge undertaking. I kept Jude, the strongest character, as the female protagonist, created a male character, Max, with the looks, personality and qualities she would be attracted to, then I built in some conflict to motivate the push/pull of the romance. That done, I reconsidered every line I'd written in terms of the female/male dynamic and made sure Max's physical movements and emotional responses reflected his maleness. How Jude reacted to Max, the male protagonist, was totally different from how she reacted to the original female protagonist, so I rewrote scenes, cut scenes, added scenes, and rewrote most of the dialogue that would be attributed to him to reflect the male perspective. It was a big, big job and a real learning experience for me. Sarah worked with me, reading drafts, critiquing them, and asking questions to help me find the inner truth of the characters. In the end, the story was the same, but the whole romantic aspect of it and the relationship between the characters was totally different."

"It sure paid off. From what little I know you've been extremely successful. Every book hits the bestseller list and stays for weeks. And I bet the one you're working on now will as well. Do you think you'll ever publish a book about two women falling in love?"

Only Maggie knew her next book was going to be a lesbian romance. She'd hurt Dana by withholding what she did for a living. And Dana feared she'd be a character in her next book. She trusted her, so why not share her plan? Knowing Dana, she'd be happy to brainstorm and be a sounding board.

She leaned in close to Dana's ear. "The book I'm planning now will be a romance between two women. Only my therapist—not my agent or my publisher or any of my friends, including Angela—knows that, so I'm going to ask you to keep it a secret."

Dana sat up. Her excitement palpable. "After I read in an article online that Calliope DeAndre was a lesbian, I moaned about her only writing straight characters every time I read one of her books. I'm thrilled. And honored to keep your secret. But why not tell your agent and your publisher? Surely you're successful enough to write whatever you want now?"

"That's true. But you know how it is. No one wants to upset the gravy train, so while they will probably print anything I write, I'm sure there would be a campaign to convince me it's a mistake to change midstream. I'm not asking permission. When I hand them a completed manuscript, they'll have a decision to make. I'm sure Sarah will support me and if my publisher refuses it, she'll sell it to someone else. Or I'll self-publish."

"Hey, if they don't want it, I'll buy a publisher and publish it."

"You have that much money?"

"I do. And once I get done with my cheating partners, I'll have even more."

"It's good to know I have a backup plan. But what would help me more is if I could use you as my sounding board on the book. You know, brainstorm, talk about characters, whatever."

"Really? You think I could help? I'd love to share that process with you."

"Great." Just as she'd expected, Dana was interested and willing to help. But damn, she hadn't thought it through. She'd just invited Dana to assume the role Abby had played. She closed her eyes, but the guilty feeling didn't materialize. Did that mean she was losing Abby? She pushed the thought away for later consideration.

"It will be fun working with you, Dana." She meant it.

The crackling of the mic got their attention. "Hey, sorry to interrupt, but I'd like to go over the plan for the next few days." Millie waited a minute while the group refocused on her. "Next stop is the Amalfi Coast for four days, including today. The thirty-four miles of the Amalfi Coast overlooking the Mediterranean are a UNESCO World Heritage Site. It's called heaven on earth by some, not just because of its sky-high cliffs, but because of the contrast of its vividly colored vegetation and multicolored towns against the turquoise waters. There are thirteen seaside towns along the coast, all connected by a single highway, the Amalfi Drive." Millie looked over her shoulder. "How much longer, Enzo?"

"Ten minutes," Enzo said.

"Okay. The Drive is a breathtakingly beautiful, world-famous road, but it's narrow and twisty and in spots barely wide enough for a bus. We'll be driving west to east, which means we'll be on the ocean side and for much of the time there will be sheer drop offs of as much as a hundred feet on our right. It's pretty scary, and when you see another full-sized tour bus headed straight for you, it can be downright terrifying. Add in people on motor scooters weaving in and out of traffic and crazed drivers screaming at each other, and well, you're the writer, Callie. What's a word more terrifying than terrifying?"

Callie laughed. "How about petrifying or bloodcurdling?"

"Either will do. But we'll be safe. Enzo has driven this bus on the Amalfi Drive hundreds of times and is still with us to drive it today. Try to relax and enjoy the exquisite views."

"After that description, you really expect us to relax?" Lou asked. "Sounds like we'll need barf bags."

Millie laughed. "Well, at least try to enjoy the scenery. To the left you'll see tall craggy cliffs with terraced lemon and olive groves built into the hillsides and yellow, pink and orange houses stepping down steep slopes. Along the edge of the road bougainvillea drapes over fences and houses. To the right, stunning views of the coast and the deep blue Tyrrhenian Sea sparkling in the sunlight. Open the windows and breathe the lemon-scented air. Any questions?" Millie made eye contact with each tour member. "Fasten your seat belts." She clicked the mic off.

Callie did as Millie suggested. She cracked the window open and inhaled, enjoying the freshness of the air and the smell of the sea.

Dana looked at her phone. "It looks like the Hotel Santa Caterina Al Mare is another hotel on a cliff. I'm glad none of us is suicidal."

Callie elbowed her. "Hotels on cliffs are romantic and, as you might remember, this is a romantic tour. I'm excited about the day trip to Capri and the visit to the Blue Grotto. And the tours of Pompeii and Herculaneum should be right up your historian's alley."

"Okay, here we go," Enzo called out.

As usual, Callie was in the window seat. She made the mistake of looking down instead of out over the water. "Yikes! Millie wasn't kidding. Bloodcurdling is definitely the right word."

Dana put an arm over Callie's shoulder, pulling her away from the window. "Don't look down, look straight out. Oops, that bus is coming straight for us."

Callie felt as if the blood was draining out of her body. Somebody screamed. The collective intake of breath in the bus sounded like what she imagined the sucking sound of a tornado would be. At least she wouldn't die alone. She'd die in Dana's arms.

But wait! Millie promised they weren't going to die here. She opened her eyes. They were still moving forward on the narrow, twisty road.

Dana tightened her grip on Callie. "Wow, this is almost as scary as the Formula Rossa roller coaster at Ferrari World in Abu Dhabi."

She leaned into Dana. "You went on a roller coaster in the United Arab Emirates?"

"Yes. I went there for a conference and Sandy was with me. She wanted to do something exciting the night we arrived and convinced me to go on the world's fastest roller coaster, the one with a top speed of 240 kilometers per hour. That's basically 150 miles per hour! It was freaking terrifying. I mean this drive is scary but…that roller coaster was insane. It took years off my life. After that Sandy could barely get out of bed. I had to hire a nurse to stay with her. I was woozy and nauseous most of the week. Luckily I was scheduled to speak toward the end of the conference, and by then I had recuperated and was able to give my presentation."

Callie glared at her. "I'm not sure whether I'm impressed or depressed that you'd do something that dangerous."

Dana flushed. "Well, it depresses me. It was just one of the many stupid things I did to please Sandy."

Callie didn't know how to respond to that, but just then Enzo pulled off the Drive into the parking area of a hotel, cutting off the discussion. Millie stood.

"Welcome to the Hotel Santa Caterina Al Mare. Lunch should be ready for us at the restaurant in the hotel's Beach Club. Follow the signs to the two elevators carved into the rock face or use the stairs to get there. Ask for the Romantic Tour table. I'll check us in, then meet you, but I've ordered an assortment of dishes for a casual lunch. Feel free to order anything else you would like. And don't wait for me and Enzo. We'll catch up."

They shuffled off the bus into the bright sunlight. Everyone thanked Enzo for keeping them safe, then stretched before filing into the hotel. While the group inquired about the elevators, Callie took a minute to survey the lobby.

"Something wrong?" Dana asked.

"I've started taking the beauty of our luxury accommodations for granted. I don't want to be that kind of person. I'm lucky to be able to afford a five-star tour, and I want to enjoy everything about it. Look at the marble floor, the vaulted ceiling, the large windows, the lovely furniture placed just so for customers, for us, to be comfortable. It's all about us, but we ignore it."

Dana scanned the lobby. "It is beautiful, but that's what we pay for."

Callie eyed Dana. "That's the attitude I'm trying to avoid."

Dana frowned.

"The elevators are back there." Lou pointed to a sign that said *Ascensori* and they followed.

They emerged into a restaurant perched on a terrace overlooking the sea with a private beach platform and swimming pool below. The maître d' greeted them and led them to two adjacent round tables, one set for six and another set for eight. Unlike on the bus, seating in restaurants wasn't fixed, and the group camaraderie was such that everyone was relaxed about who sat where. Callie moved to the crossbeam wood railing and gaped at the view.

Dana followed her. "It's amazing, isn't it? It almost feels unreal."

Callie felt the heat of Dana's body in the places it touched hers and turned to look at her. Dana's gray-blue eyes reflected the color of the Mediterranean, and they locked onto Callie's eyes, warming a place deep inside her. She looked away.

Jane inhaled the fragrance of the sea, the lemon scent on the breeze and a hint of Morgan's coconut shampoo. She leaned into Morgan, melding their bodies. Would Morgan welcome her kiss?

Callie blinked. She took a few seconds to repeat Jane's thoughts to herself so she could write them down later. *Note to self: Admit it's me not Jane and Dana not Morgan.*

"Yes, my pathetic brain is having trouble absorbing it. This place, the turquoise water, the sun glinting on the waves, the rocky walls, the mountain in the distance, it all feels almost, I want to say, romantic."

"You could say that." Dana touched her back but quickly dropped her hand. "They won't serve until we sit."

Callie followed her to the smaller table with Fran, the architect, and her wife, Susan, the history professor. Ellie slipped into the chair next to Callie while Vanesa sat next to Dana. As soon as they settled, ice water was poured. The waiter offered a choice of a beverage.

"Vorrei un bicchiere di birra." Dana ordered her beer in Italian.

"Vorrei un bicchiere di vino rosso." Callie ordered her wine. Most Italians were patient with their bumbling attempts and some helped them with it. Millie had been happy to chat with them, but they'd found many Italians, often the younger ones, wanted to speak English to improve their skill with the language.

Vanessa clapped. "Very good, ladies. Most Americans expect everyone to speak English. I speak French and some Italian, though I've been lazy about using it this trip."

Callie dipped her head. "It's intimidating but we're trying to speak as much as possible."

The wild drive along the coast dominated the conversation, but the focus turned to food when waiters delivered dishes of mixed bruschetta, seafood salad, and a large platter with a mouth-watering assortment of seven vegetables. As Callie helped herself to a moderate serving of the seafood salad and a bit of everything else, she noticed Dana was unusually quiet. Had she felt the same jolt of electricity that Callie had when she touched her? Or had she taken the comment about taking luxury for granted personally, as criticism? Or was her silence connected to the moment they'd just shared? Talking about the luxury comment would be safer, she decided.

Once the other four were engaged in a lively conversation, she spoke softly. "Dana, my comment about the lobby was criticizing my attitude, not judging yours, so if I hurt you, I apologize."

"Thanks." Dana looked up from her plate. "As usual, you made me think. I'm guilty of taking it all for granted. I was fed and clothed and sheltered but not much more when I grew up, and there was a time I was awed by five-star accommodations. Once I became wealthy and fell in with the superficial social set where I met Sandy, I became like them, entitled. I stopped seeing." She sighed. "I have so much to undo, to change in order to become the person I know I could be."

Callie squeezed Dana's thigh. "As far as I'm concerned, you're fine as you are, but I like that you want to be even better. Don't be too hard on yourself. Acknowledge what you don't like and focus on the changes you want to make."

Dana's face brightened. "Is that how it's done, oh wise one?"

"That's what my therapist says." Callie speared a shrimp from the seafood salad on Dana's plate. "I didn't get one of these."

Dana held her plate up for Callie. "Hey, my food is your food and vice versa, right?" Everyone laughed.

They were still on the first course when Millie arrived. She passed out room keys and then sat and helped herself.

The next course consisted of a pizza, what they called a folded-over pizza stuffed with ricotta, mozzarella and salami, and five other dishes. Callie noticed Susan and Fran eating from each other's plates as she and Abby had. And as she and Dana had been doing. As if to underscore that thought, Dana moved half the slice of pizza and half the grilled fish from Callie's plate on to her plate. Noticing a glob of tomato sauce on Dana's cheek, Callie removed it with her finger, then licked the finger. She heard a gasp from

Ellie. She turned and caught the look that flashed between Fran and Susan. She flushed. What the hell was she playing at? That gesture was intimate, something lovers did. Dana wiped the area with her napkin. "Am I good?"

"Yes, all good." At least one of them wasn't freaked. She ate, letting the conversation flow around her. Maggie did say she should enjoy her feelings for Dana. And there was no question that she was feeling intimate. She looked up when the waiter removed her plate and was surprised to find Fran looking at her with a small smile. She shrugged, hoping to indicate it was nothing.

And then it happened. A bird flew in and circled their table, singing a cheerful song. Waiters rushed over, trying to make it leave. Callie held up her hand. "*Aspettare. Va bene.* It won't stay long."

They stared at her. The maître d' issued a command and they retreated to watch. As Callie half-expected, the bird swirled about her head, then moved to Dana. Damn, she must be losing it. She was seriously considering that this bird, like the others, was Abby. Everyone in the restaurant stared as the bird sang its merry song, circled Callie's head then Dana's several times and, with a final dip, looked into her eyes, trilled, and flew away.

The members of the group, who had seen it before, cheered, and the others in the restaurant clapped. "Are you some kind of bird whisperer?" Ellie said when she stopped laughing. "It keeps happening. It's incredible. It almost looked like it was trying to communicate with you two."

"Yes, I felt like it was trying to tell me something." Dana ran her fingers through her hair, which Callie knew meant she was disturbed. It was time to tell her, but not now, not in the group.

Fran touched her arm. "Wow, Callie, I'm really impressed by your Italian. What did you say to the maître d'?"

"I said, 'Wait. We're not bothered.'" She lifted her shoulders. "It wasn't particularly eloquent, but Dana and I have only been studying for two weeks so I can only manage short sentences."

Dana was beaming. "You did great, Cal. And you came up with the phrases without hesitation." The praise brought a blush to Callie's cheeks. Though she was pleasantly full, when the gelato was brought out, Callie took a small serving of her favorite flavor, coffee. The food in Italy was tempting, and though she was eating more than she had since Abby got sick, she was trying to be mindful about what and how much she consumed.

"So, are you really into birds or is this some kind of coincidence?" Susan asked before taking a spoonful of the multicolored ice cream she'd served herself.

"Abby, my wife, had an unusual connection to birds from the time she was an infant and she dedicated her life to studying and teaching about them. She was a prominent and well-known professor of ornithology. I often went along with her when she went bird-watching, but it was never my thing."

"Has it ever happened before, this special attention from random birds?" Vanessa peered around Dana to see Callie.

"Milan was the first time."

"I guess Italian birds love you," Fran piped up. And then the conversation turned to what to do with the rest of the day.

"Callie and I are going to the pool. Anyone up for joining us?" Dana looked around the elevator. "And we're walking into Amalfi later to browse and find a restaurant for dinner. Meet us in the lobby at seven, if you want to join us."

It was no surprise Dana had become a leader in the group. After all, she had built a multimillion-dollar business. Her charisma and her infectious enthusiasm drew people to her. Everyone in the group seemed to feel about her the way Callie did. Well. Maybe not exactly the same.

Dana hesitated outside their rooms. "Are you as weirded out by the bird thing as I am?"

"Yes." It was definitely time to share Abby's promise to come back as a bird. "Knock when you're ready to go to the pool. I need to discuss something with you."

Callie entered her room and, as she had in the lobby, took a minute to appreciate the luxurious, airy, light-filled junior suite. She would take pictures and describe it in her journal tonight so she could refer to it when she was writing the book. Now, though, she sat on the love seat and gazed out the open doors to the large terrace overlooking the sea. The view was stunning. The suite was beautiful and comfortable. And would be romantic if she was sharing it with someone she cared about. She flushed with shame. It wasn't Abby who came to mind.

By the time Dana knocked on the door, Callie had changed into her bathing suit and caftan cover-up and packed her bag for the pool. She led Dana out to the terrace.

Dana sat at the table. "What's up?" She sounded wary.

After anguishing over whether to show the letter to Dana, Callie had concluded it was necessary for her to understand what she was going to say. "I believe I mentioned that Abby left a letter for Angela to give me if I was still mourning after a year." She extended her copy of the letter to Dana. "I'd like you to read the part near the bottom that I bracketed."

Dana swallowed. "I can't read something so personal. Why do you want me to read it?"

"I think it will help you understand what I'm going to tell you. And it's not the whole letter, just the part that's folded open."

Dana took the paper, careful to only look at the print that was exposed. She read aloud. "'Please, dearest Callie, do it for me. Go out into the world and live. Take that trip to Italy. Be happy, find someone to love, celebrate life. It's what I want for you. It's what I would want for myself if I'd lost you.'"

Dana looked up at Callie, and near tears, continued, "'But think of me as you travel through life. When you feel the warmth of the sun or the gentle kiss of rain, when you smell new mown grass or the fragrance of flowers, when you see the sparkle of new fallen snow or experience a beautiful sunrise or sunset, when you hear the rustle of leaves or the wildness of the wind. And, wherever you are, think of me when you see birds, hear the gentle flapping of their wings and their excited songs because you know, my love, if it's possible I will come back as a bird and watch over you. Shakespeare was wrong. Parting is not such sweet sorrow. It sucks, but part we must. I must die and you must live. So get your sweet ass out there. All my love forever, Abby'"

Dana handed the paper back to Callie. "That's beautiful. She must have been a wonderful woman." She rubbed her eyes. "What about that is related to what you want to talk about?"

Callie slipped the letter into the pocket of her caftan. She always carried a copy with her. "The part about her coming back as a bird to watch over me." She took a deep breath. "I know this sounds crazy but...I almost feel as if the birds flying around us since we met are Abby reincarnated. They seem to appear when I need encouragement. They look right at me, and I almost feel as if they're singing to me." She couldn't look at Dana, afraid what she would see on her face.

Neither spoke. Even though Callie was anxious about Dana's response, sitting in the warmth of the sun with the gentle breeze of the sea and the sound of the water below felt peaceful. She tried to imagine how she would have felt if Dana told her something like this, but she couldn't. She knew Dana would need time.

After what felt to Callie like an hour, Dana cleared her throat. She took Callie's hands in hers and squeezed until Callie met her eyes. "It does sound crazy. But from the first bird in Milan I've had this weird feeling that the birds are trying to communicate with you. And sometimes with me. I mean, I don't even know if I believe in reincarnation. And it's not the same bird each time. But, yeah, it does feel like it might be Abby. So maybe we're both crazy."

They burst into laughter. They sat hand in hand, looking into each other's eyes for a few more seconds, then Callie dropped Dana's hands. "Okay, crazy lady, ready to swim?"

They didn't discuss it again, but after Dana's swim Callie noticed that when Dana wasn't watching the birds flitting around the pool, she was reading the novel she'd purchased in Rome, Callie's novel, but with the dust cover removed so her photo was no longer displayed. If she had to be crazy with someone at least it was with someone who was thoughtful.

CHAPTER SEVENTEEN

Millie outlined the day's agenda at breakfast. "We have a private boat for the day. First stop will be the port of Marina Grande on Capri. From there we'll take the funicular up to the Piazza Umberto and you'll have three hours free. Then we'll return to the boat, and if the tide is right and it's open, we'll go to the Blue Grotto. After that, we'll cruise around the island, have lunch on the boat, and swim in some of the grottos."

The boat ride to Marina Grande was splendid. The breeze, the spray from the boat, and the feeling of adventure, of going someplace new, reminded Callie of a time when she threw on a backpack and set off to explore, a time when she was independent and unafraid. A time before she met Abby.

She rubbed her eyes. Where did that traitorous thought come from? They'd both enjoyed outdoorsy things like hiking, swimming, skiing, and birding, and their vacations centered on those activities. Most of the travel they did was connected to the many conferences they each were obligated to attend because of their work. Abby's idea of adventure was to take in an exhibition or two in a museum and then go back to a luxury hotel and be pampered. Callie had scoffed at that mode of travel before they met, but she'd allowed herself to be co-opted, and even when she traveled alone, she'd stopped wandering and exploring and settled for luxury. But that was on her, not Abby. However, to be fair to herself, while Abby would have loved the luxury aspect of this tour, she would never have gone along with Callie's rediscovered desire to wander and explore. But would she have let herself feel the desire again if she was here with Abby?

Callie's gaze shifted to her travel mates. To Dana, her short hair almost standing on end in the breeze, her eyes sparkling, her lovely hands expressing her thoughts, laughing, clearly enjoying talking with Lou, James, Carl, Serena, and Ellie. Abby was a bit of a snob. Though she might have been interested in Ellie, the surgeon, and Dana, the successful businesswoman, she would have been polite but disinterested in the rest of the group, even the other college professors.

On the other hand, when she realized Carl who presented himself as a simple farmer, ran the largest working biodiverse regenerative farm in the low country of South Carolina, Abby would have peppered him with questions. And Carl, being Carl, would have patiently explained that regenerative farming goes beyond sustainability, that it aims to enhance the farm ecosystem, restore the health of the soil, increase water retention, promote biodiversity and contribute to carbon negativity. Abby would have been pleased to hear it eliminated the use of pesticides and chemical fertilizers and so protects her beloved birds.

Callie bit her lip. What the hell was she thinking? Abby was wonderful. And she loved her. As did the people Abby allowed into her circle. Her memories of traveling with Abby were almost all happy. She smiled, remembering trips early in their relationship to quiet lodges or beach houses where they were alone, focused on each other, and spent most of the time in bed.

"Hey"—Dana interrupted her thoughts—"what's got you looking so dreamy?"

"Remembering vacations with Abby."

"It's great that you have good memories."

"It is, but..."

Dana waited patiently for her to finish her thought, but Callie didn't know what she meant to say. Or maybe it was how much to reveal.

"One of the things Abby said in the letter is that I should focus on all the happy memories we made, not on her loss. It's hard sometimes."

Dana squeezed Callie's hand.

Callie saw sadness in Dana's eyes. Her situation was very different. Dana hadn't mentioned any happy memories. The betrayal by her friends and her girlfriend that led to her being alone on the tour had destroyed her illusions. When she talked to Maggie later she'd talk about seeing Abby in a negative light, but right now she wanted to support Dana, to remove the shadow and the heaviness. She led Dana to the prow of the boat.

"So how about I treat you to a drink before we set out to conquer the island?"

Resilient as always, Dana smiled. "The image of us conquering Capri together like some ancient warrior queens fills my would-be historian's heart with joy, so I accept."

Suddenly aware that her thumb was stroking Dana's hand, Callie pretended to shift and let go.

When they stepped out of the cable railway system that ran up a steep slope to the Piazza Umberto I, they stopped to discuss the options. Most of the group planned to stay in Capri and visit the designer shops on Via Camerelle.

"Anyone interested in joining Fran and me going to the top of Monte Solaro in Anacapri?" Susan said. "The views are supposed to be spectacular. Then if we still have time and energy we'll go to the ruins of the Villa Jobis, the home of Emperor Tiberius, which the guidebook says is an easy walk from here."

Without consulting, Callie and Dana answered at the same time, "Yes." They burst out laughing. Susan shook her head. "You two are so connected, I can't believe you're not a couple."

"Believe it." Once again, they spoke simultaneously. They locked eyes for a long moment. A surge of warmth flooded Callie. That look was intense. Was Dana feeling it too? She hoped she wasn't blushing. She couldn't deal with anyone else's feelings about her connection with Dana right now, so she pretended she hadn't noticed Susan and Fran exchange a knowing look. Avoiding more eye contact with Dana, she looked around. "So should we get a taxi to Anacapri?"

Callie took the front seat in the taxi without consulting the others. It was rude not to ask if anyone minded, but she needed a little separation and time to clear her head. But the look she and Dana had exchanged, the feeling of warmth it generated, filled her mind and no clearing was done. Toward the end of the twelve or so minute ride to Anacapri she tuned in to the conversation in the back seat and realized they were discussing the scenery. When they exited the cab in Piazza Vittoria, Dana seemed focused on the mountain and not on her. Maybe Dana hadn't felt anything unusual in the shared look. Maybe it was only her.

When they purchased their round-trip tickets for the chairlift, Callie was relieved to learn that each rider had their own chair so she would not need to relate to Dana on the ride up. She needed the space, the time to process her feelings.

But then she felt a stab of fear. What if she had an anxiety attack suspended in the air by herself? Dana was involved with Fran and Susan, so she hadn't noticed her anxiety. Callie straightened her shoulders and breathed deeply. She hadn't had an attack in days. She could do this.

The ride was only thirteen minutes long and, it turned out, the chairs were never more than thirty feet or so above the ground so the trip wasn't at all scary. The day was sunny and clear and the higher they climbed the more impressive the views became. It was windy and chilly at the top, but they'd learned May could turn cool and pulled out the windbreakers they carried in their backpacks. They headed to the outdoor café to have a drink and enjoy the beauty of the place.

Callie cleared her throat. "Will you think I'm rude if I take a minute to write my impressions of Capri so far, before we head down?"

The no was unanimous, so Callie made some quick notes in her journal. *On the Isle of Capri. Connection with Dana intensifying. A brief moment of eye contact left me feeling weak and warm. Not sure how she reacted but I needed to separate in the cab to cool down.* She closed her notebook. "Got it. Thanks."

Little of the Villa Jovis was still standing, but some mosaics and spots of paint were still visible. Wandering through the ruins with Susan, a historian, proved to be fun and informative. The more time they spent with the two women the more Callie liked them.

Walking through Capri on the way back to the funicular, Callie stopped to gaze into the window of a clothing store. "What a beautiful blouse."

"If you don't buy that for yourself, I'm going in to buy it for you." Dana elbowed her. "Come on, you need to try it on."

Callie hesitated. This was the first time since she and Abby had purchased the sapphire dress that she had given any thought to clothing. But she did need some new things. Her appetite had increased and she'd regained some of the weight she'd lost so some of the gray, black, and white clothing she'd packed was no longer comfortable. And the somber colors no longer fit her mood. The blouse was gorgeous and just her style, but it was too soon to wear something that bright, wasn't it?

She stared at the brilliant blue blouse trying to decide, and suddenly, as if she was standing next to her, she heard Angela's voice. "Wearing bright colors doesn't mean you don't love Abby, Callie. It means you're alive." She glanced at the reflection of the four of them in the window. Not only did she feel alive, she looked alive. She wanted that blouse. And Dana, Susan, and Fran were all smiling, not judging. "All right."

The three of them took it upon themselves to bring her other things she might like and her to-purchase pile grew quickly from that blouse to two pairs of slacks, a jacket, a sweater, two pairs of shorts, two more blouses, and two casual T-shirts, all colorful, some brighter than others. She was reaching for her clothes when Dana knocked on the dressing room door, opened it a crack and stuck a hanger into the room. "Try this on."

She took the hanger, closed the door, and stared at the skimpy turquoise thing dangling in front of her. She must be kidding. "I don't wear bikinis," she said through the door.

"Be a sport and try it on. You don't have to buy it." If Dana had been pushing, she'd probably have refused but she was asking nicely. She slipped it on. Whoa. She knew she was looking better due to the weight gain, all the walking and the tan, but to her surprise she looked sleek. And sexy. Did she dare? She stepped out of the room for an opinion. The group intake of breath and low whistles from her three shopping pals made her decision. "Okay. I'm buying it." She added the bikini to her pile of purchases and dressed.

Dana, Susan, and Fran all looked so self-satisfied as they waited for her to pay for the clothing that she wondered, for a moment, whether they'd planned to get her to shop, but then she remembered she was the one to stop in front of the store.

Dana helped carry her purchases as they made their way back to the boat. "Happy with your new clothing? Everything looks beautiful on you."

Callie was pleased with her purchases. The clothing reflected who she was now, who she was before Abby got sick. But she felt uneasy, as if it meant she was moving away from her deep mourning of Abby. "I love it all and I know it doesn't mean I no longer love Abby, but I feel sad, like I'm leaving her behind."

Dana put a hand on Callie's arm to stop her. "I'm no expert on grieving, but I doubt you'll ever leave Abby behind. I bet that every step you take to reclaim your separate identity will make you sad. Didn't Abby say something like get your ass out there and live, in her letter? You know that wearing drab, too-tight clothing won't bring Abby back. And wearing clothing that looks, and makes you feel, beautiful, doesn't mean anything about Abby. It means you are alive, living as she wanted you to."

Callie kissed Dana's cheek. "Thank you. I needed that."

Hot, dusty, and thirsty, they boarded the boat. When it was Callie's turn to use the small changing room, she pulled her black one-piece bathing suit out of her backpack. It felt heavy and looked drab next to her new turquoise bikini. Could she go outside wearing just two skimpy pieces of cloth? Dana had presented her with a new challenge. She bought it, might as well flaunt it. She slipped into the suit and feeling confident, picked up her shirt in case she needed to cover up from the sun, and went out to the deck.

Lou whistled and all eyes turned to her. Ellie, Carl, and James joined the whistling. Callie grinned and acknowledged them and the verbal compliments as she moved toward the rear of the boat to get a drink. She dropped her shirt on a lounge next to Serena and reached into the cooler for a bottle of water. When she looked up, Dana was gazing at her with hooded eyes. She met Dana's eyes. Dana blinked and gave her a thumbs-up. Callie settled into the chair, not sure whether the warming of her body was caused by the attention, the sun, or Dana's gaze.

As they sailed around the island, the captain pointed out places of interest. They were only allowed to spend a few minutes in the Blue Grotto, but it was beautiful. Everyone was more than ready when the captain dropped the anchor and a simple lunch was served on the deck.

Callie leaned back, eyes half closed, enjoying the sun and listening to the quiet chatter of the group as they ate lunch. As usual, her eyes found Dana. She was sitting two chairs away talking to Carl and Loretta and trying to convince Carl to go in the water with her.

"C'mon, Carl, you can wear your life jacket and we can take a float. I promise I'll stay with you. It'll cool you off. You'll love it."

Carl glanced at Loretta. "Thanks. Unlike Loretta, who grew up in the city and learned to swim in school, I'm a simple farm boy and I never had a need to swim. I'm too old to learn." Through his thick Southern accent, his gentle voice seemed full of regret.

"Don't waste your time, Dana. He's as stubborn as a mule." Loretta patted his hand. "But he is loveable."

Callie felt a pang of loss. That's how she'd thought she and Abby would be when they celebrated their fiftieth anniversary, still in love.

Dana was talking softly to avoid embarrassing Carl. "I don't think it's stubbornness, Loretta. It's natural to be a little afraid of something you've never done. But really, Carl, I think you'd love it. We can start by sitting on the swim platform over there and putting your legs in the water. If you feel comfortable, we can ease in or if you decide not to do it I'll help you stand."

"Why do you care whether I go in the water, Dana?" Carl sounded truly curious.

"I love to swim. I do it all the time in New York City. And I'd like to share that pleasure with you because something tells me you'll love it too. But it's up to you." She stood and stripped off the shirt she was wearing over her bikini.

Dana was sexy as hell. Her breasts were fuller than she thought and so beautiful. Callie averted her eyes but ended up staring at her toned curves, smooth flat stomach, nicely rounded ass, and long, muscled legs. She'd seen Dana in her bikini several times, but before today her body hadn't reacted; the fluttering and the heat were new. She felt like a yo-yo, one moment longing for Abby, the next having thoughts about her friend that were more than friendly. She looked away.

Out of the corner of her eye she saw Carl stand, put on a life jacket, and move to the platform with Dana. With the assistance of Dana and one of the crew he sat on the platform and dangled his feet in the water. Dana sat next to him. They spoke too softly for her to hear. But at least she could admire Dana's beautiful swimmer's shoulders and back from behind and not appear to be ogling her.

Admit it, Callie. You are ogling her. She brushed that thought aside and focused on how kind Dana was, how respectful of Carl she was, how she reached out to everyone and had made friends with everyone in the group.

She turned toward the sound of a splash. Dana and Carl were in the water, he in the center of an inner tube, Dana holding on to it, and they both were grinning as they floated near the boat. She cheered along with the rest of the group. One by one they eased into the water, taking care, it seemed, to not splash Carl. Callie threw off her shirt and followed. Loretta hadn't smiled so much on the whole trip. Carl looked like he had won the lottery. Dana met Callie's gaze and smiled her gentle smile. Callie gave her a thumbs-up and swam over.

"You did it, Carl. Congratulations."

Loretta engaged with Carl, and Callie took the opportunity to compliment Dana. "You are so good with people. You make me proud."

Dana tipped an imaginary hat. "Thank you, ma'am." Her face darkened. "But judging from my two thieving partners I'm not good with all people."

Callie ran her hand down Dana's arm and intertwined their fingers. "Even you can't control other people's behavior. Take pleasure in what you accomplished today." She tilted her head toward Carl and Loretta. "He's probably always wanted to go in the water but was too afraid. I'll bet today is a highlight of the trip for him."

Once again she'd reached out to touch Dana without thinking, as if she had the rights of a lover. But friends touched all the time, didn't they? She'd been so self-involved in the year since Abby died she couldn't remember touching even her best friend. Had she touched friends before then? Yes. Off and on over the years she and Abby had discussed how she, who traced her ancestry back to ancient Venice, was touchy-feely, and Abby, a white, Anglo-Saxon, Protestant, was reserved and self-contained. She relaxed. She was just being herself, not making assumptions about her relationship with Dana.

Dana stayed close to Carl until he started to get cold, then with one of the crew she helped him and Loretta onto the platform and into the boat, made sure they had towels and a hot drink, then dove in again to toss a ball around with the rest of the group.

Everyone groaned when Millie announced it was time to head back to Amalfi, but they dutifully swam to the boat. A feast of hot chocolate, cantaloupe, honeydew, and gelato was the reward.

What a wonderful day. They were all rosy cheeked from the sun and the exercise. Callie looked around at her...she hesitated to say "friends" but more and more that's what they felt like.

The exhausted group opted for an early dinner at the hotel in order to recuperate for the next day's expedition to Pompeii. But Callie needed to talk to Maggie and arranged an appointment with her for nine p.m. Italian time, three p.m. in New Jersey. She sat on the love seat for the Zoom session.

Callie could hardly contain herself when Maggie appeared on the screen.

"Hi, Callie. Where are you now?"

"The Amalfi Coast. It's gorgeous, but I'm totally confused about Dana, about my feelings for her. And I've been having bad thoughts about Abby." She couldn't repress the sobs rushing out.

Maggie listened to her breathe and waited for her to get control. "Talk to me about Abby."

"These horrible negative thoughts come into my mind from nowhere. Like today, I was watching Dana relate to some of the others and suddenly I was thinking Abby was a snob and would have only been interested in the people she considered successful."

Maggie, as she always did, took a few seconds to consider her answer. "Do you remember that when you first came into therapy one of your issues was Abby changing, becoming like her snooty parents. But we'd only had a few sessions when she was diagnosed with brain cancer and our focus changed to helping you deal with her dying. We never got to deal with her snobbery. So was she? A snob?"

Callie felt like she'd been punched. The beauty in front of her couldn't negate the pain of the truth. "I'd forgotten how angry I was. Yes, she was becoming harsh and judgmental, like her parents. But, I loved her."

"I know you did. No one is perfect, Callie, and we love despite the imperfections. You had convinced Abby to come into couples therapy to work on the issue, but she was diagnosed as terminally ill before we could schedule our first session together and it was no longer important. It seemed at the time that the pressure from the tumor might have caused some personality changes. In any case, your subconscious reminded you about it today. Why do you think that is?"

"My attraction to Dana is getting out of control. I find myself watching her all the time and I'm reacting physically to her touch. Today we had a moment when we locked eyes, and I swear it was as if she was running her hands over my body." Callie gazed at the night sky through the terrace door, then faced her computer again. "I didn't think I'd ever love again but..."

After a minute of listening to her heavy breathing, Maggie filled in the blanks. "You're falling in love with Dana? And you feel guilty?"

"Yes. It's too soon. And I'm scared. How do I know it's real?" She laughed. "Did I tell you we had another bird incident at lunch yesterday? We were on the terrace of the restaurant at our hotel and a bird flew around us, first me, then Dana, sang its little heart out to each of us, and after a couple of loops it flew off. It's happening so frequently the others have noticed. And I think I'm going crazy, because I'm starting to believe the birds are Abby giving me her blessing."

Maggie laughed. "It is unusual, that's for sure. But woo-woo aside, finding love again after the death of a spouse is fraught with issues. It's normal to worry about forgetting Abby. Normal to feel disloyal. Normal to wonder whether you can grieve the loss of Abby and love Dana at the same time. And no wonder you don't trust your feelings. You believed you'd never love anyone other than Abby and now you're falling in love with Dana."

She took a drink of something, probably the tea she always had at hand. "There's no simple path through this, no rules. You've mourned Abby for more than a year. She knew you'd need her to set you free and loved you enough to write the letter meant to do just that. As I've said before, no one can replace Abby, but your heart is big enough to love someone in addition to her. Be patient with yourself, give yourself time to be sure that it's love you're feeling, not just the intimacy of the tour or your gratitude toward Dana for taking care of you. Give yourself permission to feel what you feel, to want what you want, and to make the choices that are right for you."

"Thanks, Maggie. My mind is willing to be patient, but my body has other ideas."

Maggie laughed. "This is where I remind you that you are in full control of both, so nothing needs to happen that you don't want to happen. Whatever you choose to do, though, take responsibility for it."

"But what about my treacherous thoughts about Abby?"

"My guess is that if you don't fight your feelings, just enjoy them, your mind won't feel the need to offer reasons why Abby was not so wonderful."

"Interesting."

CHAPTER EIGHTEEN

Dana was having a love affair with ruins and Pompeii promised to be the mother of them all. At breakfast, her excitement and that of the other history nerds in the group was palpable. Half listening to their animated conversation, Callie's mind wandered, but her gaze was riveted on Dana. She loved the breadth of Dana's interests, loved her ability to throw herself into whatever captivated her. She was so beautiful, so alive, eyes sparkling, lips parted, face soft and dreamy, flushed with pleasure. Is that how she'd look after an orgasm?

Orgasm? What the hell? Callie's heart sped up. She glanced around. *Let yourself feel what you feel. Don't fight it.* Maggie's voice in her head calmed her. She took a slow breath in and exhaled slowly. Dana did look orgasmic, so no wonder her thoughts had wandered in that direction.

"Okay, folks," said Millie, calling for their attention once the bus was moving. "We'll start today with a three-hour private guided tour of the ancient Roman city of Pompeii with an archaeologist. Pompeii has little or no shade and it can get very hot, so make sure you have a hat, sunscreen, and a light cover up if you need one.

Take a bottle of water from the cooler when we exit the bus and be sure to drink it. Enzo will meet us midway with additional water."

"The guidebook in the packet says the ground is uneven. How difficult is walking for us old folks?" Carl asked, when Millie paused.

"You will definitely need to be careful. We have canes for those who might be unsteady, some of them with seats for those who might find three hours of walking tiresome. We also have umbrellas for those who would like to use them against the sun. Pick them up as you leave the bus. If you tire, there is a café where you can wait for the group. I'll be with you so let me know if you have any problems."

Millie wasn't kidding. There was no protection from the sun and at ten in the morning it was already hot. But what was hotter was Dana. Callie knew she was playing with fire, allowing her eyes to track Dana and her brain to toss out sexual thoughts, but Maggie did say she could enjoy her thoughts and not act on them.

The archaeologist's words eventually drifted into Callie's consciousness. "Pompeii was a thriving city when it was buried under volcanic ash in the year 79 AD by the eruption of Mt. Vesuvius, the volcano near the Bay of Naples. Two thousand people died in the ash. The city lay buried until 1748 when a group of explorers looking for ancient artifacts discovered the site. It was covered with a thick layer of dust and debris but preserved exactly as it had been two thousand years before. Buildings were intact, skeletons were found wherever citizens had succumbed to the ash, household goods and other objects lay where they were dropped as people ran to escape."

Dana had enthused over breakfast that two thousand years ago between 10,000 and 20,000 people had lived in Pompeii. Now, focused on the archaeologist, she was rapt as the woman described the ancient civilization.

"Its narrow streets, made narrower by street vendors and shops with jutting cloth awnings, teemed with tavern-goers, slaves, vacationers from the north, and more than a few prostitutes."

The ruins were impressive. Callie could visualize the houses and other buildings as they might have been, picture people living and working here, and imagine them running from the fiery lava that trapped so many of them on the neatly preserved streets of the city.

"If ten to twenty thousand people lived here, how come only two thousand died?" Dana asked when the archaeologist started to move on.

The woman stilled. "In the four days leading up to the eruption, there were a number of small earthquakes, a common event in the area but a warning. We speculate Mt. Vesuvius's eruption lasted for two days. The morning of the first day things seemed normal, then around one p.m. a cloud of ashes, pulverized pumice, molten rocks, and scorching-hot volcanic gases that could be seen for hundreds of miles around shot up into the sky, then began to fall, covering the area. It became difficult to breathe."

"How do you know how the cloud looked, where it could be seen and how it felt?" Dana asked.

"We have contemporaneously written accounts," the guide said. "Most of the population fled between then and sometime overnight when the lava flowed, knocking down buildings and incinerating and suffocating any living thing in its path. For some reason those two thousand didn't leave when they could. I liken it to modern day people who are warned, for instance, about the approaching Katrina Hurricane, and decide to stay for some reason—they have no place to go, they want to protect what they have, they don't believe the warnings, and so on." The archaeologist turned. "Let's move on."

Callie knew Dana probably had a thousand questions, but she dropped back, allowing the others to walk with the guide so they could ask their questions. Callie smiled. Despite her enthusiasm, despite her need to know everything about the ancient civilization, Dana's kindness, thoughtfulness, and decency wouldn't allow her to monopolize the woman.

Dana acknowledged Callie's presence with a smile as she moved beside her to walk behind the archaeologist. But it was clear Dana was trying to overhear the questions and answers, so Callie was silent, content to watch her absorb it all. Dana's single-mindedness, her ability to focus on something, and shut all else out must certainly be at the base of her success in business. And probably the reason for her less than desirable personal life. While pouring everything into her business, she'd accepted whatever crumbs life brought personally.

Dana leaned close to Callie. "The road ahead looks bumpy. Let's help Carl and Loretta." She stepped between the two older people, asked Carl about something they'd seen, and, without fanfare, took his arm to steady him on the bumpy parts. Callie moved to the other side of Loretta and took her arm.

Loretta smiled. "Thank you, Callie." She tipped her head toward Dana. "She's really good with him. You know he'd never ask for help or accept it from most people, but she's managed to get past his defenses. He likes her a lot and, more important, he trusts her. I should be jealous. Except for me, he never lets his guard down, even with our grown children."

"Are you jealous?"

Loretta laughed. "You know, if anyone had told me that Carl would be friends with a young lesbian millionaire, I'd have laughed myself silly. But she's managed to connect with him and he with her. I think it's because she's genuinely interested in knowing him while most younger people just write off us old folks as boring. Having her on the trip has made all the difference for him. And for me. So no, I'm not jealous. I trust her too. She's a treasure." She squeezed Callie's arm. "And we hope you'll hold on to her."

Before Callie could respond, they arrived at the next lecture spot. Callie stared ahead, blankly trying to absorb the fact that these two older strangers saw Dana for who she was and obviously had discussed her in relation to Dana. Suddenly lightheaded, she inched closer to Dana, knowing she would catch her if she fell. Without turning, without speaking, Dana touched her hand, acknowledging her presence. The hyper-focused woman could also multitask.

Pompeii was wonderful and their guide was fabulous. But three hours of standing in the sun, walking on uneven streets, and focusing on the information being imparted was exhausting. Everyone seemed turned inward as they exited the site, and there was little conversation. The appearance of the air-conditioned bus prompted a cheer as did the bottles of cold water Enzo handed to each of them as they entered. They sank into their seats with various sounds of appreciation. As the bus rolled away from Pompeii, Dana drained her bottle of water and pulled one of her history books on Pompeii and Herculaneum from her backpack.

"Aren't you hot and tired, Dana?" Callie couldn't help but ask.

Dana turned to her. "Yes, but I want to prepare for Herculaneum. Don't worry, I'm used to pushing myself. Did you enjoy the morning?"

Callie was exhausted, but she'd enjoyed learning about Pompeii and watching Dana's passion for history blossom. "I did. But I wish the museum with all the artifacts was open. I'd love to see those to get a real sense of how they lived."

"I read that the museum—it's called the Antiquarium—has been closed for more than forty years, but they're projecting it will open soon. We'll have to come back when it opens to see the plaster casts of the people who died there and the jewelry and household items found at the site." She shifted slightly. "You look wiped out. You should sleep. I'm going to read."

Callie closed her eyes but was aware of the light pressure of Dana's thigh against her, the sound of Dana's breathing, and the tangy smell of her sweat mixed with the citrusy hotel soap. She was sure Dana was attracted to her, but it made her happy to hear that Dana expected they'd be together and do things after the tour was over. Her heart fluttered.

Millie's voice woke Callie from a very pleasant dream of walking hand in hand with Dana through the ruins of Pompeii at sundown, stopping to kiss every now and then.

"Okay, folks, our table is outside in a grove with fig, peach, quince, and lemon trees. Order from the menu as you like. We'll be here for about three hours, so after eating relax with a cool drink in the comfortable chairs scattered around the grounds."

Callie didn't open her eyes, trying to hold on to the turned-on feeling from the dream.

"Cal, time for lunch." Dana touched her shoulder.

"I'm awake. I just, um, need a minute. I'll meet you at the table."

As Callie neared the group of history nerds, she heard Dana's awed voice. "Did you read about the pyroclastic surge? Can you imagine the terror, seeing superheated poison gas and pulverized rock pouring down the side of the mountain at one hundred mile per hour, coming right at you?"

"All right, ladies and gentlemen, they're ready to take orders so please sit." Millie gently herded them to the table.

Callie and Dana sat together and each took several pieces of the bruschetta from the plate the waiter offered. "It's wonderful to see you so immersed in and enthusiastic about ancient history," Callie said. "Have you considered going back to school when we get home?"

Dana stopped with a bruschetta halfway to her mouth. "That's an interesting question. I've been so focused on trying to get my business back that I haven't thought about anything else. But I haven't felt this kind of excitement and need to know since my first computer programming class. So, while I haven't thought about it, I will now." She grinned. "You have the best ideas, Dr. DeAndre."

"How do you know about that? It was just an honorary doctorate awarded by my alma mater."

"Aha, you forget I was a fan before we ever met. As I recall it was awarded to recognize your outstanding achievement in literature. I knew a lot of facts about you before, but I've learned many interesting and intimate things about who you really are since we met."

"Intimate?" Callie blushed. Of course, she could say the same about Dana. A really good way to get to see the real person is watching how they interact with others. And she liked what she was seeing.

Dana blushed. "Sorry. I meant hearing about your feelings and fears and hopes, not anything sexual."

Callie's whole body heated. "I didn't think you meant sexual." *But you might if you could read my mind.* "Um, the waiter is approaching. Do you know what you want?"

"Oops, better look at the menu."

To Callie's surprise, after a relatively light lunch followed by a brief nap she was ready for the guided tour of Herculaneum. Perhaps because it was closer to the Bay of Naples or because it was later in the day and the sun wasn't so strong, it was cooler and she enjoyed exploring the site. She was fascinated to learn that unlike in Pompeii, wooden roofs, beds, and doors as well as other organic-based materials such as food had been protected because the ash and other material that covered it had carbonized. She didn't understand what carbonized meant, but she did understand that it preserved organic things. Not people, of course.

Callie and everyone in their little group oohed at the Roman baths with separate male and female spas, the deep pools, marble seats, and stucco friezes and reliefs on the walls, and hearing the archaeologist's vivid description of their use. In other buildings they viewed many statues, a wooden screen, and parts of murals that were preserved, but the highlight for Callie was the amazing mosaic depicting Neptune, god of the sea, and his wife, Amphitrite, in warm colors.

"Wow, this is so vibrant it seems impossible that it's two thousand years old."

Dana placed her hand on Callie's shoulder. "It really is incredible. Looking at these ruins, at what's left, and wandering these ancient cities makes me feel connected to the past. I want to know all about the people who lived then and what their everyday lives were like. I'm fascinated by how archaeologists deduce things from what they dig up. I might have to study archaeology too."

Standing in the warmth of the late afternoon, savoring the gentle pressure of Dana's hand, Callie enjoyed their easy connection, the feeling of sharing something meaningful. Wanting to see Dana's face as she examined the artifact, she turned and was surprised to find Dana looking at her rather than the mosaic. Their eyes locked and for a moment everything around them faded. It was just the two of them speaking through their eyes. Overwhelmed by the need to kiss Dana, Callie leaned in.

"Okay, folks, let's move on." They both blinked as the voice of the archaeologist leading the afternoon tour shattered the illusion of privacy. Without a word they followed him.

Jane was finding it harder and harder to resist Morgan. Every touch, every look stoked her desire. Watching Morgan feed her passion for history seemed to feed Jane's passion for Morgan.

"Are you up for a quiet night? A hot tub or the sauna, then dinner at the Beach Club?" Dana asked Callie, on the drive back to the hotel.

"That sounds perfect." Callie pulled her journal out of her backpack, glanced at Dana to make sure she was not reading over her shoulder, and quickly jotted down the snippet for her book.

Callie and Dana skipped having a drink in the bar when they got back to the hotel and, as a result, apparently missed the group's plan to walk into Amalfi for dinner. She wasn't complaining. Being alone with Dana in the hot tub wasn't a hardship.

"I've been meaning to tell you how much I like the inscription in my copy of your book. I hope the part about liking having me in your life means you want us to see each other after the tour."

So Dana really did want to stay in contact. She sure as hell wanted it. "It does. I can't imagine not seeing you." *Every day.* Her attraction to Dana was growing exponentially. Some days she thought Dana felt the same. Other days, not so much. "I'm ready for dinner. You?"

"Sure. Let's go get out of these wet bathing suits."

The look on Dana's face when Callie walked out of her room wearing her new brilliant blue blouse eliminated any question about whether she should be wearing bright colors. Though maybe it was the amount of cleavage showing rather than the color. It had been a while, but Callie enjoyed feeling appreciated by a woman she appreciated.

They were shown to a table for two near the edge of the terrace of the Beach Club's restaurant. The velvety evening sky, the dim lighting, the candlelight, and the lovely music playing softly in the background all added up to intimate and romantic. At least to Callie. And maybe to Dana as well.

Ordering meals in Italian was relatively easy since it only required set phrases and the names of the dishes they selected, but the goal was to get used to speaking the language and they were taking advantage of every opportunity. Dana ordered wine and several dishes to share and then, after the waiter walked away, she turned to Callie. "I had a great time with you today. I've never experienced the kind of connection we have, nor the kind of intimacy there is between us, even with women I've been in a relationship with. I love that we talk so easily about everything, that sharing thoughts and experiences with you seems so natural."

Callie put her water down. "I feel the same with you, Dana. This tour, you, have done wonders for me. I'm so glad we won't lose each other when we go home." Their eyes locked as they had earlier in front of the mosaic, and Callie felt the same bolt of electricity as earlier. She wasn't ready for this, for these feelings. "So have you given any further thought to whether you'd consider doing anything other than being CEO of your company?"

Dana blinked. Perhaps the electricity between them had vaulted her mind to the same place as Callie's. She took Callie's hand. "I think my brain has been working on the idea of doing something else without my realizing it. I've been interviewing high-level people to replace my thieving partners and eventually me, so I could step away from the day-to-day running of the business once Linda and Artie are arrested. I'd planned to stay on as chair of the board, but the time commitment would be minimal so I could go back to school if that's what I decide to do."

Dana seemed surprised by her subconscious thoughts, but Callie had sensed the shift in her. "What do you see in your future?"

"The idea of studying for a PhD in ancient history and archaeology and someday teaching on a college level excites me." Dana met Callie's eyes. "And someday I'd like to settle down and have a family." She looked away.

Was Dana asking her to settle down with her? To have children? Callie couldn't be sure. "You should follow your heart, Dana."

Dana met her eyes again. Callie thought she saw love and desire, but then the waiter placed their appetizers on the table, breaking their contact. When she looked at Dana again, she thought perhaps she'd projected her own feelings onto the other woman. Dana laughed. "I know what my heart wants, but I'm not sure it can have what it wants. I guess we'll see."

Callie reluctantly let go of Dana's hand and, as she served them each some of the appetizers, attempted to steer the conversation away from topics that involved intimate eye contact.

"So what were your favorite parts of Pompeii and Herculaneum?"

CHAPTER NINETEEN

Another beautiful, sunny day. Callie stood at the railing of her terrace, tasting lemons on the gentle breeze and feasting her eyes on the deep blue sky, turquoise water, and lush greenery. This was truly God's country. Her phone vibrated with a text from Dana. *At your door. Ready for breakfast?* On time and raring to go, as usual.

At the breakfast buffet on the terrace, Callie helped herself to some cheese, a hardboiled egg, a croissant, and an orange. Dana did the same but also included several slices of prosciutto and a slice of cake. They both ordered cappuccinos. Slowly members of the group wandered down.

Dana had enjoyed the boat trip to Capri so much she'd booked a private full-day boat excursion for their free day, their last in Amalfi. They would cruise the coast, visit Positano, have lunch on the boat, swim in lagoons, snorkel and swim in grottos and caves only accessible by sea. Everyone was invited to come along as her guest. Millie opted out, but the group seemed to relish the idea of a relaxed day on the water with minimal optional sightseeing. Spirits were high and after breakfast they headed for the boat.

Leave it to Dana. She managed to hire a fifty-foot boat with a female captain and crew. According to Captain Gina Cavaliere, the boat was a classic. It had a cabin, a partially covered outdoor area, and enough comfortable outside lounge chair seating for the twelve of them. Stacks of soft towels were placed strategically in the cabin and on the deck as were coolers with beer, wine, carbonated and uncarbonated water, and juice. The rental came with melon, prosecco, and Limoncello, but Dana asked that they be held for the end of the day.

The first stop was Positano, known as "the Jewel of the Amalfi Coast," to do a little sightseeing and pick up the lunch Dana had ordered from a top restaurant. The view of Positano from the water was postcard-worthy with colorful houses in layered rows starting high up, seeming to tumble down the cliffside, stopping on the beach at the church of Santa Maria Assunta, its majolica-tiled dome glowing in the sunlight.

At the dock, they split up. Most of the group ambled into the heart of the town while Callie and Dana went in search of the restaurant. After confirming that lunch was on schedule to be delivered to the dock in about a half hour, they strolled the narrow streets but avoided the boutique clothing stores and the shops selling ceramics and the lemon-themed items of the Amalfi region. It was already getting hot and crowded, so they headed back to the appointed meeting spot on the dock and waited for the others and the lunch delivery.

It turned out the others in the group weren't interested in shopping either and slowly drifted back to where they were seated. Once the food arrived and everyone was accounted for, Dana texted the captain and a dingy came to bring them back to the boat.

With what sounded like a group sigh of relief at being back on the water, everyone stripped down to bathing suits, applied sunscreen, donned hats, took a cold drink, and sat in the circle of chairs as they headed out into open waters.

"Hey, Dana, this was a great idea." Lou looked around at the others. "But we think you shouldn't pay for it all. We'd like to chip in."

Dana stood with both hands in front of her as if pushing back. Which of course she was. "Listen up, folks. I planned to do this whether it was just me, me and Callie, or, as it turned out, the whole group. I know you know I can afford it so just accept it as my gift to all of us." She grinned. "Besides I had to get Carl out in the water again. I'll make a swimmer of him yet."

"Hah, I knew it was a trick. But I appreciate it and happily accept your gift." Carl lifted his water as if toasting. "And so should you all. Say 'thank you, Dana.'"

"Thank you, Dana," the group shouted.

"Okay, enough of that. Captain Gina says our route will show us the real beauty of the coast in a way that you can't see from the crowded, narrow streets of the towns. She's taking us to grottos and lagunes in different parts of the coast where we can swim and snorkel. Let's just sit back and enjoy the day."

They cruised and swam and played. Several times during the day, Dana got Carl into a life jacket and in the water with her. She already had him treading water. Dana and Callie floated side by side while Dana kept an eye on him hanging onto a tube with Loretta.

"Look at Carl, already comfortable enough to not have you next to him in the water. Good job, Dana."

Dana grinned. "All I did was encourage and support him. He really wanted to be in the water and once he realized he wasn't going to drown, he relaxed."

Callie splashed her. "So modest. Take the credit you deserve."

Dana splashed back, and after a brief water fight, Callie managed to get close enough to wrap her arms around Dana. "Had enough?"

Dana looked into her eyes. "I'll never have enough of you."

The words and the way Dana looked into her eyes made Callie weak. Maggie had said feel what you feel but, damn, she might drown if she didn't get some space. "Yeah, yeah." She dropped her arms, splashed Dana, and swam to the boat. Relieved that Dana didn't follow her, she sank into a lounge chair, closed her eyes, and pulled her hat over her face. She needed an ice bath, but the cool breeze would have to do. *You're in control of your emotions and your body.* Maggie's words echoed in her mind. *Right.* She pretended to sleep.

"Callie." She must have actually fallen asleep. She opened her eyes, glad it was Ellie, not Dana waking her. "Time for lunch."

She sat up. The crew had laid out the sumptuous spread. The variety and colors of the offerings made it visually pleasing. Callie's mouth watered. Looking uncomfortable, Dana was sitting as far from Callie as she could get. She probably thought she'd offended her. Callie wasn't about to tell her she'd turned her on, but she also didn't want her to feel bad about something she didn't do. She smiled and waved, hoping Dana would get the message that she wasn't angry.

Dana waved and smiled, then seemed to count heads. Everyone was back on board. "Okay, folks. Let's eat."

Ellie settled next to Callie, put her beer in the drink holder on her chair, and displayed her plate. "It all looks delicious, so I took a little bit of everything."

Callie lifted her beer. "It's tempting." Her gaze shifted to Dana leaning against the railing, plate in hand, having a lively discussion with her history buddies. Her long, lean body was relaxed, and the red bikini hid none of her assets—muscled arms, full breasts, flat stomach, curvy waist and hips. Her face was alive, so expressive as she listened attentively. As if feeling Callie's gaze, Dana looked up, met her eyes momentarily, then smiled and turned back to her group.

Brief as it was, Callie felt the heat of that gaze again. *You're in control of your emotions and your body.*

"She's quite the catch." Ellie spoke softly for Callie's ears.

"She is, but you know—"

"Yeah, yeah, I know. But from outside, you appear to have a real and intense bond that's more than friendship, and I, we, don't understand why you're not a couple."

Callie stared at Ellie. "It isn't the right time for either of us."

Ellie took a swig of beer. "It looks to me that's what your heads are saying, but your bodies are sending a very different signal. I understand, though, why you might be reluctant. It sounds as if you and Abby had a solid marriage." She stared at Dana for a long moment. "You know, if it was a different time in my life, I might fight you for her."

"Really?" Callie felt a surge of jealousy. Ellie was attractive, poised, confident, and, she'd learned, a prominent surgeon. She was a catch. Callie swiveled to face her. "I thought you were straight." She hadn't meant it to sound like an accusation, but it did.

Ellie laughed. "I'm bisexual. Prior to falling in love with my asshole ex in our first year of medical school, I dated women and men. I was physically monogamous until he walked out, but I wasn't always mentally monogamous since I was tempted to have affairs with several women."

"Were you totally blindsided when he left?"

"With hindsight I realize our relationship started to go downhill when he didn't make the cut for surgery. He was devastated. I would have been too. He wouldn't talk about it, but it was there, a shadow between us. When I was named Chief Resident, he insisted we get pregnant, even though he knew the responsibilities and pressures of the job demand one hundred percent. I was in a rage at the time, but agreed to go off birth control." She took a bite of the fish salad. "But I believed, whether it was conscious or unconscious, he wanted me to fail, so I actually didn't stop until I joined the surgical practice I now run."

"Wow." Callie's gaze flicked to Dana. Dana met her gaze and raised her eyebrows. Callie smiled.

"That's what I mean, Callie. A really strong bond. I can sympathize about not being ready, but in the time we've been together I've observed you emerge from your grief—" Ellie held her hand up. "I'm not saying you're not still feeling the loss of Abby, but you've blossomed from a withdrawn, worn-out shell into a beautiful, sexy woman who, in my opinion, is glowing from the beginning feelings of a new love. I encourage you to go for it."

Callie opened her mouth to protest but realized Ellie was right. "Thank you, I'm getting there. I'm not sure that Dana feels the same."

Ellie laughed, a deep belly laugh. "Believe me, it's mutual. I'd put money on it."

Dana wandered over and sat at the end of Callie's lounge. "You two look so serious. What are you plotting?"

Callie and Ellie looked at each other and burst out laughing. "Just talking about life," Ellie said.

The engine sputtered, then caught and the boat started to move. Each place they swam and snorkeled was more beautiful than the last and all had picture-perfect views of the towns and the mountains. Callie's favorite was the Bay of Maiori. Not only was it gorgeous, but while they swam a member of the crew took the skiff to the dock and brought back delicious lemon granita as a treat.

High-energy Dana was the last one out of the water at the end of the day. Sun and water-soaked, everyone sprawled on their lounge chairs sipping prosecco and eating cantaloupe and honeydew melon with their granita.

"This has been such a romantic day," Marian said at a lull in the conversation. "Thank you again, Dana."

"Hear, hear," a few people responded.

Callie jumped in to get some opinions on the question at the heart of her book. "It's interesting you say that, Marian. Since I'm writing a book that takes place on a"—she sketched quote marks with her fingers—"'romantic' tour, I'm interested in understanding what makes a city or town or any place romantic. Anybody have an opinion?"

"I have a better answer today than the last time you asked me." Marian smiled. "Today has felt romantic to me because I'm sharing this beautiful place"—she waved her arm, encompassing the coast and the water—"with Lou and with you all, who have become friends in a very short time. And all the laughing and talking, really talking, makes me feel close to everyone. Also, because it's unusual for me to be sipping prosecco and nibbling melon on a yacht in the middle of the day with nothing more pressing than enjoying myself."

Callie tipped an imaginary hat. "Well said. Anyone else?"

"Yes, me." Fran took Susan's hand. "Pretty much being anywhere with this woman makes it romantic."

"Aaw." Everyone responded the same way.

Fran laughed. "But, as an architect, I have to say that sharing places like the ones we've visited, cities built on a human scale, and walking around and in ancient buildings that have inspired architects across the centuries, feels intimate and romantic."

"For me," Vanessa interjected, "it's age. Over time a city accumulates a layered history. Even cities ruined by wear or war or a place like Pompeii. The solid stones still stand, fragments of art and daily living survive. We can imagine life as it existed there. Like with people, age gives a city depth and its history adds to the spirit, beauty, and romance of the place."

Callie clapped. "The historian speaks. Anyone else?"

"I came on this trip to keep Ellie company, not for the romance," Serena said. "But I've felt the romance in the vibrant colors of the sky and the water and the sunrises and sunsets. And the buildings." She pointed toward shore. "Look. The turquoise water, the lush greens of the lemon trees and other plants, the deep blue sky, and the colorful buildings. Do you remember Cinque Terra's colors? It's also the materials used in the buildings, the different color stones, things like the green and yellow and blue tiles on the dome of the Church of Santa Maria Assunta in Positano. Maybe it's because I'm an artist, but the colors touch my soul and add to the romance of a place. Sometimes it's overwhelming and I want to reach out and touch someone." She locked eyes with James.

Callie and Dana had wondered whether something was happening between Serena and James and now it seemed it was. Serena had really exposed herself.

Callie broke the silence. "That was beautiful, Serena. I didn't know you were an artist."

"You're not the only famous one." Ellie threw an arm over Serena's shoulder. "My sister hides behind her librarian persona, but she's a wonderful, wonderful painter with a big following."

"If Serena tells you her pseudonym, you'll all recognize it," Dana said, before looking at Callie and lifting her shoulders.

Callie assumed it was an apology for not telling her about Serena, but she would expect no less of Dana. It was ironic that she who believed she only lived on the surface had made intimate connections with so many of the group. What an incredible woman.

"Thanks for outing me, ladies." Serena smiled. "I started painting before I was married, so I continued to use my maiden name, Serena Redman."

Callie gasped. "I have one of your paintings. You don't have much of a public face, do you?"

Serena grinned. "Well, *Calliope*, like you, I enjoy my privacy. And like you, I was a young widow. By avoiding photos and publicity and working a few hours a week at the library as a cover, I've managed to live a quiet life with lots of time to paint."

Everyone laughed.

Callie held up her hands. "Okay, I deserved that poke. Anyone else want to talk about what makes something romantic?"

Dana raised her hand. "I learned this from you, Callie. It's walkability. If a city is walkable, we slow down and notice things we wouldn't notice in a car or from a tour bus, things we couldn't see in a museum or church or any building. We notice the buildings, for sure, but we also notice the people and the smells and the sounds and the decorations and our minds are free to imagine the lives of the people who lived there centuries ago. And, most important, a walkable city gives us time to share what we are seeing and what we feel about what we are seeing and there is time to look into each other's eyes and connect in an intimate and romantic way." Dana gazed at Callie.

"Wow, I taught you that?" Callie felt like, like she wanted to cry. Dana really did get her like no one ever had. Not even Abby.

"Yes, you did. A city isn't romantic because of its buildings or ruins from long, long ago. I think you get the vibe of a city when you walk it, especially when walking it with someone you care about. It can be magic." Dana stood. "Now I'm getting fanciful. Anyone need another drink?"

"Thanks to you all for sharing. And I'm always open to hearing about what you think makes a place romantic." Callie was feeling overwhelmed. Was Dana giving her a message?

As she was getting ready to leave her room to go to dinner, a text pinged. Dana. *Feeling woozy. 2 much sun so I won't be joining the group for dinner.*

Callie was tempted to knock on Dana's door but thought better of it. She texted back. *Too upset to eat? Or should I send something up?*

Dana's reply came right back. *Pls send something. Thx. See u in the am.*

Dana must have assumed she'd send a waiter with a tray, but Callie needed to see with her own eyes that she was okay. She knocked. "Dana. It's Callie. I have a tray for you. Should I leave it out here?" There was no answer. *Must be sleeping.* If she left the tray out here the staff might think Dana was done with it and take it away. She knocked again.

Dana opened the door. "Hey."

She looked sleepy, but she was still fully dressed. "Hey, Dana, I hope it's all right that I brought you dinner." Callie thrust the tray at her. "I wanted to make sure you were all right."

Dana took the tray. "Come in."

"Are you sure? I don't want to intrude."

Dana smiled. "I'm sure. Let's go out to the terrace."

They sat at the table. Dana removed the covers from the dishes. "Everything looks and smells fabulous. Thanks. I fell asleep, but I'm hungry." She poured a glass of beer. "Want some?"

"No, it's for you. I've eaten and had wine. Are you feeling better?"

Dana looked down at the food. Callie deduced she was buying time while deciding how much to reveal. She twirled some seafood pasta on her fork, put it in her mouth, and chewed slowly while gazing at the sea. Finally, she faced Callie.

"I'm better." She took a deep breath. "I had an anxiety attack, the first one in months."

"Oh, Dana, I wish I had been with you. But I know it's not possible to make a phone call or text in the grips of the attack." She watched Dana eat a small piece of the pizza included on the tray. "Do you want to talk about what set it off?"

Dana gazed out at the blue-black starlit sky, then turned to Callie again. Her beautiful face was open and so vulnerable Callie had to stifle the impulse to hold her. She knew Dana trusted her, but she seemed to be struggling. Dana sipped her beer and avoided looking at her.

Jane felt Morgan's pain as if it was her own. She was overwhelmed with need, the need to comfort and soothe Morgan, the need to kiss and make love to her.

Callie blinked. She was thinking sex when what Dana needed was comfort.

"When I got back to the room I felt like a fake, a phony using my money to get people to like me. I felt worthless, just an empty shell with no substance." Putting the fork down, she squeezed her eyes, trying to keep the tears in.

Callie didn't hesitate. She stood behind Dana and wrapped her arms around her. Dana leaned back and rested her head on Callie. Dana's body was vibrating so the sobs didn't surprise Callie.

Callie tightened her arms and rocked her. Neither of them pulled away when the sobs subsided. Callie kissed the top of Dana's head and spoke softly. "You are so much more than an empty shell, Dana. You didn't buy anyone off. All of us already loved and appreciated you before you gifted us with one of the most wonderful days of the trip." She moved back to her chair so she could see Dana's face, and took her hand. "You're not a fake or phony, sweetheart. You're one of the most authentic people I know. You are kind and loving and you've managed to touch the hearts of every single one of us in one way or another. Everyone was worried about you at dinner. I practically had to physically block Ellie from coming up here to check you out. I promised I'd call her if I thought you needed a doctor."

Dana used her napkin to dry her tears. "I need a psychiatrist, not a surgeon."

"I don't think you need either. You need to focus on feeling the love coming from all of us, not on the false picture you have of yourself."

Dana sniffed. "I—would you hold me, Callie?"

Callie pulled Dana onto to one of the lounge chairs, wrapped her in her arms, and held her tightly as the sobs erupted again. "You're not alone, Dana. You are loved. I'm here," Callie murmured over and over.

Long after her sobs stopped, long after her tears dried, Dana sighed and pulled away. "Thank you. I've soaked your shirt. I'm sorry. You must be tired."

Callie smiled and stretched. "You've held me physically and emotionally since the minute we met, Dana. I'll never tire of holding you. It's what good friends do for each other. And I'm sure the other ten people on this trip would happily hold you and comfort you anytime."

Dana moved to the table, picked up a piece of cold pizza and took a bite. Callie sensed she needed the time to think, and watched her chew but remained silent.

"I don't think I need a psychiatrist, but I think it's time to schedule a telephone session with Jean, my therapist. She said I'd know when I was ready to dig deeper into my feelings. Inevitably when I think I'm okay, I find I have more to unpack."

Callie stood. "I think it's part of the process. At least it has been for me." She pulled Dana into a hug. "Would you like me to stay with you? I can sleep on the sofa."

Dana kissed Callie's cheek. "I'm all right now. Thank you for listening."

Callie cupped Dana's chin and gazed at her. She was tempted to kiss her but decided this wasn't the time. "Don't forget it's a two-way street with us." She closed the door behind her.

CHAPTER TWENTY

Callie was sad to leave the Amalfi Coast, but for the setting and atmosphere in her romance to be authentic she needed to have a sense, the feel, of each romantic city/area they visited. She didn't need to see and do everything in every place.

Dana slid into her seat and Callie immediately felt the heat of her body everywhere flesh met flesh. The seats in the bus were comfortable and built for people larger than them, but recently they seemed to gravitate toward each other, so their bodies touched. While Dana appeared to be her usual cheerful self, Callie kept flashing back to the vulnerable Dana of last night. She'd felt like a fragile kitten in her arms, and Callie had been overwhelmed with tenderness and the desire to protect her. She flushed, remembering her not-so-innocent feelings as well. Having Dana clinging to her, her soft breasts pressing and her warm breath on her neck, was a turn-on. Of course she wouldn't act on those feelings in a situation like that. In fact, she wouldn't act on them until they were both less needy.

Dana settled her backpack and pulled out a book. "You're quiet this morning."

"I was wondering what, if anything, could top the last few days." Callie put her hand on Dana's thigh. "Did you sleep?"

"After you left, I called Jean to see if we could set up a time to talk tonight. It turned out she was free, so we had a session." Dana covered Callie's hand, and her thumb gently stroked it. "It was helpful. I have a lot to think about. I'd be happy to share with you when we have some privacy. If you're interested."

Did Dana realize what she was doing? Callie forced herself to focus. The heat of Dana's hand, the caress of her thumb, caused a flurry of butterflies in the lower region of her body and a feeling of warmth all over. More and more her body's response to Dana was unmistakably sexual. Her body knew what it wanted and she was finding it nearly impossible to keep from kissing Dana. She shifted and reached for her backpack, freeing her hand and moving slightly away from Dana, trying to lower her temperature.

"I'm definitely interested in whatever you feel comfortable talking about."

Her treacherous body was longing to move close to Dana again. She needed a diversion. The daily information packet she'd stowed in the outer pocket of her backpack caught her eye. She pulled it out and scanned the cover page.

"Matera looks interesting, but I'm not sure about sleeping in a cave."

Dana lit up. "It's supposed to be fabulous." She shifted slightly so she could face Callie while they talked. "How better to experience what the original inhabitants felt?"

Callie snorted. "I'll bet our digs, no pun intended, will be a lot more luxurious than those of the original inhabitants."

"You're probably right, but it will still be fun. And, ooh, maybe scary. I mean caves don't have windows, right?"

Callie shivered. "No windows?"

Dana patted her arm. "Don't worry. You can stay with me if you're afraid."

Callie punched her lightly. "I'd probably be more afraid of you." Or, truthfully, afraid of her own lack of control if they shared a room.

Jane imagined lying next to Morgan in a dimly lit cave, hearing the soft puffs of her breath, seeing the gentle rise of her lovely breasts, smelling her arousal and mapping her body with her hands and her mouth.

At this rate the book was going to write itself. The chemistry between Jane and Morgan was clear but she was confusing herself, thinking of them as her and Dana. The story would come from them. She needed to think more about who they are, who they were before and how they change on the tour. She reached for her journal.

They settled into their usual quiet space, reading, sketching, or writing, but Callie's gaze kept going to Millie, who was talking on her phone constantly and seemed uncharacteristically agitated. Something was wrong. She scanned the bus. Everyone else seem relaxed so maybe it was a personal problem. *Interesting.* She hadn't thought much about Millie's life. Millie had been so wonderful to her in Rome, been there as a support for the group and facilitated their travel. She'd been spending time every day talking with her and Dana, helping them converse in Italian, yet she'd taken the younger woman for granted. She resolved to make an effort to be more appreciative.

The mic crackled and Millie spoke. "We should be arriving in Matera in about forty-five minutes. We'll be there for two nights, so you'll have a day and a half to explore and two evenings to enjoy the romantic atmosphere. In the past we've found that some of our guests felt claustrophobic staying in a windowless underground cave room, so our hotel, the Corte Cava San Pietro, is a luxury cave hotel that will give you the cave experience in rooms with a window and a glass door that opens to the outdoors rather than an inner hallway. The hotel has a wonderful spa and a fabulous restaurant on site. Any questions?" She paused. "Okay. In a few minutes Enzo is going to stop for gas and a fifteen-minute break at a little café with a beautiful view of the valley. Dana and Callie, I'd like to talk to you when we arrive." She shut the mic off.

"What do you think this is about?" Callie whispered.

"I don't have the vaguest." Dana raised her eyebrows. "Did you do some wild thing over dinner when I wasn't there to control you last night?"

Callie poked her with her elbow. "I'm always good, you know that."

"Hah. We'll see."

As soon as the bus stopped moving, Callie and Dana exited and waited for Millie to join them. She didn't waste any time getting to the point.

"We have a problem. Callie, you booked the trip two weeks before departure because we had a late cancellation, right?"

"Yes. I've since learned that it was Dana's friend who couldn't make it. What's the problem?"

"We had one room booked for Dana and her friend. At the time you reserved the office staff booked an additional room at each stop. This hotel confirmed the additional room but didn't reserve it. Last night I was reviewing the reservations with the staff at the hotel and realized we're short a room. I've been on the phone since then and, believe it or not, there's not one luxury room available in Matera for the rest of this week." She took a deep breath, "I would get a room at a different hotel and give one of you my room, but I'm required to stay with the group. And giving my room to one of you doesn't solve the problem because it's a single and I'd have to share the double room. So the only solution seems to be for you two to share a room with a king bed and, if I can arrange it, a cot."

There was a moment of stunned silence. Sharing a room, possibly a bed, with Dana felt dangerous, but she'd rather share with her than with Millie. She turned to Dana. "Can you stand two nights in the same room with me?"

"I'll bet you snore, but I'll chance it." Leave it to Dana to use humor to break the tension.

"I beg your pardon." Callie sniffed. "Well, I'll only agree if you skip the loud parties both nights."

Dana pretended to think about it. "It will be boring, but I can do that."

Callie turned to Millie. "I guess we're good."

With a big smile, Millie pulled them into a three-way hug. "Thank you. I didn't sleep at all last night. I should have known you'd both be gracious and cover for our mistake. We'll refund you both for two nights lodging, of course."

"I don't know about Callie, but don't worry about a refund for me."

"Or me. You've taken good care of us, so forget it."

Back on the bus, Dana turned to Callie. "Are you okay sleeping in a king bed with me? It would probably be more comfortable than one of us sleeping on a cot."

Callie blushed. "A king should be large enough for us to sleep separately. Right?" She hadn't slept in the same bed with anyone since Abby needed a hospital bed to be comfortable. Hopefully she wouldn't automatically gravitate to the warm body in the bed.

"You're safe with me." Dana grinned. "But we can put a line of pillows down the middle of the bed to be sure."

Good idea. But would saying she wanted the separation reveal too much to Dana? Better to keep it light. "Sounds good. But your devious mind would probably figure out a way to breach the barricade and poor me would be helpless to fight you off."

Dana laughed. "Sounds like a plan."

"Argh, you're incorrigible." Callie leaned in and whispered, "I'd rather share two nights with you than with Millie." She blushed. It was true. Really true. But she hoped Dana thought she was joking.

Her face soft, lips hinting at a smile, Dana closed her eyes and didn't comment. What was Dana thinking? A surge of warmth shot through Callie. She closed her eyes, imagining tonight, allowing herself to feel the twinge of anxiety combined with anticipation.

"Okay, folks, we'll be entering the Sassi, the stones, in a few minutes. It's very dramatic. Don't miss it." Millie's announcement woke Callie. She opened her eyes, moved off Dana's shoulder, and gazed out the window. Dana groaned and stretched so she must have dozed off too. Callie's eyes widened. Though they'd talked about Matera being a UNESCO World Heritage Site, Callie hadn't pictured a magical city of gray stone houses carved out of the rocks, one on top of the other so that the roofs of some seemed to be streets for those above. It looked like something out of a fairy tale. Damn. Why did her treacherous brain have to flash on a picture of her in a cave, in a bed with Dana now? She blew out a breath. One step at a time. Bedtime was a long way off. And she'd often slept next to Dana in the bus and it hadn't been a problem. She'd be fine.

"Holy mackerel. This is fantastic." Dana leaned over Callie, trying to get a better view. "I can't decide whether it's menacing or beautiful." She pulled back with a mischievous grin. "Yep. I'll bet sleeping in those caves is scary. Don't worry, Callie, I'll protect you."

Callie elbowed her.

"Ouch." Dana rubbed her side. "What was that for?"

"You poke a bear and the bear pokes back. Now be good or you'll have to explore without me and you know that would be awful."

"I agree. Who else would put up with my pretending I know something about what we're seeing?"

Millie spoke again. "When we arrive at our hotel in a couple of minutes wait by the bus while I get your room keys. The rest of today and tomorrow are free. I've reserved a table for dinner in the hotel restaurant at eight tonight. Please text me by five to let me know whether you plan to be there so I can adjust the head count if necessary. Breakfast is served in the courtyard. Check your packets for information and call or text me if you have questions."

As they waited for their room assignments, Callie and Dana arranged to meet up with the group after going to their room to lighten their backpacks. The twelve of them would start out together and then, based on interest and or endurance, people would split off along the way. Callie loved that the group had come up with a way to include everyone but allow them the freedom to go it alone.

Millie handed out room keys. "The doors to all rooms open off a terrace or courtyard." As she took her key, Dana whispered, "We decided a king is big enough to share without crowding."

Millie looked thrilled. *"Voi due siete i migliori."*

Dana translated Millie's compliment. "You two are the best?"

Millie clapped. *"Molto bene."* She leaned in and spoke softly. "They just told me they don't do cots here so if you wanted one, I was going to have to go shopping this afternoon. Instead, I'm going to the spa. Ciao."

They walked up an outer staircase to a private terrace and stopped to take in the view before opening the door to their room. Callie was nervous but followed Dana into the dim room. Her jaw dropped. She hadn't expected an actual cave carved out of stone and lit by candlelight. The floor, arched ceiling, and walls were all stone. Though the floor and ceiling were smooth, parts of the walls were rough and unfinished, and other parts were polished and even. The high-end designer bed and other furnishings were rustic and suited the interior as did the soft white colors used throughout. It wasn't scary at all. In fact, the candlelight bouncing off the pastel stone was very…romantic.

She walked to the bathroom visible through the arched doorway. Large, soft-looking towels were piled on a block of stone and two robes hung from nearby hooks. It had a double stone sink, an open shower, and a sunken tub that looked perfect for two.

Callie felt a full body flush as her mind immediately furnished images of being in that tub, Dana embracing her from behind and gently kneading her breasts. She suppressed the moan prompted by the fantasy and cast a furtive glance at Dana. Also focused on the tub, Dana appeared flushed and her expression was...

Callie gasped. She must be having similar thoughts. Dana turned suddenly, her eyes wide, and gazed at Callie for a moment before looking away, and scanning the room.

"There are light fixtures and lamps so there must be a..." she said, her voice deeper than usual. She strode to the door and suddenly all the fixtures and lamps lit up and the candles went off. Dana had found the light switches and apparently the candles were electric. Callie relaxed. In the glow of the lamps and wall fixtures the room looked lovely, but not as romantic.

Dana dropped onto the love seat in the sitting area of the suite, pulled her bottle of water from her backpack, and took a long drink. "Do you think we can be comfortable here for two nights?"

Fearing she would give in to the need to touch Dana if she sat next to her, Callie sat on the bed. "Absolutely." She could endure anything for two nights. She'd lain awake many nights after Abby died, so she knew she could get by without sleeping. "We should go meet the others."

The group wandered through narrow alleyways up and down uneven paths and crude steps hewn into the rock, stopping occasionally to enjoy the view. Though they paced the walk to the slowest members of the group, the terrain required attention and walking was difficult. Carl and Loretta dropped out when Loretta fell onto the steps. Callie and Dana, who were walking behind her, helped her up and braced her between them. Ellie diagnosed a twisted ankle plus scraped knees and palms and insisted she accompany the older couple back to the hotel so she could wrap and ice the ankle and cleanse the scrapes. Callie and Dana supported Loretta going down the steps to the road, but Carl and Ellie insisted they could manage from there.

"Wait," Vanessa said. "I'm going back too. My fear of falling is causing my back to tense and making it difficult to enjoy what I'm seeing."

By the time they stopped for a late lunch, everyone was exhausted from the difficult terrain and the unexpected heat of the day. Being inland was a lot hotter than being by the sea. They chose a small restaurant on a terrace with umbrellas for shade and shared some pizzas and appetizers along with beer and nonalcoholic drinks. They relaxed and chatted for a long time about what it must have been like to live in a cave, not like they were going to live, but in the old days with no electricity or running water.

"The marvel of it all," Susan said, "is that the rooms inside the buildings are caves carved into the limestone cliffs. Think about the effort required to excavate one cave and then extrapolate it to this entire city. What an amazing feat."

As they neared their hotel, they encountered a group of three-wheeled vehicles with awnings, known as tuk-tuks, looking to pick up tourists for tours. No one else was interested. But Callie wasn't anxious to spend any more time in the room than necessary and Dana as usual wanted to see everything, so they stopped to get information.

Dana nudged Callie. "I've got this." She turned to a woman standing next to one of the tuk-tuks. *"Quanto dura e quanto costa."*

The rapid stream of Italian in answer to the question of how long and how much, went right over both their heads. They exchanged a bewildered look.

The woman laughed and responded in English. "Sorry, your accent was good so I spoke naturally. The cost of a forty-five-minute guided tour of the Sassi with stops for photos is thirty-one dollars each, a ninety-minute tour is forty-five dollars."

They opted for the longer time.

Thrown together on the sharp turns as they whizzed through streets and narrow alleys, places they would never have seen on foot, Callie ended up tucked against Dana and anchored by her arm. The close contact made her feel safe on the bumpy route.

The woman, Mari, spoke excellent English and was a terrific guide. She stopped often to point out a view or something unusual or share an interesting bit of history. It turned out she was a history and archaeological graduate student and extremely knowledgeable. Once she realized Dana was truly interested, she was more than willing to impart what she knew. They didn't go into the buildings or churches she stopped at, but she always described what she found exciting about the interior and suggested which ones would be worth revisiting on foot. She even marked them on Dana's map.

At one of the most picturesque stops, the Piazza San Pietro Caveoso, they got out of the tuk-tuk and followed Mari to the low wall overlooking the ravine bordering the Sassi. The view was breathtaking. Mari pointed out the dark eyes of the abandoned ancient caves dotting the cliff on the opposite side of the ravine and talked about some of the original inhabitants of Matera who had lived in them. Dana was enchanted with the history. Callie was enchanted with Dana. It seemed natural to lean into her with an arm around her waist.

Mari pivoted and drew their attention to the Church of San Pietro Caveoso on other side of the piazza.

"San Pietro is one of Matera's major historical attractions, but in my opinion the most interesting is behind it. Look up," Mari said. "That is the rupestrian church of Santa Maria de Idris. The inside is a cave dug into the large limestone rock. Originally there were many frescos, most, but not all, of which have been removed to protected environments to preserve them. On the left of the altar of Santa Maria is a tunnel that connects to the Crypt of San Giovanni, where valuable frescoes dating back to a period ranging from the twelfth to the seventeenth century are stored."

Callie stared at the church. It looked like a normal church, at least the entrance part, but then it seemed to grow out of the rough rock behind and towering high over it. A church in a cave. She'd never seen anything like it.

Dana frowned. "What does 'rupestrian' mean?"

Mari nodded. "It means art done on cave walls. Rupestrian churches were caves dug into the soft tufa that had frescoes painted on their walls. Matera has over one hundred and fifty rupestrian churches. They go back nearly a thousand years, from antiquity through the medieval period. This entire area of caves has been continuously inhabited since paleolithic times."

Before Dana could launch into her next hundred questions, Mari held her hand up. "We must start back now, but before we go would you like me to take a photo of you here with the ravine or the churches in the background?"

Callie had been taking pictures with her phone so she could refer to them while writing. She handed the phone to Mari. Without discussing it, they embraced and posed first in front of the ravine and then with the churches in the background.

Mari dropped them off in front of their hotel. "I am available all day tomorrow for a private tour if you would like."

"Would you do a group?"

"Yes, though the smaller, the better."

"What do you think, Callie?"

Callie had not only enjoyed Mari's presentation of a lot of information in an easily understandable way, but as usual, she'd enjoyed Dana's fascination with the subject. "Let's do it. Would you do a morning and an afternoon? We'd buy you lunch in between."

Mari grinned. "I'm not cheap."

Dana smiled. "Neither are we. What's your rate for the day?"

"Seventy-five euros an hour for up to eight people, more for more. Some attractions close for four hours in the afternoon, so the number of hours is up to you."

"You know, Dana, with Loretta's twisted ankle and the others who can't handle all the steps and the rocky terrains, we'll probably be nine or less."

"If you can work around the closures, try to avoid too many steps, and plan it so we visit the most wonderful places and see as much as we can, I'll make it a hundred euros an hour for up to twelve people, though as Callie says some may not come or only do part of the day."

"If you like, I would offer up to four of your people, the ones who can't do it on foot, the ninety-minute tuk-tuk tour during the four-hour afternoon break."

"That's terrific. How would you like the payment? Check? Cash? Credit card? I'll pay you after the morning tour and then at the end of the day."

Mari's eyes widened. "If you pay me in euros, I will love you for life."

Dana extended her hand. "It's a deal. Let's meet here about nine tomorrow morning." Mari shook hands, then sped away in her three-wheeled vehicle. "What do you say to a drink, then a long soak in the tub before dinner?"

Callie gulped. "Uh."

Dana's mischievous grin indicated Callie's attempt to hide her alarm at the suggestion was a failure. "Don't worry. I meant with bathing suits."

"Sounds good." Callie followed Dana into the cocktail lounge, glad for the dimness to cover the full body flush that seemed omnipresent whenever she was around Dana lately. Since she learned they would be sharing a bedroom, her mind had been running an almost continuous slide show of X-rated pictures. She was confident Dana felt the same way, but that only made her more anxious.

They were greeted with cheers. The group had convened for cocktails ten minutes before, but neither of them had checked their phones and they didn't see the group text. They sat at the table and both ordered beer. Dana raved about the tour they'd taken with Mari.

Callie waited until the questions tapered off before putting out the invitation Dana had asked her to extend. "Dana and I have hired Mari to give us a private tour tomorrow. We'll do a morning and an afternoon session, and since she says the group can be up to twelve, you're all invited to join us. And by the way, she offered a ninety-minute tour like the one we took today for up to four people who can't do the walking. That will be between the morning and afternoon sessions."

It was agreed that Carl, Loretta, Vanessa, and Serena would take the tuk-tuk tour, though Serena said she might also try to do the morning expedition. They were so into talking to each other and joking and teasing that they lingered in the cocktail lounge until it was time to go into the restaurant for dinner. Callie was relieved but disappointed that they'd avoided the soak-in-the-tub issue.

The candlelight dinner was served on the terrace overlooking the Sassi, a hauntingly gorgeous sight. Dana sat next to Callie, their arms and thighs casually touching. Callie joined in the conversation but spaced out from time to time when the contact with Dana increased, causing the always ready embers to flare.

She sighed. It was romantic, definitely romantic. Was it the candlelight? The overall atmosphere? The company of friends? Or the company of someone she cared about? Yes, she confirmed to herself, that was it. She cared about, for, Dana. And they would be sleeping in the same bed tonight. How could she not touch her?

They were dealing with their fears differently. Callie had pulled into herself as the evening wore on while Dana had expanded out, telling stories, listening and laughing with the group. And drinking. By the time the group headed off to their own rooms, Dana was flying high. With Ellie's assistance, Callie managed to get Dana to their room and onto the bed. "I can stay with her until she falls asleep," Ellie said.

Callie was glad she'd inadvertently switched the candles on because her sudden flush was hidden in the dim light. After an awkward few seconds, Callie explained about the room mix-up and the need to share.

Ellie's smile was sly. "Well then, she's all yours. See you in the morning."

And then they were alone in the room. The moment she'd feared all day. But she needn't have worried. Curled in the fetal position, Dana was sound asleep. No threat, no temptation. Staring at her in the warmth of the candlelight, Callie realized her feelings for this beautiful person went beyond sexual attraction. She felt protective and…loving. She hadn't expected to find love again. Tears trickled from her eyes. She wasn't sure whether she was crying for Abby or because she was happy to have found Dana. She removed Dana's shoes, then gathered her own pajamas and went to take a shower.

She was brushing her hair when a buzzing sound caught her attention. It seemed to be coming from Dana's pocket, probably her phone, but Dana continued to sleep peacefully. Callie leaned over her, figured out that the phone was in a pocket she could reach, and pulled it out. It was Ellen, Dana's attorney and best friend. Callie stepped into the bathroom and accepted the call. Oh, she hadn't notice it was FaceTime. "Um, hi. I'm Callie. Dana is asleep."

"Hi, I'm Ellen." The phone pulled back from Ellen's face. "And I think you know this woman."

"Hi, Angela." Angela's eyebrows shot up. She glanced at Ellen.

"Sorry, Cal, we didn't expect you to be…Um, this is awkward. Are you all right? It looks like you're in a cave."

Callie laughed. "I *am* in a cave, in a cave hotel in Matera. Check it out and you'll understand."

Angela looked confused. "Did I miss something? Are you and Dana sharing a room these days?"

Callie laughed, then explained. She walked into the bedroom and turned the phone so they could see Dana sleeping on the bed. "As you can see, nothing nefarious happening here."

"None of our business, right, Angela?" Ellen shifted the phone so Angela's smiling face was in the center of the screen. "Not our business, but I think we both wholeheartedly endorse any sexual thing you two want." Angela smirked.

"Leave her alone." Ellen smacked Angela's arm. "We had an appointment with Dana to talk business tonight. Tell her we'll talk tomorrow night. Good night, Callie."

Callie ended the call. At least it was both their best friends, so not too embarrassing. Angela looked relaxed, happy, and she and Ellen seemed connected. Was there something going on with them? She turned off the lights and climbed into bed. As soon as she closed her eyes, her mind filled with memories of the day. She smiled, crawled to Dana, a shape backlit by the bathroom nightlight, and lightly kissed her lips.

"Good night, sweetheart."

CHAPTER TWENTY-ONE

Callie stretched, opened her eyes, and rolled to her side. Dana was watching her from the other side of the bed. And she was wearing pajamas instead of the clothing she'd had on last night. Did that mean they'd…? Of course not. She wasn't the drunk one, so she would remember.

"Good morning, sunshine. Sleep well?" Dana didn't sound like she had a hangover.

"I did. What about you? How are you feeling?"

"Pretty good. When I got up to use the bathroom last night, I noticed a call from Ellen on my cell and since it was still early in New York City, I called her back. Angela was with her, and they told me they'd spoken to you about forty-five minutes before. After we talked, I took a shower, drank lots of water, swallowed a couple of Tylenol, and slept soundly the rest of the night."

"You were so buzzed last night I needed help getting you here. Just so you know, Dr. Eagle Eye figured out we're sharing a room and was smirking when she left."

Dana raised herself onto one elbow. "I'm sorry I flaked out on you. I was scared to share a bed with you, afraid what I might do, so I drank too much. Not consciously, of course, but I don't usually drink myself to oblivion so I'm certain that's why I did it."

Callie was moved by Dana's willingness to own up to her fears and her behavior.

"I was scared too. Abby and I always slept close, so I thought I might roll onto you or grab you in the middle of the night and get, um, intimate."

Dana rubbed her eyes. "You've probably sensed that I'm attracted to you, Callie. I know nothing can ever happen between us, but I thought I might lose control being in bed, so close to you." She sat up and reached for her phone. "It's almost dawn, want to go out to the terrace and watch the sunrise? It's private so we won't have to get dressed."

"That sounds great." Callie's heart flipped upon hearing Dana say aloud what they'd been dancing around for a while now. She sensed the intimacy and exposure were too much for Dana. She needed to break the tension.

They grabbed their jackets, shuffled outside, and shoulder to shoulder leaned on the wall, watching the sky slowly brighten. Callie's belly tightened. She was about to make her own confession.

"Why do you think nothing can ever happen between us? I'm attracted to you. I'm not ready to act on it just yet, but I'm hoping there's some kind of future for us."

She heard Dana gasp and felt her tense. Maybe she'd misunderstood. Maybe Dana meant she didn't want anything to do with her. She was after all, still dragging Abby's ghost behind her. She'd exposed too much.

Dana's gaze remained on the beautiful dawn breaking in front of them. Her voice was low and filled with pain.

"I'm not worthy of you, Callie. I don't think I've ever had a real relationship. In fact, I don't know how to love or even what it means to love someone. I've told you about myself, about how I live my life on the surface while I'm empty inside. Maybe we'd enjoy a couple of nights of hot sex, but why would you even think about a future with me?"

Tears tumbled down Dana's cheeks. Callie didn't know how to comfort her. Or whether her touch would be welcomed.

"You are so wrong about yourself. You're brilliant and kind and thoughtful and caring, yet you can be ridiculous and you're always fun to be with. Because of your gentleness and genuine interest in people you connect on a basic level with everyone, no matter how different. I've never met anyone so full of love. You have so much to offer."

The sun popped up and then—*whoosh*—a flock of screeching birds rose and swirled overhead, swooped, and dove around them before flying off.

Dana laughed and turned to Callie. "Lots of wing flapping and noisemaking. They seemed to like us. Do you think it was Abby?"

Callie was delighted that Dana didn't dismiss her fantasy about Abby watching over her. "Definitely. It was Abby signaling her approval. Obviously, she also thinks you're wonderful and loveable."

Dara stared at her for a second. "You think I'm loveable?"

'Yes." She took Dana's hand. "Let's get dressed and take a walk before breakfast. We can talk more about us if you feel up to it."

Callie turned toward the door to their room. Their room. She liked the sound of that. "C'mon. You can have the bathroom first." She patted Dana's shoulder as she moved past her into the bedroom. "You were funny and endearing last night, so you'd better brace yourself for lots of teasing over breakfast."

It turned out that neither of them was ready to say more than they'd already said, so they held hands and walked in comfortable, connected silence through the quiet of early morning Matera.

Ellie waved Callie over when they entered the breakfast area. "Sit and tell me how it went last night. Don't leave out the good stuff."

Callie shook her head. "Your dating fantasies are certainly different than mine, Ellie. Even if I was ready for a relationship with Dana, I would never have sex, forget make love with her, when she was drunk. That's pathetic."

Ellie covered her face and peeked between her fingers. "Sorry, Callie. Neither would I. Have sex with a drunk, that is." She dropped her hands and stared down at her plate. "I guess I'm rooting for a happy ending for you two to give me hope for my future."

"We're meandering, but we'll get there." Callie put her arm over Ellie's shoulders. "I thought I'd never be attracted to anyone but Abby. Be patient. You have a lot to deal with right now, but

I'm sure when you're ready your person will come along and scoop you up."

"Thanks for not treating me like the ass I am."

"You're welcome." Her willingness to take responsibility for her behavior, and her sense of humor were two of the reasons Callie liked Ellie.

Dana put a plate in front of Callie. "I got you some of your favorites to start." Their eyes met as Dana sat across from her. Dana's thoughtfulness was one of the reasons she was falling for her. Just one of the many.

"Hey, Dana…"

And so the ribbing started. Dana was a good sport and gave it right back until it was time to meet Mari. She had asked to meet the group in the courtyard of the hotel so everyone could sit while she gave a brief lecture about Matera's history before heading out. After greeting and meeting everyone, she started.

"The Sassi di Matera is a complex of fifteen hundred cave dwellings honeycombing one side of the steep ravine created by the Gravina River, which, you'll see, is now just a small stream. It is believed, though scholars still debate it, that Matera has been settled and occupied since the tenth millennium BC, making it potentially one of the oldest continually inhabited settlements in the world."

She stopped to give them time to absorb what she'd said. "Many of the dwellings are little more than small caves, and you will see that in some parts of the Sassi a street lies on top of the dwellings. It is estimated that only thirty percent of the Sassi is visible and the other seventy percent is underground."

"Did the people who dug these caves just die out and leave them empty?" James asked.

"No. The people of Matera lived in these caves in relative obscurity for centuries until 1945 when the Italian artist and author Carlo Levi published his memoir, *Christ Stopped at Eboli*, about his year of political exile in Basilicata under the Fascists. In it, he exposed the extreme poverty, lack of running water and electricity, the poor sanitation, meager working conditions, and rampant disease. There was an uproar in Italy and the Sassi became the shame of the nation. In 1950, Sassi residents were forced to abandon their homes and relocate to new housing built for them nearby."

"So did the government then bring in water and electricity and modernize the caves?" Fran asked.

"No. Toward the end of the 1950s several dozen young students who had grown up in the modern housing united to reclaim their heritage. Eventually these young people became part of the political class—lawyers, businessmen, et cetera—all with the shared goal of restoring the Sassi. At first they worked with volunteers clearing out caves and cisterns, then in the early 1980s the government got involved. Several years later a law providing protection and funds was passed. And here we are today." She waved her arms. "Come, I will introduce you to this wonderful historic place."

"It was exhausting, but worth it. Do you agree?" Callie asked. They were sprawled on their bed, resting after trudging three-plus hours around the Sassi with Mari. The group would meet for lunch after the others got back from the tuk-tuk tour.

"I do." Dana rolled to her back and closed her eyes.

Callie took advantage of the opportunity to study Dana up close. Her tanned flawless skin, soft, kissable lips, high cheekbones, straight nose, and round jaw added up to a strong but beautiful face. Callie closed her eyes and, lulled by the silence and the comfortable bed, drifted off until Dana's voice jolted her awake.

"Wasn't the reconstructed typical cave dwelling with furniture and tools of the time gut-wrenching? Seeing how whole families and their animals lived in one or two small cave rooms made me claustrophobic. And thinking about the smells, the lack of privacy, the lack of running water and electricity, the heat and the cold, and the unsanitary conditions made it more understandable that the government and the Italian people felt it necessary to rip these people from the only homes they'd ever known."

Dana yawned and stretched. "But with hindsight it's easy to see that instead of wholesale relocation the government could have installed electricity and running water and enforced sanitary conditions rather than wait almost thirty years to start to reclaim the area. What was your favorite place we visited this morning, Callie?"

"Materasum Ipogeo, the underground neighborhood inhabited by families sharing resources, things like cisterns, granaries, ovens, and churches. So huge. And so magnificent. I can't imagine what it took to dig such a complex underground structure."

"You sound as if you've caught the history bug."

"Not like you but I'm fascinated. Think about it. These poor uneducated peasants scraped homes out of the rock with rudimentary tools, built this underground community and who knows what else we haven't heard about yet. It was considered a national shame, but when you step back, it was actually an amazing feat. If they hadn't been so isolated perhaps they would have learned about sanitation and electricity and running water."

"It *is* amazing." Dana hesitated. "This is amazing too. Being together in our room talking about our day feels homey. Intimate." She flushed. "I've never experienced anything like it."

Callie gazed at Dana, not sure how much to reveal. Honesty, she reminded herself. "I feel it too. The intimacy. It's the good part of being in a relationship, either with a close friend or with a lover."

"I need a nap." Dana closed her eyes again. "Don't worry, I set the alarm so we can meet the others for lunch."

Callie understood Dana needed space after revealing her feelings. She found it difficult to share her own feelings, so it must be even more difficult for Dana who was experiencing real intimacy and closeness for the first time. Besides, they had another demanding afternoon among the rocks ahead of them.

Mari tailored the afternoon as mostly a walking tour, with occasional stops at some of the cave churches, including Santa Maria de Idris, where they saw the remains of ancient frescos. After two hours the group had had enough. Mari led them back to the hotel and joined them for a drink. Everyone was tired but happy. They'd seen and learned a lot about the Sassi. Those who'd stayed behind joined them. Callie was seated next to Carl. Dana was at the other end of the table peppering Mari with questions.

"Thank you for arranging the tuk-tuk tour." Callie started at the sound of Carl's voice. "Loretta and I had resigned ourselves to not seeing much of this place because of the uneven terrain, but Mari did such a wonderful job of showing us places and describing what life must have been like that I have a real sense of it. She even brought us to an easy-to-access cave and painted a verbal picture of how the people lived. It was wonderful."

"She's a wonderful guide. I'm so glad we found her." Despite her best efforts, Callie's gaze kept wandering to Dana, enchanted as always by her flashing eyes, her intensity, and her passion as she engaged with Mari. Would she be a passionate lover? She blinked. *Down, girl.*

"She's something, isn't she?"

"What?" Callie turned to Carl.

He jutted his chin toward Dana. "Our girl Dana. So enthusiastic, so interested in everything. Her zeal is contagious. She's like a magnet."

"I don't—"

"Come on, Callie." He gently elbowed her. "Even though it's been more than fifty years since I fell in love, I can still remember what it felt like, wanting to spend all my time with Loretta, not being able to take my eyes off her when she was in the room. Sometimes it seems like there's an invisible wire connecting you two."

"Is it that obvious?" First Ellie, now Carl. Knowing this group, they'd discussed it and everyone was aware of what she apparently couldn't keep off her face. "I'm starting to come to terms with my feelings, but I'm not there yet."

As if Dana sensed Callie's thoughts, she shifted her gaze from Mari to Callie and smiled.

"See what I mean. You two belong together." He laughed. "I'd love to see the expressions on my kids hearing me giving love advice to two lesbians, one a best-selling author and the other a millionaire entrepreneur. But they'll have to deal with the fact that this trip has been transformative for me. We never know what life has in store for us, do we?"

Callie thought about that. Would she have come on the Romantic Italy tour if she knew she'd find love among the ruins? Probably not.

CHAPTER TWENTY-TWO

Callie attributed the unusual quiet on the bus this morning to the steady downpour, the first real rain they'd had. She'd had a hard time waking this morning, a hard time getting out of bed, and an even harder time not rolling over to snuggle with Dana. She watched Matera disappear through the rain-spattered window with mixed feelings. Sharing the room with Dana had brought them closer, but neither of them was ready to move forward on the feelings they'd finally acknowledged. A couple of days relaxing at the beach would do them both good.

"Ouch." Callie rubbed her thigh and glared at Dana. "Why did you pinch me?"

"To wake you, of course." Dana seemed pleased with herself. "If you sleep now, you'll be groggy all day. Talk to me. Are you looking forward to Polignano a Mare?"

She was always groggy and sleepy on dark rainy days so she wasn't surprised the sound of the rain and the hum of the bus had lulled her to sleep. She drank some water and straightened up. "I had a great time in Matera, but I'm looking forward to the beach. Even if it rains every day, walking on the beach in the rain, doing nothing but reading and maybe a little writing, sounds like heaven."

"Me too. Matera is wonderful. But I love the water, and I'm looking forward to swimming in the Adriatic."

Callie loved that Dana was so flexible. Or was adaptable a better word? No, neither captured Dana. She'd recently come across a word that described her perfectly. She closed her eyes, visualizing the Wikipedia page. Ah, yes, Dana was a "multipotentialite," someone with many different interests and creative pursuits, someone with the ability and the intellectual or artistic curiosity to excel in multiple fields and pursue them sequentially or simultaneously.

"Hey, you're not falling asleep again, are you?"

"Just thinking." Callie wasn't ready yet to let Dana know just how often she was in her thoughts.

The mic crackled. "Okay, folks," Millie said. "The sun is breaking through, so I can honestly say we're approaching sunny Polignano a Mare, one of the most beautiful seaside cities on the coast of Puglia."

Dana's smile was as bright as the now sunny sky. She really loved this woman. *Wait. Love?* Was it possible to fall in love in just three weeks? Like the characters in her books? But that was fiction, not real life or real people.

She shifted so she could watch Dana's face as she listened to Millie describe the area and their next hotel and was surprised to find Dana watching her. They both quickly turned to Millie. "The Hotel Puglia a Mare enjoys a stunning location—"

"On a cliff," Dana whispered.

"Stop it." Callie squeezed Dana's knee as Millie continued.

"—on a cliff overlooking Polignano and the Adriatic Sea. It has a private beach, and all the usual amenities including a highly rated restaurant that serves locally caught fish and seafood as well as other traditional local dishes on a terrace facing the sea. It's just a few minutes' walk to the beach or the center of Polignano a Mare."

Millie paused.

"In keeping with the last few days, we'll have dinner tonight in a restaurant in a cave formed over a million years ago. It's considered one of the most romantic sites in the world. We'll be outside on the cave terrace and our reservation is timed to enjoy the sunset to the tune of waves crashing against the rocks. It's a dress-up restaurant, not gowns and tux formal but not casual either, so leave your shorts, jeans, chinos, flip-flops and bathing suits at the hotel. We'll go and return by our bus so please be outside by the appointed time."

Marian raised her hand. "Um, Millie, it's still early. Will we be able to use the pool?"

"Yes. I'll be passing out temporary passes so you can use the spa, fitness room, the pool, or the beach before we're checked in at four p.m. Your other options are to hang out in the lobby or the terrace café or walk into town. Look for me any time from four on and I'll have your room keys. And, since this is a romantic tour, I recommend you plan on taking time to watch the unbelievable sunsets." The mic clicked off.

Most of the group headed to the pool, but Callie and Dana went to the fitness center. After a half hour on the treadmill, Callie did a full free-weight workout, showered, and changed into her bathing suit. At the pool she dropped her backpack on a chaise next to Marian and dove into the water, swam a few laps, then dried off and applied sunscreen.

"Where's your honey?" Marian's eyes were hidden behind her sunglasses, but she was smiling.

My honey? After her talk with Carl yesterday, she realized it was pointless to act like she didn't understand the references to her relationship with Dana since their travel mates seemed able to read her like one of her books.

"In the fitness room finishing up her weight machine circuit."

"Need some help putting sunscreen on your back?" Marian extended her hand.

"Thanks." Callie handed her the sunscreen and swiveled. "You know we're not a couple, right?" She pulled her hair up to give Marian access to her back.

"Whether you acknowledge it or not, we all see you as a couple." Marian rubbed the creamy lotion in slow circles. "And speaking of couples, Lou and I are still trying to figure out what makes something romantic. Have you come up with an answer?"

"I'm realizing it's not one thing."

"Okay, we're done." Marian handed Callie the tube of sunscreen.

Callie dropped her hair and faced Marian. "It can be atmosphere like the candlelight in our rooms in Matera or it can be sharing something beautiful or meaningful with someone you...care about."

"Hey." Dana dropped her things on the chaise next to Callie. "I'm going to do some laps." Callie watched her dive off the side of the pool, pop up, and begin to swim. She was so graceful.

"Or new love."

"What?" Callie pulled her gaze from Dana.

Marian put her hand on Callie's knee. "I was referring to our conversation about what makes a place romantic."

Callie opened her mouth to protest her innocence, then reminded herself it was futile.

"Yes, new love definitely puts a romantic filter over one's eyes." Unsure whether to write in her journal, which had evolved from just story ideas to include her thoughts and feelings about Dana, or to read one of the books downloaded on her Kindle, Callie closed her eyes. Happily, Marian took the hint and didn't attempt to pursue the conversation.

"Callie." She smiled hearing Dana's gentle voice, but she was reluctant to leave her dream. "Callie." She opened her eyes. Dana was sitting beside her. "It's time for lunch and you're getting overexposed to the sun. How about grabbing a bite in the terrace café then exploring the town?"

Callie stretched to give herself a few seconds to squelch the urge to kiss Dana. She extended a hand and Dana pulled her to sitting position. "How long was I asleep?"

"An hour or less. I covered you with a towel, but you really should get out of the sun."

They gathered their things and went in search of the café on the terrace. Carl waved them over to the large, shaded table the group had taken over. As usual, Callie and Dana shared. They ordered an appetizer of mussels in a tomato, wine, garlic and basil broth, a main course of grilled octopus, fried calamari and shrimp, and, while they waited, nibbled on the olives and assorted marinated vegetables provided for the table.

"I'm afraid I'm getting used to this luxury lifestyle." Fran said, sipping her white wine.

"I'm afraid you are too," Susan said, poking her. "Along with the usual post-vacation adjustment to a new school year, we'll need to get used to doing our own cooking, cleaning, shopping, and laundry again."

Marian elbowed Lou. "We'll have to adjust to married life at the same time we adjust to not living in luxury."

Lou took Marian's hand and looked into her eyes. "I'm loving married life and our lifestyle is luxurious enough for me. But students seem to be getting more and more fragile and demanding every year so going back to work will be hard."

Callie opened her mouth to agree with the difficulty of having to adjust to a less luxurious lifestyle but realized there was no reason she couldn't continue to live this luxurious lifestyle in Italy. She had the money, the business of publishing was basically done online, and she was able to write anywhere.

Similarly, if Dana hired people to run her business day-to-day, she could afford to live this luxuriously anywhere she chose. She mentally slapped her head. Her subconscious already had them living together in Italy. She peeked at Dana. How would she feel about having her future planned for her?

Dana didn't comment. For obvious reasons, she'd only shared the drama going on in her business back in the States with Callie. She was considering stepping away from the company to go back to school. If she did study ancient history, would she be tied to the States until she received her degree? Could she study in Italy? Or would she consider spending half time in Italy? Callie shook her head. She really was getting ahead of herself.

Polignano a Mare was small but quaint and relatively crowd-free this early in the season. They wandered through the whitewashed buildings and web of alleyways in the lovely historic center, stopping to rest at one of the outdoor cafés in the Piazza Vittorio Emanuele II. As usual, conversation flowed between them, and as they walked, Callie threw out the question to satisfy her curiosity. "Would you ever consider living in Italy?"

Dana studied Callie before answering, as if trying to understand the question. "You've probably noticed I'm in love with the country, its history, its people and its language." She grinned. "But I have a lot to unravel and put in place within my company before I can think about making any serious life changes. That said, I've started looking into the possibility of studying ancient history and several of the most highly rated universities are in Italy. What about you?"

Callie's heart leapt. Maybe her fantasy was a possibility. She stopped moving and faced Dana. "I love it too. And I've been fantasizing about living here all or part-time." Their eyes locked. They both smiled and looked away.

Dana gestured to the bridge they were standing on. "This is the Ponte di Polignano, a Roman bridge. It's amazing how everything is so old in Italy." She looked toward the sea. "And I think that's Lama Monochile." The clear pristine turquoise water of the sea between two huge, magnificent limestone cliffs was filled with swimmers, some leaping off the cliffs at various levels, others wading into the water from the small beach. "I'm going to jump off those cliffs and swim there before we leave."

Callie felt the warmth that came when you love something about someone you love. Dana's delight and desire to experience everything and her enthusiasm were contagious, and even Callie, who was normally laid-back, was pulled in and experienced the joy of it.

Dana snapped a picture of Callie standing on the bridge with the water and cliffs behind her, then glanced at her phone before pocketing it. "We can check in any time now. Let's head back to the hotel so we can unpack, rest, and get ready for this evening."

Millie was waiting in the lobby. She handed them their room keys. "You're back to singles, but I have to warn you I found another glitch and you may have to share again."

"No problem," Callie and Dana responded simultaneously, then burst out laughing.

No surprise. As in all the other hotels, Callie's room was gorgeous and the view was even better. She considered her clothing as she unpacked. After shopping in Capri she'd bought additional better-fitting and more colorful clothing along the way for herself and left behind the too-tight, too-drab black or gray things she'd worn every day at home. She pulled her two black dresses from the suitcase. The one she bought online for the unveiling of Abby's memorial ceremony next month was too tight now, but the one she'd worn to Abby's funeral fit her again.

She held the funeral dress and memories of Abby's last days and the crushing pain of losing her washed over her. Clutching the dress, she sank into a chair, expecting to be overwhelmed by tears and a sense of desolation as usual. Instead, she felt sadness and the comforting warmth of her love for Abby mixed with the hopefulness of her new love for Dana. She was stunned by the shift.

A few minutes later she hung up the dress. She would wear it tonight. With a necklace, some bracelets, and a bright scarf, it would be perfect. She opened her second suitcase, hung up the blouses, sundresses, and slacks, and moved the folded things into drawers. The last item was the sapphire dress she'd discovered in her bag when she'd totally unpacked for the first time in the Cinque Terre. It seemed so long ago that Angela had encouraged her to take it, but it had looked horrible on her then and she was sure she'd never want to wear anything so bright again. When she called Angela on it, she'd confessed to sneaking the dress into the bag, hoping she would change her mind at some point on the trip.

She fingered the dress, held it in front of her, then slipped it on. Her eyes widened as she stared at herself in the mirror. The day she'd tried on the dress while packing she was skeletal and shrunken into herself. The dress had been at least a size too large and hung on her like a shroud and the beautiful sapphire blue had cruelly emphasized her pasty skin and hollowed out eyes. Now she was almost back to her pre-mourning weight and the dress fit her perfectly, hugging every curve and displaying just enough cleavage to tantalize. The sapphire was vibrant against her tanned and glowing skin and made her blue eyes sparkle and pop. Just like Dana's eyes would pop this evening. She hung the dress in the bathroom and turned on the shower to freshen it and steam out the few wrinkles. *Thank you, Angela.*

Callie was not disappointed. Dana's jaw did drop when she walked out of her room. She flushed but didn't comment. Was she speechless? Or did Callie not look as good as she thought after fixing her hair, doing her light makeup, choosing her jewelry, and shimmying into the glove that was her sapphire dress?

Dana seemed to have taken special care too. "You look beautiful," Callie blurted. The blue silk shirt she wore brought out the blue of her eyes and the perfectly tailored navy pantsuit subtly emphasized the best features of her body.

Dana's eyes fluttered. "Thanks." She cleared her throat. "I, uh… Don't move so I can…" She aimed her phone, snapped Callie's picture, and then held the phone so Callie could see the photo. "You look spectacular. That blue is definitely your color. And that dress is definitely…um, yours." Her voice was deeper than usual. Could Dana be feeling aroused?

Callie leaned over and placed a soft kiss on Dana's lips just as the elevator doors opened. *Oops.* The elevator was nearly full and the clapping and cheering indicated the crowd approved of the kiss. Trying to hide her smirk, she strutted into the elevator and faced the door. She side-eyed Dana and saw the same smirk on her face. Dana took her hand.

Callie was ready to skip dinner, take Dana back to her room, and make love to her all night. She'd spent enough time ogling her in her bikinis to be able to visualize the beautiful, strong body under the well-fitted clothing. Now she wanted to know how that body would feel naked against her, how responsive it would be to her touch, to her tongue. As she imagined lipstick images of her lips all over Dana's body she felt the color rise from her toes to her scalp. She didn't know whether to pretend it was too warm or just leave people to their own assumptions. One thing she did know: her writer's imagination had improved, because the scripts she was writing in her head were so much more developed than those she'd written when she was courting Abby. Is that what she was doing? Courting Dana? *Yes.* And Dana was courting her.

Getting into the bus was very different in a tight dress than in the comfy casual clothes she usually wore. As soon as they were seated Dana took Callie's hand again and held it in her lap on the short drive to the parking lot where the restaurant shuttle would pick them up. Callie was intoxicated and she hadn't even had a drink yet. She would have to watch her liquor tonight.

The Grotto Palazzese more than lived up to its reputation. A terrace inside a natural cave in a limestone cliff open to the ocean, it was dimly lit, magical, enchanting, elegant and, without a doubt, romantic. They were seated at a table near the edge of the terrace, immersed in the wonders of nature—the open cave itself, used as a restaurant continuously from the 1700s, the sound of the waves crashing against the rocks, the stunning views and smell of the clear blue water of the sea, and, as dusk fell, the seagulls swooping and swirling against the backdrop of the gorgeous colors of the sunset.

They were served a seven-course fixed menu with accompanying local wines. The dishes were a sophisticated mix of Italian specialties using local seafood, fish, and vegetables. Each course was delicious, presented beautifully and sized so that the seven courses were not overly filling.

Callie studied the group in the flickering candlelight, eating, drinking and talking together like a family or old friends. She had moved from a year of almost total isolation to living with these eleven strangers and feeling close to each and every one of them. She tried to focus. It would have been easier if she and Dana had been sitting next to each other, but they'd ended up at opposite ends of the table. She struggled to be present with Loretta, Carl, Serena, and James while images of her with Dana flashed in her mind and her eyes of their own accord sought out Dana. And every single time she'd glanced at Dana, she was looking at her. This thing between them, this attraction was heating up.

Damn but Dana was sexy. Was she feeling it? Callie felt warm, loving and a little dizzy. It was a good thing they weren't sharing a room tonight because either this place was so romantic it was turning her on or maybe the wine and the rich food was the culprit. In any case, her body was awake in a way that it hadn't been for at least eighteen months.

She gazed out at the sea, trying to remember the last time she and Abby had made love. It was the day she'd bought the dress she was wearing, she realized, one of the last good days before Abby's rapid decline and death.

"Are you planning to stay the night?" Dana's whisper in her ear ran through her body like an electric shock. It took a few seconds for the words to penetrate her foggy brain. Dana took her hand and pulled her up.

"Um, stay the night." Callie turned into Dana's arms.

"Why, Callie, I do believe you're drunk. Come on before the shuttle bus leaves without us." Dana sounded amused, not romantic.

Callie opened her eyes. Waiters were clearing their table for the next party. What had happened? "Oh, sorry, sweetheart, I must have spaced out for a second." Did she just giggle? No, she never giggled.

"Just let me guide you." Dana put an arm around her waist, pulled her close, and grasped her hand. As they moved through the restaurant, Dana's body heated every place it touched her. Outside, standing with her friends, their soft laughter and conversation swirled around her, but she could only lean into Dana and enjoy the tingling in her body.

CHAPTER TWENTY-THREE

Callie struggled to consciousness as if she were swimming through quicksand. She must have fallen in the bathroom and hit her head. It was pounding. She needed help. Afraid what she might see when she opened her eyes, she lifted one eyelid, then the other. She gasped. Dana was sleeping next to her. Covered by the sheet. Was she naked? It was too dim to tell. Callie jerked to a sitting position.

Oh, damn. She buried her head in her hands. And remembered. She drank too much at dinner. Way too much. Had she fallen asleep at the table? Had she and Dana…? She carefully lifted her head and checked. She was wearing her slip and underwear. She squinted. That spot of color on the sofa must be her dress.

"Morning. How are you feeling?" Dana stretched. The sheet slipped off, revealing her sleeping shorts and tank top.

"Not so great."

"I'll bet. I tried to get you to drink some water and take a couple of Tylenol last night, but the minute I sat you on the bed you passed out."

"So why are we in the same bed again?"

"You were so out of it I was afraid to leave you alone in your bedroom, so I brought you in here where I could watch you while I did some work. Don't worry, I was a gentlewoman."

"You're not the one I was worried about. Did I do anything to embarrass myself here or at the restaurant?"

"No. You were cute and cuddly, not loud or aggressive. But you should be prepared for some teasing this morning."

"Tell me."

"Nothing too bad. You were just very affectionate in the bus and the elevator. And, you demanded I take you to bed."

Callie covered her face. "Oh, no. I'm sorry."

Dana pried Callie's hands away from her face. "We're good. Don't worry. How did you end up drinking so much?"

"I'm not sure." Callie thought back on the evening. "They served so many different wines and the waiters were constantly topping off the glasses. I must have lost track of how much I was drinking. It was accidental, but it sounds like I embarrassed myself and this headache is still a killer. I apologize if I embarrassed you. Is it time to get up?"

"It's still early. There's water and Tylenol on the night table. Take that and try to sleep a little more. I'll wake you in time to get ready." Dana watched her swallow the tablets.

"Callie, time to get up." Dana's voice woke her. She opened her eyes. Dana was sitting next to her on the bed, dressed and ready for the day. Her headache was much better, but she wasn't sure she was ready for a day of sightseeing.

"The idea of wandering among cute stone houses doesn't fill me with joy. I'm going to skip today."

Dana laughed. "It seems like others in the group feel the same. They decided last night they'd rather spend the day outside on the water so they've hired a boat for the afternoon and we're invited as their guests." She looked at the clock radio on the night table. "It's nine now and we're not leaving until eleven. You can sleep another hour or shower, dress, and go down to breakfast with me."

Callie's gaze went to the door to the terrace. Another beautiful sunny day. Eating now would give her stomach time to adjust before they got on the boat.

"Breakfast. I need about twenty minutes to shower and dress. And speaking of dressing, please hand me mine so I can make the dash of shame to my own room."

Dana laughed and brought the dress and her shoes to her. "I'll check to make sure the coast is clear so you can dash next door in your slip."

Callie got out of bed. Dana had taken the dress off her so she already knew how tightly it fit but shimmying into it in front of her would be embarrassing. She dug into the purse Dana handed her to get the keycard for her room, grabbed the shoes, and placed the dress over her arm. "I'll pick you up when I'm ready. You check the hall and I'll dash." She stood behind Dana at the door.

Dana peered out. "Go."

The shower was restorative, and by the time she knocked on Dana's door the Tylenol had kicked in and she was almost back to normal. They were the last to arrive at breakfast and, as Dana predicted, Callie was teased about her condition last night. Apparently, she'd been all over Dana, whispering in her ear and trying to kiss her, something Dana had failed to mention.

Callie blushed but gave as good as she got, asking whether they could blame her and insisting they were jealous because she chose Dana and not any of them. Confirming that Callie was all right, Dana went to select items for their breakfast while Callie ordered their cappuccinos.

After a few more minutes of teasing, Millie asked for their attention. "I booked four hours on the boat as you asked, but the captain can extend an hour at a time it if you want to stay longer. You'll visit the caves in the area and swim. The boat will have paddleboards, noodles, air mattresses, and innertubes, enough toys to have a good time. Water and nonalcoholic beverages will be available throughout the day and they'll serve a light lunch. They provide towels but be sure to bring sunglasses, sunscreen, hats, a light covering, and anything else you need to be comfortable."

"Are you coming with us?" Serena asked.

"No, I'm doing a spa day."

"Taking a break from us?" Lou asked.

"Yes. Taking a break from you." Millie smiled. "Tomorrow instead of driving directly to Otranto we'll do the things we planned to do today and check into our hotel in Otranto after dinner in Lecce. Dinner tonight is on your own, so make a reservation in the hotel restaurant or try one of the places recommended in your packet. Any questions?"

She waited a few seconds. "Enzo will be in front of the hotel at 10:45 to drive you to the pier. Give him a call when you're on your way back to the pier and he'll pick you up. Enjoy your breakfast and have a great day."

The day was exactly what Callie needed. Naps in the sun combined with vigorous water play. Captain Paolo was terrific. He cruised along the coast, giving them a sense of its beauty and drama and stopping at caves and rocky outcroppings along the way so they could swim. At Dana's request, he stopped at the mouth of Lama Monochile.

"I'm going to dive off those rocks and swim. Who's coming?" Dana stood hands on hips, a challenge in her voice, looking sexy as hell.

All eyes were on Dana, Lou, Ellie, Fran, and James as they swam in and climbed the rocks, not to the top of the cliff but higher than Callie liked. She tensed. Her focus narrowed to Dana. Callie's breath caught as Dana's arms rose over her head and she dove off the cliff. A beautiful dive. When Dana's head popped out of the water, Callie took another breath. She turned to Serena, who had the superzoom lens on her professional camera focused on the five adventurers. "I'd love copies of those pictures."

Serena continued to snap until all five were in the water. "Sure."

Callie relaxed and watched the five swim a bit, then tensed again as they climbed back up to the ledge. They dove again, high-fived each other in the water, and swam to the boat. Callie reached for her journal and her pen.

Watching Dana dive off the cliffs in Polignano is a turn-on. She is fearless and a naturally charismatic leader who inspires without trying. I admire her more and more each day. And each day, I fall deeper and deeper in love.

She stashed the journal and pen in her backpack and tracked the adventurers swimming to the boat. They were all smiles as they climbed aboard.

Her gaze on Callie, Dana grabbed a bottle of water. Callie's thumbs-up was rewarded with a huge grin. Dana turned to Carl.

She must have invited him to join her in the water, because he put on his life jacket, tossed his tube in, and slipped off the platform.

Dana talked nonstop, arms waving, and Carl laughed and splashed her, and some of the others joined in the water fight that ensued. They all loved seeing the sights and learning the history, but no question the water was this group's happy place. And Dana was lead water nymph. They would have to live near a lake or the ocean. *Oops.* She was getting ahead of herself again. But she was catching up.

"What are you looking so happy about?" Ellie dropped into the chair next to Callie.

Ellie was another one transformed by this trip. At the start she seemed unhappy and depressed. Who wouldn't be after being dumped without discussion by their spouse of eighteen years? And now, she seemed like the attractive, aggressive, confident surgeon she probably had always been. At this moment she looked pleased with herself.

"I was thinking that this group's happy place is the water. We enjoy all the sights and the history and the great meals and the luxury, but we seem to burst with happiness in the water."

"You're right. Even my sister blossoms in the water. Look at her having fun. She's always so focused, so serious. This trip, this group, has done wonders for both of us. She and James seem to have really hit it off and her softer side, the part that got hidden after the death of her husband, has emerged again. I hope they continue to see each other when we get back to Chicago."

She accepted a bottle of water from a member of the crew. "Thanks." She took a long drink. "Our gal Dana is responsible for the spark, the energy that motivates all of us. It wouldn't have occurred to me to dive off those rocks if she hadn't challenged us to do it, but you know what? I feel terrific about accepting the challenge and doing it successfully. Twice. It reminded me of how I feel facing a difficult surgery and the exhilaration after. Serena encouraged me to take the tour and I agreed because I wanted to run away and hide. I was broken when I arrived. I never expected to heal and find myself again. That's what this group has done for me."

She struck a pose. "Recovered surgeon. Maybe I should ask Millie if they want to put me in their brochure?" They burst out laughing.

Callie and Dana were lounging on the terrace in Callie's room with a beer, rehashing the day.

"You're right, Callie. My favorite place is in the water. I've thought from time to time about buying a second home on a lake or on the ocean, a place to enjoy the water, read, write, and recuperate from the pressures of business. I don't think I admitted to myself that I needed to get away from the demands of my social life, but that was part of it."

"But you didn't?"

"Sandy and our friends would never leave the city unless they were going to someplace where they could rub elbows with the rich and famous, and I was afraid I'd be alone and even more lonely than usual. Have I told you how much I love being with you because we can read, write, sketch, or just be silent together?"

Callie smiled. "You have. And I feel the same way."

That evening the group ate at a small family-owned cave-like restaurant near the beach in Polignano. It wasn't a real cave like the fancy one last night, but the group shared many different dishes, the seafood was super fresh, and everything was cooked perfectly. Relaxed and sated, they chatted as they walked back to the hotel.

Callie took Dana's hand. "I'm amazed of how fond I've become of everyone. And even more amazed that a random group of twelve people has become so close. I feel like I'm with family."

"Not quite what it was like in my family," Dana said softly. Hearing the sorrow in Dana's voice and feeling the energy leave her body, Callie brought them to a halt.

"It sounds like you had an unhappy childhood. Want to talk about it?"

Dana shook her head. "I'd rather not. At least not now. This group is the family my family has never been. And I feel like I'm becoming the person I might have been had I had love and support from those who should have given it freely." She shrugged. "What was your family like?"

Callie really wanted to hear about Dana's family but she knew Dana would talk about it when she was ready.

"There are five DeAndres. Mom, Dad, then me, Todd, and Brooke. Mom taught third grade. Dad was a mailman. We lived in a three-bedroom house in a small town in New Jersey and were the kind of family that had dinner together every night, shared our days, and talked about books and things happening in our community." She paused. "I guess that's why the group feels like family to me. My parents are both retired now and live in California near Brooke and her family. I'm still close to them, but while I forced myself to speak to my mom once a week during the year I was in mourning, I asked Brooke and Todd to get updates from her." Callie kissed Dana's knuckles. "I'd love to hear about your family some time when you feel like talking about them."

Dana's phone alarm buzzed. "You're not the only one." She turned off the alarm. "My therapist has been encouraging me talk about that very subject. And that was a reminder for my therapy session in a half hour."

CHAPTER TWENTY-FOUR

Callie woke with Dana snuggled in her arms, her head tucked into her neck, her warm breath comforting. She lay still, enjoying Dana, the soft in and out of her breath, the feel of their bodies melded together, the smell of her shampoo and soap, and the sight of her relaxed in sleep. She smiled. All her senses were tuned in to Dana. Well, not all. Taste would have to wait. She'd been aroused since yesterday and sleeping with Dana had turned up the heat.

She still wasn't sure it was possible to fall in love after knowing Dana a little more than three weeks. But she'd known almost immediately with Abby, so maybe three weeks wasn't so fast. She hadn't been touched in so long. Could she be feeling lust, not love? Whatever it was—sex or making love—would wait until they were both whole. Passion, not neediness, would lead them.

Poor Dana was needy last night. She'd been surprised to get a call from her, sobbing and asking her to come to her room. She was even more surprised when she got there and found that Dana was still in her Zoom session with her therapist. Jean hadn't wanted Dana to be alone after they said good night and had suggested she call someone she trusted to be with her. Dana had called her.

That level of trust overwhelmed Callie at the same time as it confirmed for her that they were both feeling love and trust. And, she, a sense of completeness that she'd been missing since Abby's death.

Callie was curious about the memories that were so painful that Dana's therapist felt she needed someone to hold and comfort her, but after the therapist ended the session Dana was exhausted and fell asleep almost as soon as they got into bed. And Callie wasn't far behind. She would wait for Dana to share if and when she was ready.

Dana opened her eyes and quickly rolled off Callie. "Sorry. I didn't mean to crowd you."

Callie heard Dana's discomfort. "You didn't crowd me. Remember I promised to hold you?"

Dana looked away. "I remember. About last night. I don't want to talk about it. I need time to process everything."

Callie touched Dana's chin and turned her head so they were face-to-face. "Hey, it's me. You don't have to talk about it now. Or ever."

Dana's eyes filled. "Thanks." Her breathing was the only sound in the room. "I'm going to take a shower and get dressed. Wouldn't want to miss the cooking class." She rolled off the bed and attempted a smile.

"So I'm dismissed?" Callie attempted to defuse the tension with humor. "I didn't realize you were the type to lure women into your bed, then toss them aside in the morning. I guess I'll go to my room and get ready for the day."

Judging by Dana's face, she didn't get the joke.

"The tossing aside was a joke, Dana. We're still good. I hope." She got out of bed. "Knock when you're ready to go down for breakfast."

"Callie?" Dana strode to the door and hugged her. "I'm sorry for being an ass, but I don't know how to handle all my thoughts and feelings. Thank you for rescuing me last night." She leaned in close, clearly intending to kiss Callie, but hesitated, giving Callie a chance to withdraw. Callie leaned into the kiss. It was brief but tender.

Callie could see Dana struggling to be present and engaged as usual during breakfast, so she jumped in to divert attention away from her by telling funny stories about her abortive cooking experiences. She could fry an egg, boil water, and cook pasta that she served with sauce from a jar, but that was it. Abby didn't cook because, well, because people of her class just didn't, so they paid someone to prepare and serve dinners. They sometimes managed cereal or toast and eggs for breakfast and sandwiches for lunch, but they often ate both breakfast and lunch out. She was pleased with herself. Not only had she covered for Dana, but she even got her to laugh a couple of times.

Of course Eagle Eye Ellie saw through her ruse and zeroed in on her as they left the breakfast area. "Dana seems withdrawn this morning. Did you two have a fight?"

Callie knew Ellie would persist until she got an answer. "She's dealing with some personal issues she isn't ready to talk about." She hoped that would keep Ellie from pressing Dana.

They had a couple of hours before their noon cooking class and most of the group headed to the pool. When Dana suggested they go to the café overlooking the water to read and write, Callie remembered Jean, Dana's therapist, suggesting Dana take some time today to write down her thoughts and feelings about what had come up during therapy. She happily accepted Dana's suggestion now. Not only did she want to stay close to Dana, but she wanted to write down her own thoughts and feelings about her part in Dana's therapy session.

They ordered cappuccinos, took out their journals, and each focused on writing. From time to time they looked up, locked eyes for a moment, then went back to their journals.

Our connection is strong even without words.

The thought surprised Callie. But it was true.

I love her when she's strong and when she's needy, when she's smiling and when she's sad. I'm amazed to love again.

The cooking class turned out to be fun. Having something physical to do and something new to master seemed to pull Dana out of her funk. They learned to make typical Puglia pasta, with varying degrees of skill. Of the men, Carl did the best, and of the women Dana and Ellie, the two most competitive, excelled.

At the end of the class the pasta was cooked and served as part of their lunch. As usual, there was much laughter and Dana seemed almost back to herself. Callie again wondered what terrible experiences digging into her memories had brought up for her. She might never know, but she was happy Dana was so resilient.

Back at the hotel, Dana suggested they put on bathing suits and walk on the beach. Callie knew Dana found it easier to talk while walking. She changed into her bikini, put on sunscreen, grabbed a shirt and hat, and knocked on the door to Dana's room. They made their way down to the beach, headed to the water's edge, and walked with their backs to the sun.

Dana broke the silence. "Thank you for covering for me this morning at breakfast."

Callie considered denying it but thought better. "You're welcome."

"And thank you for not pretending you weren't making yourself a target to give me some space." Dana took Callie's hand. "Is this okay? Touching you calms me."

Callie threaded her fingers with Dana's. "I like it too."

Callie enjoyed the warm sun on her back, the water sloshing around her feet, and the sense of togetherness she felt as they silently strolled down the beach. Dana didn't speak again until they reached a part of the beach with fewer people.

"I've felt alone my entire life. I've been lonely my entire life. Until I got to know you and the emptiness filled, I thought everyone felt that way. But I've also felt worthless and unlovable for most of my life and that hasn't changed. I went back into therapy to work through my feelings of not being good enough for you."

Callie had a lot to say about those last two sentences, but this wasn't about her so she went with silence and kept walking.

"Last night I told Jean how the group of people on the tour feels like a loving family, something I didn't have growing up. She asked me again to talk about my family and I recalled some things I'd repressed."

"You don't have to tell me this, Dana."

"I do. But stop me if it's too much for you." Dana closed her eyes for a second. "She said start anywhere, and Sharee Wright's face popped into my mind. I was a high school freshman. She was a junior. We were both on the basketball team. She was one of the most popular girls, the team star, pretty, smart, nice, and from one of the wealthiest families in town. I was madly in love with her.

"She didn't know I existed until one day I noticed her pacing around her car as I was leaving school. I asked if I could help. She laughed and said she doubted it. Her car wouldn't start. Growing up with six older brothers taught me two things, how to play basketball and how to fix cars. I fixed her car and she insisted on driving me home. After that, she was friendly during practice and sometimes sat with me at lunch. In bad weather she often dropped me off at home.

"The nicer she treated me the more enamored I became. I convinced myself she felt the same. One rainy day she offered me a ride. Her best friend and her football player boyfriend were making out in the back seat. Stupid me took that to mean Sharee intended us to do the same. I made what I thought was a cool move and put my hand on her thigh while she was driving. She pulled over, put her hand on mine, and said, 'What are you doing?' Totally misunderstanding, I leaned in and tried to kiss her. She pushed me away. Still not getting it, I said, 'I love you.'

"The couple in the back sniggered. She moved my hands into my lap. 'I'm sorry if I gave you the impression that I'm into girls, but I'm not.' She wasn't mean or nasty, she was matter of fact, not judgmental, but the two in the back seat started calling me names like dyke, cunt, a piece of shit not worth the dirt under Sharee's feet and other things I don't remember. She told them to cut it out, but I was stunned and embarrassed so I got out of the car and started walking. The guy came after me and attacked me, punching, then kicking me when I went down. I heard Sharee screaming, but by the time she pulled him off me, I was bleeding from my nose and lip, had cuts over my eyes, and was doubled over on the ground throwing up. I must have passed out, because when I opened my eyes, at least as far as they would go, I was in Sharee's arms, looking into her worried face. 'I'm taking you to the emergency room. Alan'—she lifted her chin toward the guy sitting nearby with his head in his hands—'is going to pay whatever it costs, but if you tell them what happened, he'll get into trouble.'

"I tried to nod, but it was too painful. 'I'll say I didn't see who did it.'

"She stayed with me in the ER, paid the bill, then drove me home and told my two brothers who were there that I was attacked by a couple of guys but couldn't identify who they were. They were so relieved I wasn't raped that they never pressed me on it. And neither did the police. Sharee visited me at home a few times until I was fit to go back to school. We never talked about my coming on to her or the attack. She was still friendly but the rides home and eating lunch together stopped.

"I don't think she said anything, but despite my covering for Alan, I believe he and Alison spread the word. Though I'd been too geeky and weird to be popular, I did have friends, but when I returned to school bruised and battered not one person asked what had happened. Even the outcasts avoided me. Worst were the comments said just loud enough for me to hear but not know who said them, things like dirty lezzie, pervert, and descriptions of what should be done to people like me."

Callie took Dana's hand. "Did you talk about this to anyone? Your parents, one of your brothers, a teacher, or a school counselor?"

"Last night was the first time I told anyone. In fact, I was surprised when Sharee's face popped into my mind. I hadn't given her or what happened a thought since I left town the summer before my sophomore year."

"You moved away?"

"My dad had a massive heart attack at work and died. The boys pulled straws and my youngest brother, Derek, got the short one, so I went to live with him. He's twelve years older than me and worked in construction during the day and played bass in a band at night so he wasn't around much. He and the others made sure I had money and occasionally one of them took me out for a meal but for the most part, I was on my own. I started at a new high school where I didn't know anyone. I was friendly but avoided making friends. I threw myself into studying and spent all my free time reading and fooling around on the computer. I think that's why I was able to get a full scholarship to Stanford."

"What about your mom?"

Dana chewed her lip. "She died three days after I was born so I never knew her."

"Was her death related to your birth?"

"I killed her. Apparently when she found out she was pregnant her doctor advised her to have an abortion because her health was precarious. But I was the girl she'd been waiting for and she insisted on going through with the pregnancy. She lived long enough to hold me and name me, but childbirth was too much of a strain."

"I'm so sorry, Dana."

"It's all right. I never knew—" She burst into tears.

Callie held Dana while she sobbed. Finally, she caught her breath and dried her tears on the tail of her shirt. "Sorry, I don't know why I cried. I never knew my mom."

Callie knew why. Unexpressed feelings.

"Were you able to talk to your dad and brothers about her? Maybe an aunt?"

Dana lifted a shoulder. "I don't have any aunts or uncles. Eric, my oldest brother, got drunk at my dad's funeral and told me Dad blamed me for my mom's death. He told my brothers to put me up for adoption or raise me themselves but he didn't want to have anything to do with me. The boys weren't sure what to do, so they paid a neighbor with four young kids of her own to take care of me until I was old enough to go to day care. Two or three of them always lived at home and they took care of me the best they could. I have no memory of the woman or anything until I was about six."

They started walking again.

"Jean helped me understand that I feel guilty because my mom died giving birth to me, that my dad's rejection made me feel worthless, and that, while my brothers provided the necessities, none of them took responsibility for me so I was essentially alone. That was when she said I shouldn't be alone and suggested I call someone I trust."

"And you called me. I'm honored. I couldn't be there for that fourteen-year-old girl, but I'm here for you now."

"Everybody would have been better off if she'd had an abortion." Dana sobbed again.

Callie pulled Dana into her arms. "Don't forget that your mom chose to have you, knowing she might die giving birth." She kissed Dana's forehead. "And I, for one, would not have been better off if you hadn't been born. Whether it was the universe or Abby that brought us together, I'm so happy we found each other. I'm just sorry your mom didn't live to see you grow up and become the remarkable woman you are. I'm sure she would be proud." Callie kissed her forehead again. "And for the record, I have no qualms about your worthiness."

Dana leaned back and searched Callie's face as if confirming she meant it. "You're the only woman I've let myself want since Sharee. The women I've been involved with, including Sandy, all came after me. I've never been as open or as vulnerable with anyone as I have with you. But I'm damaged, and I have work to do so I can be fully present. Confronting the past is painful, but I believe you're worth it so I hope you're all right with waiting for me."

Dana brought their lips together briefly, then pulled away to look at Callie. Seeing a welcoming smile, she leaned back in and kissed her with passion. Callie returned the kiss. And the passion.

CHAPTER TWENTY-FIVE

Callie remembered her doubt that first day when Dana reassured her that seating on the bus would be no problem. And it hadn't ever been. No matter what, no matter how close they got, no matter how much fun they had at their last stop or their hotel, everyone always took the same seats on the bus. Such a smart lady. And so much more. She tightened her arm around Dana's waist and shifted to keep her from bouncing around in her sleep.

Callie was sorry to be leaving Polignano, but that wasn't new. So far she'd been sorry to leave every place they'd visited and had loved the next place, so she didn't doubt she would be happy in a new hotel in a new place tonight. Dana's gentle breathing in her ear was comforting. And a turn-on. Between Dana's Zoom meetings with Angela and Ellen, the hours she spent checking on the activity in her company's computer systems, and her recently added nightly therapy session, she didn't get a lot of sleep. And, Callie assumed, the nightly therapy probably brought up issues that made sleep difficult during whatever time was available.

"Arriving in Alberobello in ten minutes, folks." Millie's quick announcement woke Dana and, from the flutter of movement behind them, others.

Dana rubbed her eyes. "Sorry. I toss and turn all night, yet the minute I'm next to you on the bus I conk out on top of you."

"It's probably the movement." Callie loved being so close to Dana. It brought out her protective feelings and she found herself kissing the top of Dana's head frequently.

After the bus stopped, Millie stood. "We'll meet back here in two hours. Set your timers. I'll be sitting at the café over there. Join me or text if you need me."

They stood in a clump, staring at the strange little houses. "Looks like a freaking theme park," Carl muttered, and they all laughed. *Exactly.* Because of its large concentration of "trulli," whitewashed stone structures with conical roofs, Alberobello was a UNESCO World Heritage Site. But it didn't look real.

"Where are the Hobbits?" Vanessa giggled.

"Wait a second," said Fran, the architect. "They may look cute to our jaded eyes, but from an architectural perspective, trulli are really interesting. They were built to be easily dismantled, using local limestone boulders and drywall or mortarless construction—which is a prehistoric building technique still in use in this region."

"Why would you need to dismantle a house?" James asked.

"Money, of course," Fran said. "The feudal lords in the 1500s ordered the peasants to build their houses without mortar so if the king ordered an inspection they could be quickly dismantled and the landowners could avoid paying taxes on them. They built this way until the 1700s when the king made Alberobello a royal town and it was no longer subject to the whims of its lords. Despite being built to be temporary, hundreds of trulli are still standing all over Puglia, especially here." She waved her hand in the direction of the thousand trulli. "And Carl's theme park comment is to the point. These are mostly gift shops or B&Bs rented to tourists who want the experience of sleeping in a trulli. No one lives here." She took a deep breath. "Okay, that's my spiel. Why don't we walk around see them close up."

"There's another section nearby where people actually live in the trulli." Dana blushed. "I read that somewhere."

Fran nodded. "I read that too. We can wander over there, if you'd like. And I also read that it gets really crowded here as the day goes on, so I suggest we get moving."

An hour and a half later everyone had joined Millie at the café and was relaxing with cold drinks in front of them.

"I'm glad we came to Alberobello," Callie said. "It's unusual and very pretty, but after you've seen one trullo, you've seen them all."

"I agree." Dana had been quiet as they meandered through the streets lined with the neat white, pointy-topped trulli. "Alberobello is pretty and an interesting oddity for tourists to visits. I'm glad we came. But what fascinates me is the ingenious ways poor, uneducated peasants adapted to their environments. Think about it. The trulli, built with rudimentary tools using the materials at hand, were designed to be easily dismantled yet have survived intact for centuries. Some are still lived in today. And the peasants in Matera, again using rudimentary tools, dug caves in the rocks to make homes that are still inhabited, though not by the peasants. It's amazing."

"I see a PhD dissertation in your future, Dana." Vanessa laughed. "You have definitely been bitten by the history bug. I'd be happy to write a recommendation to go with your application."

"So would I." The academics in the group spoke as one.

Dana stood and bowed. "I'm seriously considering it, so I may take you all up on your offers." She turned to Millie. *"Dove andremo dopo?"*

Carl punched her shoulder lightly. "Damn, I'm impressed. Three weeks and already speaking the language."

Dana laughed. "Yes. At the level of a two-year-old Italian." She grinned. Knowing the importance of speaking the language, she and Callie had reconciled themselves to sounding like children while they were practicing.

"Abbi pazienza, Dana," Millie replied. "Be patient. You'll get there. But to answer your question, Locorotondo is next. It was voted one of the most beautiful small villages in Italy. We'll take about an hour to wander around and then continue on to Lecce, a beautiful baroque university city for lunch, sightseeing, and dinner." Millie stood. "There's Enzo with the bus. Time to go."

Once they were settled, Dana read from the daily packet. "'Archeological finds at the site of Locorotondo indicate it's been settled since between the third and seventh century BC. Now it's known for its wines and its beauty. It was built on a circular plan with narrow concentric streets and alleys lined with white pitched roofed terraced houses unusual for Italy.'"

Dana frowned. "So why did they build those roofs? And why would they build it circular?" She reached for her notebook. "This country is fascinating. Whether I go for a degree or not, I'll study its history." She clicked her pen and started writing.

Callie enjoyed seeing the ruins and learning about the citizens of the various ancient civilizations, but she didn't share Dana's passion for history. And though she'd loved Abby's passion and dedication to the study of birds, she hadn't shared that either. Dana's passion would make her a wonderful professor, like Abby had been. Although she hadn't thought about it before, she was obviously attracted to passionate women. Abby's passion had infused their lovemaking. She assumed the same would be true of Dana. She gazed out the window at the countryside, at the intermittent trulli, at the vineyards and olive groves all against the blue sky she'd come to expect.

She blinked. They were approaching a blindingly white city on a hill surrounded by a wall. She poked Dana and pointed out the window. "That must be Locorotondo."

"Wow." Dana looked up from her notebook. "It's not so far from Alberobello. I've noticed lots of trulli on the drive so you would think the two would be similar. Though now that I think of it, 'not far' for us would probably be a very long way in ancient times. But I still wonder why they built such different homes." She shook her head and jotted a note.

Callie laughed. "Vanessa was right." She narrowed her eyes and touched her temple. "I, too, see a dissertation in your future."

Vehicles were not allowed in the historic district of Locorotondo, so Enzo dropped them off nearby and they walked in. The streets, really walkways, were a narrow circular labyrinth, the houses were all whitewashed and sparkled in the sunlight, and red geraniums were on every balcony and in front of every door. It was unlike anything they'd seen in Italy. Like Alberobello it was too neat, a bit unreal, like a movie set. Yet also magical and beautiful. Most of the houses had been renovated and were part of a horizontal hotel, so there were tourists and a few residents but not a huge number, at least that Callie could see. It reminded her of photos she'd seen of Greek islands, except no water was in sight.

It was like a maze. They followed the walkways, entered dead ends and backed out, stumbled across restaurants with a few tables outside, until eventually they emerged into Piazza Vittorio Emanuele, the elegant main square, and off to the side a small park that seemed to be frequented by locals and tourists.

They met Millie in the park, as planned, near the short wall overlooking the valley.

Callie and Dana stood shoulder to shoulder on a natural balcony that offered a panoramic view of a valley dotted with trulli, scrub forest, and vineyards surrounded by stone walls. Their hands brushed as Dana pointed to the fortified farmhouses found on the estates in this region. Overcome by the sheer beauty of the vista, Callie gave in to her need to touch Dana and entwined their fingers. She was rewarded with a gentle pressure, the heat of Dana's body as she leaned in, and a soft smile acknowledging the contact.

This was romantic. And Callie felt it from her toes to the top of her head. She'd slowly come to believe that what people found romantic was personal, not universal. And for her, it was sharing something beautiful and meaningful with...Dana. *All right*, she acknowledged what she was feeling again. But could she trust that feeling?

Back on the bus, Millie asked for their attention. "Just a few notes. Lecce is very different than any city we've seen in southern Italy. It's called the Florence of the south because of the rich baroque architectural monuments found here. But it's no imitation Florence. Its Baroque architecture, known as *Barocco Leccese*, is unique, intricate, and lyrical. Most of the many churches and buildings and the sculptures decorating the beautiful facades in the old town are made from Lecce stone, a soft, local limestone that has a unique, warm golden hue.

"I could go on and on, but I think it best to let you discover it yourselves. Your packets include what I consider 'don't miss' sights, but there are amazing sights around every corner so just strolling around, if that's what you choose, will still fill you with joy. Lunch is on your own, so I included some restaurant recommendations. We'll meet at eight for dinner at the restaurant noted and then go on to our hotel in Otranto. Everything is marked on the map."

They milled around a few minutes after the bus dropped them off, figuring out who was doing what before they split up. The group consensus was lunch, then sightseeing. Callie craved time alone with Dana, but Dana was always hungry and would probably opt for lunch with the group. As if their connection needed confirmation, Dana whispered, "Are you okay with spending the day alone with me? We can walk for a while and find a place to eat lunch by ourselves."

Callie felt the smile split her face. "Absolutely."

"All righty, folks, Callie and I are going off by ourselves. The historic center doesn't look that large on the map, so I'm sure we'll catch up with you somewhere along the way."

Disregarding the hoots, whistles, and lovebird comments, they walked away from the group and turned right onto the first street they encountered. Dana seemed deep in thought. Callie assumed she was thinking about how this city differed from the others they'd visited today. "All the buildings look golden. Is it me or does it seem magical?"

"Magical and romantic." Dana took Callie's hand. "Is this okay?"

Callie brought Dana's hand to her lips. "It's perfect." Their eyes locked for a second and Dana flashed the sweetest smile.

They strolled through the narrow, winding cobblestone streets, passing row upon row of buildings built with the rich, earthy-colored stone, and balconies displaying pots of multicolored geraniums. They let the city seep into their pores, listened to the sounds of birds, the clanking of silverware, and the low rumble of conversations from small sidewalk cafés. They inhaled the smells of cooking and coffee and admired the glowing buildings. They hadn't walked together like this since Rome. But there she had run away when their travel mates thought they were a couple. Now she wasn't running.

They stopped at a small restaurant with a few shaded tables outside, ordered sparkling water, a carafe of the local white wine, an antipasti platter, and two local specialties—fava bean puree with chicory and pasta with broccoli rabe.

They ate slowly, shared bites of the food, and talked about the beauty of Italy. Dana marveled at the wonder of the three towns they'd visited today. "You know, I'm in love with Italy, particularly the south. I'd love to live in Puglia. Could you be happy there?"

All ambient sounds drifted away, leaving a deadly silence.

Jane froze. Is Morgan asking her to live with her in Puglia? No wait, this is about her and Dana.

Was Dana just making conversation? Or, if she was asking her to live in Italy with her after only sharing two or three kisses... didn't she find it strange? A few seconds passed before Callie dared look at Dana, who was staring at her with a soft smile and loving eyes. She exhaled. And suddenly they were surrounded by noise again.

"Puglia would be perfect. But anywhere near the water with you would be wonderful." Callie smiled. "Let's get the check and continue walking."

They clasped hands and walked, turning down random streets until they stood with jaws hanging open in stunned silence. "Whoa." Dana regained speech first. She looked at the map in her hand. "This is the Basilica of Santa Croce."

Callie still hadn't pried her eyes off the magnificence before them. "It's breathtaking. Look at the dragons, griffins, bears, and men supporting the balcony on their shoulders. And just about every inch of the façade is decorated with figures of sheep, weird mythical birds, cherubs, and, maybe, dodos. How did they carve them so lifelike? It must have taken years."

Dana consulted the notes on her phone. "You're right. It took more than a century to finish the church. Apparently the limestone found exclusively in this area is so soft and pliable that stonemasons can create the embroidery-like carvings and the precise sculptures of flowers, fruits, vegetables, figures, wreaths, and spiral columns we see here. But listen to this. Once Lecce stone is exposed to air and the elements, it loses its suppleness, becomes durable, and lasts much longer than other types of limestone carvings. I guess that's why the work hasn't deteriorated."

Callie gazed in wonder. "I've never seen anything like it."

"Neither have I."

Callie took some phone photos and Dana used her more powerful camera to take closeups of particular sculptures. Then Dana took Callie's hand and they continued walking.

"I have the same question I had earlier today. How did three relatively close communities develop such different architecture? Why is Lecce more like a northern city than the others? It's so interesting. Did I tell you that Mari, our guide in Matera, said Sapienza University in Rome is the number one college in Italy to study classics and ancient history? Harvard, Yale, Oxford, and Cambridge also rank in the top ten."

"You're serious about applying?"

"I am. But I have to get rid of Linda and Artie and hire and train replacements for the three of us before I commit to anything else. If I can get a good candidate to replace me it would be a lot easier." Dana turned to Callie. "Ellen has suggested I hire Angela as my replacement."

"Really? She's been so busy we haven't had much contact in the last few days. I don't know what the job entails, but I do know you won't find a more capable, loyal, honest employee. Does she know you're considering her?"

"I don't think so. Client confidentiality is important to Ellen, so even though they're into each other, I trust Angela doesn't know. I've interviewed the top candidates and she's definitely the best. I'm going to offer her the job. I hope you won't say anything."

Callie's eyes widened. "You've been doing job interviews at night? No wonder you've been so tired lately."

"Between the therapy, the job interviews, strategy sessions with Ellen and Angela, and romping through my computer systems every other night or so, I've been awake into the wee hours." She shrugged. "Enough about me. We have wonderous sights to see."

"So where are you applying?"

"I'm hoping for Sapienza, but if not there either somewhere else in Italy or England. I want to be near the places I'll be studying."

"So you might be studying in Rome?"

"If all goes well, yes." She cleared her throat. "I'm hoping you'll join me at some point. Does it matter where in Italy?"

Callie squeezed Dana's hand. "I can write anywhere. And the business of publishing is all virtual these days."

Dana's face lit up. She leaned in and kissed Callie, not a deep passionate kiss, but a tender kiss that promised more to come. And then the cheering and clapping started. They jerked apart. Ellie, Serena, Loretta, Carl, Vanessa, and James surrounded them. Carl stood between them and draped his arms over their shoulders. "Don't let them get to you. They're just jealous. It's wonderful to see you both looking so happy."

"I agree." Serena snapped a picture of the three of them. "And I got a great picture of that kiss."

Callie couldn't decide whether the heat she felt was from embarrassment, sexual turn-on, or being embraced by Carl in the heat of the day, but she knew the teasing came from a place of caring.

"A photo can't replicate the feeling of kissing Dana, but please send me a copy anyway."

Laughing along with everyone else, Ellie took pity on them. "Come on, let's leave the lovers to their…whatever." She started to move away. "But if you're still interested in seeing the sights, ladies, turn the next corner and take a look at the Piazza del Duomo. You won't be disappointed."

Carl kissed them both on the forehead. "Go in peace and in love, my children." He laughed and walked away with the group.

Dana stared after them. "I imagine this fond teasing is what one endures growing up with lots of siblings and other relatives."

Callie put her arm around Dana's waist and steered them toward the corner. "I had a little of that with my brother and sister, but you didn't, so enjoy it now."

They stood in the center of the airy, spacious piazza, and Dana read from Millie's notes.

"The bell tower, the seminary, the Bishop's Palace, and the cathedral with a façade facing the piazza and another looking westward are all superlative examples of the lecce baroque. It's magical at night, because the lighting highlights the golden color of the stone and, get this, the sensuous lines of the buildings."

Callie studied the buildings. "They're beautiful and I appreciate the baroque façades, but I don't see sensuous lines, do you?"

Dana gazed at Callie. "Truthfully? The only sensuous thing I see in this piazza is you."

If these blood-heating moments kept coming, Callie would be burnt to a crisp by dark. People always said she was pretty, intelligent, and nice, but no one had ever said she was sensuous. At least to her face. Callie leaned in and kissed Dana more intensely than earlier. Someone nearby whistled, but she was distracted by the gentle probing of Dana's tongue. She opened her lips. And enjoyed the sweetness of Dana as their tongues touched and swirled around each other. When they broke for air, she wasn't sure where they were or how long they'd been kissing, but her body was on fire. She blinked. Focused. They were on the street. She thought she couldn't possibly get hotter, but the giggles of the two teenagers being rushed away from them brought another flash of heat, this time a blush of embarrassment. "Dana. We're—"

Dana backed away. "Yeah. I'm so sorry. I didn't mean to—"

Callie placed a finger on Dana's lips. "You didn't do anything. I'm the one who started it." She looked around. A few amused faces. A couple of smirks. "Let's get out of here."

Dana looked at the map. "How about we find the Church of Saint Clare? From what I read, it sounds as if it's worth going inside."

Neither spoke as they followed the map to the church. Callie was glad for the time to pull herself together. What was she doing? There had been plenty of sexual tension and passion with Abby, but she'd never felt this...this wanton with her. Dana's surprisingly erotic kisses stoked her lust. And her body hadn't wanted to stop.

Forcing herself to do some breathing exercises and focus on their surroundings, she side-eyed Dana. As far as she could tell, Dana seemed equally discombobulated by the kiss. At least she wasn't the only one.

By the time they arrived at the church, Callie had regained control and focus. They paid the fee and stood just inside the entrance trying to take it in. Dana spoke first. "Lecce keeps astounding."

"It's the baroque. It's extravagant. We're not used to such ornate work." Callie's eyes swept the church. It was over the top and beautiful at the same time, sort of how she was feeling about the kiss. "I don't know that I could live with it in my home, but I really like it here." They started with the main altar, then stopped to study each of the six side altars. "I'm in awe. Every surface and niche is embellished with swirls, twisting columns, and ornate statuary. It must have taken a small army to decorate this place."

"Wow," Dana said. "The beams on the ceiling and all the statues are made of paper-mache, not wood." She read from her phone. "'The craft of *cartapesta*, paper-mache, is unique to Lecce in Puglia and was developed in response to the expanding demand for religious statues and monuments in the seventeenth and eighteenth centuries. Since artisans in the region didn't have access to the traditional and expensive materials like marble and bronze or the tools necessary to work with those materials, they were forced to find a new medium and turned to papier-mâché.'"

She spun around. "Don't you find this fascinating? It's another example of Italians adapting to their environment."

"This is…mind-boggling." Callie gazed at the ceiling, then moved to examine some of the larger statues. "These are stunning." She took pictures with her phone as they moved around inside the church. "I'm ready for a cup of coffee or a drink, though."

"Me too."

Dana took out her map. "Millie noted that the Piazza Sant'Oronzo has lots of cafés and restaurants and is considered the center of Lecce's old town. And it overlooks a second-century Roman amphitheater. It's close. Let's head there."

Callie expected part of a wall and maybe a row of seats, not the intact small portion of the second-century AD Roman amphitheater right there in the piazza. It wasn't open to visitors, so they leaned on the railing surrounding the partially exposed amphitheater and marveled at it.

At a nearby café they each ordered Lecce's specialty coffee, espresso over ice with almond milk. While they sipped their drinks, Dana read from Millie's notes.

"No one knew the amphitheater was under the ground until 1900 when construction workers excavating to build a bank uncovered it. Estimates are that the full theater could hold fourteen to twenty-five thousand people. Can you believe they actually hold musical and other events here now?"

Dana was adorable when she was fired up over history.

"Yes, I can."

They listened to the rapid-fire, lyrical Italian conversations floating around them and talked about what they'd seen, as the color of the surrounding buildings slowly shifted with the changing light. Though neither mentioned the kisses or the feelings percolating underneath their conversation, Callie was having a hard time keeping her eyes away from Dana's lips. They'd talked about living together and kissed twice in the streets of Lecce today. And she wasn't panicking. Was Dana? Bathed in the soft light of the setting sun, Dana looked happy, not fearful.

The restaurant Millie had chosen for dinner specialized in "cucina povera," the regional cuisine based on the way the poor cooked of necessity. The group shared a variety of Lecce's specialty dishes made with fresh, simple, and cheap local ingredients. Everything from crunchy fried pasta to horsemeat.

Only a few brave souls tasted the horse meat. From time to time, Dana offered her fork with some delicacy she wanted Callie to taste. She took the fork into her mouth and slid the tidbit off, keeping her eyes on Dana as she slowly chewed. Dana held her gaze. It felt sensual. She knew the others were watching, but she really didn't care. Dana's flush was the only thing that interested her.

The dessert, a pastry filled with custard, was scrumptious. But for Callie, the highlights of the meal were the intense connection she felt with Dana, the delicious warmth where their legs pressed together, and the feel of Dana's hand on her thigh. She wasn't sure which of them had initiated the contact, but it heightened her awareness and meant she was totally present for the teasing and commentary that accompanied each dish.

CHAPTER TWENTY-SIX

They leaned into each other in the bus, fanning the embers that had been smoldering all day. Ready to burst into flames, Callie was happy that by the time they straggled out of the bus Millie was standing in the lobby of the hotel with their room keys in hand.

"Tomorrow is free, but Enzo is available to transport you back to Lecce or to the beach. Just let me know whether you need him. And don't forget, the next day we're traveling from Otranto to Taormina, Sicily, and we need to get on the road early in order to make our late afternoon ferry reservation. I'll text reminders, but please allow time for breakfast and be on the bus before we depart at seven a.m."

Leave it to the universe to toy with them. Not only were she and Dana the last to receive their keys, but it took forever for Millie to answer questions and chat with the others.

Finally in the elevator, Callie closed her eyes. Judging by the heat emanating from Dana's body and her flush, her need for Callie was as undeniable as was Callie's need for her. They stumbled out of the elevator into a blessedly empty hallway and moved quickly to Callie's room. Callie was shocked when Dana brushed her lips lightly, said, "Good night, Callie," and started to turn away. *No, no, no.* She wasn't sure whether she'd said it out loud, but she grabbed Dana's arm, holding her in place while she waved her room key over the card reader. The lock clicked, the light turned green, and she pulled Dana inside with her.

"What is it, Callie?" Dana sounded alarmed.

The door clicked shut behind them. Callie's heart pounded against her ribs. She cupped Dana's chin, stared into her eyes, and, seeing the reflection of her need, pressed their lips together. Dana put a hand on Callie's chest and pushed gently. Oh, God, had she misinterpreted the signs?

Callie withdrew. "Is this all right?"

Breathing heavily, face flushed, heat radiating from her body, Dana nodded. "More than all right. But are you sure? I don't want to do anything that will cause you to feel guilty in the morning."

Callie was relieved. It was only Dana being Dana, thoughtful, considerate, caring, one of the reasons Callie adored her. Adored her? Yes, she did. Right now though, she needed the other part of Dana. Her passion, the part Callie knew was there, but Dana only expressed in relation to ruins and history.

"Are you freaking serious? Don't you feel it? If we don't do something to quell the fire flowing through my veins and the drum beating between my legs, I think I'll die."

Dana's eyebrows shot up. A grin split her face.

"It would be my pleasure to stoke, I mean quell the fire and, um, check the problem between your legs."

Callie's fingers traced that grin, then leaned in to capture Dana's lips. She'd missed this, the wanting, the intimacy, the love.

Dana was an expert kisser. Their tongues danced together like ballerinas, circling, touching, together, apart. Dana tasted of wine and garlic and something sweet. And though she would love to kiss all night, her whole body was throbbing now. She needed more.

Apparently so did Dana. Those long beautiful fingers slipped underneath Callie's sweater and caressed her bare skin. They both moaned. And then with no fanfare, Dana unhooked Callie's bra, freeing her breasts, then cupped her hand around one and gently rubbed her thumb over the nipple.

An exquisite spike of pleasure shot through Callie, weakening her knees, but strengthening her need. Panting for air, frantic to touch Dana, she pulled at her shirt and tugged at the buttons on her pants. Dana trapped her hands between their bodies.

Still kissing, still caressing Callie's breast, Dana slowly propelled them across the room until Callie tumbled onto the bed. Dana crawled on top of her. Her lips swollen, her eyes glassy, love and raw want painted on her face, she stared into Callie's eyes and then feathered her jaw with soft kisses.

The fire inside Callie flared. She started unbuttoning Dana's shirt, but her fingers were clumsy and she ripped it open in frustration. Buttons flew in all directions. "Get these damn clothes off before I tear them to shreds."

Dana pulled back. "Okay, tiger." She slipped off the bed, shrugged her shirt off, pulled her sports bra over her head, and started undoing her belt.

Instantly, Callie was on her feet in front of Dana. "I'll do that." She undid the belt, then the single button, and pulled down the zipper. With her eyes on Dana's face, she pulled her pants down, letting them pool at her feet. She cupped Dana through her soaked boy shorts, then knelt and peeled them off.

She'd seen this lovely body before, albeit with the good parts covered by a bikini, but she'd never touched the nearly flawless skin, never breathed in its inherent fragrance. Callie's body burned, but she wanted to go slowly, to kiss and touch and love every inch of Dana. She reached up and squeezed her breasts, ran her hands over her stomach and her ass, then buried her nose in Dana's crotch, inhaling her arousal. She nipped Dana's thigh and pushed her onto the bed. Dana's eyes glittered in the dim light as she watched Callie slowly undress herself.

Watching Dana watch her fanned the flames of Callie's desire. They moaned in unison as their naked bodies met for the first time. And then the gentle ballet of their tongues changed to a tango, each vying to be the one to give pleasure to the other. They kissed and rolled and bit and touched. Callie had missed this, the passion, the loving.

"Let me make love to you, Dana."

She looked panicky. "I've never..." Then, as if she sensed Callie's overwhelming need, she nodded.

Callie trapped Dana's hands under her, then kissed her eyes, her nose, her jaw, her lips, her neck, and down to her breasts. She kissed each breast, then wrapped her hand around one and took its nipple into her mouth. She could feel Dana's heart pounding under her hand.

Dana thrashed and moaned. "God, Callie, I'm on fire."

Callie hesitated. "Are you still okay with this?"

"Now you ask?" Dana laughed unsteadily. "Stop at your own risk."

Callie got to her knees and kissed her way down to Dana's crotch and slipped between her thighs. Once again, she buried her nose in the wetness, then entered her, first with her tongue, then with a finger. Dana bucked and pushed herself into Callie's face.

Drunk on Dana's smell and taste and feeling powerful, Callie added another finger. Using the bucking and pressing of Dana's body to guide her, she licked and sucked as she slowly moved her fingers in and out. Dana's breathing sped up. Callie felt herself nearing orgasm, but she focused on Dana, on what she needed, until Dana stiffened and screamed.

"Callie, Callie, oh God, Callie."

With her fingers still inside Dana, Callie used her other arm to hold Dana close as her body tensed, trembled, then relaxed as the aftershocks of the orgasm rippled inside and outside of Dana.

Dana was still, then she pulled Callie up and kissed her deeply. Dana's face was wet. Not sweat. Tears.

"What's wrong?"

"Nothing is wrong." Dana seemed to glow. "Everything is right." She raised herself on her elbow and gazed into Callie's eyes. "I'm pretty sure I just had a huge orgasm. And I've never had one before."

Callie was shocked. "What?"

Dana kissed her tenderly. "I've never felt about anyone the way I feel about you. I've never trusted anyone the way I trust you. I've never opened myself, made myself vulnerable, to anyone but you. I didn't know sex could be this way."

"That wasn't sex, Dana. I made love to you."

"That's why it felt different. We were making love." Dana grabbed Callie and flipped her. "My turn."

Callie touched Dana's face. "I came when you came. I'm fine."

"You might be fine, my love, but unless you'd rather skip it, I need to make love to you."

Callie rarely came more than once, but her orgasm hadn't stopped the drumbeat in her core. "I'd like that."

Dana's lips and her warm breath against her skin traced an agonizingly sweet path to her mouth. Her kisses were like butterflies, light and fluttery, then her tongue joined the party and gently swept Callie's lips until they parted. Callie moaned. Dana's kisses were deep and intense and communicated all the love she hadn't spoken of yet. Callie shuddered as her arousal came to a boil again.

Dana's hands explored Callie's body, fingers and lips touching her everywhere, tracing delicate paths across her face, her neck, her shoulders, her breasts, her stomach, and descending to her hips, her thighs, and her calves. It was torture by loving. Callie felt as if she was floating. Now the throb of arousal drumming in her center had spread through her body, and she was on edge with anticipation.

Dana seemed to sense the shift. Her hands and tongue continued the sensual massage, moving upward, increasing the pressure, but avoiding the places on Callie's body that were screaming to be touched. When Dana stretched on top of her, breasts to breasts, stomach to stomach, thighs to thighs, Callie moaned and shifted, trying to get Dana to ease the throbbing. Dana kissed her breast, licked it, and then sucked the nipple into her mouth. Callie whimpered. The feelings were excruciating and pleasurable at the same time. Dana grinned. "You like that?"

Callie rolled her eyes. "Oh, yeah."

"Then I'd better do the other one too." She shifted to the other breast and made love to it. Callie was aware she was moaning, but she had no control over any part of her body. Dana raised her head and held her gaze as she slowly slid down Callie's body. She positioned herself between Callie's legs, stretched a hand up to massage a breast, then using her mouth, her tongue, her breath, and her fingers, she pleasured Callie.

Happy to be proven wrong about never having more than one orgasm, Callie snuggled next to Dana and dozed. She woke and watched Dana sleep for a while until desire overwhelmed her again. Dana moaned softly as Callie covered her body with soft kisses, but her eyes popped open when Callie's tongue stroked her clitoris. It didn't take long for Dana to experience another orgasm and turn the tables on Callie. They alternated dozing and making love until the early hours of the morning, slept a few hours, and picked up where they left off.

They spent their free day in bed, making love, dozing, talking, and eating meals ordered from room service.

CHAPTER TWENTY-SEVEN

Callie woke with the alarm in the dark, her first thought about the ticking of a different clock. Five days from today they would fly home from Catania. At least that was the plan for the tour. But she wasn't ready to leave Dana now and couldn't imagine being ready in five days. Should she try to convince Dana to stay longer?

Dana moaned and opened her eyes. "It can't be time to get up."

"It is." Callie kissed Dana. "Good morning." Embers quickly turned to flames again as tongues got involved and the kisses became passionate. Callie pulled away. "We'd better get moving. We still have to pack and we should have breakfast before we begin the trek to Taormina."

Dana moaned. "Can't we just stay in bed for the rest of the trip?"

"We could, but then we wouldn't have a chance to say goodbye to everyone. Besides, if we sleep on the bus we'll have energy tonight."

Dana pinched Callie's leg. "Great idea. Let's get going." She got out of bed, grabbed her clothing from the floor, and pulled on her pants and buttonless shirt. She put her jacket on to cover the shirt. "I can't find my underwear. Pack it in your suitcase if you find it. I'll knock when I'm ready." She dashed for the door.

Callie showered and dressed, quickly packed her things and Dana's underwear, locked her suitcases, and left them in the entry for Enzo to pick up and load onto the bus. Aware that she and Dana were glowing, Callie steeled herself for the inevitable teasing. But because of the early hour, everyone was sleepy and breakfast was all business with little conversation and none of the usual good-natured joking. Callie was thrilled that no one noticed and happy to not have to deal yet with the intrusive outside world.

The group filed out of the hotel and into the bus like zombies, everyone yawning and moaning. Though Callie was dreading the long hours in the bus only broken up by bathroom breaks, lunch, and the hour or so ferry crossing, it meant that she and Dana could be close all day, their bodies, hands, heads touching as much as they desired—though they would have to be careful to remember where they were. Callie was asleep before the bus left the hotel parking lot. She woke several times to find either she was sprawled on Dana or Dana was sprawled on her, and immediately fell back to sleep.

Millie woke them after two hours. "I know you're sleepy, but we're stopping for a bathroom break. We'll be there for twenty minutes to give you time to pick up coffee at the café, but I encourage you to use the time to exercise, walk around, do some stretches, whatever feels good, because otherwise you'll be stiff and uncomfortable by the end of the day. We'll stop again in two hours."

The group grabbed coffee and was sitting outside with it when Dana began to do yoga stretches. Callie and Ellie followed her lead and, in a few minutes, the entire group was stretching with them.

They got some weird looks from other people stopping at the café, but that didn't deter them. Back on the bus, they agreed they would stretch each time they had a break.

At the next stop, Dana insisted others take turns leading the stretching with her and everyone took a shot at it, some accompanied by much laughter. In the bus Callie and Dana held hands, read and wrote and dozed. After lunch Callie was awake enough to make the first note in her journal.

We made love for the first time in Otranto, the night before last. We couldn't get enough of each other, and, except for dozing and room service meals, we were at it until this morning. It was fantastic. D even more passionate than I imagined. And what joy knowing she experienced her first orgasm with me. I am definitely head over heels in love. How lucky am I to have found such love, such passion twice?

"We'll be at Villa San Giovanni where we catch the ferry to Messina in about twenty minutes." Callie was shocked. The day had flown by.

Millie continued, "Crossing the Strait of Messina takes about thirty minutes but loading and unloading vehicles adds considerable time to the trip. Once we're in line you can get out and stretch or run to the loo, but please stay close to the bus so you can get in when we start loading. After we park on the ferry, you're free to go up on the deck until they make an announcement about going back to vehicles."

She stopped, seemed to consider a thought, and then went on. "I want to thank you all. Usually this day is a nightmare for me and Enzo. Even though we warn people about the length of the drive when they sign up for the tour, I always get a million complaints and some people get nasty. But you all rolled with the punches and entertained yourself. You are by far the best group I've ever had the pleasure of leading. I've never had a group that got on so well together, one that included everyone. Except for the incident at the very beginning, we've had no interpersonal problems. And none of you has ever kept the bus waiting. I appreciate you."

They cheered, whistled, and clapped. Millie smiled. "Drinks and dinner are on me tonight." That got a laugh because that was true every night. She switched off the mic, then switched it back on. "I almost forgot. As you know we Italians are not into orderly lines and that applies in spades here, so Enzo will be jockeying to get us on and also off the ferry. You know he's a great driver, so don't get anxious if you see vehicles headed right for us. Trust him."

She wasn't joking. Getting onto the ferry was a scary experience. It was right up there with the Amalfi Drive as a white-knuckle event. But they made it without incident.

After strolling around the deck, Callie and Dana considered going back to the bus and making out, but they decided it was too high-schoolish. Besides, Enzo would probably be there guarding the luggage. So they held hands at the railing and watched the lights of Messina as they approached Sicily.

"How would you feel about sharing a room in Taormina?" Dana sounded tentative, but Callie had thought the same thing. They were two consenting adults, so there was no need to hide the fact that their relationship had reached the place that everyone had assumed it was during the last two weeks.

"I had the same thought. Let's talk to Millie."

The air was fresh and invigorating, the setting sun was gorgeous. And it seemed natural to kiss. They were really into it when Callie became aware of people standing around them. She pulled back. "We're busted, Dana."

"What?" Dana opened her eyes. "Oops."

The group laughed. And offered their congratulations. Ellie grinned. "I thought you guys were acting different this morning, but I chalked it up to not enough sleep. But I'll bet you two had even less sleep than the rest of us."

Both their faces were flaming, but they made no effort to deny it. Dana put her arm around Callie, pulled her close, and smiled sweetly.

On the way to the bus they spoke to Millie about sharing a room for the rest of the tour. She laughed. "Funny you should mention it. Taormina is the other place that was booked incorrectly so it's already arranged. And, uh, congratulations."

CHAPTER TWENTY-EIGHT

"The Sant'Andrea Palace Hotel is in central Taormina, near the ruins of a Greek theater and in walking distance of everything else. It has three restaurants an outdoor pool, a spa, a fitness center, and a sauna. Your rooms all have a terrace or a balcony with spectacular views of the sea, the town and Mt. Etna," Millie announced. "The rest of today is free. Tomorrow we drive to Palermo and stay overnight. The day after we get back we'll tour the ruins at Siracusa and stop at a Mt. Etna winery. I want to send you home sun-drenched, relaxed, and happy so I've hired a boat for our last full day in Taormina. Our final day we'll leave right after an early breakfast for the airport in Catania, where you'll catch your flights home. Now I know you're tired after traveling all day, so I've arranged an early dinner at the hotel for tonight. Let me know at dinner which, if any tours, you'll be joining."

They stood in the entry to their room, suddenly shy with each other. Their four suitcases were stacked on the luggage racks, so it was official. They were a couple. Callie glanced at Dana. They'd made love. But were they together?

Dana cleared her throat. "Sharing a room feels different than it did in Matera. Then we were friends. But now we've...we're...are we a couple?" Blushing, she faced Callie. "I'd like to think we are."

Callie cupped Dana's face and looked into her blue-gray eyes. "So would I." She smiled as the tension melted away, and they both leaned in for a kiss, then another, until breathless they pulled away. "I've been dreaming all day of picking up where we left off this morning, but I'm tired and grimy after being cooped up in the bus all day. How would you feel about a shower and a nap before dinner?"

Dana ran her hands down Callie's body. "Shower together?"

Callie laughed. "If we do that we'll never make it to dinner and we won't have energy for what I plan to do to you tonight."

"In that case, do you want to take the first shower?"

When Dana crawled into bed to nap, Callie rolled into her arms and settled with her head on her chest. The steady thrum of Dana's heart, so unlike the pounding beat in the midst of lovemaking, lulled her, but sleep did not follow. Her mind wandered to Abby.

After she graduated from college, she'd taken a full-time job as a barista in the off-campus coffee shop where she'd worked throughout college. The pay was low and she was forced to live with three roommates to get by, but it left her free to write. The September morning she met Abby, a graduate student, she'd received five rejection letters and was depressed and distracted, which was the reason she tripped and basically threw a cup of coffee at Abby. At least it was an iced coffee.

Abby was upset but not nasty about being soaked. She laughed and tossed the ice cubes she retrieved from inside her bra at Callie. A few days later, Callie knocked the tip jar over, covering Abby with coins, some of which again found their way close to her breasts. And a week or so later right before closing, Callie was deep in thought about a problem in her manuscript while mopping the floor and knocked over the bucket of water just as Abby was walking by, soaking her shoes.

"Damn, woman, what have I ever done to you?"

Callie looked up. "Oh, my God, I'm so sorry." Resigned to losing her job, she asked, "Do you want to talk to the manager?"

The woman stared at her. "Not now. I want to talk to you. Meet me in front of the library when you finish work." She walked out.

Callie wasn't sure what was going on, but at least they were meeting in public, so it was unlikely the woman was going to kill her.

She remembered the woman liked iced coffee and that her name was Abby, so she prepared one and took it with her. When she saw her sitting on the library steps she extended her hand with the coffee.

"Just put it over there." Abby watched her place the coffee on the concrete pillar at the bottom of the staircase, then got up, retrieved the coffee, and patted the step next to her. "Sit."

Callie sat next to her. "I really am sorry."

"What's your name?"

"Callie."

"Well, Callie, you looked graceful approaching me just now so I don't think you're clumsy, I'm pretty sure you're not coming on to me, and I know you're not in any of the classes I teach, so it's not a vendetta. Tell me what's going on."

Callie stared at her hands tightly clasped in her lap. "Nothing's going on. I'm just clumsy lately." She shrugged.

"Look at me, please."

Callie swiveled her head so they were face-to-face.

Abby stared into her eyes. Callie felt like she was touching her soul and really wanted to understand. And that was all it took for her to open up and talk about her dream of being a writer, of working a boring, low-paying job to have the time to do it, and feeling like she was failing. At some point they started walking while they talked about their lives and their dreams. Before they separated hours later, Abby invited Callie to her apartment for dinner the next night.

Callie fell in love that night. It took Abby a little longer, but in a matter of weeks they were an exclusive couple and two months later they were living together.

Callie smiled. She'd fallen in love with Dana quickly, but not more quickly than falling for Abby. She'd never thought about it before, but she had a type—brilliant, passionate women who inspired others and were warm, caring, and kind. She was incredibly lucky to be loved by not one but two such extraordinary women.

Dana woke Callie with kisses. "Time to get ready for dinner."

Callie stretched and rolled out of bed. While brushing her teeth, she thought about the limited time they had left in Italy and decided she wanted to spend it alone with Dana. She hoped Dana felt the same. As they were dressing, Callie put her thoughts out there.

"We only have a few days left in Italy. Rather than go on any of the tours Millie mentioned, I'd like to spend the time alone with you in Taormina. In our room."

"My thoughts exactly. But so we maintain the connection with the group, let's join them for dinners when they're in Taormina and on the boat the last day."

They kissed and headed out to dinner, where they got lots of hugs, kind words, and, of course, more gentle teasing. And lots of hoots when they explained their plans for the next few days. They didn't mention the bedroom, but it seemed as if everyone understood. It was sweet and wonderful.

CHAPTER TWENTY-NINE

Callie was exhausted. After their lovemaking marathon they'd been stuck in the bus all day, and now, though she'd eaten lightly, she had had more wine than she should have because of the many toasts offered for their happiness. It appeared her body hadn't gotten the "tired, must sleep" memo, though. Because when Dana put her arms around her in the elevator she was sure the two of them would burst into flames.

As soon as the door to their room closed, Dana kissed her and, without a word, slowly undressed her and led her to their bed. Never losing eye contact, she quickly stripped, climbed on the bed, and stretched out on top of her. "Me first tonight," she whispered before she kissed her.

Callie made no objection. She closed her eyes, enjoying the kiss and the sensation of their bodies meeting skin to skin once again, their breasts touching, and the heat between them. She felt the loss when Dana ended the kiss but recovered quickly as Dana's mouth and those lovely long fingers slowly explored her body. She shivered in anticipation as Dana slowly slid down. She sighed and opened her legs as Dana ended up exactly where she wanted her and moaned as Dana dragged a finger through her wetness, then inserted a finger and then another. Dana made eye contact again before lowering her head and putting her tongue to work. Callie's moans grew louder and louder in response to Dana slowly increasing the speed of thrusting and withdrawing her fingers and the pressure of her tongue on Callie's clitoris. She grasped Dana's head and held her in place until the tension built and she could do nothing but thrash and beg Dana for release. She came, screaming, "Dana, Dana, Dana."

When Callie caught her breath, she pulled Dana up and rewarded her with a kiss. Being exhausted was no longer an issue. She had no trouble making love to Dana. After several rounds in the next few hours they fell asleep wrapped in each other's arms.

Callie opened her eyes to bright sunlight. She didn't know how long they'd slept, but judging by the light she guessed it was late morning. Her body was pleasantly achy. Today was a free day for the group, but she was in no rush to leave their nest. Inching away from Dana, she took a minute before leaving the bed to admire her glorious, naked, toned and tanned body and her beautiful face soft with sleep. She took a quick shower, then took her phone out to the terrace and ordered coffee, fruit, and pastries from room service.

The room service delivery woke Dana, and as soon as Callie signed and closed the door she got out of bed. "Good morning, sunshine." She hugged Callie. "Do I have time for a quick shower?"

"We have time to do whatever we want today." Callie kissed her. "I'll be on the terrace."

Callie looked up when Dana walked out to the terrace wearing shorts and a T-shirt. Her breath caught. Would she ever get used to seeing Dana so relaxed, so vibrant, so sexy?

Dana walked behind Callie and hugged her. "You are so beautiful. You glow in the sunlight." She kissed the top of Callie's head. "Ah, coffee."

They sipped their coffee, nibbled on fruit and pastries, and chatted about their lives, wanting to know everything about each other. After a while, Dana excused herself to check her email for new developments in New York. She shared the results with Callie when she returned to the terrace.

"The FBI raid is set to happen two days after we get back to New York City."

Reality settled over them like a heavy blanket. Callie took Dana's hand. "I'm sure seeing your friends arrested will be hard, but you'll have the support of Ellen and Angela. And I'll be with you as much as you want."

"Thank you." Dana put a hand on Callie's knee. "I'm so thankful that we found each other. Ellen and I didn't work as a couple, but she's the only one I've ever felt really cared for me. Feeling so connected to you, just being together after making love is more wonderful than I could ever have imagined."

Callie lifted Dana's hand to her lips. "I'm happy too." She pulled Dana up. "Let's go back to bed."

It was getting dark when the pinging of their phones woke them. Dana laughed as she read the barrage of texts. "They want us to join them for dinner at a local restaurant. Ready to face the world. And the group?"

Callie laughed. "I'm not sure I can walk, but if I can, I'm game. What about you?"

"I'm starving. Let's go." Dana rolled off the bed. "I'm calling dibs on the shower."

Callie's gaze followed Dana's lithe, naked body as she dashed across the room. She couldn't remember ever feeling this insatiable. The slightest touch, a look, a whispered word stoked her desire. The need to touch Dana was overwhelming. Hopefully, a shower, the evening air, and the teasing of their probably-by-now-raucous tour mates would help her keep her distance.

CHAPTER THIRTY

Except for a brief interlude in the middle of the night when Dana woke her to make love, they'd actually slept last night and woke at their normal time. They decided to take Carl's advice to go out for a Sicilian breakfast and were sitting under an awning at the Bam Bam Café dipping warm brioche into granita, partially frozen ices made from water, sugar, and fruit. It sounded weird, but as Carl had insisted, it was good.

As they fed each other bits of brioche, they mapped out their day based on recommendations received last night. Vanessa encouraged them to visit the ancient Greek theater while Serena said they had to spend some time in the English-style public gardens gifted to Taormina by a Scottish noblewoman and Ellie suggested they do what they loved, wander around the small town, and take in its beauty.

Dana geeked out over the ruins of the ancient Greek theater just as she had over the ancient Roman ruins. They went from there to the public gardens, which were amazing. They wandered paths shaded with towering trees and lush magnolias, hibiscus, bougainvillea, and lawns, walked by delightful fountains and whimsical nineteenth-century ornamental towers or pavilions known as "Victorian follies," and rested in the shade on a bench overlooking the Ionian Sea.

"How would you like to walk on the beach, Callie?"

Callie frowned. "I looked at the Taormina beach in the info packet. You have to take a cable car to get down to it and it looked pretty small, not somewhere we could walk."

"I saw that. I was thinking about taking a taxi to Letojanni, which is about seven miles north of here. It has a real beach with lots of restaurants right on it. What do you think?"

"I'd love it."

The evening was warm and they walked until they tired, then sat on the sand holding hands and watching the sunset. They talked about the beauty and wonder of Italy, the book Callie was planning and the books they were each reading. They didn't talk about the future. When they were hungry, they strolled along the beach until they found the restaurant the concierge at the hotel had recommended. On the beach, with dim lighting, soft music and nicely distanced tables, it felt intimate. The ever-present thrumming in Callie's body, the need to touch and make love to Dana, sparked as they fed each other from their plates, sipped wine, and stared into each other's eyes. Dana kissed Callie's palm. Her voice rough, she said, "Let's go back to the hotel. I want to make love to you."

The next three days felt slow and luxurious, filled with lovemaking, walking, talking, and, when they were available, meals with others in the group. At the same time, the days seem to be speeding by. It was fitting that their last full day was spent on a boat where the group was happiest. They swam and had fun as usual, but under it all was sadness that their time together was coming to an end.

Their last group dinner was filled with laughter and toasts as they talked about their first impressions of each other. And tears because this was the last night of their wonderful vacation together. Callie thought about how this random group of twelve people had become so close, about how far she'd come in just a month. About how the tour, meeting Dana, had changed her life. She squeezed Dana's hand. Sad to have the night and the tour end. Anxious to get back to their room.

CHAPTER THIRTY-ONE

They packed before they went to sleep and set the alarm to get up early. They wanted to enjoy their last morning in Italy, at least for now, before they left for the airport. Dana woke Callie with kisses long before the alarm, and they'd made tender love before dressing and eating a quick breakfast. Then with less than two hours before Enzo arrived with the bus to drive them to the Catania Airport, they'd come to the public park with their books, journals, and sketchbooks. Callie was seated on a bench facing the water and Dana was perched on the wall overlooking the water.

Callie had always romanticized love, believing you only loved once in a lifetime, that there was only a single soulmate for each person. Abby teased her about being a romance writer who believed the tropes of her genre.

Callie's gaze went to Dana, sitting on the wall sketching, with the gorgeous view of the water behind her. Abby was right. And thanks to Abby's encouraging her to get her ass out there, she'd found Dana. Another soulmate.

A bird dipped and swooped behind Dana, seeming almost to be celebrating her or trying to draw Callie's attention to the beautiful oblivious woman. The sound of Abby's laugh, followed by her cheerful voice, jolted Callie. She swiveled looking for the person responsible for the sounds before realizing the voice was in her head. It was Abby promising to come back as a bird to guide her.

Callie closed her eyes, listening to the wind in the trees. She smiled, remembering the wonderful times she and Abby had shared. She opened her eyes and found herself looking into the quizzical stare of a bird perched on the edge of her cup of iced cappuccino. The bird chirped, then dipped its head and drank from the cup.

Dana's hearty laugh pulled Callie's eyes away from the bird. A grinning Dana walked toward her—saunter was a better word—totally at ease in her body, sure of her place in the world, confident that Callie would welcome her.

The bird shook its head, splashing her with cappuccino. It didn't fly away when Dana sat next to Callie, instead it twisted its little head from side to side, as if trying to evaluate what was going on between them. Then it flitted onto Dana's shoulder and, once again, stared at Callie. She couldn't help herself, she lifted her phone and took a picture.

Dana made no attempt to brush the bird away.

Callie shook her head. "I've never seen a wild bird do that."

Dana laughed. "If it's Abby, I hope she likes me and has good bowel control."

The bird flew up, circled their heads a few times, then perched on the branch of a nearby tree and sang while staring at them.

Dana touched Callie's hand. "You look so far away. Are you thinking about Abby?"

It was amazing how sensitive Dana was to her moods. "I want to return this cup to the hotel before we get on the bus. Let's walk and I'll tell you."

She glanced at Dana. She seemed relaxed walking beside her, not pressing her to talk, giving her the space to organize her thoughts, something she'd always loved about Abby and now valued in Dana.

Callie made no attempt to stem the tears falling. "That bird fluttered over your head when you were sitting on the wall, almost as if it was trying to get me to look at you. Then it flew to me. It stared into my eyes, drank my coffee, something Abby always did, flicked coffee on me, and then sat on your shoulder." She sniffed. "It felt like a direct communication."

Dana put her hands on Callie's shoulders. "Do you think I passed muster?"

Callie looked into Dana's eyes. "If it *was* Abby's spirit, I would say you definitely passed. What do you think?"

Dana started walking as she considered the question. "We've had too many unusual interactions with birds on this trip for it to be accidental. I believe this bird, like the others, was delivering a message. I think it was Abby blessing our relationship."

CHAPTER THIRTY-TWO

Fourteen Months Later

In early June, a few days after they got back to New York City the FBI raided Integrated Bank Financial Software and arrested Linda, her associates, and Artie, plus two of their auditors, who it turned out were part of the scheme. Because the company dealt with software for banks, it was big news across the country and the public relations firm Dana hired went into action immediately, putting Dana out there as the face of the company. She talked about uncovering the theft and how Fortuna, Melloni, and Carter, Angela's financial consulting services firm's audit had exposed the extent of the crime and the criminals. At the same time she introduced Angela and the new executive team, discussed the restructuring of the company and, with Angela, met face-to-face with every customer to reassure them.

Callie was surprised how quickly and easily their lives had melded. After weeks of living with one foot in Dana's apartment and the other in the house she and Abby had owned in Montclair, New Jersey, Callie officially moved in with Dana. Angela remained at the house and Erin and Bonnie were planning to move in whenever Callie finished sorting through all of her and Abby's possessions. She wasn't ready to sell the house so they would rent for now.

Callie loved living in the city, writing on the terrace, swimming in the terrace pool, and taking long walks in Central Park every day. Except when Dana was traveling for business, they had lunch and dinner together, often with Angela and Ellen, who were now a couple, and Erin and Bonnie. As Callie knew she would, Dana connected with her three closest friends and the six of them spent as much time together as schedules allowed.

Callie allocated time each week to sort through Abby's belongings, laughing, crying, and remembering their life together. At the end of June, the six of them attended the dedication of the memorial to Abby at her university and Callie's speech honoring Abby resulted in many tears and much laughter, both of which Abby would have loved.

And even as Dana focused on the business she managed to apply to and be accepted into the Sapienza University Ancient World Studies PhD program. The two of them had resumed studying Italian when things quieted, but now Dana hired a native Italian speaker from the Italian embassy and together they began to dedicate hours each day to learning the language and becoming fluent by giving small dinner parties and attending events where only Italian was spoken. When Dana learned the head of Sapienza's Department of World Studies would be a guest lecturer at Columbia University starting in February, she received permission to enroll in two of the courses she was teaching and accrue the credits toward her PhD.

While Dana worked and studied, Callie wrote the romantic Italy book. The story seemed to flow out of her; she finished it in four months, a record for her. Though surprised by the lesbian characters, Sarah loved the book and had no problem letting Danville House Books know that if they didn't want it, she would take it elsewhere. They hemmed and hawed for a few days, then accepted the manuscript and rushed it into the publishing pipeline.

Now, fourteen months after they left Italy, Callie and Dana were back. And for the next two weeks they would be hosting friends and family here, at the cliffside hotel they'd taken over near Polignano a Mare. Everyone invited had been instructed to call a number provided to make plane reservations. They had no idea that first class tickets and transportation to and from the airport on both sides of the Atlantic would be paid for by Callie and Dana. And most of them still had no idea they were here to celebrate Callie and Dana's wedding.

Guests had been trickling in. Angela, Ellen, Erin, Bonnie, and all their tour mates arrived yesterday. Callie's parents, her brother and sister, their spouses and her nieces and nephews arrived last night. Various other friends were expected over the course of today. The excitement was palpable.

At breakfast Callie and Dana sat with their friends from the tour enjoying the usual teasing and playfulness.

"James and I were thrilled to find personalized copies of your new book about us, oops, I mean *Love Among the Ruins* in our room," Serena said. "Did everyone get one or just us?"

Callie gazed at the people sitting with her. She and Dana weren't the only ones whose lives the tour changed. Serena and James were engaged. Ellie had healed and moved on. Fran was on a leave of absence and Susan, a sabbatical, and they were spending a year in Italy writing a book together about the history and architecture of Southern Italy. Carl and Loretta had moved closer to their children and their lesbian daughter had felt comfortable coming out to them. And Dana had reached out to her six brothers, hoping to connect. They were still getting to know each other, but during the last year Callie and Dana had spent many tearful and joyous days visiting with the six of them individually and as a family. The six, their wives, their children, and grandchildren were arriving today.

"All the adults got a copy of the book. After all, it's what led us here."

"Fran and I were surprised and thrilled to see that it's a lesbian romance. Did your publisher give you any grief about that?" Susan asked.

"Some. But our contract didn't stipulate a heterosexual couple and after Sarah, my agent, let them know we'd bring it to another publisher if they rejected it, they got on board. It meant reworking the marketing plans they'd put in place but, ultimately, I think they're happy with the book. In fact, early reviews are fantastic and they're predicting it will be another bestseller. The official release is next week."

"Will you be doing events in the States?" Marian asked.

"More than I wanted but fewer than my publisher wanted. I'll fly back for several weeklong tours over the next few months, but they're spaced so that I'll never be away from Dana for more than a week. There are a few appearances in England. And, since I speak Italian now, we've scheduled some events in Italy."

"What's your next book about?" Loretta said.

"If you want to write a mystery about a murder on a romantic Italy tour, I have lots of ideas from some of my groups before and after you guys." Millie said.

The group laughed.

"I'll find you when I'm ready to write that. Actually, I've started doing research for a historical in Venice. I'm not sure whether it will take place during the fourteenth, fifteenth, or sixteenth century or whether the characters will be lesbians or heterosexuals."

"Ooh, I can't wait for that," Vanessa chimed in. "And what are you up to, Dana?"

"In three weeks, I start classes at Sapienza University in Rome. Callie and I have purchased a large apartment near the Spanish Steps, close to the university. It has plenty of light and separate workspaces for each of us, as well as three bedrooms, a living room, a dining room, and a modern kitchen. So let us know when you all want to visit. Callie will research and write. I'll attend classes, study, and continue as the chair of the board of directors of IBFS. I'll probably fly to New York a few days a month, but I'll mainly work remotely via Zoom." Dana, as usual, didn't want to hog the limelight. "Now how about you bring us up-to-date on what you all are doing," Dana said, turning the focus of the conversation onto their guests.

Later, on the terrace overlooking the pool and the ocean, Callie was chatting with Ellie and Megs, the internist she'd been seeing for three months.

"Thanks for including my daughters. They're excited to be in Italy and hanging out with the other teenagers here. And I'm excited that you've provided activities and guides to expose them to the various places we visited so Megs and I can enjoy the time too." She laughed. "Is Dana trying to make history converts of them?"

Callie's gaze found Dana.

Ellie elbowed Callie. "You still can't take your eyes off her."

Callie laughed and pulled her gaze back to Ellie. "It's true. My eyes seem always to end up on her."

"So all these people"—Ellie waved an arm to include the crowd—"are your guests for two weeks? I assumed we were coming to a tour group reunion, but the people Megs and I have spoken to have included relatives and friends. It seems as if every male I speak to claims to be Dana's brother. Just how many does she have? And what's really going on?" She leaned in. "It smells like a wedding to me."

Callie blushed. They'd actually legally married before they left New York with Angela and Ellen as the only witnesses. This ceremony would be a celebration with friends. "I knew we couldn't put anything over on you. Have you said anything to anyone?"

"No, but now I understand Carl's joke about becoming a minister. Is he officiating?"

"Damn, Ellie, you are perceptive."

Ellie laughed. "Well, since the asshole caught me off guard and dumped me, I've been paying more attention, tuning into those around me. Right, Megs?"

"I'll say. I've never been with someone who really pays attention to me, who really sees me. It's wonderful."

Ellie put an arm over Callie's shoulder. "I learned that from watching you and Dana. So, when are you going to tell people?"

Callie watched Dana talking to Carl, Loretta, and their daughter Jodi and her partner Anne. They'd been together for five years but Jodi hadn't felt safe to come out to her parents until Carl raved about Dana and Callie. Leaving them, Dana hopped from group to group, hugging, kissing, and hands in motion, talking and laughing.

"We're both so excited. We wanted to share our love with everyone close to us. We'll announce it tonight at dinner. All our guests will be here by then. And, since you asked, Dana has six brothers."

Callie stood on the balcony of their room gazing out at the sea. Her eye sought out the small wooden platform near the edge of the cliff where they'd be married under the simple frame the florist built and decorated with branches and red flowers. The setting was gorgeous and the contrast of the red with the vast expanse of the blue sea in the background was fantastic. In front of the platform enough chairs for the guests had been arranged in rows on two sides of an aisle covered with a white carpet. Planters filled with arrangements of colorful flowers lined the sides of the chairs. And in the chairs were all the important people in their lives, dressed, as instructed, in comfortable casual clothes like everyone in the wedding party.

Callie's heart skipped as Dana, wearing a gauzy white pantsuit in the same style as her own gauzy white dress, came into view on the terrace with Ellen beside her. Dana looked up, mouthed "I love you," and smiled.

Callie blew her a kiss.

Dana and Ellen moved into position to walk down the aisle. Carl, who had been sitting up front with Loretta, Jodi, and Anne, stood and moved onto the platform with a small book in his hands. Dana smiled at him and he gave her a thumbs-up.

They'd picked the recessional song together but they'd each selected their own processional music and hadn't shared their choices. Dana nodded in the direction of the DJ and Callie waited to hear what Dana had chosen. As Etta James began singing "At Last," Dana looked up, threw her a kiss, then slowly walked down the aisle with Ellen, her maid of honor.

Angela tapped Callie on the shoulder. "It's time for us to go." They held hands as they walked out to the terrace and moved into position. After Dana and Ellen stepped onto the platform, Callie took a deep breath and signaled the DJ. She squeezed Angela's hand as Marvin Gaye began singing "How Sweet It Is" and for the second time in her life walked slowly down the aisle toward her soulmate. Tears filled her eyes at the overwhelming love flowing toward her from the crowd and from Dana. Fourteen months later and the electricity between them was stronger than ever.

"You look beautiful," Dana whispered, as Callie took her place next to her. They held hands and faced Carl.

Carl looked out at the crowd. "Please be seated. Welcome, everyone. I'm Carl Alston. And I have the honor of officiating the marriage of Callie and Dana. But before we get to that I want to say a few words.

"I met these two wonderful women a little over fifteen months ago on a month-long tour of Romantic Italy. You're probably wondering what an old guy like me was doing on a luxury tour with romantic in its title. Well, my wife, Loretta, and I were celebrating our fiftieth wedding anniversary and our six children gave us the tour as a gift. The people on the tour, more specifically Dana and Callie, changed my life. If you're curious about what that means talk to Loretta or my daughter Jodi and Jodi's soon-to-be wife, Anne.

"At first, I felt a little out of place. I'm a simple farmer from South Carolina, and suddenly I was talking to and hanging out with an architect, a surgeon, an investor, several college professors, a millionaire entrepreneur and, although I didn't know it until partway through the tour, a famous artist and a *New York Times* best-selling author. I've always been reserved and held back with everyone except Loretta. And I've never felt comfortable with strangers, even strangers whose lives are like mine.

"But this group was different. In a matter of days, I was not only comfortable but the group felt like family. And do you know why?" He paused and looked straight at the audience. "Dana. And Callie. Ask anyone in our group. We love these two and wish them a long happy life."

He opened his book and smiled at Dana and Callie. Dana put her hand up to stop him and spoke to the audience. "For the record, there's nothing simple about Carl. He's taught us the importance of being flexible and open to change, no matter your age. He's very special to us." She faced Carl and smiled.

He looked out at the crowd. "She's really annoying sometimes." He glanced at his book again, then, once the laughter stilled, he addressed the crowd.

"Callie and Dana have brought all of us, family and friends, to this paradise to share their happiness and witness and celebrate with them as they commit their lives to each other in marriage. They understand it's a sacrifice and they appreciate your willingness to spend two weeks in Italy to share this event with them."

Once again he paused until the laughter died down. Carl focused on the couple. "Dana, please take Callie's hand and repeat after me, 'I, Danielle Elizabeth Wittman, take you, Calliope Marie DeAndre, to be my lawfully wedded wife.'"

Dana's voice was filled with emotion as she repeated the vow and then continued, "Callie, my love, you are beautiful inside and out, and whether it was the universe or Abby that brought us together I will be forever grateful. I was broken and unable to trust when we met, but your love healed me and made me strong. Being with you makes my life joyful and I promise to work always to bring joy to you and to our life as long as I shall live."

Carl led Dana through the rest of her vows. "In the presence of our family and friends, I promise to be your faithful partner in good times and in bad, in sickness and in health, and in joy and sorrow. I vow to love you unconditionally, to honor and respect you, and to cherish you for as long as we both shall live."

"You may put the ring on Callie's finger."

Ellen handed the gold band to Dana. She slipped it onto Callie's finger and gazed into her eyes as she spoke. "Callie, love of my life"—her voice broke—"with this ring, I thee wed and pledge you my love now and forever. Accept this ring as a symbol of my eternal love and commitment. As it encircles your finger, may it remind you always that you are surrounded by my unending love."

Callie used a tissue to dry the tears streaming down Dana's face.

"Callie." Carl's voice got her attention. "Please repeat after me. 'I, Calliope Marie DeAndre, take you, Danielle Elizabeth Wittman to be my lawfully wedded wife.'"

Callie repeated the vow, then spoke from her heart. "Dana, my love, mourning the loss of my wife and soulmate, Abby, I was crippled by anxiety attacks and sure I would never love again. But you saw my fragility and stepped up to care for and comfort me. I fell in love with your humanity, your kindness, your generosity, and your passion. How lucky am I to have found another soulmate and another love? I promise to try to make you happy, to nourish your passion for life and for ancient history"—she waited for the laughter to settle—"to emulate your kindness and caring and to make you joyful as long as I shall live."

Callie looked to Carl. After repeating the rest of her vows, she turned to Angela for the ring. She placed the ring on Dana's finger and looked into her eyes. "Dana, with this ring, I pledge you my love now and forever and give my heart and soul to you. Wear it as a symbol of my eternal love and commitment and as it encircles your finger, know that you are always surrounded by my unending love."

"May these rings be the symbol of your endless love and remind you to be faithful and loving always. May you share a long and happy life together." Carl grinned. "It is my pleasure to pronounce you wife and wife. You may kiss the bride."

The crowd cheered and whistled as the kiss turned passionate. They separated and turned to walk down the aisle, but hearing flapping wings and chirping, they looked at each other, smiled, then looked up. A flock of birds circled high in the sky, swooping and diving several times before flying off over the water. The crowd cheered.

Callie and Dana locked eyes, kissed and turned to face their guests. As the DJ blasted Hall & Oates singing "You Make My Dreams Come True," they clasped hands and boogied down the aisle to their future.

Bella Books, Inc.

Women. Books. Even Better Together.

P.O. Box 10543
Tallahassee, FL 32302
Phone: (800) 729-4992
www.BellaBooks.com

More Titles from Bella Books

Mabel and Everything After – Hannah Safren
978-1-64247-390-2 | 274 pgs | paperback: $17.95 | eBook: $9.99
A law student and a wannabe brewery owner find that the path to a
fairy tale happily-ever-after is often the long and scenic route.

To Be With You – TJ O'Shea
978-1-64247-419-0 | 348 pgs | paperback: $19.95 | eBook: $9.99
Sometimes the choice is between loving safely or loving bravely.

I Dare You to Love Me – Lori G. Matthews
978-1-64247-389-6 | 292 pgs | paperback: $18.95 | eBook: $9.99
An enemy-to-lovers romance about daring to follow your heart, even
when it's the hardest thing to do.

The Lady Adventurers Club - Karen Frost
978-1-64247-414-5 | 300 pgs | paperback: $18.95 | eBook: $9.99
Four women. One undiscovered Egyptian tomb. One (maybe) angry
Egyptian goddess. What could possibly go wrong?

Golden Hour - Kat Jackson
978-1-64247-397-1 | 250 pgs | paperback: $17.95 | eBook: $9.99
Life would be so much easier if Lina were afraid of something
basic—like spiders—instead of something significant. Something like
real, true, healthy love.

Schuss – E. J. Noyes
978-1-64247-430-5 | 276 pgs | paperback: $17.95 | eBook: $9.99
They're best friends who both want something more, but what if
admitting it ruins the best friendship either of them have had?